WOMAN IN THE MIRROR

MICHAEL O. GREGORY

BOOKSIDE Press

Copyright © 2023 by Michael O. Gregory

ISBN: 978-1-77883-250-5 (Paperback)

All rights reserved. No part of this publication may be reproduced, distributed, or transmitted in any form or by any means, including photocopying, recording, or other electronic or mechanical methods, without the prior written permission of the publisher, except in the case brief quotations embodied in critical reviews and other noncommercial uses permitted by copyright law.

The views expressed in this book are solely those of the author and do not necessarily reflect the views of the publisher, and the publisher hereby disclaims any responsibility for them. Some names and identifying details in this book have been changed to protect the privacy of individuals.

BookSide Press
877-741-8091
www.booksidepress.com
orders@booksidepress.com

CONTENTS

DEDICATION V
WOMAN IN THE MIRROR SYPNOSIS VI
CHAPTER ONE 1
CHAPTER TWO 8
CHAPTER THREE 15
CHAPTER FOUR 25
CHAPTER FIVE 31
CHAPTER SIX 39
CHAPTER SEVEN 46
CHAPTER EIGHT 52
CHAPTER NINE 59
CHAPTER TEN 66
CHAPTER ELEVEN 72
CHAPTER TWELVE 80
CHAPTER THIRTEEN 85
CHAPTER FOURTEEN 93
CHAPTER FIFTEEN 97
CHAPTER SIXTEEN 103
CHAPTER SEVENTEEN 110
CHAPTER EIGHTEEN 116
CHAPTER NINETEEN 121
CHAPTER TWENTY 129
CHAPTER TWENTY-ONE 134
CHAPTER TWENTY-TWO 147
CHAPTER TWENTY-THREE 158
CHAPTER TWENTY-FOUR 164
CHAPTER TWENTY-FIVE 175

CHAPTER TWENTY-SIX...183

CHAPTER TWENTY-SEVEN 188

CHAPTER TWENTY-EIGHT 194

CHAPTER TWENTY-NINE 202

CHAPTER THIRTY..210

CHAPTER THIRTY-ONE..216

CHAPTER THIRTY-TWO..224

CHAPTER THIRTY-THREE 229

CHAPTER THIRTY-FOUR 239

CHAPTER THIRTY-FIVE 251

CHAPTER THIRTY-SIX...266

CHAPTER THIRTY-SEVEN 273

CHAPTER THIRTY-EIGHT...280

CHAPTER THIRTY-NINE..286

CHAPTER FORTY...295

CHAPTER FORTY-ONE..303

CHAPTER FORTY-TWO 310

CHAPTER FORTY-THREE..316

CHAPTER FORTY-FOUR...324

CHAPTER FORTY-FIVE 333

CHAPTER FORTY-SIX..341

CHAPTER FORTY-SEVEN 349

CHAPTER FORTY-EIGHT..357

CHAPTER FORTY-NINE 363

CHAPTER FIFTY..373

DEDICATION

I dedicate this book to the memory of my sister-in-law Joane Berry. It was first published in 2004 with the title 'The Dead Years'. It was my first book and Joane helped me by proofreading the manuscript. After I finished chapter thirty, I thought that I had an excellent novel. Joane then asked a question, 'what was the young woman doing in the motel room in a coma'. I wrote the last twenty chapters to answer that question. As I was getting the book ready for publication Joane was diagnosed with cancer. We prayed for a miracle. The one we got wasn't the one we asked for, but it was the best one for Joane. The end was quick and without much suffering.

WOMAN IN THE MIRROR SYPNOSIS

Karl Boyle, age seventeen is injured in a diving accident and becomes quadriplegic. Years later he is given a second chance for a normal life; however, he will have to have his brain transplanted into another body; he accepts. The body they get for him is a woman of about twenty-five years. Thinking that it is just suicide by surgery, but a way out of a miserable life, he accepts. To his surprise he wakes up in the body of an attractive young woman. Determined to make the best of it, Karl takes the name, Catherine White and starts to get acquainted with her new body. At the same time she forms a close bond with Nurse Helen Schofield. After a period of recovery she is discharged and takes a job at the clinic where the surgery was done as a nurse's aide. Nurse Schofield invites her to move into her apartment and share the expenses, Catherine accepts. After a slow start at a social life and dating, Catherine meets a man, Samuel Tankersley. Their relationship slowly develops, with Sam wanting to push it along, and Catherine wanting to go slow. The relationship slowly changes from platonic to romantic interest. One day at the mall a woman addresses Catherine as Amanda Jenkins. The woman excuses herself when Catherine denies being Amanda. After a few days, Catherine goes on with her life when nothing seems to come of the strange encounter. Meanwhile, the woman at the mall, having gotten Catherine's license plate number, gives it to her friend, Elizabeth Jenkins, whose daughter Amanda has been missing for over six years. Through a private investigator Elizabeth learns that the young woman calling herself Catherine White recently awoke from what the doctors had believed to be a non-reversible coma with complete amnesia. Elizabeth is now certain that Catherine is her daughter Amanda. Catherine loves Sam and would like to make a full commit to him, but she feels uncertain; there's still that woman at the mall that thought she was Amanda Jenkins. Out of desperation, Elizabeth makes direct contact with Catherine. This led to a crisis of conscious and some soul searching. Catherine realizes that Karl is no more. A third personality has emerged, a new Amanda. She now knows in her heart she is Amanda Jenkins; and that she has a family that loves her, and that she could love. With all this settled, Amanda moves in with Sam, and they are soon engaged.

Amanda and Sam marry, and are soon expecting their first child. On her first visit to the OB/GYN she learns that she has given birth before. She does not know where the child was borne, the gender, the age or where it is now. All she knows is that she must find her child. With the help of a private investigator they pick up a trail at New Orleans where Amanda went by the name of Victoria Bujold. The trail leads from New Orleans to Lexington, Kentucky. She learns that there she gave birth to a daughter, almost five years old now named Cheryl. In Lexington she learns that the father, David Zamora, a drug cartel boss, has fled to Mexico, taking Cheryl with him. The private investigator puts her in touch with Patrick Fitzgerald who arranges to have her daughter kidnapped and returned to her. David Zamora, enraged at learning that Victoria kidnapped Cheryl, swears to hunt her down and kill her. David Zamora is able to track her down to Atlanta, Georgia, and learns her real name. There's a final confrontation where Sam kills David in Amanda's defense. Amanda gives birth to a son, Sam Jr. Her life is now complete.

CHAPTER ONE

The sun blazed in a partly clouded sky on a typical hot and humid Georgia summer afternoon, with a temperature of ninety-seven degrees and heat index of one-hundred six degrees, and no breeze to give relief from the heat. On a day like this everyone's concern would be to stay out of the heat as much as possible. Everyone who could had found some place to be cool.

Karl Boyle swam about lazily in the pool. He had been thinking how fortunate on such an unbearably hot day as today, to have a friend like Bobby, whose folks had a pool where a friend could find relief from the heat.

Karl and Bobby had been best friends since they were in the third grade together. They now went to the same high school and would be in the senior class when school started in two weeks. They would be going out for the football team again this year. They tried hard each year, but they were not very gifted athletes. It seemed the only time the coach let them play would be when their team had such a commanding lead that they couldn't lose. They kept hoping that next year would be their year to excel in sports. They wanted so much to gain a reputation as athletes of great prowess, so that they could attract and date the more attractive and popular girls.

Bobby's sister Gail had also taken advantage of the pool this day. At sixteen Gail was a year younger than Karl. Gail had become the object of all of Karl's dreams. When Karl and Bobby were younger they had went everywhere together. Gail had always wanted to go with them, but they never invited her along. After all, who wanted a girl tagging along when you were doing guy things? At the time Karl wasn't interested in Gail, or any other girl. Then three years ago Gail started to change. Now Karl had become very interested in her. He now looked for any opportunity to be noticed by her. Gail had become a beautiful young woman, possessing a marvelous personality, with a fabulous face and body. In her bikini she looked gorgeous. Her beauty had captivated Karl. However, being very shy when it came to girls, he didn't know what to do. When they were young, he could talk to her, but now he didn't know how. Their relationship had come full circle; before she had wanted to follow him, now he wanted to be close to her.

Karl would like to ask her for a date, but she now thought herself above him socially and hadn't shown any interest in him. He had the impression that the reason that she hadn't shown any interest in him was that he hadn't tried to date her. That had been because he feared rejection from her and hadn't worked up the courage to ask her for a date. As a cheerleader at school Gail had become a very popular girl, especially with the jocks. He felt intimidated by her popularity and had been waiting for a sign from her that his overture toward her would be welcome. He always looked for ways to impress her. If he could only find a way to show her that he was deserving of her attention, then he may be able to get a date with her.

Gail relaxed in the shallow end of the pool. She had been aware of Karl's attentions toward her for quite some time now, and that he wanted to date her. She knew that he could be trusted to show the proper respect to her, but he just didn't have the social standing that she looked for in a boyfriend. She knew that he continually tried to impress her. Every time that Karl tried to get her to notice him, she would look away, pretending not to notice.

Bouncing up and down on the diving board, Bobby feeling restless, wanted to get some kind of competition going with Karl. Karl treaded water in the pool, while daydreaming about Gail. Bobby called out, "Hay, Karl, wake up! Let's do some diving. I bet that I can do a better cannonball than you can."

Karl snapped out of his reverie. "You're on Bobby; you go first."

Bobby took a couple of bounces, got a good take off and hit throwing water all over the pool.

Karl called out, "I can do better than that!" He left the pool and mounted the board. He bounced two times, got a good takeoff and hit throwing water all over the pool.

Gail, seeing their silly competition, had moved as far into the shallow end of the pool as she could to stay out of the way; thinking that boys just didn't want to grow up. They kept this up for a few minutes, each one trying to outdo the other.

After a while Karl got tired of the game. He looked at Gail in the shallow end of the pool. In a moment of bravado, he thought. *Playing childish games with Bobby is no way to impress her. I must do better than this to attract her attention.* He mounted the board and stood at the very back. He had in mind to attract Gail's attention; to show her his prowess as a man and earn her respect. He got a running start and hit the end of the board, getting a takeoff for as much distance over the pool as he could. He did a swan dive and entered the water at a steep angle.

The dive had carried Karl too close to the shallow end of the pool; he hit the bottom of the pool hard. Light bulbs exploded behind his eyes; bright spots were swimming in his vision. He thought that he must shake this off and push back to the surface, but he couldn't move.

Bobby and Gail had watched Karl make the dive and enter the water. When Karl didn't surface, they looked and saw him lying motionless on the bottom of the pool. They immediately knew that something had to be wrong.

Gail exclaimed loudly, "Oh my God, something's wrong with Karl!"

Gail and Bobby dove together to the bottom of the pool, grabbed Karl by the arms, and carried him back to the surface. They could see that Karl had done nothing to help himself.

In a worried tone of voice that quaked with anxiety, Gail asked, "What's wrong with him Bobby?"

"I don't know." In a loud voice Bobby asked Karl, "Karl, what's wrong? Do you hear me?" Looking back at Gail, Bobby said, "I think that he was knocked out on that dive." He didn't think that it could be anything worse.

Gail, on the verge of panic and frightened that something terrible had happened to Karl, started to cry. She spoke with a pleading voice, fighting to stem the flow of tears. "Oh, God! What do we do now?"

Bobby said with a voice that tried to convey more confidence than he felt inside. "Take his right arm and hold his head up out of the water. I'll get him on the left and do the same. We must get him out of the pool."

Gail did what her brother said. Together they walked Karl to the steps at the shallow end of the pool and dragged him out of the pool onto the pavement.

Gail, still crying, asked in a sobbing voice, "Oh, God, is he breathing?"

Bobby looked at Karl then exclaimed, "Quick run and have Mom call 911!"

Gail jumped to her feet and took off for the back door of the house running as fast as she could screaming. "Mom...Mom!"

Gail burst through the door into the kitchen. Her mother, having heard her daughter coming, stood at the back door. "What's wrong Gail?"

Gail, almost breathless and still crying exclaimed, "Karl was diving and hit the bottom of the pool knocking himself out! Call 911!"

Gail's mother grabbed the phone to call 911. At the same time Gail's father, having heard the exchange between Gail and her mother, bolted from the family room, through the kitchen and out to the pool. He dropped to his knees beside his son. "Is he breathing Bobby?"

"I don't know Dad."

Bobby's father took a quick look at Karl. "His breathing is shallow and labored. While I assist him in breathing, you run to the house and get some blankets. We can't have him going into shock."

Bobby jumped to his feet and hurried to the house for blankets.

WOMAN IN THE MIRROR

The paramedics arrived quickly and took charge of Karl's treatment. Bobby and Gail stood by the pool with their father and watched the paramedics as they got Karl ready for transport to the hospital. Their father tried to comfort then without much success. Gail couldn't stop crying and Bobby just stood in shocked silence.

In a few minutes Karl had been immobilized on a backboard, on a respirator and in the back of an ambulance speeding to the hospital. Bobby's mother called Karl's parents on the phone to let them know what happened, and where they were taking Karl.

Karl's first sensation had been that of light. Looking around nothing looked familiar to him. He tried to sort out his surroundings. He tried to move his arms and legs but couldn't. Panic gripped him. Why couldn't he move his arms and legs? He heard a voice and could see that there were people close to him. He heard someone speak. "Karl, are you awake?"

He looked to where the voice had come from and saw a woman dressed in green scrubs. Karl asked, "Who are you? Where am I? What's wrong with me?"

She sensed the tension in his voice and could understand his bewilderment. Looking Karl in the eyes, she said, "I'm Dr. Judith Richards. You are in the recovery ward of the Redmond Regional Medical Center. Do you know who you are?"

Karl tried to nod his head but couldn't move. He fought down a feeling of panic, then spoke, "Yes, of course, I'm Karl Boyle."

Suddenly Karl was overcome by a wave of nausea. A nurse helped him, and he threw up in a bowl provided. Karl started to get lightheaded, and the room dimmed. He slept again.

Karl became aware of a voice. "Karl, are you awake?"

Karl opened his eyes to see a man in a white lab coat standing beside his bed. "Yes, I am now; and who are you?"

The man looked at him, then spoke, "I'm Dr. Paul Jaskowski. I'll be your doctor during your recovery here at the hospital. You are in a semiprivate room, although there's no one here to share it with you.

MICHAEL O. GREGORY

We'll make it as comfortable for you as we can while you're with us."

Karl still didn't know what had happened to him. Looking at Dr. Jaskowski he asked, "Doc, I was swimming and I know that something happened to me; I can't move. What's wrong with me? How bad is it?"

Dr. Jaskowski grabbed a chair and dragged it up next to Karl's bed. He took a seat, adjusted his lab coat, looked out the window for a minute, and then turned to face Karl. In all his years in medicine he had never learned an easy way to tell someone that their body had now become useless; that their life as they knew it had ended. He knew that there could be no easy way to say it. Before he spoke, Dr. Jaskowski looked at Karl to try to gage just how strong a person he was. "Do you remember anything about the accident?"

Karl tried to shake his head but couldn't. "I was swimming with Bobby and Gail. Then I woke up here. That's all I know."

With a nod Dr. Jaskowski responded, "Well Karl you were diving, and you hit your head on the bottom of the pool. Your neck is broken at the fourth vertebra. It has been stabilized by surgery, but there has been damage to your spinal cord."

Karl was depressed to hear this, he thought. *Spinal cord injury! How bad is it, and how long will it take me to get over it?* He wanted to know. He hadn't yet considered the fact that it could be permanent. He took a deep breath. "Tell me Doc, how much damage? Will I be okay again?"

Dr. Jaskowski didn't respond right away. He looked into Karl's eyes to try to see how well he would take it before he spoke. After a few seconds he concluded that Karl could handle the truth of his predicament. Making hard eye contact with Karl, he said, "I had planned to speak to your parents first before going into it with you. I think you're ready for it now; besides your parents have already been told the worst by the surgeon. Karl, your injuries are very serious. Your spinal cord has been severely damaged. Just how much we won't know until you've had time to heal."

Karl just had to ask the big question, "Will I be able to walk again?"

Dr. Jaskowski sat motionless for a few seconds before he spoke. This had always been the hardest part. He took a deep breath and continued. "I would like to say that it's possible, but I don't think it would be fair to you. You may recover some use of your arms and hands, but baring a miracle, that's about all that you can expect."

The news devastated Karl, he thought. *This can't be happening to me. If only I could have that last day to do it over again. I wouldn't need the whole day, just those last few minutes. If I could just have them back, I would do it right this time. It's not fair that just one mistake leaves me like this.* "But Doc this just can't be happening to me. There must be something that you can do to make me walk again?"

Dr. Jaskowski just looked at Karl knowing the turmoil that assailed his mind. "I'm sorry, there's nothing that can be done. Would you like to see your parents now?"

Karl had no desire to be with anyone right then. He just wanted to be alone so that he could come to grips with this. With a sigh he said, "No, Doc, I'd like to sleep now. Would you please turn out the lights?"

Dr. Jaskowski nodded. He understood that when a person first learned how bad it was, they needed some time to adjust to it. "All right, if you need anything just call out for the nurse. They will hear you at the nurse's station."

Dr. Jaskowski got up from the chair and walked to the door. He looked back at Karl once, turned out the lights and left, closing the door behind him. In the dark Karl began to cry.

CHAPTER TWO

The Evans Clinic had a large comfortable conference room, with dark blue carpeting, white-painted wainscoting and light blue painted walls. A large oak conference table dominated the room, with comfortable high-backed chairs upholstered in dark-blue leather. A coffee urn and a tray of pastries rested on a sideboard in a corner of the room.

Dr. Bruce Evans, age fifty-two and director of the clinic sat at the head of the table. He always dressed in dark-blue or dark-gray suits. At six-foot three-inches, two-hundred-thirty pounds, with salt and pepper hair, he projected a very commanding presence. He had started his medical practice as a neurosurgeon, but he wanted to be able to do more than just limit the damage to the human brain and nervous system after injury. His answer had been clinical research to find a way to rejuvenate the brain and nerve tissue after injury. To this end, making use of a personal fortune, he built the clinic and assembled the best team that could be had to staff it. His management style was to delegate authority to his competent staff, give directions, then let his staff make it happen.

To his right sat Dr. Grace Weston Assistant Director, age forty-five, light brown hair, petite, trim, and a smart dresser. She always projected an air of authority. She had a background in research. As a facilitator she was able to keep the team efforts focused on the goal. She knew how to get things done.

On Dr. Evans left sat Dr. Steven Martinovich Chief of Surgery, age forty-seven, a balding man a little on the heavy side. He was a brilliant surgeon with remarkable skills and dedication to his profession. He had been credited with pioneering many innovative surgical techniques.

On Dr. Weston's right sat Dr. Frank Anderson Chief of Research, age thirty-nine, a trim man with dark blond hair. His main area of research had been in brain and nerve disorders. He also had a background in genetics and nanobots, molecule size biological machines programmed for a specific task.

On Dr. Martinovich's left sat Dr. Walter Lokey Chief of Clinical Trials, age forty-two, brown hair, very slim. He also had a background as a neurosurgeon.

On Dr. Anderson's right sat Dr. Maryanne Prater assistant to Dr. Lokey, age thirty-three, a black woman of trim figure with fine features and impeccable taste in clothing. She was the team's resident psychiatrist.

Dr. Evans pressed the button on the recorder. "Doctor's let's bring this meeting to order. First, is there any unfinished business from the last week's meeting?" He looked around the table to see if anyone had anything to say. When no one spoke up he continued. "Okay, Dr. Lokey, what do we have on clinical trials this week?"

Dr. Lokey looked down at his notes before he spoke. "We received a medical transfer from Dillon, South Carolina last Thursday afternoon. An Afro-American male, age twenty-eight, a brick layer. He fell two stories from scaffolding. The second vertebra lumber spine is broken, with spinal cord damage. We received him thirty-one hours after the injury occurred. The vertebra has been repaired by surgery. Spinal cord treatment is going well. He should be walking again in rehab in about two weeks. All other patients are progressing as expected."

Dr. Evans turned next to Dr. Martinovich, "Now surgery Steven, what do you have?"

Dr. Martinovich looked at his notes, then said, "I've checked the surgery of the patient that we received from Dillon, and it looks good. There's also Mrs. Johnson, the lady from Highland, North Carolina. The one who fell down the stairs, she's healing well. I foresee no complications to her full recovery. That's all I have of surgery."

Dr. Evans looked around the table. "Does anyone else have any urgent business?" No one indicated that they had anything to say. He switched off the recorder then continued. "We're off the record now. Let's get to project 'Trade In'. As usual there will be no recordings, or personal notes of the minutes of this meeting. We can't allow unauthorized material outside the project. First surgery, Steven, are you ready?"

Dr. Martinovich looked down at his coffee cup as he gathered his thoughts, then back up at Dr. Evans. "Yes, we've planned and trained for the procedure. We've performed it on lab primates with excellent results, and we've practiced on cadavers. Surgery is ready." He felt confident that he had done everything that he could to be ready. He also felt confident in the proficiency of the team.

Dr. Evans nodded to Dr. Martinovich. He knew that he was the best in the field and would be capable of doing the job. He turned next to Dr. Anderson, "Frank, are there any questions from research?"

Dr. Anderson looked up. "No, our treatment for nerve damage already had FDA approval for clinical trials. The treatment has been successful with nerve tissue, and also brain tissue. 'Trade in' is just an extension of our approved trials. Research is a go!"

Dr. Evans now turned to Dr. Lokey. "Walter, is your department ready?"

Dr. Lokey looked over to Dr. Prater to see if she had anything to say before he answered. With a nod from Dr. Prater Dr. Lokey spoke, "We're now sitting up the special ward for 'Trade In'. We've selected personnel for 'Trade In' and now have them in training. We'll be ready in four weeks."

Dr. Evans nodded. "Good, keep me informed if you encounter any problems."

Dr. Evans got up and went to the sideboard for a fresh cup of coffee. Taking his time and sipping his coffee, he returned to his chair. He picked up a stack of papers from in front of him and tapped them on the table as he studied the faces of the others at the table. He could tell by the expectant looks on everyone's faces that his team was ready. He put the papers back down on the table. "As you know, up until now this has just been a research project. Once we go beyond this point and bring a candidate into it we're committed. Is there anyone here who doesn't think that we should go forward with the project?"

Dr. Evans took a minute to allow anyone who wanted to speak do so. Everyone held his or her breath in anticipation. Finally Dr. Evans broke the silence. "Okay, 'Trade In' is on."

As one they all sat back in their chairs. The release of held breath was almost audible.

Dr. Evans said, "Good, now we need a candidate. Grace, what do you have for us?"

Dr. Weston checked her notes. "We have three possibilities. Number one Miss Darlene Smith, black female, age twenty-seven, quadriplegic, injured at age twenty, thrown from a car in an auto accident. She lives with her parents in Macon. They have assisted home care. She has two brothers, ages twenty-nine and twenty-one.

Number two Mr. Thomas Lambert, white male, age thirty-three, paraplegic, injured at age twenty-four, construction accident. He lives in Douglasville and works as a packer for a company that sells fasteners, like screws, nuts, bolts, and other fasteners wholesale. Divorced, a son, age eleven. His parents live here in Atlanta.

Number three Mr. Karl Boyle, white male, age thirty-eight, quadriplegic, injured at age seventeen, accident diving in swimming pool, home town Adairsville, Georgia. Father deceased nine years ago. Mother has remarried seven years ago and moved to Jacksonville, Florida. Subject now lives in nursing home in Marietta. He has no other close relatives."

Dr. Weston put down the notes that she had been reading from and turned to face Dr. Evans. "Well Bruce there you have it. I recommend that Maryanne do a psychiatric work-up on our candidates and give her recommendation as to who we should go with."

MICHAEL O. GREGORY

Dr. Evans nodded. "Good, thank you Grace. Maryanne, how long will it take you to get a psychiatric work-up on our candidates?"

Dr. Prater cleared her throat before speaking. "I can have it done by the time that the 'Trade In' ward is ready."

Dr. Evans nodded, "Good, then take care of it."

"Yes, Dr. Evans." Dr. Prater responded.

Dr. Evans looked at everyone before he spoke, "If there's nothing more for now, our next meeting will be after Maryanne has completed her work-ups. Then we will decide if or when to proceed with the next step in operation 'Trade In'."

Dr. Evans reached down and switched the recorder back on before he spoke again, "Now for housekeeping. Grace, do you have the report on our pharmaceutical supply service?"

Dr. Weston reached for a folder on the table in front of her.

Four weeks later they were all present at another staff meeting. Dr. Evans was speaking, "Thank you for your report, Walter. Go ahead and make the necessary staff changes and keep me informed. Now, is there any more urgent business for today?"

Dr. Evans looked to see if anyone else had anything to say. He then turned off the recorder. "I'd like to remind and caution everyone here again that recordings and personal notes of the meeting shouldn't be taken. Walter, is everything ready with the new ward?"

Dr. Lokey put down his coffee cup. "Yes, the 'Trade In' ward is completed and fully equipped. The staff is ready to take up their duties when needed."

With a nod Dr. Evans said, "Good work Walter, thank you. Now Maryanne have you completed your workups yet?"

Dr. Prater opened a folder in front of her. "Yes Dr. Evans I have. Number one Miss Smith's work-up was done at her clinic in Macon. Her psychological profile is good, but her close family ties wouldn't make her my first choice."

Dr. Evans nodded. "What about number two?"

Dr. Prater continued to read from her notes. "Number two Mr.

Lambert's work-up was done on an out-patient basis here at our clinic. I believe that he should be rejected. He isn't, in my opinion, adaptable enough to handle 'Trade in'."

Dr. Evans nodded, "Alright, he's out. What about number three?"

Dr. Prater checked her notes again then looked up. "Number three Mr. Boyle. I had him transferred from his nursing home to our clinic for his work-up. His psychological profile is good, and he has no close family ties. I'd say that he's the best candidate for 'Trade in'."

Drumming a pencil on the table, Dr. Evans surveyed the other doctors at the table. The time had come. "Ladies and Gentlemen, we've come to the point of no return. From here we must bring the candidate into the project. After that there will be no turning back. Do we go for it? Grace?"

Dr. Weston didn't hesitate, "Yes!"

Dr. Evans looked at Dr. Martinovich, "Steven?"

Dr. Martinovich took a sip of coffee and put his cup down. Slapping the table he exclaimed, "I say, go for it!"

"Thank you, Steven. Frank?"

Dr. Anderson answered immediately, also with a slap on the table. "Let's do it!"

"Thank you, Frank. Walter?"

Dr. Lokey answered right away. "Yes!"

"Thank you, Walter. Maryanne?"

"When do we start?" Dr. Prater responded.

Dr. Evans sat back in his chair with both hands on the table as he surveyed everyone at the table. All his work was about to pay off. Everyone waited for now would be the okay from him. Clearing his throat, he said, "Thank you Maryanne. Now that we are all in agreement we began." Dr. Evans looked at Dr. Weston, "First we must bring Mr. Boyle into project 'Trade In'. Grace, I believe that you're the one best to brief Mr. Boyle and bring him onboard. How about it?"

Dr. Weston took a couple of minutes to check her appointment book, "I can make time for him the day after tomorrow, in the morning.

MICHAEL O. GREGORY

I'll see him then."

Dr. Evans nodded. "That's good, take care of it. Well, people, after Grace brings Mr. Boyle onboard things will start to happen. Any other questions?"

No one spoke. Dr. Evans restarted the recorder. "Now housekeeping, I've a report from the chief of nursing that we are having problems with linen delivery."

CHAPTER THREE

Dr. Weston sat on the sofa in her office across from her desk. The morning sun streamed in through the windows flanking her desk giving the room an atmosphere of warmth and cheerfulness. Mr. Karl Boyle sat in his wheelchair at the corner of the sofa facing Dr. Weston.

Karl had been asked to this meeting with Dr. Weston. They had only told him that Dr. Weston wanted to discuss his medical condition and ideas for treatment. He had had many such meetings like this over the years, they all ended the same way. Sorry, but there's not much that we can do for you. By now he had developed a pessimistic view of the medical profession.

As soon as the attendant that had brought him left, closing the door behind himself, Dr. Weston said, "Good-morning Mr. Boyle. I'm Dr. Grace Weston. I'm the Assistant Director for the Evans Clinic. You may call me Grace if you like. May I call you Karl?"

Karl nodded saying, "Yes, you may call me whatever you like Dr. Weston, and good morning to you." He wondered what she had to say about his medical condition, as if it made any difference.

Dr. Weston looked at Karl. She could see that he expected to be disappointed. She wondered how he would react to 'Trade In'. "Okay Karl let's get down to business. I have asked you here today to discuss your treatment. As you know we had you transferred to our long-term treatment facility from your last place of residence for us to conduct tests and develop a plan of treatment for your heart condition. Oh, by

15

the way, before I go on I'd like to ask you if you're pleased with your accommodations with us."

Waiting to hear what Dr. Weston really had to say, Karl said, "Yes, I'm very pleased. In fact, it's much better than I'd expected."

Dr. Weston smiled. "Good. If you need anything just let us know."

Karl nodded. "You can count on that, Doc."

Picking up a manila folder from the coffee table, Dr. Weston continued. "All right, now for what we're here for. Our test results show that your heart is functioning at about forty percent of normal. Of course, we're only confirming what your own doctors have told you."

Karl had heard all this before. "Yes, that's right doc."

"Also, we can't stop or reverse the degeneration of the heart. I believe that your doctors told you that too."

Karl nodded. "Yes, they did."

Dr. Weston took a sip of coffee and put the cup back down on the coffee table in front of her before continuing. "We can develop a treatment program that will slow the progress of the degeneration of your heart and make you as comfortable as possible. That I believe was your doctor's conclusion."

Karl wondered just where this conversion was heading. He had a feeling that he had not been called into the Assistant Directors office just to hear again what they both already knew. "Yes it was. You were holding out hope for me, but it looks like you can't do anything more for me than they could. Although you can hope for a miracle, I really wasn't expecting one."

Dr. Weston held up her hand in supplication and said, "Hold up now don't give up yet. Miracles, even little ones, can happen sometimes."

Dropping the manila folder back down on the coffee table, Dr. Weston picked up her coffee cup, took a sip of coffee, and placed he cup back down on the coffee table. "Your injury is a contributing factor to your heart condition and other ailments. Let's talk about it. Now you have been in that wheelchair for how long?"

Karl said with deliberate firmness, "About twenty-one years, long-hard years!"

"And you have some use of your arms and hands, I presume."

Karl spit out the words. "If you want to call it that! If I try hard enough, I can get a spoon from my plate to my mouth, but I can't hardly call that use!"

Dr. Weston nodded; she could understand his bitterness. "It must really be hard for you in that chair."

Karl looked hard at Dr. Weston as if she didn't have a clue to his plight and said with anger in his voice. "Doc, you don't know the half of it! This isn't a chair; it's a prison and I have a life sentence! I don't have a life, I just exist! I used to count time, but time has no meaning for me anymore! I've even stopped counting my birthdays! I've wanted to kill myself countless times, but I don't have the ability to do so!"

Karl's statement moved Dr. Weston. She could really understand his bitterness and anger. In her profession she had seen enough pain and misery to know that life wasn't fair, just indifferent. "Thanks for being so blunt and honest. If you had told me otherwise, I wouldn't have believed you."

Dr. Weston picked up her cup, took another sip of coffee, and put it back down on the coffee table. "Your diving accident, what happened anyway?"

Karl said with as much of a shrug of his shoulders as he could manage. "It's no big mystery. I was showing off for a girl and crashed into the bottom of the pool breaking my neck."

"There must have been something wrong to have hit the bottom of the pool with such force?"

Karl nodded. "Your right doc, there was something wrong. The board was too large for the pool. I hit right where the bottom makes a sharp rise from the deep end to the shallow end. At least I had a good lawyer. He went after everyone, the board manufacturer, the contractor who installed it and the pool owner. He got me a good settlement. More important though, he kept my mother from getting control of it. He set up a trust that has supported me through the years. I've used most

MICHAEL O. GREGORY

of it to maintain myself in nursing homes, so there isn't much left."

Dr. Weston finished the coffee in her cup and put the cup back on the coffee table, "That's a good story Karl. Now I have a question for you. Do you know what we do at the Evans Clinic?"

Karl had inquired about the Evans Clinic when they had asked him to transfer to it. He had found out that they were on the cutting edge of nerve damage repair. "I know that you have a long-term care facility. And that you are also conducting research into spinal cord damage."

Dr. Weston nodded. "You've covered it in a very general way. We do have a very good long-term care facility. We are also involved in research into spinal cord and nerve damage. In fact we're developing new surgical techniques and revolutionary treatment for the repair of spinal cord and major nerve damage."

Dr. Weston now had Karl's full attention. "Did you say to repair spinal cords?"

Dr. Weston noticed Karl's increased interest. "Yes, I did, and we have been given FDA approval to conduct clinical trials."

Karl had now become very interested. "And you plan to start conducting trials soon?"

With a smile Dr. Weston responded, "We started clinical trials about seven months ago."

Karl now saw hope, perhaps there could be a way out of his wheelchair. "So, what you're saying is that you may be able to help me after all. Right?"

Dr. Weston regarded Karl for a few seconds before she answered. "Perhaps we can, but there are problems to treating you."

The hope started to dim for Karl. "Like what?"

Dr. Weston would now show him the downside. "For starters, your body hasn't been used for twenty-one years. The muscles of your body are atrophic. Even if we could restore the signal to them, they will no longer work. As for our spinal cord and nerve damage treatment, it's best that the treatment be started within days of the time of injury, at the most about four weeks. After that the effectiveness of the treatment

WOMAN IN THE MIRROR

slowly declines until there's no longer any noticeable effect from the treatment."

Karl now felt that he had been getting the run around, that all of this was going nowhere, he thought. *More false hopes and broken promises. First, they give you a big buildup, then jerk the rug out from under you.* "I thought you said that you could help me. Now you say that you can't. Then someone, please tell me what I'm doing here!"

Dr. Weston got up from the sofa and went to the coffee maker on a corner table. After making herself another cup of coffee, she returned to the sofa. Taking a sip of coffee, she looked into Karl's eyes, then put her cup on the coffee table. "Karl, I would like to ask you a couple of questions. Now don't answer me. I want you to give them some thought and answer to yourself. Now, what would you do to get out of that wheelchair? What sacrifices would you be willing to make to have a normal life again?"

Dr. Weston gave Karl a minute to think about the questions then continued. "Now Karl, before we go on you must swear that every word spoken in this room from now on will stay in this room. You will confide in no one." Karl was really perplexed. Dr. Weston repeated, "Karl, promise me, not one word."

Karl nodded. "Okay, I promise, not one word."

Dr. Weston smiled. "Thank you, Karl. Now let's first review the prognosis of your current condition. Your heart is only forty percent effective now, and despite our best efforts will continue to decline. You have five years, but not ten. Is that what your doctors told you?"

Karl nodded. "Pretty close doc, actually they gave me three to five years."

Dr. Weston looked hard at Karl. The time had come to present the alternative of 'Trade In'. "Then the only way for you to overcome your problem is if you had a new body."

Karl's mouth fell open. His ears must be deceiving him. With an astonished look, Karl said, "What did you say?"

Dr. Weston continued to look directly into Karl's eyes. "The only way out of your predicament is that you're given a new body."

Karl shook his head. "You're kidding. This is some kind of a joke."

Dr. Weston kept looking at Karl. "No, I'm not kidding, and this is no joke."

Karl then said sarcastically, "Then what am I going to be, the six-million-dollar man, robo cop? No thanks!"

Dr. Weston tried to be reassuring. "I know that it sounds incredible."

Karl answered with forcefulness, "You're damn right it sounds incredible! It sounds impossible!"

Dr. Weston raised her hand to have his attention before she spoke again. "Please Karl, even if you find this hard to believe, just hear me out."

Karl looked back at her and thought. *This is bazaar, but what the hell. I'll go along with her.* With a nod he said, "Okay, why not. I don't have any place to go right now."

Dr. Weston got up from the sofa, went to her desk, and picked up a thick folder that had been sitting on the corner of her desk. She took it back to the sofa and dropped it on the coffee table. She then faced Karl. "Listen Karl, we have developed a treatment that is injected in and around the damaged nerve and spinal cord. We can even repair nerves and spinal cords that have been completely severed. What is injected is what you may call an exotic medical cocktail. It's a pinkish gel consisting of a nerve stimulator, and a growth medium, along with nanobots that are tiny molecular-size biological machines that are programmed to make new neurological pathway connections. There's also some genetically engineered material that acts like a genetic blueprint so that each wire on one side is plugged into the right wire on the other side, so to speak. It not only works with nerve tissue, but also with brain tissue. We can give you a new body."

Karl looked at Dr. Weston and thought. *These people are crazy. They're talking nonsense.* Karl considered asking to leave, but he had become curious and decided to play along. With a nod he said, "Okay, so it works, I believe you. I seem to recall a story that I heard about that was on television back in the nineties. It was about some doctor who cut off the head of one monkey and stuck it on the body of another monkey. I believe that it lived for about two weeks. Is that what you have in mind for me? Get some brain-dead stiff and stick my head on his body?"

Dr. Weston shook her head with an amused smile. "No, that's not what we plan to do. I remember that show. That was Dr. Robert White. It wasn't much more than a cheap parlor trick. The job of hooking up the plumbing to get a blood supply and keep the brain alive was easy to do, but the rest of the body wasn't plugged into the brain, so it wouldn't work.

"Now there was one other unexpected benefit from our treatment. We found that the treatment was so good at making new neurological pathway connections that we could join the halves of two brains together to make one brain. With this technology we can perform a brain transplant, or as some call it, a total body transplant. Regardless of the phrase that you use it's the same thing."

Dr. Weston reached out to tap the folder on the coffee table with her finger. "In this folder is a summary of what we have done and what we plan to do. If you decide to go with us, you will have a chance to review it with our staff and all of your questions will be answered.

"What we will do is obtain the body of a brain-dead donor with a brain case of the right size. Then we transplant your brain into the donor's body. When it's all done no one will know the difference. When you repair a nerve or spinal cord you can't have a scar. A scar will block the signal from the brain. With this new treatment there won't even be a scar to give it away. We have already done this with lab animals. We have two live and healthy chips, and other animals to prove it.

Karl still had a hard time believing all of this. "I must admit that you do have my interest, but it all sounds so risky. What are my chances?"

Dr. Weston felt that Karl had started to come around. "I'll be straight with you Karl. All surgery is a risk and there are no guarantees, but if I didn't believe that we have an excellent chance for success we wouldn't be willing to go through with it. If you decide to go through with the surgery, it will go like this. You'll be put under. Then you and the donor's body will be cooled down. Then we will open up both brain cases, remove the dead brain from the donor's body, and transplant your brain in its place. We will then make all the connections, close up, and bring the body temperature back up to normal.

"We will then keep you in a chemical-induced coma for twelve days to two weeks. By then good neurological connections would have been forged. We will then wake you up. Well Karl that's about it in a general way. Take as much time as you need to think about it and let us know if you're with us, or not."

Karl still thought that these people were crazy. What they were talking about sounded like something out of a science-fiction novel. He couldn't see how it would ever work, but if they killed him, what the hell, he would finally be rid of this miserable life. With a nod he said, "Okay, doc, I don't need any time to think about it, let's do it. One way or the other I'll be out of this wheelchair."

Dr. Weston smiled. She had expected Karl to want to take some time to think about it, but it didn't matter that he had already made up his mind. Looking into Karl's eyes Dr. Weston said, "That's good Karl. Now I have some questions for you, but first let me explain. We can't just sit around waiting for your brain-dead twin to show up. It just won't happen. You must take what you can get. The donor must have the right size brain case, be medically fit, and a good match. The donor will most likely be an unidentified transient who won't be claimed. Now I have two questions for you. First, would you be willing to accept a donor of another race? Second, would you be willing to accept a donor of the other gender?"

Karl took a few seconds to think about it before he answered. "Well doc, I hadn't thought of that."

Dr. Weston responded quickly, "I'm asking you now Karl. What do you think of it?"

Karl thought for a few seconds more. The question made him realize that any new body would most defiantly be strange. With a sigh he said, "Well doc, I don't know. That's quite a leap to make. I don't know how, or if it would work out for me."

Dr. Weston knew that this could be one of the hard points. She tried to be reassuring. "I believe that I know your misgivings, but I wouldn't ask this of you without a good reason. Look Karl, any donor is going to be hard to come by and to limit us to just a white male who is a good match for you may make it impossible for us to help you. I know that there are profound differences between the races and sexes, but they aren't as great as you may think. As for race, the main difference is the individual's perception of society. Now for the difference between genders. Aside from the physical differences we're much the same. In behavior and how the mind works there are some things that are gender specific, but even in those areas there's some overlap between genders. The individual that's all male or all female in their psyche is rare. Most of us have both genders in our psyche, one being dominate over the other. There can also be profound differences between religious beliefs or politics. I assure you that whatever donor we use, whatever values and beliefs you have when we put you to sleep, will still be your same values and beliefs when you wake up. If you're a jerk when we put you to sleep, you'll still be a jerk when we wake you up."

Dr. Weston's humor got a laugh from Karl and broke the tension. She continued, "Look Karl, if you're thinking that if you end up with a donor of the other gender, you will end up a man trapped in a woman's body, that won't happen. In order to keep the cranial nerves intact, and also the pituitary gland, we keep the donor's hypothalamus and pituitary gland. They control reproduction, flight or fight, self-preservation, appetite, sleep, body temperature, regulation of sexual function, and control of water balance. In other words, you'll be the same between the ears as you are between the legs. To put it another way, part of your brain would be female to start out with. That would help the transition to your new gender. So, Karl, what's your answer to the question? You will still have the final say on the use of any donor."

Karl had already made up his mind. After all, what difference did

MICHAEL O. GREGORY

it make? This crazy thing wouldn't work anyway. He just saw it as a way out of his wretched life. With a nod he responded, "Okay doc, the answer to questions one and two is yes."

Dr. Weston smiled. They had their candidate. "Thank you, Karl, and welcome aboard. Now there are things that we need to take care of. The first is for you to make out a will. You may dispose of your property as you see fit, but anything that you would like to keep will it to the Evans Clinic. Anything willed to us will be transferred back to you after the surgery. You will also request that you be cremated. This is to protect all of us. Oh, by the way, this enterprise is called project 'Trade In'. That seems to be our director's attempt at humor."

CHAPTER FOUR

The morning dawned overcast and dark, with a cold wind and rain that chilled a person to the bones. The wind blew the rain on Sarah, as she moved from one room to the next to clean them. After three days of rain, she yearned to see the sunshine again. Her boys were getting cabin fever having to stay in out of the rain. They needed to get outside to run off some of their excess energy, and she needed a break.

Sarah pushed the cleaning cart to the next room. There she knocked on the door and called out, "Housekeeping!" After receiving no answer to her call, she took the passkey at her wrist and opened the door to go in. She took one step and stopped; the room was still occupied. A young woman lay sleeping on her back on the still made-up bed. The young woman was dressed in a green-knit pullover sweater, denim skirt and pantyhose, but no shoes.

Sarah started to excuse herself, "Excuse me, Miss I…" She froze, something looked very wrong here. The young woman seemed to be unusually still and had started to turn blue. Sarah rushed to the bedside to check on the condition of the young woman, then grabbed the phone. As soon as the desk clerk answered she yelled, "George, call 911! I have a dying white girl in room 104! I can't tell if she's breathing or not, hurry!"

Sarah then grabbed the young woman by the shoulders and shook her vigorously shouting, "Come on, girl! Don't give up on me!"

When she got no response, Sarah dragged the unconscious young

MICHAEL O. GREGORY

woman from the bed to the floor and rolled her onto her back. She then started to give the young woman CPR. Soon Sarah heard the wailing of a siren coming closer.

Five hours later the young woman lay comatose in a hospital bed all wired up and on a respirator. Dr. Williams and Dr. Newman were standing next to her bed in conversation. Dr. Newman let out a sigh and turned to Dr. Williams. "We have her stable for now, but a whole hell of a lot of good it's doing her."

Dr. Williams nodded. They had worked hard to save the young woman, but when she had stopped breathing in the motel room she had gone too long without oxygen. He replied, "Yea, I believe you're right. Her coma is irreversible. The lower brain is viable. The body will live, but the higher brain functions are gone. She's in a permanent vegetative state. By the way, what did the police have to say about her?"

Dr. Newman looked at the young woman as she lay unmoving in her bed. He thought that what a tragedy it was that a young woman with so much of her life still ahead of her had to do this. He answered, "She had been registered at the motel as Miss Susan Smith from Columbia, South Carolina, but they believe this to be an alias. She had just fourteen dollars and seventy-three cents in her purse, and no identification. They're trying to get a positive identification on her now. The police are reporting it as an intentional overdose. She was trying to kill herself."

Dr. Williams nodded in agreement. "It looks like she was successful. I will never understand why people think that the only way out is death. With so many people trying to live, it seems a waste."

Dr. Newman kept looking at the young woman as he answered, "You can say that again. She's such a beautiful young woman. I wonder what it was that drove her to do this?"

It was early afternoon on a clear and cold day. Karl's curtains were closed against the bright afternoon sun so that he could watch the soap operas on the television from his bed. He heard a knock at the door and called out, "Come in!"

The door opened and in walked Dr. Evans, followed by Dr. Weston, Dr. Martinovich and Dr. Lokey. Dr. Evans spoke first. "Good-afternoon Karl. How are you doing today?"

"About as well as can be expected Dr. Evans."

Dr. Evans reached for a chair. "May we have a seat? We have something to talk to you about."

Turning down the volume on his television, Karl nodded. "Yes, go ahead."

Everyone dragged chairs up to Karl's bed and took their seats. As soon as everyone had gotten comfortable, Dr. Evans looked at Karl. "We have good news for you Karl. We have a donor."

Karl suddenly became very excited. He turned off the television and looked at Dr. Evans. "A donor! When did you get him?"

Dr. Evans continued, "It's a transfer from Nashville. The donor is in an irreversible coma. We had the donor transferred here from Nashville for long-term care. The donor is a white female. Age…"

Karl interrupted, "Just hold it! Did you say female?"

Dr. Evans gave Karl a stern look that told him not to interrupt. "Yes, I did say female. Now, if you will please hold your questions until I'm finished, then I'll answer your questions. As I was saying, the donor is a white female, age early to mid-twenties, five-foot eight-inches tall, one-hundred and thirty-four pounds, black hair and green eyes. She was found in a motel room in time to resuscitate the body, but the brain is gone."

Karl shook his head, let down that the donor had turned out to be a female. Even though it had been a possibility he had never considered it. "A female you say."

Dr. Evans gave Karl a reassuring smile. "Yes, Karl, a female. You did say when we accepted you for 'Trade In' that a change of gender would be acceptable. Are you now having second thoughts about it?"

Karl started to reject the donor when he thought. *Why am I so concerned about what gender the donor is? After all this crazy thing isn't going to work anyway. It's just suicide by surgery.* Shaking his head, Karl

MICHAEL O. GREGORY

answered, "No, I just want to know if this is my best option."

Dr. Evans felt sure that Karl would accept the donor with the right explanation. "Okay, Karl, before this one there were three others. One seemed good until the test showed him to be HIV positive. Another had a brain case too small. The third looked good, but the police were able to identify him, and the family claimed him. Let me put it to you this way. Donors aren't so easy to come by. Most potential donors are identifiable and have someone who cares for them and will claim them. Others turn out to be unacceptable for other reasons. This may not just be your best option, but your only option. It's up to you Karl. Do you want to take this donor?"

Karl quickly made up his mind. After all, what did it matter anyway? So, what if the donor was a girl, he doubted that he would really become her. With a chuckle he responded, "You can't blame me for asking the question. I had a fantasy that you might be able to get me someone like Arnold Schwarzenegger, but I guess that in a not-to-perfect world, you must take whatever you can get. Of course, I'll take it."

With Karl's acceptance the tension in the room eased. Dr. Evans smiled, relieved that they could now go forward with the surgery. "Thank you for your acceptance, Karl. Now let's get down to the business at hand. The donor will be here this afternoon. We already have blood samples from the donor. We will get a fresh sample from you, and then we can start to tailor the treatment to match you and the donor's DNA. That will take two days. Then we will do the surgery. The start time for the surgery will be six AM, on…let's see, this is Wednesday. That will make it Saturday. Dr. Martinovich will be doing the surgery, Dr. Weston will be assisting and Dr. Lokey will be your anesthesiologist. I will also be assisting in the surgery. Now, the night before the surgery, after you have been prepared for surgery, you will be given a sleeping pill so that you can get a good night's sleep. When we wake you up in the morning, you'll be given an injection to relax you before you're taken in for surgery. I believe that you have already been briefed on the surgery?"

Karl nodded. "Yes I have."

Dr. Evans continued, "One other thing, would you like to see the donor when she gets here, before you have the surgery?"

Karl shook his head. After all she meant nothing to him. Why should he want to see her? Looking at Dr. Evans, Karl said, "No, I don't feel that I should see her now before the surgery. I want to see her for the first time in the mirror. That way she will never have been another person to me. I do have one question. Is she good looking?"

Dr. Lokey smiled at Karl, "I went up to Nashville to do tests on her. I can assure you that she's a very attractive young lady."

Dr. Evans remarked, "It's a good idea that you meet her for the first time as yourself. Everyone will be leaving now, except for Dr. Lokey. He wants to go over the anesthesia procedures with you. See you Saturday morning."

Everyone except Dr. Lokey got up and left the room. Dr. Lokey moved to the chair closest to Karl. Settling into the chair he said, "Well Karl, looking forward to the big day Saturday?"

Karl nodded, "Yes, but I'm a bit nervous."

"That's understandable." Dr. Lokey said, "Now as to what will happen on Saturday. When they bring you into the operating room, I will be waiting for you. You will be placed on the table face down. We will then place your arms on boards that stick out from the table at right angles from the shoulders. After your arms are secured to the boards, I will start an IV. I will then tell you to start to count back from one hundred. I will then say to you, good night Karl. The next thing you will know is that it will be all over with. Now, any questions?"

Karl shook his head, "No, I have no questions. I've been through surgery before, it's much the same for me."

Dr. Lokey leaned forward in his chair, moving closer to Karl, "Listen Karl, there's something else that I want to talk to you about, and this is just friend to friend, not doctor to patient. Do you have any reservations about what you're about to do? You're about to make the most extreme identity change there is. You will not only be another

MICHAEL O. GREGORY

person, but you will also have to adapt to the other gender. You will have to live your life as a woman. You may be giving up something that later you may decide that you didn't want to."

Karl understood what Dr. Lokey was trying to say, but what did it matter. He didn't expect to survive it anyway. It would just be a way out of an unbearable life. With a nod Karl replied, "Thank you for your concern, but I have no reservations about what I'm about to do. And what if anything that I'm giving up, if you think it's hard to adapt to being a woman, try adapting to life in a wheelchair. Besides, what does it matter to be a man if you can't even feel your manhood, or do anything with it?"

Dr. Lokey nodded in understanding, I can see what you mean Karl. Well, good luck Saturday."

With a nod Karl responded, "Thanks, doc."

Dr. Lokey got up from his chair and left the room, leaving Karl alone with his thoughts.

At four-thirty AM Saturday they awoke Karl and gave him an injection. At five-thirty AM they wheeled him into the operating room and transferred him to the operating table. Dr. Lokey stood there waiting for him. "Good-morning, Karl, today's the big day. How do you feel?"

Even sedated Karl still felt very apprehensive. He felt sure that this would be his last moments of consciousness. That he would never wake up from the surgery. "Ask me later, doc."

Dr. Lokey secured Karl's arms to the boards. He then took the IV and started to insert it. "Are you comfortable Karl? I'm going to start the IV, then we will be ready."

Karl wondered if he was doing the right thing. Perhaps he should shout, "Stop it!" But no this had to be the right thing to do. He just closed his eyes and nodded his head as best he could.

Dr. Lokey started the IV, "Now I want you to start counting backward from one hundred."

"Okay, doc, one hundred…ninety-nine…ninety-eight…"

"Good-night, Karl."

Chapter Five

Karl's consciousness slowly spiraled up from a great-dark depth. At first, he felt confusion and anxiety as his brain tried to figure out what his senses were trying to tell it. Out of the confusion he heard a voice calling from far away. He also had an awareness of light through his still closed eyelids. His first thought had been that they didn't do the surgery. That had to be it, being that he still lived. The voice still called, "Karl, wake up! Karl, wake up!" Karl tried to answer, but a strange voice kept talking. It was a feminine voice that sounded soft yet strong, clear and with a somewhat dulcet quality to it. It seemed that every time he spoke, this feminine voice mouthed the words. Suddenly Karl snapped awake. "Is that me? Is that my voice?"

Dr. Lokey and Dr. Prater were standing next to the bed. Dr. Lokey said, "Yes, Karl that's your voice."

Karl looked down at her body. The two protrusions that showed from under the single sheet that covered her body could only be a woman's breasts. The rest of the profile under the bed sheet also seemed different, unlike anything she had ever seen before. To say that she was amazed had to be an understatement. She exclaimed, "Oh my! Oh my! You did it! You really did it!" Karl still struggled with the implications of what she was experiencing. Even with the proof of what her eyes and ears were telling her, she still had a hard time believing it.

Dr. Lokey smiled at her. "Yes, we did. And do you know where you are?"

Karl nodded. "Yes, I do. I'm in my room, in my bed." Karl glanced

31

MICHAEL O. GREGORY

down at her body once again, just to make sure that it wasn't a dream. Her mind finally had to accept what her senses were telling it. Her life had just changed in ways that she had been completely unprepared for, Karl thought. *I'm a girl! I'm a girl! What do I do now!* Karl fought to maintain control as she came to terms with her new self.

Dr. Lokey put a restraining hand on Karl's shoulder to reassure her. "Good, now don't try to move yet. We want to check you out first. First off, how do you feel?"

Karl did feel different, but she found it hard to put words to it, "I feel…well…different in some way, I don't know. It's hard to understand and put words to it."

Dr. Lokey asked, "Different, like how?"

Karl still tried to sort it out. She felt like her senses were trying to tell her something, but her mind was having a hard time processing it. "I guess that you might say not like my old self. I'm still trying to sort it out."

Dr. Lokey had a pin in his hand. He raked it along the bottom of Karl's foot and got an immediate reaction. "Wow! Wow!"

Dr. Lokey chuckled. "You felt that?"

Karl could barely contain herself. "You're damn right I did! Wow!" She had a broad smile on her face as tears rolled down her cheeks. "Oh my God, it worked! It really worked! I can feel my legs! I can feel everything! Oh, thank you, God! Thank you!"

By then everyone had started to get teary-eyed. Dr. Lokey said, "Now are there any problems with your vision, hearing, or sense of smell?"

Karl shook her head. "No, everything seems to be working just fine."

Dr. Lokey held the index finger of his right hand in front of, Karl's face and had her follow it with her eyes as he moved his finger from side to side, and up and down. He then removed the bed sheet that covered her. Karl had on a shapeless green hospital gown that closed at the back with ties. He then had Karl touch her nose with the index finger of each hand. Karl noticed immediately that she could do it without any effort. He then had her draw up her knees, first the right, then the left. It had been such a long time that Karl had to try to remember how to use her legs.

Dr. Lokey nodded satisfied at Karl's performance so far. "That's good. Now are you ready to sit up."

Karl looked at Dr. Lokey. This would be the big moment that she had dreamed of, but never thought could happen again. With a nod she said, "Okay, doc, let's do it."

Dr. Lokey motioned to Dr. Prater. "Dr. Prater and I will help you sit up."

Dr. Prater took her by the left arm while Dr. Lokey took her by the right arm. They lifted her to a sitting position, then rotated her so that her legs were hanging over the side of the bed.

Dr. Lokey gave Karl a reassuring pat on the back. "How are you doing so far.?"

Karl beamed with joy. "Just great, doc."

Dr. Lokey turned to Dr. Prater. "Okay, Maryanne, just hold onto her while I get the walker. Letting go of Karl's arm, Dr. Lokey reached behind himself, picked up the walker, and placed it in front of, Karl. With a smile, Dr. Lokey said, "Okay, Karl, it's time to walk. I want you to place your hands on the walker. Dr. Prater and I will help you."

Karl reached out and grabbed the handgrips of the walker firmly. With a determined look, Karl said, "I'm ready, let's do it."

While keeping a loose grip on her right arm and Dr. Prater having a loose grip on her left arm, Dr. Lokey said, "Good, now stand up."

With the help of Dr. Lokey and Dr. Prater, Karl got to her feet. Karl exclaimed with unbridled joy, "Look, I'm standing! Really standing! Oh, thank you God, thank you!"

Dr. Lokey pointed to a chair by the window, "Now let's walk over to the chair by the window."

Karl, still gripping the hand grips firmly, said, "Okay, doc." With first one hesitant step then another, gaining confidence with each step, Karl walked over to the chair by the window and sat down.

"You're doing well Karl." Dr. Lokey said, "With a little help you will

MICHAEL O. GREGORY

soon be walking on your own without that walker. Dr. Prater and I must talk to you. But first, would you like to see what you look like now?"

Karl, eager to see herself, said, "Yes, doc, I'd like that."

Dr. Prater went to the night table, took a hand mirror from the drawer, returned to Karl's side and handed it to her.

Karl took the mirror and held it up to her face. In the mirror she saw a very attractive woman in her mid-twenties. She had an oval face framed with lustrous-black hair that cascaded down over her shoulders past her breasts, Vivid-green eyes with long lashes, a finely shaped nose, full lips and finely drawn jawline. The sight of herself in the mirror took her breath away for a moment. She thought that the voice went well with the face in the mirror. Karl said, "Say, I'm beautiful. I love it."

Smiling, Dr. Prater said, "Then you are pleased with the results?"

Karl was beside herself. "Am I pleased? I couldn't possibly be more pleased." She then chuckled. "This would be the face of Karl's dream girl. Now I'm the dream girl."

Dr. Lokey and Dr. Prater laughed a little at Karl's humor. Karl took one last look, taking care to memorize every aspect of her new face, then passed the mirror back to Dr. Prater.

Dr. Prater said, "You can no longer use your old name. Karl died thirteen days ago of a heart attack. I believe that you have been thinking of a new name. We can't keep calling you, Jane Doe."

Karl had given no consideration to a new name, having thought that it wouldn't be needed. Karl said, "No we can't use Karl anymore, but I'd like a name close to Karl."

Dr. Prater then offered names that Karl passed on. "Then what about Karla?"

Karl thought for a moment, then shook her head. "No, it sounds too ordinary."

"What about Kay?"

Karl rolled the name around on her tongue silently for a couple of seconds before she answered. "No, I don't like that one either."

"What about Kitty?"

WOMAN IN THE MIRROR

Karl raised her eyebrows and rolled her eyes at the thought of anyone calling her such a frivolous name, "Oh Lord, no! Do you think that I look like a, kitty?"

Stifling a laugh, Dr. Prater said, "Okay, then what about Catherine?"

Karl tested the name and smiled, "Yes, Catherine sounds like a lovely name. I like it. My new name will be Catherine." The name had character, a noble ring to it, she really liked it.

Dr. Prater also thought that the name suited her well. "Okay, Catherine, now for your last name. What would you like?"

Catherine thought for a moment. "Let's keep it simple. A name that will be easy to remember like White. I like that."

Dr. Prater nodded approval. "Then Catherine White it is. From now on that's who you will be known as. Now, Dr. Lokey has something to speak to you about."

Nodding, Dr. Lokey said, "Catherine, I like that name. We need to talk about your cover story. For anyone who asks, you haven't any memory of anything before you woke up in this room just now. You have been told that you were found in a motel room in Nashville, and that's all that anyone knows about you."

Catherine approved of the cover story; it being simple with nothing made up to remember. "Yes, that's easy enough. That way I don't have to invent anything."

Dr. Lokey continued, "Now, you can be open to the doctors in Project 'Trade In', and one other nurse Helen Schofield. She will be the one closest to you during your recovery. She will help you through the trials of adjustment to your new body and instruct you in any special concerns of women. As for all the other nurses, two other nurses know the secret of Project 'Trade In', but to be on the safe side keep your cover with them all."

Catherine nodded. "Yes, I understand."

Dr. Lokey then said, "The Nashville police sent down all of Jane Doe's clothing and personal effects that were in the motel room when they found her. They are now in your closet. You may go through them

MICHAEL O. GREGORY

and keep whatever you want. They are yours now."

Dr. Lokey then looked at Dr. Prater. Dr. Prater went over to the night table, retrieved a gift-wrapped box and handed it to Catherine. "Catherine, this is just a little something for you from Dr. Lokey and me. I know that a girl likes something better than these hospital gowns to wear."

Catherine took the gift and opened it. Inside she found a red nightgown with black-lace trim, a pink-fleece robe and a pair of pink bedroom slippers. Catherine smiled, "Oh, thank you, I love it." She felt the satin fabric and lace of the nightgown between thumb and index finger. It felt soft and cool to the touch. Karl would never have considered wearing such a garment, but now as Catherine it seemed appropriate, and to be truthful she really did like it. The robe and slippers were a dark pink, what some called hot pink. They were all very pretty. With a smile she said, "Thank you very much, I really love it."

Dr. Lokey and Dr. Prater were pleased that Catherine liked her gift. Dr. Lokey said, "We enjoyed giving it to you. Now, one last thing, your birthday. You will have to give one when you go to get identification, like social security, or driver's license. Now, you are between the ages of twenty-four to twenty-six. Let's say, twenty-five. Now for a birth date."

Catherine thought for a moment, they said, "Yes, twenty-five seems about right. What's today's date?"

Dr. Lokey replied, "Today's Thursday March sixteenth."

Catherine looked at Dr. Lokey. "Since today is the first day of my new life, then it seems reasonable that it should be my birthday. Today's my twenty-fifth birthday."

Dr. Lokey and Dr. Prater said, "Happy birthday Catherine."

Catherine smiled, now that she had a name and a birth date, she had started to feel like a real person and accept her new identity. All of her life's experiences up to now had been as a man, as limited as they were. Now she would have to put it all behind her and become what she now was. She would have to look at it as not losing something, but rather gaining much more. Looking at Dr. Lokey and Dr. Prater she said, "Thank you. I was just thinking of a book that I once read. It was about Julius Caesar. What comes to mind is what he said when he crossed the Rubicon River on his way back from Gaul to Rome, 'the die is cast'. Those words seem to be appropriate for me now. For me the die is cast. What is done can't be undone. For better or for worse this is who I am for the rest of my life."

Dr. Prater patted Catherine on the forearm and gave her a reassuring smile. "Let's hope it's for the better."

With a nod Catherine responded, "Yes, let's hope so. As I remember in the book, they had Julius Caesar's words in Latin. I wish that I could remember them now."

Dr. Lokey thought for a moment, then said, "I took Latin in college. As I remember in Latin there's more than one way to say that. The words he used were *Jacta alea est*. Is that what you wanted?"

Catherine thought for a moment, "Yes, that sounds like it. I'll have to try to remember that."

Dr. Lokey put his hand on Catherine's shoulder. "We will be going now. Do you want to go back to your bed, or stay here at the window?"

Catherine replied, "I believe that I'll be just fine where I'm at."

Dr. Lokey continued, "Nurse, Schofield is waiting at the nurse's station. Do you want her now?"

Catherine shook her head. "No, not now. Give me about fifteen minutes, then send her in."

After Dr. Lokey and Dr. Prater left the room, Catherine took a minute to just sit and look out the window as she marveled at her transformation. It excited her to have the freedom of a complete and healthy body again. At the same time, she feared that someone would see through her ruse; figure out that she was something other than what she seemed to be. She had a woman's body, but she as yet had to learn what being a woman entailed. Slowly she got to her feet. With the aid of the walker, she then took the nightgown, robe and slippers and walked to the bathroom where they had a full-length mirror.

Standing next to her walker in front of the mirror, she loosens the

37

ties at the back of her hospital gown, and lets it slip to the floor. She now stood nude in front of the mirror. She took a long look at herself, the face and hair, the full breasts, the narrow waist and the broad-rounded hips. It was the image of a young, healthy and very attractive young woman. She took a couple of minutes to study in detail this body that was now hers, but still alien to her. After the inspection she found it thrilling the challenge of becoming this person. She hadn't expected the surgery to work, but it did and no one had been more surprised than she had been. Now she must make the best of the situation and learn to live in her new body.

She spoke to the mirror. "Well hello woman in the mirror. We may be strangers now, but we'll soon know ourselves very well, for you are now me and I'm you."

After a last look at her new body, she put on the new nightgown, thinking that she looked good in red. After putting on the robe and slippers, she walked back to the chair by the window to wait for Nurse Schofield.

CHAPTER SIX

The next two weeks for Catherine were just marvelous. Catherine's walking though unstable at first, improved by the hour. As she gained confidence in herself, she had been able to discard the walker. After that she carried a cane for a couple of days, not making much use of it.

Catherine had spent her first day in her private suite with Nurse Schofield and the Doctor of Project 'Trade In'. All the doctors were very inquisitive. They poked and prodded her, drew blood, took a urine sample and gave her a physical examination. They also had questions, many questions, they didn't stop; they wanted to know everything. A lot of the questions were about her feelings and what she was experiencing, some were very personal.

The second day they encouraged her to leave her suite and to start walking about the clinic. It was an ordeal at first for her to leave the comfort and security of her suite and face the other people who worked or were patients at the clinic. She couldn't help it that she felt different. Everyone that looked at her, she wondered if they could sense the difference in her. After a while she realized that no one had started to pay any special attention to her and started to relax. However, she soon noticed how young men looked at her and followed her with their eyes. It became disconcerting for her at first, but she soon realized that they were just admiring a pretty girl. That realization she found amusing, and helped to raise her confidence and self-esteem in herself.

By the evening of the second day Catherine had acquired from

MICHAEL O. GREGORY

Nurse Schofield two sweatshirts, two sweatpants and three casual frocks of a cotton/polyester floral-print. With these she wouldn't have to wear a nightgown and robe around the clinic.

Her physical rehabilitation consisted of walking about the clinic, and swimming in the rehabilitation swimming pool. For this she had been provided with a not very flattering one-piece navy-blue swimming suit. She had started to become accustomed to and appreciative of her new body. She still had memories of Karl's body before the accident. In standing, walking, sitting, posture and other things there were minor differences between Karl's body before the accident and this new body of hers. Most of this was due to the female's different center of balance, wider pelvis and pelvic tilt. She could also remember that Karl's body at seventeen years had more upper-body strength than she now had with her new body.

Another thing new to her was the fluctuating hormone levels and almost daily changes in her body during her cycle. Six days after she woke up she had her first period. Nurse Schofield had to instruct her about feminine hygiene and the use of pads and tampons. At least she didn't need the lecture about female reproduction and boys.

There were other things like the care of her long and thick hair that fell well below her shoulder blades, almost down to her waist. She had to get used to the weight of it and it falling over her ears and in front of her face if she didn't keep it pinned back. And it became a lot of work to keep the tangles out. She took to brushing it out and wearing it with a headband to keep it pulled back from her face, or in a ponytail. Then there was the shaving of the legs and underarms. A chore that had to be repeated often. It amazed her how many little differences there were. Some were insignificant, but they all had to be learned. Once things started to sort themselves out, Catherine started to enjoy her new role. She had accepted her new character and embraced it. She had started to like being a woman. She found it no better or worse than being a man, just different. She need not dwell on the past; there could be no looking back. As soon as she could, she started with aerobics and light weights in the rehabilitation center gym. It would be good for general good health, strength and toning. It also let her know and get use to how her new body moved and reacted.

Nurse Schofield, very attractive, well-groomed, blonde, five- foot three- inches and in her late twenties had become a good friend to Catherine. She became a confidante, big sister and teacher to Catherine. Nurse Schofield gave Catherine all the help that she needed, and she really needed and appreciated it. For Nurse Schofield no question from Catherine was too trivial, too bizarre, or too embarrassing. Nurse Schofield instructed Catherine in everything that she needed to know. That even pertained to the most personal things. Whenever Catherine needed her she was there; they had all their meals together and were always talking about something.

The first two weeks of Catherine getting to know her new self-proved to be a time of hard work, adventure, pleasure and discovery. They went by too quickly. By now she reacted instinctively to her new name. She had also started to lose that feeling, except for the young men, that everyone was watching her. It seemed normal to look in the mirror in the morning and see the image of herself reflected back at her. Catherine by now had started to know the woman in the mirror very well.

It was Thursday, the first day of the third week for Catherine as her new self. She had just finished her aerobics session, had taken a shower and had started to get ready for lunch, when Dr. Weston knocked and entered her suite. With a smile, Dr. Weston said, "Hello, Catherine, how are you today?" Dr. Weston then took a seat in a chair.

Catherine, continuing to get ready for lunch responded, "Just fine, Dr. Weston, I'm getting ready for lunch now." Catherine wondered what Dr. Weston wanted to talk about and took a seat in a chair close to Dr. Weston. She then said, "I have time, Dr. Weston, go ahead."

Dr. Weston gave Catherine a reassuring smile to put her at ease. "We are really pleased with your performance. You are fully recovered now, and you need to start getting out in public. Easter is not far off.

How would you like to go shopping at the mall for a new Easter outfit?"

Although Catherine felt at ease in the familial environment of the clinic, she still felt very self-conscious of herself and shy around people that she didn't know. Given a choice, she had rather remain in familiar surroundings where she felt most comfortable. However, she also knew that she must eventually face the public as her new self at some time. She considered rather-or-not she should go to the mall. Even though she felt apprehensive about it, she decided to go anyway. With a nod Catherine responded, "I'd like that Dr. Weston, but how am I to get to the shopping mall?"

Dr. Weston had a ready answer. "I can have Nurse Schofield go with you. She will drive you to the mall, and you can take all the time you want. Just look at everything you want and have a good time. We just want you to enjoy yourself."

Catherine thought about it for a few seconds. As the first time out in public, a trip to the mall wouldn't be such a traumatic event. Finally, Catherine said, "Okay, then I'd love to go to the mall."

Dr. Weston felt pleased that Catherine had agreed to go. "I will get with Nurse Schofield. You just be ready to go after lunch." She then said good-bye to Catherine and let herself out.

Catherine thought that if she were going to the mall, the casual frock that she had just put on wouldn't do. She went into her closet where Jane Doe's clothing had been put for her use. She went through them looking for something suitable to wear. As nervous as she was, she dare not wear a miniskirt. Wearing a skirt was still a new experience for her. She only felt comfortable wearing a skirt or dress that had a hemline below the knee. Anything above the knee made her feel insecure about showing so much of herself. The idea of wearing a miniskirt in public horrified her. All of Jane Doe's dresses and skirts were short, except for a denim skirt; it would have to do. It being cold outside, she also took a green-knit sweater. All the regular shoes had high heels and she didn't trust herself to wear them. She already had on a pair of Jane Doe's running shoes so they would be just fine.

Dr. Weston sat at her desk working when a knock came at the door. "Come in!" Dr. Weston exclaimed.

Nurse Schofield entered and stopped in front of Dr. Weston's desk. "You wanted to see me Dr. Weston?"

Dr. Weston looked up at Nurse Schofield. "Yes, Helen, I have an assignment for you. I want you to change into street clothes and take Catherine shopping at the mall for a new Easter outfit." Dr. Weston then pushed a credit card across her desk to Nurse Schofield. "Here's a Master Card, you can charge it to the clinic."

Dr. Weston's voice and manner now became more direct. "Now, Helen, this outing is very important for Catherine. She has become accustomed to her surroundings here at the clinic, but this will be her first time out in public. She will be very nervous and self-conscious. She will be feeling that every eye in the store is on her. Just relax and have a good afternoon of shopping. After a while Catherine will realize that no one is paying any more than normal attention to her. She will then relax and start to enjoy herself. This outing is for her to gain confidence at getting out in public."

Nurse Schofield picked up the credit card, "Is there anything else Dr. Weston?"

Dr. Weston shook her head, "No, nothing else. Catherine will be ready to go after lunch. So just take all the time you want and have a good time."

"We'll do just that Dr. Weston. I'll make sure that Catherine has a wonderful time." Nurse Schofield left Dr. Weston's office, changed into street clothes, then went to have lunch with Catherine.

After lunch Nurse Schofield drove Catherine to the Lenox mall. There they entered Macy's department store to begin their shopping. Catherine felt nervous, but eager to be shopping with her good friend Helen. The walk from the car to the store had been an agonizing venture for Catherine. Every time that anyone even glanced in her direction, she felt as if their eyes were boring into her and wondered if they were looking at her. Once inside everything seemed to be normal. Everyone

MICHAEL O. GREGORY

seemed to be looking at the merchandise instead of her. After a few minutes Catherine started to relax and enjoy herself.

They started in the dress department. They looked at everything once, then started to look again. Helen and Catherine were of different personalities and had very different tastes in clothing. Helen had an outgoing personality and felt comfortable with people. Her choice in clothing could be said to be in keeping with her personality. She didn't feel self-conscious about wearing something that made her stand out. Catherine felt very different. She was a caring person but lacked confidence in her mind. Her desire would be to find something conservative. She wanted to dress correctly without attracting attention to herself. This of course made a difference in what Helen thought Catherine should get and what Catherine was looking for. Catherine finally decided on a dress. It was a light-cotton floral print on a lavender background with white-on-white embroidered collar.

At the cosmetics department Helen persuaded Catherine to have a makeover. Up to now Catherine had been reluctant to use cosmetics, not knowing the art of its use. About all that Helen had been able to do was to get Catherine to try lipstick. After the salesgirl had finished, she showed Catherine the results in the mirror. After seeing the results of what cosmetics could achieve Catherine was hooked. She ended up buying a whole line of cosmetics.

After the cosmetics Catherine needed a white purse to go with her dress. She found a white-leather purse of a convenient size for her, with a shoulder carrying strap.

In the shoe department Catherine got a pair of white low-heel shoes to try on. "How do you like them?" Catherine said as she stepped and turned to get the feel of the shoes, and to let Helen see them.

Helen looked at the shoes and shook her head saying, "Well, I don't know. You really have shapely ankles. You should show them to the best advantage. Here, try these on." Helen opened another box, took out a pair of white high-heel shoes and handed them to Catherine to try on. Catherine put them on, then took a few steps, trying not to fall. She could see that wearing high-heel shoes seemed to be an acquired skill.

She sat back down and removed them, "No thanks Helen. Perhaps I may try high-heel shoes later, but not now."

Helen opened another box and took out a pair of white pumps and handed them to Catherine to try on. Catherine put them on, then stepped and turned to try them out. "How do they look?" Catherine said.

With a smile Helen responded, "They look good on you. They give your ankles a better line than the flats do. I think that you should get them."

Catherine then made up her mind. "Okay, then I will take them."

After paying for the shoes, they left the store and went for a cappuccino at Starbucks. After the cappuccino they returned to the clinic where Catherine put away her purchases. Catherine and Helen then went to dinner. It had been a wonderful day shopping at the mall with Helen. Catherine felt that this had been a test for her, and that she had passed. She felt good about herself.

CHAPTER SEVEN

At ten o'clock the next morning Catherine entered Dr. Weston's office. When she entered, she noticed that Dr. Lokey and Dr. Prater were there. Looking at Dr. Weston, Catherine asked, "You want to see me Dr. Weston?"

Dr. Weston stood up and came around from behind her desk. Dr. Lokey and Dr. Prater also stood up. Dr. Weston put out her right hand towards Catherine. "Congratulations Catherine, your treatment is complete. You are to be discharged as a patient today." Dr. Weston, Dr. Lokey and Dr. Prater then shook Catherine's hand. After a brief exchange of well-wishes, they all took their seats. Dr. Lokey settled himself into an over-stuffed chair, Catherine sat on the sofa with Dr. Prater. Dr. Weston took her chair behind her desk.

When everyone was comfortable Dr. Weston addressed Catherine. "We have some things for you Catherine. First, we have obtained a Social Security card for you in the name of Catherine White." Dr. Weston then took a card from in front of her and placed it on the corner of her desk so that Catherine could reach it. Dr. Weston continued, "Second, the money that you put in trust with us. We have placed eight-hundred dollars in a checking account, and the rest in a passbook savings account for you in the name of Catherine White at the Wells Fargo Bank." Dr. Weston picked up two cards from her desk, "You need to sign these two cards were indicated by the 'X' and return them to the bank." Dr. Weston then picked up two bankbooks from her desk. "Also, here is your checkbook and savings passbook." Dr. Weston placed the cards,

46

checkbook and passbook on the corner of her desk with the Social Security card. She then continued, "Third, Nurse Schofield will take you down to the Department of Motor Vehicles today so that you can get a picture ID."

Catherine got up from the sofa, stepped up to the desk, gathered up the cards, checkbook, passbook, and returned to her seat on the sofa. She regarded the cards and bankbooks in her hands with pride. She had become a real person now; she had a real identity.

Dr. Weston now had other things to talk about. "Catherine I would now like to talk to you about employment." Catherine refocused her attention on Dr. Weston. Dr. Weston continued, "Now I know that you are eager to get away from the clinic, to find a job, a place to live and to start living your life. I also know as well as you that you have no work history, no education records and no credit history. Without those you will find it hard to find employment, or an apartment to live in. Now you don't have to accept it if you have other plans; I would like to offer you employment with the Evans Clinic as a nurse's aide in our long-term care facility. We will pay you the current wage for a nurse's aide. What do you say Catherine? Do you want to come to work for us?" Dr. Weston regarded Catherine with an expectant look awaiting her reply.

Dr. Weston's offer had caught Catherine by surprise. A nurse's aide wouldn't be Catherine's first choice of employment. She had had enough of hospitals, clinics, nursing homes and doctors. She just wanted to get away from them. However, Dr. Weston had spoken the truth, Catherine knew that she had nothing to fall back on. What would she do if she left the clinic, be a waitress in a dinner, become a domestic, serve drinks at some club or bar? And where would she live? Most likely in some place where she didn't want to live. Catherine also felt an obligation to the people here at the clinic that had helped her so much. After some thought she found the offer very attractive. With a smile she replied, "Thank you Dr. Weston. I had given it some thought as to how I would be able to find work and I was a bit worried about

MICHAEL O. GREGORY

it. I would love to work here at the clinic."

Dr. Weston smiled relieved that Catherine had accepted their offer. "That's good Catherine, glad to have you with us. We will start you on the day shift. This is Friday; you will report to the head nurse of the long-term care facility at eight AM Monday ready for work. I will call personnel and have you put on the payroll. When Nurse Schofield takes you to get your ID card at the DMV, she can also take you to the uniform shop that carries our uniforms so that you can get the uniforms and shoes that you will need to work here.

"Now, as for your living arrangements, you may stay on in your private suite here at the clinic until you find a place to live. There will be no charge for the use of the suite. Is that all right with you?"

Catherine found the arrangement acceptable, but hoped that it would only be temporary, until she could find a place of her own. She responded, "Thank you, Dr. Weston that will be just fine."

Dr. Weston continued. "I know that this may not be your choice of a carrier, but it will give you a work history. We can also get you a high school equivalency so that you can get into a trade school, business school, or college, whatever you want. Now, one last thing, how much driving experience do you have?"

Catherine thought for a moment recalling experiences of many years' past. "I had a learner's permit at age fifteen and had started to drive on my own for a little more than one year before the accident."

With a nod Dr. Weston said, "All right, we will get you tested for a permit and give you the training for you to get your driver's license. Do you have any questions?"

Catherine shook her head. "No questions Dr. Weston."

Dr. Weston said while getting up from behind her desk. "Good, I will send Nurse Schofield to meet you in your room. We will see you Monday morning."

Catherine shook hands again with Dr. Weston and the others. She then left the office.

Helen had already been waiting in her room when Catherine got there. Catherine changed clothes and put all the items that she had received from Dr. Weston in her purse. Looking at Helen Catherine said, "I also have to stop by the Wells Fargo Bank to drop off these cards."

Helen replied, "All right, it's not far from here, and not too much out of the way. Are you ready to go?"

Catherine started for the door. "Yes, let's get going."

On the trip to the Bank and the Division of Motor Vehicles Catherine talked with Helen about her new job. For Catherine it would be the first real job that she had ever had, she felt really excited about it. She also talked about getting her own apartment and being able to live on her own for the first time in her life. Helen listened to Catherine and encouraged her to express her desires and dreams. They really enjoyed each other's company.

At the Department of Motor Vehicles, they looked at her Social Security card, asked her a few questions then took her picture for her ID card. When they finally handed her the temporary ID card, she took a good look at her picture on it and smiled with satisfaction. At last, she felt like she had really become a real person. The clerk at the Department of Motor Vehicles informed her that her permanent ID card would come to her in the mail in a few days.

At the uniform shop Catherine purchased five uniforms that the nurse's aides wore at the Evans Clinic. This consisted of five white-cotton/polyester blouses and five red jumpers. She also purchased a pair of white nurse mate shoes. Helen had told her that would be enough to start out with. She could get more uniforms later as she needed them.

After the uniform shop they got into the car and started going back to the clinic. Helen said, "Okay Catherine, I need to stop off at my apartment on the way back. You don't mind, do you? It's not far from here."

Catherine had been enjoying the trip so far and didn't mind the detour. She was also curious to see Helen's apartment. She replied, "No, Helen, I don't mind, go ahead."

They drove to Helen's apartment. When they got there Helen

invited Catherine in to see her apartment. Helen had a large two-bedroom apartment, tastefully furnished and very comfortable. Helen gave Catherine a tour of the apartment, and introduced her to Tiger, a large male yellow tabby cat. Catherine loved animals and Tiger immediately took to her. Catherine picked Tiger up and started to pet him as she followed Helen around the apartment. Tiger settled into Catherine's arms and purred with contentment. Helen noticed right away how Tiger took Catherine. They ended up in the kitchen where Helen started to make coffee.

Later they were seated at the kitchen table drinking coffee. After taking a sip of coffee and sitting her cup back on the table, Helen said, "Well, Catherine, how do you like the place?"

Catherine put her cup down on the table and glanced around the kitchen. "Oh, Helen, I love it. I'd like to find an apartment just as good as this that I can afford for myself."

Helen reached out taking Catherine's hand in her own and looked into her eyes, "Catherine, I've the extra bedroom and I've been looking for a roommate. How would you like to live here with me?"

Catherine grabbed Helen about the shoulders and gave her a hug. "Oh, thank you Helen I'd love to!"

When Catherine finally broke her embrace, Helen said, "All right Catherine since Tiger and I both want you it's a deal. We'll go fifty-fifty on the rent and expenses."

Catherine put forth her right hand. "It's a deal. Let's shake on it."

After they shook hands, Helen said, "You go out to the car, get your things, and put them in your bedroom. After that we'll go back to the clinic to get the rest of your things. Then we'll go out to dinner tonight. Do you like Chinese? There's a good Chinese restaurant close by that has a wonderful buffet. The food and service is really good."

By now Catherine had become so excited that it didn't matter where they went for dinner. She responded, "Yes, I do like Chinese."

Helen said, "Good, then Chinese it is. By the way, can you cook?"

Catherine with a smile replied, "If I read the instructions I can

WOMAN IN THE MIRROR

defrost." Catherine got a good laugh from Helen.

When Helen stopped laughing, she said, "That's okay, I'll teach you."

That night Catherine had the pleasure of sleeping in her own bed, in her own home, for the first time in her life. It had been a memorial day for her. She didn't know what life had in store for her, but at least she had gotten off to a good start.

CHAPTER EIGHT

April just had to be the most beautiful month in Georgia. Spring had arrived and nature had started to come alive again. There could be seen bright-green foliage on the trees, greening lawns, cool nights and pleasant days. The red bud and dogwood were in bloom. The azaleas were a blaze of color from white through pink, lavender, salmon and red. It seemed as if nature had been reborn.

Catherine also had a feeling of rebirth. She loved her work. It gave her a wonderful feeling to be doing useful work, rather than be dependent on other people for her well-being. She found the work of a nurse's aide hard and at sometimes monotonous, but she loved every minute of it. For Catherine life had become a wonderful experience. Everyday seemed like a new adventure for her. Her personality had also started to change. A softer more feminine side that had been suppressed had now started to come forth. She now felt free to express her feminine side.

Catherine and Helen went everywhere together. To the market, shopping at the mall and out for dinner. They were fast becoming best friends. Catherine looked to Helen for guidance whenever she encountered something that she didn't feel sure of. Helen would always be available when Catherine needed her. Catherine was grateful to have someone to lean on when she felt insecure about anything.

The next Tuesday, after, Catherine moved in, Helen took her down to the Department of Motor Vehicles, so that she could take the written test to get her learner's permit. Helen had also been helping

Catherine to catch up on her driving skills. Catherine's driving skills were coming back quickly. She felt that she would be able to pass the driving test and get her driver's license by the end of the month. Helen had also started to teach Catherine to cook. Catherine had never had much experience at cooking, but she had proved to be a quick study and made swift progress.

Catherine thought of what to do with Jane Doe's clothing and personal effects. Everything fit, and she was sure that everything had been chosen with great care. However, they were not to her liking. Catherine could see that Jane Doe had had a very different personality than hers. Most of the clothing had been meant to show as much of the legs and cleavage as could be considered decent, or with most of the clothing as far as Catherine was concerned, not so decent. Most of the clothing had also been snug fitted to show off the figure and used bold colors to attract attention. The lingerie had been chosen more for sexual display and titillation, not for comfort or practicality. There were even some items that Catherine didn't even want to dwell on their use. Catherine wanted her clothing to be conservative and good taste. She didn't want her clothing to show a lot of thighs or cleavage, or be suggestive of anything. She wanted her clothing to be feminine without being provocative, to use color to compliment, but not to attract undue attention.

At first Catherine had to use Jane Doe's clothing because she had nothing else. She had now started to replace Jane Doe's clothing as quickly as she could. Catherine wanted everything in her closet to be hers. Helen helped her shopping for new clothes and Catherine even let her choose some things for her. However, Catherine had some rules that were absolute, skirts and dresses had to have hemlines below the knee, to mid-calf and pants couldn't fit so tight as to be like sausage skins. There had been some jewelry, nothing expensive, costume jewelry mostly. She decided to keep three rings and a silver cross set with turquoise on a silver chain. She also kept a denim skirt, a pullover knit-green sweater, a dark-red knit cardigan sweater, a black-leather belt

MICHAEL O. GREGORY

and a black-leather coat. The rest of the clothing being too revealing or too provocative and some that she wouldn't even wear on a dare she threw out. All of Jane Doe's personal effects, to include the jewelry, except for the few pieces that she had decided to keep, were also thrown out. She was Catherine White now, Jane Doe no longer existed as far as she was concerned. Catherine still couldn't help but wonder what sort of a personality and lifestyle Jane Doe had had.

Helen had an active social life. She currently dated a high school English teacher. They would go out for dinner and a show or dancing every weekend and sometimes for dinner during the week. Catherine yet had no social life. She had her work and would go to the market, shopping at the mall, or out to dinner with Helen. Other than that, she just stayed home.

Helen, with the help of her boyfriend James, had been trying to fix Catherine up with a date and make it a foursome, but for the first two weeks Catherine resisted, still being in the process of sorting out what it meant to be a woman, and she didn't yet have a desire for, or feel comfortable around men. Helen had however been very persistent, so Catherine relented and accepted a dinner date for a Wednesday evening. That way the date would end early because of work the next morning. Helen had told James that Catherine had awakened from a coma and that she had amnesia and couldn't remember anything from her past.

James had a friend who would come as Catherine's date. He was an insurance salesman with whom James played racket ball with at the health club. Helen had insisted with James that whomever he got for Catherine would be of good character. James had assured her that his friend Robert had a reputation for being a gentleman with the ladies that he wouldn't try to impose himself on Catherine. James felt sure that Robert would be a good first date for Catherine.

Come Wednesday Catherine and Helen were ready to go at seven PM. Catherine had on her new outfit that she had gotten at Macy's that first day. Helen wore a form-fitted, red-knit dress with a hemline just above the knee, with red shoes and red purse to match. When the doorbell rang Helen answered the door and admitted two men. They were both six-foot tall and of athletic build, both wearing dark-blue suits. Taking one by the arm that Catherine recognized as James, Helen said, "Oh, James, you know Catherine. Why don't you go ahead and make the introductions?"

James, placing his hand on his friend's shoulder and facing Catherine said, "Catherine, this is Mr. Robert Stuart, we call him Bob." Glancing at his friend, James continued, "Bob, this lovely lady is Miss Catherine White."

Catherine and Bob shook hands and exchanged greetings. Catherine noticed how Bob made a quick appraisal of her with his eyes. She had noticed this behavior with a lot of the men that she had met. Perhaps it was an unconscious action with most men. She wondered if she would ever get used to it. She realized that women got their first impression by studying a man's face. Most men got their first impression by assessing the woman's body. She looked into his eyes and thought that she saw a gentleness that she could trust.

Helen took charge of things. "Hay, you have two ladies here who are hungry and ready to go to dinner. Where do you plan to take us?"

With a little chuckle at Helen's boldness, James said, "How would you like Italian tonight?"

Helen looked at Catherine. Catherine gave a nod of approval. "That's fine with us." Helen replied.

With a nod, James said, "Alright, girls, then it's the Olive Garden."

Helen then responded, "Just let us get our purses, then we can go."

They all went in James's car. James and Helen in the front seats, with Bob and Catherine in the back seat. During the drive to the Olive Garden, they passed the time talking about work and current events. It gave Bob and Catherine a chance to get to know each other.

At the restaurant, after they had been seated and had ordered, the conversation continued. Bob started to tell Catherine about himself. As a native of Swainsboro, Georgia, he grew up in Swainsboro and attended Georgia Southern University. He majored in history but found out that he could make a better living selling insurance than teaching school.

From the way that he talked about it, Catherine could see that Bob liked the insurance business. With a bit of levity Catherine remarked that she hoped that he wouldn't try to sell her any insurance tonight.

Bob smiled at Catherine's humor and gave his word that he wouldn't. He liked that in a person. James had briefed Bob about Catherine's condition, so he had been considerate enough not to ask her any questions about her past, or where she came from. Catherine had been tense at first, worried that she would commit some social blunder and embarrass herself. After a few minutes when nothing happened, she started to relax and enjoy herself.

The evening passed with casual conversation as everyone enjoyed a very good meal with friends. Occasionally, when Catherine looked in Helen's direction, Helen would flash her a reassuring smile. By the end of the evening Catherine no longer felt concerned with being able to interact with people in a public setting.

Upon returning home after dinner, everyone said his or her good nights at the door. James and Helen embraced and kissed and talked to each other, while Bob and Catherine said good night.

Bob took Catherine's hand in his as he looked into her eyes. "Catherine, I have had a wonderful time this evening. It has been such a pleasure to enjoy your company for dinner."

Despite a shaky start for her, the evening had turned out rather well. She had had a wonderful time. Catherine gave Bob a warm smile. "So have I Bob and thank you for the dinner."

Bob had taken an interest in Catherine. She was a beautiful woman and he very much wanted to see her again. Looking into her eyes, he said, "Oh, Catherine, may I call on you again?"

Catherine continued to look at him as she considered his request for another date. He did seem to be a kind and considerate person, a real gentleman, and handsome. She had really enjoyed his company. She decided to accept his offer and go on another date with him.

WOMAN IN THE MIRROR

Continuing to smile at him she replied, "Why yes, Bob, I would really like another date with you."

Bob felt pleased that Catherine had taken an interest in him and had been thrilled that she had accepted. "Then how about Friday for dinner? I'll pick you up at seven."

Catherine nodded acceptance. "Okay, Bob, Friday at seven it is. I'll be ready."

Catherine and Bob said their good nights. James and Bob then took their leave and headed back to the car. Catherine and Helen entered their apartment.

Once Catherine was inside and the door closed, she leaned back against it. It had started out as a trying evening for Catherine. She had been so afraid that she would commit some social blunder and embarrass herself. She had been so relieved that the date had gone so well. She had decided, even before the evening was over, that she would give another date favorable consideration. It wouldn't be because she had found interest in him as a man; it being too early for that. All that interested her now would be a platonic relationship. She still had gender identity conflict and couldn't see men as being of sexual interest to her. She realized that she had to start getting out and meeting people. Bob for her would be just a friend and a good first step.

Catherine and Helen changed, then went into the kitchen to make coffee. After Helen put the coffee on, they had a seat at the kitchen table. Helen was curious and wanted to know if Catherine had enjoyed herself. With an expectant look, Helen asked, "Well, did you have a good time this evening?"

Catherine sighed and a gratifying smile appeared on her face. "Yes, I did. My first date out with a man and I found it very enjoyable. At first I had a fear of falling on my face, but I soon found my fears not to be justified. Bob has even asked me out again."

Helen gave her an inquisitive look. "Are you going?"

Catherine, still smiling said, "Yes, I am. Bob seems to be a nice man. I don't think that he'll try to push me into any kind of a relationship

MICHAEL O. GREGORY

that I'm not ready for yet. I'll just have him as a friend for now. I'll see where the relationship goes from there."

Helen placed a hand on Catherine's wrist and spoke to her in a reassuring manner. "Catherine, If ever you need me I'm your friend and I'm here for you."

Helen's show of support really moved Catherine. "Thank you, Helen, it's so good to have such a good friend as you."

CHAPTER NINE

The fifth of May became Independence Day for Catherine. On that day she passed the driving test, receiving her driver's license from the Department of Motor Vehicles. Catherine and Helen celebrated by going shopping at the mall. They kept going from store to store until they were about to drop from exhaustion. They then went to refresh themselves with a cappuccino at the coffeehouse. They ended the day with the pages of the classified ad spread all over the living room floor. Catherine needed to find a good used car. After nine days Catherine found the car that she had been looking for. She bought a late-model red Ford Taurus from a reputable dealer. She felt proud of her car; it was a beautiful car. To her it meant complete freedom.

As for Catherine's weekly sessions with Dr. Prater, or Maryanne as she wanted Catherine to call her, they were starting to uncover some personal identity conflicts. They tried to smooth things out, but sometimes the road was bumpy. The person that now called herself Catherine had been the result of the most extreme metamorphosis imaginable. That there would be problems had been expected. It would just take time to work things out.

The day after Catherine got her new car, both she and Helen had the day off. They were in the kitchen having their morning coffee. Helen looked at Catherine. "Oh, Catherine, what do you have planned for today?"

Catherine put down her cup. "I plan to wash my hair, do my laundry, and then maybe in the afternoon go shopping. Why?"

"I have an appointment with my beautician this morning. Why don't you put off the laundry until later and come to the hairdresser with me?"

Catherine had never thought about going to a beautician. She had gotten use to caring for her long hair. After brushing it she would braid it, wear it in a ponytail, with a headband, or just pin it back away from her face. She sipped her coffee as she pondered rather or not to go with Helen. "Well, I don't know if I really need to go."

Helen appealed to Catherine. "Come on, Catherine, you can keep me company. Besides, I know that even though you can manage it well enough now, long hair is a problem for you. You should get it cut and styled. I can assure you that you will look and feel better afterwards."

Catherine was a little hesitant. She knew that it could be expensive to go to a beautician and she hadn't decided if it would be worth it, but if Helen thought that she should go. She asked, "So you think that I should get it cut and styled?"

Giving Catherine a reassuring nod, Helen said, "Yes, I do. You will look a lot more attractive with a new hairdo. Afterwards you'll find that it's a lot easier to care for."

Catherine thought for a moment as she sipped her coffee. She then put her cup on the table, having made up her mind. Touching her hair, she said, "This is how it was to start with. I've gotten used to it this way, but no harm in looking at what can be done. After all, I don't have to do anything unless I want to." Catherine would go with Helen to the beautician.

The beautician proved to be very accommodating. She had an opening in her appointment schedule, so she could do Catherine's hair. The beautician even had a computer that took a person's face and showed them on the monitor screen how they would look with many hair styles. Catherine choose a style with a relaxed curl that covered the back of the neck but was just below the shoulder. Everyone agreed that it made quite an improvement over the old look. It would also be easier to care for. Helen had also suggested that Catherine should see how it would be to be a blond. Catherine thought it enough for now just to have her hair cut and styled. Some day she may get the crazy idea to become a blond, but not now. She had to decline Helen's suggestion.

Catherine couldn't help feeling good about herself. The next day when she went to work everyone complimented her on her new hairdo. It made her feel very good about herself, and to feel that every cent that she had paid had been worth it.

Catherine had a ten AM appointment, her regular weekly session with Dr. Prater. At ten AM she knocked at the door to Dr. Prater's office and was admitted. Catherine and Maryanne exchanged greetings. Catherine then took a seat on the other end of the sofa from Maryanne.

Maryanne looked at Catherine's hair, "I see that you have a new hairdo. It's so beautiful. It makes you look so much more attractive, and it should be a lot more comfortable this summer."

Catherine felt pleased and at the same time a little self-conscious of the attention. With a self-satisfied smile, she said, "Why thank you Maryanne. Helen talked me into having it done. I'm glad because I like it too."

Maryanne now got down to business and started the session. "That's good Catherine. Now what have you been doing this week? Are you having any problems?"

Catherine was quick to make an announcement. "I've good news. I just completed the test for my high school equivalency from the state. Now I can enroll in Business College." Catherine felt proud. Every accomplishment helped to boost her confidence and self-esteem.

Maryanne also felt pleased to hear of Catherine's accomplishments. "What do you plan to take in Business College?"

Catherine replied with delight. "I plan to take administrative office management. I think that's a good career choice."

"I think that you'll do well in it. It's a whole lot better than staying a nurse's aide. There's no future in that."

"You're so right Maryanne." Catherine said with a nod.

Maryanne changed the subject. "Okay now Catherine, what else do you have to talk about?"

Catherine looked down at her hands in her lap. "Well, on the downside, it looks like my relationship with Bob is over."

"Oh, what happened?" Maryanne said with a concerned look.

Still looking down at her hands, Catherine replied, "It started out well enough. I found him to be a very nice man, a real gentleman; he treated me like a real lady. He had an interest in me and we enjoyed going out with each other. We had five dates, and I liked being with him. The problem was that every time he tried to advance the relationship, I'd back away until he just quit calling."

Maryanne had been aware that Catherine had these problems. She needed to bring these problems out and talk about them so that she could deal with them. Maryanne said, "If you like him so much, why keep him at arm's length like that?"

Catherine looked up to Maryanne as she spoke, "I guess that I still see men as just friends, nothing more. I still find it hard to see men as a romantic interest, and even harder the idea of having sex with a man."

Maryanne then asked a provoking question to see what reaction she would get from Catherine. "Then what about relationships with women?"

Catherine wasn't confused about this issue. "Well, Maryanne, I don't see women as rivals or objects of interest, just as friends and coworkers, nothing more. I guess that I'm just in a sexual limbo. One way to put it, my psyche is in flux. I no longer have the interest in women that Karl had, but I have yet to have felt any passion for men. However, this I can say, in my psyche in all other things I now see myself as female."

Maryanne nodded, acknowledging that she understood. "Yes, we expected that there may be problems in adjusting to the new persona. The most difficult being physical attraction to members of the opposite sex and sexual desire. That's why we have these weekly sessions. I want to help you work through all this."

Catherine sighed. "Yea, this metamorphosis isn't as easy and straight forward as I had expected it to be. The physical part of my new persona

WOMAN IN THE MIRROR

was the easy part. Who and what you are determines your role in society. How you dress, act and what you do, that's easy to adapt to. It's the mental persona that's hard to achieve. Old attitudes and experiences tend to confuse the emotions."

With a nod, Maryanne said, "I'm glad that you are at last coming to grips with it. Given time you will be able to set aside your old attitudes and become a complete person again. Anything else?"

Catherine now changed the subject to a dream that she had been having. "I've been having a dream lately."

Maryanne had found Catherine's dreams to be very interesting. "Yes, what about the dream?"

Catherine started to relate the dream. "Well, in the dream I'm out some place like the market, the mall, or at work. I happen to look down and I'm dressed in the wrong clothing. I should be dressed in women's clothing, but I'm dressed in men's clothing. I say to myself, no problem, I'll just go back home and change into the proper clothing. However, as hard as I try, I can't manage to find my way back home. I panic and start running around looking for my proper clothing. Then I look down and notice that the men's clothing that I had been wearing is gone. I'm standing in nothing but a T-shirt. I'm shocked and desperately start trying to pull down the T-shirt to cover my nakedness. That's usually where the dream ends."

Maryanne covered her mouth with her hand to stifle a laugh, masking it with a short cough. "That's really a good one. What do you think it means?"

Catherine again looked down at her hands in her lap. "Oh, Maryanne, I just don't know."

Maryanne thought for a few seconds, then asked, "Do you think that it means something about you dressing in women's clothing now?"

Catherine shook her head. "No, I don't. After all, clothing is as much a costume as anything else. If you're a cowboy in New Mexico, you don't dress like a cod fisherman in Maine. If you're a brick layer you don't wear a three-piece suit to work. If you're a soldier you wear

63

a uniform. It's only natural that I dress as myself. I have no problem dressing in women's clothing. After all, I now have the figure for it. What I do have a problem with is my purse. I must continually keep reminding myself of it so as not to forget and walk away from it. I guess that in time carrying a purse will become second nature to me."

Maryanne thought for a minute before she responded. "Then perhaps the clothing in your dream has another deeper meaning. Maybe it has something to do with gender identity."

Catherine nodded agreement. "Maybe you're right. I'd like to know what it's supposed to mean."

"I'm sure that someday you will come to know what it means."

Catherine sighed. "I hope so."

Maryanne felt that the session was about to end. "Anything else Catherine."

Catherine looked at her. "Yes, one other thing. When I was in a wheelchair people would pity me, patronize me, ignore me, or avoid me. Now as a woman I'm still being patronized and treated different at times."

Maryanne knew all too well what she meant. "Well, Catherine, that's life. We must all live in a society full of archaic rules of social order and dominance that we didn't make but must live by until we can change them. Anything else?"

Catherine thought for a moment, then spoke. "Yes, there's one thing else that I have to say. I'm trying very hard, but it's difficult. I'm having to learn behavior and other things right away that other women have had a lifetime to learn."

Maryanne knew how hard Catherine had been working to adjust. "I know that it has been a lot of hard work. For what it's worth Catherine, I think that you are doing marvelously. Just keep it up and you will get there. Now, is there anything else?"

Maryanne said as she started to get up from the sofa. "Then that's all for today. I will see you at the same time next week. If you really need to talk to me about any problems before then, I'm on call. Good-day Catherine."

Catherine got to her feet. "Good-day Maryanne."

CHAPTER TEN

By late May the weather in Atlanta had started to turn hot. The swimming pool at their apartment complex had opened for the summer. Catherine and Helen had decided that they had to start working on their tans. The only bathing suit that Catherine had was that unflattering navy-blue suit that she had gotten at the clinic. Helen also wanted to get a new one. At the first opportunity they went shopping for bathing suits.

At the mall they started looking at bathing suits. Catherine had in mind a one-piece suit for herself. After checking the racks, Catherine picked out a one-piece suit in aquamarine trimmed with white. Helen took one look at the suit and made a sour face. "You're not planning on getting that, are you?"

Catherine had the suit in her hand while deciding if she should try it on. "I may. I like the color and it's a one-piece."

Helen took the suit from Catherine and hung it back on the rack. "You don't want that. If you want a good tan, you need a bikini, like this one." Helen took a yellow bikini from the rack and showed it to Catherine.

Catherine shook her head. "No, that won't do. I rather have a one-piece."

"Why?" Helen said with a questioning look.

Looking at Helen, Catherine replied, "I don't want to attract that much attention. I rather that people not notice me that much."

Helen laughed, giving Catherine a pat on the back. "Oh, Catherine,

WOMAN IN THE MIRROR

do you have a lot to learn. Now look Girl you're a woman, a very pretty woman and that's all you have to be for the men to look at you, no matter what you are wearing."

Catherine blushed at Helen's remark. She knew Helen to be right, but she had yet to get use to the unwanted attention from men. With a sigh she said, "I know what you're getting at Helen, but I still don't feel right showing that much of myself in public."

Helen winked at Catherine and smiled. "Don't you want the men to notice you?"

Catherine shook her head. "No, not really. I feel uncomfortable when I sense a man looking at me like that."

"Like how?" Helen asked.

Catherine replied, "Like they're trying to undress me with their eyes."

Helen put her arm around Catherine's shoulder and took on the role of big sister. "Maybe you feel like that now. However later on you will feel different about that, believe me you will. Besides most everyone wears bikinis anyway, and it's not as if I'm asking you to wear a thong. You won't be attracting any more attention than anyone else will. Get a bikini, you'll love it."

Catherine thought about it and had to admit to herself that Helen was right as usual. She relented and deferred to Helen's counsel. "Okay, I'll get a bikini. I want to get a good tan, and who cares who looks anyway."

Hele laughed and hugged Catherine. "That's the way! Now, one last, but very important thing."

"What's that?" Catherine replied with a questioning look.

"For your own good forget what went through Karl's mine when he looked at a pretty girl."

Catherine blushed, then laughed, "Ok you! Alright I'll try."

Together they went through the racks and chose several bikinis to try on. Finally, after trying several on, they made their choice. Catherine ended up with a fetching yellow bikini with navy-blue and deep-orange accent stripes. Helen got a red bikini just as flattering.

Afterwards they continued to shop. Catherine had to build her summer wardrobe. She ended up buying two pairs of white shorts, three polo shirts and three strapless sun dresses. She also got a pair of running shoes to replace the pair that had belonged to Jane Doe. She now felt ready for summer.

Catherine and Helen started to spend time at the pool in the afternoon after work to work on their tans. There were also some young men at their apartment complex that also spent time at the pool.

Catherine soon met a handsome young man, a Mr. Dan Cummings. He lived in the apartment block on the other side of the pool and tennis courts from their apartment. She took a few days to get to know him. Helen agreed with Catherine that he seemed to be a good man, and that if he asked her for a date that she should accept. When he asked Catherine out on a date she accepted.

For their first date he took her to the Outback Steak House for dinner. He seemed very courteous and considerate, a real gentleman. He also proved to be a good conversationalist at dinner. They talked about each other; Catherine already knew that he worked for the Georgia State Highway Department. She found out that he was a country and western music fan. He liked motor sports like auto and motorcycle racing. He even liked drag racing and tractor pulls. He also liked to hunt and fish. He was also a civil-war buff and felt angry that they had changed the state flag. She had the idea that under his civilized veneer lurked a redneck.

Catherine used her cover story to avoid talking much about herself. She was satisfied to let Dan do most of the talking. By the end of the date, she felt sure that they could have a good relationship. Catherine had enjoyed the whole evening. When Dan asked her for another date she accepted.

The second date didn't go so well. It started out well, much like the first date, but there appeared a slight difference in his demeanor. She began to wonder if his true character had started to show through, that before he had been on his best behavior. During dinner Dan started to drink a lot and his speech started to become somewhat crude and vulgar. Catherine became disgusted with Dan's behavior and decided that it was time to go home.

In the parking lot Dan grabbed and held her, trying to kiss and grope her. They struggled until Catherine got an opening. A strategically placed knee, then a quick dash back to the restaurant and she had gotten away from him. Dan didn't try to go after her. He just got into his car and left her there.

Catherine had to call Helen to come and pick her up. Catherine hadn't been frightened as much as she had been angry and upset with herself for being so unsuspecting and being caught off guard. She had to face the fact that she lacked social experience. Karl had stopped living life after the accident. After that he had just been an observer on the outside. Helen cautioned Catherine to be more careful from now on, but not to give up on men. There were a lot of good ones out there, so she had to keep trying. It was a good lesson for Catherine that as a woman she now had something to protect that she didn't have before.

The second Sunday in June Catherine drove with Helen and James up to Chattanooga to see Lookout Mountain and Rock City. They found it an enchanting place. The place was a wonderland with lots to see and do. They had a marvelous time.

They arrived back home at about five-thirty PM. Helen and James had decided to go out for dinner and invited Catherine to come along. Catherine didn't feel like being a third party intruding on their space. She knew that Helen and James had offered the invitation out of courtesy, but that they rather be alone. She made her excuses and bid them a good evening.

By seven Catherine had started to get hungry and had begun to regret not taking them up on their offer for dinner. She didn't want to open a can, or nuke something from the freezer in the microwave for dinner, so she decided to go out to Captain D's for takeout.

Catherine arrived at Captain D's and took her place in the drive-through line behind a white Honda Accord. She placed her order then

MICHAEL O. GREGORY

drove around to the pick-up window. She got her order and started to leave.

The white Honda Accord still waited at the exit ramp for the traffic to clear. Catherine pulled up behind him and stopped. The traffic cleared and the driver in the Honda started to pull out of the drive into traffic. Suddenly a car whipped out of another drive-in front of him. The driver of the Honda had to slam on the brakes and stop short. The sudden stop took Catherine by surprise and she bumped into the back of the Honda. Catherine was shocked that she had done this to someone.

A tall-athletic looking man in his late twenties, with dark-brown hair and blue eyes got out of the car. He wore a red Georgia bulldog T-shirt and denim cutoffs. She could immediately see that he was very angry. He shouted, "Idiot! Imbecile! Why don't you try to drive with your eyes open?"

Catherine knew that she should get out of her car and face this man that she had offended, but she couldn't bring herself to move. She felt too intimidated by him.

The driver of the Honda now stood at the back of his car looking for damage as he said, "Where did you get your license, from the school for the blind?"

Catherine stuck her head out of the window, "Please, Sir, I'm sorry that I hit your car. I hope it's not damaged." The other driver was now down on his knees running his hands along the bumper of each car and looking underneath. Catherine decided that she had to face him. She opened the door of her car and got out. Looking at the driver of the other car she said, "I'm sorry, Sir. I hope I didn't hurt you or your car."

Getting to his feet, the driver of the Honda brushed off his hands and knees, then turned to face her. Most of his anger seemed to be gone. He replied, "No, I'm not hurt, and I don't think that there's any damage to either car." He seemed to regard her now for the first time and his facial features softened as he lost his anger. His face reddened as he became embarrassed by his rash behavior.

Catherine felt his eyes on her, appraising her, but this time, for some unknown reason that she failed to comprehend, she took no offence. She took some time as she looked into his face. She had to admit to herself that he was a handsome man. Then she too became embarrassed by the realization that she had been appraising him as he had been appraising her.

Getting her purse from her car, Catherine took out a pen and small note pad. She wrote her name and telephone number on it and handed him the slip with her name and number. "Here, Sir, this is my name and telephone number. If anything's wrong just give me a call and I'll take care of it."

He took the slip of paper, looked at it, then reached for his wallet. He placed the slip of paper in his wallet, then took out one of his cards. "I don't think that there will be any problems, but just in case here's my card." He then handed his card to Catherine, and she took it. They got back into their cars and went their own way.

After arriving back home Catherine went to the kitchen to eat her dinner, after giving some to Tiger to keep him happy. After she finished dinner, she got the card out of her purse to look at it. The card read,

MR. SAMUEL E. TANKERSLEY
Attorney at Law

She looked at the card and thought of the handsome young man again. There had seemed to be something different about him, at least in her mind there had been. She blushed again at her own thoughts and put the card back in her purse. She then got up from the table and made coffee.

CHAPTER ELEVEN

Sam Tankersley sat at his desk with the late afternoon sun streaming in through the window behind him. He kept looking at a piece of paper that had been on his desk in front of him all day. The piece of paper had a name and telephone number on it.

Ever since his encounter with that girl at Captain D's Saturday evening, he couldn't get her out of his mind. That lovely face and vivid-green eyes, he couldn't forget them. If only he hadn't lost his temper and shouted at her like a madman. Most likely she wouldn't have anything to do with him now. He wanted to call her and ask her out to dinner, but he feared that she would say no.

His law partner Fred Zimmerman had watched him for most of the afternoon sitting at his desk agonizing over her telephone number. Finally, he asked, "Well, are you going to call her?"

Sam kept looking at the piece of paper on his desk. "Mind your own business, Fred."

Fred came over to Sam's desk, dragged up a chair and had a seat beside Sam's desk. He looked at Sam and the piece of paper for a few seconds before he spoke. "Well, are you going to call her?"

Sam didn't look up. "I don't know, maybe."

Fred slid his chair closer to Sam. "She must be a really good looker. You have been looking at that piece of paper all day."

Sam snapped, "Don't rush me!"

Fred held up his hands in supplication. "Okay, just settle down. Now what's making you so uptight?"

"Nothing." Sam responded.

Fred looked hard at Sam, "Don't give me that nothing bit, the way that you have been acting lately. What is it?"

Sam looked at Fred and sighed. Fred had seen Sam fall for a girl before, but he had never seen him like this before. He must be infatuated with her. Sam said, "Well, I met a really beautiful girl and what happens, I have to be angry and acting like an ass."

Fred's eyebrows came up in mock surprise. "Oh, why the loss of temper?"

With a forlorn look, Sam said, "It's this latest client of mine. He's so guilty that there's no way that he could win at trial. I've been able to get him a good plea bargain, but he's intransigent. He wants to go to trial and have his day in court, even if it will cost him more in the end. I had just become frustrated by it all. He's digging himself a deeper hole and I can't do anything about it. I just took my anger out on her. I know that I acted boorish, and I shouldn't have done it, but I just couldn't help myself. She didn't deserve it. I just didn't think until it was too late."

Fred picked up the phone from the corner of Sam's desk and placed it in front of him. "Call her."

Sam picked up the phone and put it back on the corner of the desk, "I doubt that she would want to take my call anyway. She probably thinks that I'm a jerk."

Fred took the phone and put it back down in front of Sam. "Call her."

Sam put the phone back in the corner. "Maybe later."

Fred picked up the phone and sat it down hard in front of Sam. "Sam, call her now, so that we can get some work done around here."

Sam slammed both hands down on the desk. "Okay!" Sam picked up the phone and dialed the number, then waited for someone to answer. When he got an answer he said, "Hello, is this Miss Catherine White?"

Wondering what the call was about, Catherine replied, "Yes, I'm Catherine White."

Sam took a deep breath. He hoped that she wouldn't hang up on him as soon as he identified himself. "This is Sam Tankersley, you know, from Captain D's the other evening."

Catherine had a mental picture of Saturday evening. She remembered the handsome man who had been driving the Honda Accord. She also remembered just how rude he had been to her and wondered if she should speak to him. Her first impulse had been to hang up the phone on him. She did, however, detect some quality in his voice that made her hesitate. He also may have a legitimate reason for calling her. "Yes, I know who you are Mr. Tankersley. What do you want?" Her voice seemed cold and formal.

Sam was relieved. He had half expected her to hang up on him, but she remained on the phone, even if she didn't sound too friendly towards him. He said with his most pleasant voice. "I'm calling to ask if everything is okay. I would also like to say that I acted like a jerk the other evening. I would like to apologize to you for my rude behavior."

Catherine could sense the tension in Sam's voice. She felt relieved that he had called to apologize. She also got the feeling that he hadn't called just to apologize, but for some other reason. Catherine answered with a warmer, more informal voice. "Oh, that's okay Mr. Tankersley. You had the right to be angry. I should have been more attentive. It was my fault."

Sam felt relieved that her voice now sounded softer and more pleasant. Perhaps she did forgive him for his bad behavior Saturday. He steeled his nerve and went for everything. "Miss White, I feel bad about the way that I behaved the other evening. I would like to make it up to you. I would like to take you to dinner."

Catherine thought. *He does seem sincere and contrite for our last meeting. But should I take a chance with him?* She could still remember her last experience at dating. She didn't want to go through that again. "I don't know if I should Mr. Tankersley. After all I don't even know you. I recently had a bad experience with a date from hell. I like to know the men that I go out to dinner with better now."

WOMAN IN THE MIRROR

Sam was quick to reassure. "Miss White, I can understand that. If you give me a chance, you'll find me a very likeable person. I would like to take you to dinner to show you how nice I can be."

Catherine hesitated for a few seconds. The accident the other evening had been her fault, and she felt that she should make it up to him. However, she did want to maintain some measure of control. She decided on a compromise. "Okay, Mr. Tankersley, I'll not let you take me out to dinner, but I'll meet you for dinner wherever you want."

Sam became elated that she had accepted. "Oh, good. What would you like for dinner? How about steak?"

"Steak sounds good." Catherine responded.

Sam looked at his watch. "Okay, it's six O-clock now. Can you meet me at Ryan's Steak House at say seven thirty? It's just two blocks down from Captain D's where we met the other evening."

Catherine thought for a second. "Yes, I know the place and seven thirty is just fine. So I'll see you there at seven thirty. And I'd rather that you call me Catherine than Miss White."

"Okay, as long as you call me Sam."

Catherine starting to hang up said, "Well, good-bye Sam. See you soon."

Sam had started to get up from the chair. "Good-bye Catherine." Sam hung up the phone and gave Fred a thumbs up. "I've got to get moving. I've a date in just one and a half hours."

Fred returned the thumbs up. "Good luck Sam."

When Catherine arrived at the steak house, she found Sam waiting for her just inside the entrance. He was wearing a light-gray suit with a white shirt and teal and golden-yellow striped tie. Catherine wore a floral print on a yellow background sundress, with a white purse and pumps.

Catherine remembered him in a T-shirt and cutoff denim shorts. She didn't fail to notice how much more handsome and intelligent he looked in a suit. This was the first man that she had ever looked at with more than just casual interest. She felt her pulse quicken and the

75

palms of her hands get damp.

To Sam she looked even more beautiful than he had remembered her looking Saturday. He sensed something special about her. He had a feeling about her that he had never had for a woman before. Suddenly he felt like a teenager on his first date and wanted very much to impress her.

They didn't have much conversation other than the exchange of greetings until they had their table. Catherine had felt Sam's eyes on her, apprising her when they first greeted each other, but this time she didn't mind. After they were seated Sam started the conversation. "Thanks for coming to dinner with me."

Catherine decided to use humor to put Sam at ease. "I figured that I owed it to you after bumping you with my car Saturday. I thought it a good idea since you're a lawyer, and I don't want you to sue me."

Sam was quick to reply. "Why would I sue you?" He looked at Catherine and could see that she was having a little fun with him. It pleased him. He liked a sense of humor in a person.

Catherine continued, "You're a lawyer and lawyers sue people, don't they?"

Sam pretended shock. "Good God, no! Lawyers don't sue people, people sue people. We just work for them. Besides, that's not the kind of law that I practice."

Catherine had started to become interested in Sam and what he did. "Oh, then what kind of law do you practice."

Sam had started to become more at ease with Catherine. "I'm a criminal defense attorney. I defend mostly people who can't afford an attorney."

Catherine was being very attentive to Sam. "If they can't afford an attorney, then how do they pay you?"

Sam continued to be at ease with her. "I'm assigned the cases by the court, and I'm paid by the court on an hourly basis."

Catherine kept looking at Sam. She watched his every move and listened to his every word with interest. "Your work sounds really interesting."

Sam felt that now would be a good time to tell her a little about herself. "Perhaps then I should tell you more about myself. I'm twenty-eight years old. I'll be twenty-nine on October the fourth. I'm from Augusta, or Martinez. It's part of the Augusta metro area, but mostly in Columbia County, not Richmond County. My family has been in Columbia County since before the Civil War. I attended Lakeside High School. I received my bachelor's degree from Augusta University, and my law degree from the University of Georgia. I have spent the last four and a half years building a practice with another attorney, Mr. Fred Zimmerman. I like baseball, football and tennis. I watch the first two and play the third. I also run when I can. I also like soft rock and country and western music. Well, that's who I am." Sam now expected Catherine to follow his lead and talk about herself, but she asked a question.

"Does everyone call you Sam?"

Sam said smiling. "Most everyone. My mother calls me Sammy, except when she gets angry with me and then it's Samuel. That's enough about me. I'd like to know something about you."

Catherine always felt nervous about talking to other people about herself. She could only say so much about herself before she had to fall back on her cover story. "Well, there isn't much to know. I work as a nurse's aide at the Evans Clinic. I like soft rock, Jazz and some of the classics. I like our cat, Tiger. I also like working out at the health club."

Sam waited for Catherine to continue. When she didn't, he said, "Are you from here in Atlanta?"

Catherine shook her head. "No."

Catherine seemed to be evasive about her past and Sam had started to become curious about her. "Then where's your hometown?"

Catherine started to get tense and her voice started to sound a little defensive. "I don't know my hometown."

Sam gave Catherine a sideways look and said in a patronizing voice. "What do we have here, a mystery lady?"

Catherine became defensive. "Don't laugh it's not funny."

Catherine's reaction took Sam by surprise. She really had told the truth. Now his voice became conciliatory. "Please forgive me. I didn't mean to be insensitive."

Catherine started to relax again. "How could you have known? Actually, it's no big mystery. You see, I was in a coma for almost a month. I have no memory of anything before I woke up this March sixteenth at the Evans Clinic."

Sam didn't know what to think about all this. "Even if you have no memory, they know who you are. You must have some information about yourself."

Catherine shook her head. She was about to use the cover story and wondered how Sam would take it. "No, they don't know who I am. You see Catherine White isn't my real name. I was found in a Nashville motel room in a coma from an overdose of sleeping pills. I had no identification on me. I was registered under a false name. I didn't want to be known as Jane Doe, so I made up the name of Catherine White. I'm between twenty-four and twenty-six years, so I give my age as twenty-five. I use the date that I came out of the coma as my birth date."

Sam sat back in his seat and let out an audible sigh. She was a woman without a past, a real mystery lady. "I say, you really are a mystery lady."

Catherine looked into Sam's eyes and could see concern in them. "I don't feel like a mystery lady. I just feel lost. I'm making new friends and building a new life, but it takes time."

Sam reached across the table and took Catherine's hand in his. "Catherine, I would like to be your friend."

Catherine could see the sincerity in his eyes. "Thank you, Sam, I appreciate that."

Catherine and Sam finished their meal with a conversation of current events and items of common interest. Before departing they made a date to meet at the Olive Garden Friday at seven PM for dinner. Then Sam walked Catherine out to her car. They said their good-nights and drove home.

When Catherine got back home, she found Helen waiting for news of the date. As soon as the door closed, she asked, "Well, how did it go?"

Catherine stepped out of her shoes and reached down to pick them up. With a smile she said. "It went very well. We talked for a long time. He told me a lot about himself, and we found that we've a lot in common. He calls me his mystery lady."

"So, you told him about the coma and memory loss?"

"Yes, and he believes me. He said that he wants to be my friend and I believe him."

Helen was curious. "Are you going to see him again?"

Catherine started for her bedroom to change into something more comfortable. "Yes, we have a date for Friday at the Olive Garden."

CHAPTER TWELVE

When Sam got to the office the next morning Fred wanted to know how the date went. Sam put his briefcase on his desk. "Not yet Fred. Let me get my coffee first." Sam poured a cup of coffee from the coffee maker, then sat at his desk and sipped his coffee. Sam got a perverse pleasure from making Fred wait to hear about how the date had gone the night before.

Fred also took a fresh cup of coffee, pulled up a chair next to Sam's desk and took a seat across the desk from Sam. "Alright, tell me. How did the date go?"

Sam put down his coffee cup. "Okay, I won't keep you in suspense any longer. It went very well."

Fred slammed his hand down on the edge of Sam's desk. "Ha! Was I right? Now are you glad that I made you make the call? So, are you going to see her again?"

Sam laughed. "Okay, you were right, I'm glad that I made the call. As for the answer to your question, yes, we have a date for Friday at the Olive Garden, but she still won't let me pick her up for the date. She wants me to meet her there. She needs time to start trusting people again."

Leaning forward with his elbows on Sam's desk, Fred said, 'Why, what happened?"

Sam picked up his cup and leisurely took a sip of coffee, as he watched Fred sitting on the edge of his chair with an expectant look on his face. Sam put his cup back down on his desk. "Well, Fred, she's my mystery lady."

Fred's eyebrows went up in surprise and wrinkled lines started to show on his brow. "Mystery lady?"

Sam just had to smile at Fred's surprised look. "Yes, she has had a severe trauma, and she's really a mystery lady. She woke up from a coma three months ago, on March sixteenth to be exact. She has no memory of anything before she woke up from the coma. Catherine White isn't even her true name. It's just one that she came up with."

Fred took a sip of his coffee and put it back down on the desk. "What are you going to do? Are you going to keep on seeing her?"

Sam leaned back in his chair, folded his arms in front of his chest and looked at Fred. "Why of course I am! She seems to be a wonderful person, and great looking too. Besides she intrigues me. One thing for sure, I'll have to let her set the pace of this relationship. With the problem of her amnesia and her insecurity; because of it I don't want to push her."

Fred felt a little concerned about all this. "Aren't you concerned that there may be some dark and unsavory secret in her past? You don't know who she was before. She could even be an ax murderer."

Sam slapped his knee and roared with laughter. "Fred, you're too much of a cynic. I think that I'm a good judge of character and I say that she's a good person. And one other thing, I also saw that movie and she's no ax murderer." Sam took the time to take a sip of coffee, then went on. "I can't explain it to you. I can't even explain it to myself. It's like there's some special quality about her, something beyond the usual senses, like something that you feel inside. I don't know how to describe it, but it's there. She's the one, the woman that I've been looking for. She's the woman that I want to fall in love with and grow old with. She doesn't know it yet, but she's to be my wife."

Fred didn't feel so sure that his friend was thinking right. "What if there's something in her past" you say that you have a feeling about her. What if you're wrong?"

Sam had thought about that and had already made up his mind.

MICHAEL O. GREGORY

"If there's something in her past, we will face it together. She's the one and that's all that matters."

Fred shook his head, amazed at how crazy his friend seemed to be. "You're crazy, but in a nice way. I guess a person has a right to be a little crazy when they fall in love."

Sam smiled. "Yea, I'd say that it runs in the family. It was the same way with my father and grandfather. My father told me that he proposed to mother on their second date. My grandfather knew the moment that he saw my grandmother that she was the woman for him. I must tell you the story someday of how they met, it's a good one."

Fred laughed; he already knew the story. Sam had told him the story about two years ago. Given the family history Sam's behavior didn't surprise him. "Perhaps you're not so crazy after all. I wish you good luck."

"Thanks." Sam said.

After the third date Catherine let Sam start picking her up for their dates at her apartment. They started to see a lot of each other on weekends and sometimes during the week. Catherine felt secure in a relationship where she could enjoy the company of a good friend and remain in control. Sam understood and had the patience to wait on her. He knew that she had issues in her life to work out. He was in no hurry to advance their relationship.

Catherine felt more confident now. Her sessions with Maryanne had been going well. She seemed to be adjusting well in most, but not all areas. In relationships with men, she had made some progress. Maryanne could tell from how Catherine talked about Sam that she had started to develop a romantic interest in him, even if she didn't fully realize it yet. In every other way she had become a woman. Now all that she had to do is come to terms with her sexuality. Maryanne was seeing this as the only stumbling block to her complete transformation to her new self.

The second Saturday after the fourth of July Sam took Catherine to Stone Mountain. They visited the Civil War and antique automobile museums. They rode the railroad around the mountain. After the train ride they were ready to eat, so they had some fried chicken at the restaurant.

After lunch they rode the cable car to the top of the mountain, then walked around the top. Catherine found the view just breathtaking. She could understand why Sam liked it so much up here. From atop Stone Mountain she could see for miles in every direction. She could even see the buildings of the Atlanta skyline from here.

After they got down from the top of the mountain, they went for a ride around the lake on the paddlewheel riverboat. Then back to the parking lot in front of the restaurant and train depot. There they had some funnel cake.

By then it was late afternoon. They went back to the restaurant to have dinner. After dinner they returned to the car. Sam took a blanket from the trunk of the car, and they found a good spot on the grassy mall where they could spread the blanket and get comfortable for the laser light show that started after dark.

When they arrived back at Catherine's apartment, they were both tired, but happy. Catherine had really enjoyed herself and felt reluctant for the day to end. Instead of saying good night, they stood at the door and talked about the day's events. Catherine looked into Sam's eyes as she spoke. "It was all so wonderful, Sam. I really had a great day."

Sam stood very close and looked back at Catherine. "I'm glad that you enjoyed it. Stone Mountain is one of my favorite places."

"And mine too now. Oh, the view from up there, you can see everything. I want to go again."

Sam took her hands into his. "Then we'll go again soon, that's a promise." Sam just stood there holding Catherine's hands and looking into her eyes. "Well, it's late now."

Privately Catherine wasn't eager to see the day end. She wanted to hang onto the experience of the day. "Yes, it is."

Sam didn't want it to end either. "Then I believe that it's time to say good night."

Catherine nodded. "Yes, good-night Sam."

Sam kept looking into her eyes. "Good-night Catherine."

On impulse Sam took Catherine in his arms and kissed her with passion. Catherine let herself be carried along by the impulse of the moment and returned the kiss with equal passion. Sam had his hand in her back and pulled her close to him. Catherine pressed her body hard against his. Her heart pounded in her chest, and she felt a warm feeling deep down in her loins. When the kiss ended, they remained in each other's embrace for a while, like two dancers who were not moving. Nothing more had to be said. Catherine reached for the doorknob as they disengaged. Sam gave her one more kiss, then she passed through the door, and he turned to go.

Catherine closed the door and leaned back against it. She was still breathing hard and still had that warm feeling deep down in her loins. Although Sam kissing her had been unexpected it had been a pleasant experience. When Sam's lips touched hers something inside of her stirred for the first time. She found his lips on hers to fire passions in her. In a way she had encouraged him and had welcomed it. Sam was a wonderful man, and she would rather be with him than with anyone else that she knew. However, she wasn't sure if she was ready for a serious commitment yet. She must talk to Maryanne about this during their next session.

Chapter Thirteen

Catherine entered the office and closed the door. "Good-morning, Maryanne."

Directing Catherine to the sofa Maryanne said, "Good-morning, Catherine. Please have a seat."

Catherine took her usual seat on the sofa. Maryanne had started to make herself a cup of coffee. "Would you like a cup of coffee Catherine?"

Catherine shook her head. "No thank you. I just had a cup in the break room."

Maryanne took her seat on the sofa, took a sip of coffee, put the cup on the coffee table then turned to face Catherine. "Well, how are you feeling today?"

Looking at Maryanne, Catherine replied, "Oh, I'm feeling just fine."

Maryanne reached for her cup again and took a sip of coffee. "That's good to hear. How did your week go?"

Catherine had started to get comfortable on the sofa. "It went all right. I've enrolled in the business college and will start taking evening classes beginning the last week of August."

Maryanne gave Catherine a pat on the forearm. "That's good, and good luck to you. I know that you'll do well."

It pleased Catherine that Maryanne approved; she really valued Maryanne's opinion. "Thank you."

Maryanne took another sip of coffee and put her cup back down on the coffee table. "Is there anything else that you would like to talk to me about? You have been telling me about Sam. How's your relationship with him?"

Catherine smiled, recalling Saturday night when Sam had kissed her at her apartment door. "It's going very well. We went to Stone Mountain on Saturday. That's a really big place. You need more than one day to see it all."

When Catherine paused to put her thoughts in order, Maryanne asked. "What is it? Something about Sam?"

Catherine nodded. "Yes, it has something to do with Sam and I."

"Yes, go on." Maryanne said with interest.

Catherine ordered her thoughts before speaking. "As you know, after our disastrous first meeting we've formed a good relationship. I want just a friend to spend time with. Up to now that's what he's been to me. He didn't try to push me. He just let me set the limits of our relationship, but Saturday night he went beyond those limits."

Maryanne sat up straight on the sofa, her curiosity piqued. "Oh, how's that?"

Catherine sat back in the sofa, folded her hands in her lap and looked at Maryanne. "When he brought me home from Stone Mountain Saturday night we were in a really good mood. We didn't want the day to end. We didn't say good night right away. Instead, we lingered for a while talking about the wonderful time that we had had that day. When at last it came time to say good night, we were standing close together looking into each other's eyes. Then all at once he just took me in his arms and kissed me. It had just been an impulsive act, and I allowed myself to be carried along by it."

Maryanne had become excited. "So, he kissed you."

Catherine nodded. "Yes, but it wasn't just a friendly good-night kiss. It was a long and passionate kiss. One that implies that more is desired and expected."

Maryanne found this very interesting and had moved a little closer to Catherine on the sofa. "Are you saying that even though you enjoyed the kiss that you wished that he hadn't done it?"

Catherine shook her head. "No, I didn't say that. In fact, I did enjoy it. More than that it awakened feelings in me that I have never experienced before. Feelings that I have to sort out and learn to control, but that's not the point. What I'm saying is that he has changed our relationship from a platonic one to one of romantic involvement, and I don't know if I'm ready for that yet."

Maryanne took a sip of coffee, put the cup back down on the coffee table and faced Catherine. Maryanne could see that the problem wasn't the fact that Sam had kissed her. Catherine had admitted that she had enjoyed it. Maryanne believed the problem to be that Catherine feared losing control of the relationship. "You said that you weren't ready for it. Yet you say that you enjoyed it. So I take it that you may be open to a romantic, or even a sexual relationship with a man at some time?"

Catherine had been thinking about this for a while. "Yes, I'd say so. However, I'd have liked to have had more time to adjust to it."

Maryanne could see that passion had started to be awakened in Catherine, that she had started to experience the sex drive of a normal female. These were feelings that she would have to sort out for herself over time. "You knew that this was coming, that you would have to deal with it someday."

Catherine nodded agreement. "Yes, I know, but I'm still trying to get used to my new self. I now enjoy the company of men. I even enjoyed being kissed by Sam. I enjoyed it very much, but sex is another matter. I don't know when I'll be able to go that far."

Maryanne could see that Catherine needed encouragement, that she needed to have a little direction. "Catherine, when we took you into the program, we went over all of this with you. We talked about how much of an adjustment you would have to make to accommodate your new identity. That you would have to lose your old self in your new identity."

Catherine looked out of the window behind Maryanne's desk for a few seconds, then looked back at Maryanne. "To be honest with you, I didn't know how seriously to take it at first. I perhaps only half believed that it would work, and to just be warehoused for the rest of my life. The five to eight years that you gave to me was still too long. I would have grabbed at any chance given to me. Even if it failed, I'd be better off than I was before. Wow was I surprised! It worked beyond my wildest dreams. I had mobility again. I had freedom to do whatever I wanted. I had a life again. I didn't look past that."

Maryanne put her hand over Catherine's hands and spoke to her in a warm, friendly manner, like friend to friend. "That's good and I'm happy for you, but you must now look past that. You must become a complete person. As you have told me, the outside changes were easy. You can act the part very well, but you must completely become the person that you are now. That means that you must also experience your passions and learn to control them. You must acknowledge your sexuality. When you became Catherine White, Karl Boyle died. Understand?"

Catherine nodded. "Yes, I understand."

Maryanne patted Catherine on the back of her hand and spoke with a soothing voice. "That's good. I'm here to help you, but you must also help yourself. Enough of that now. Are you still having that dream that you told me about?"

Relieved that Maryanne had changed the subject, Catherine asked, "Do you mean that dream about the clothes?"

Maryanne nodded. "Yes, that's the one."

"Yes, once in a while. There's another dream that I have been having lately."

Maryanne became very attentive. She liked to hear about Catherine's dreams, they were an insight into her psyche. "Would you like to tell me about it?"

Catherine sat back on the sofa and became more relaxed. "Well, it starts out I'm walking down the street, or down a hallway. Everything is familiar. I know where I'm going and how to get there. I turn a corner or walk through a door and things no longer look familiar. No problem I tell myself, I'll just go back, but everything has changed. I no longer know where I am. I try to find my way again, but every time I turn a

WOMAN IN THE MIRROR

corner, or walk through a door I'm more lost than I was before. That's usually where the dream ends."

Maryanne didn't find anything unusual about the dream. "That's a dream that most people have from time to time."

Catherine nodded. "Yes, I know that. It's not the dream that's strange, it's me. Always before in my dreams, no matter what they were about I was always, Karl, and I was always male. Now in my dreams I'm still me, but the 'me' in my dreams is somewhat vague. I'm there, I know that, but I can't quite make out my identity. I'm there, but I can no longer see myself, or determine my gender."

Maryanne had an idea what the dream had meant, but she wanted to hear it from Catherine. "What do you think it means?"

Catherine uttered a sigh. "Well, I think it means that I still have a ways to go."

"I also believe that it means that you are making progress."

"Do you really think so?" Catherine asked.

Maryanne nodded. "Yes, I do." They sat quite for a few seconds. Maryanne continued, "Anything else?"

Catherine shook her head. "No, that's about it." They both got to their feet and Catherine started for the door.

All that week for some reason Catherine felt depressed. She didn't know why. It seemed to be just one of those things that happened from time to time. It was something that she would just have to get through.

By Thursday she still felt low. After work she decided that the best way to get herself out of this slump would be to go shopping and treat herself to a gift. She decided to go to Macy's at the Lenox Square Mall.

She started out in the dress department, where she looked at and tried on several dresses. She then went on to sportswear and ladies' accessories. She looked for a brown leather purse but didn't find anything that she liked. From ladies' accessories she went to the shoe department. She purchased a pair of white high-heel shoes that Helen had been urging her to get. She then decided to get a very pretty pair of black high-heel shoes that caught her eye. She would have to spend a lot of

89

MICHAEL O. GREGORY

time wearing them around the apartment before she could feel that she had mastered them enough to wear in public. She then decided to go over to the jewelry department to look at all the pretty things there.

After a while she found a nice pair of earrings. They were silver crescents on a short length of silver chain with a turquoise bead in each crescent. Catherine stood in front of a small mirror that sat on top of the counter, holding the earrings up to her ears to see how they would look on her.

"Amanda! Amanda Jenkins!"

Catherine looked up from the mirror. A middle-aged woman stood next to her. Catherine responded, "Pardon me. Are you addressing me?"

The woman gave her a concerned look. "You are Amanda Jenkins, aren't you?"

Catherine suddenly got cold inside. This woman believed that she knew her. She felt that she must do something to get away from this woman as quickly as she could. "You must be mistaken. I'm not who you believe I am."

The woman excused herself, "Oh, please forgive me. I thought that you were someone I know."

Catherine felt all knotted up inside from anxiety but tried to sound casual. "Oh, think nothing of it."

Catherine took her purchases and left the store as quickly as she could. She went to the parking lot, got into her car, and drove straight home.

Helen was in the kitchen cooking supper when Catherine got home. Catherine was still visibility upset and Helen picked up on it right away. "What's wrong?"

Catherine took a seat at the kitchen table and looked at Helen. "Something strange and a little frightening just happened to me at Macy's."

Helen took a seat across the table from Catherine, anxious to hear what she had to say. "Tell me, what happened?"

Catherine recounted the experience. "I was at the jewelry counter

90

looking at earrings when a middle-aged woman came up to me and addressed me. She called me Amanda Jenkins."

Helen became very concerned about this. "Tell me, how sure are you that this woman believed you to be Amanda Jenkins?"

Catherine shook her head. "I'm not sure. When I denied being Amanda Jenkins, she quickly excused herself. Then I left the store as quickly as I could."

Helen needed to know everything that Catherine could remember about the encounter, "Think, how sure are you that she believed you to be Amanda Jenkins?"

Catherine tried to recall as much of the encounter as she could. "I don't know if I convinced her that I wasn't Amanda Jenkins or not. However, I'm reasonability certain that she believed that she had recognized me as Amanda Jenkins."

Helen was quite for a few seconds in thought before she spoke, "It's a very unlikely event, but there was the possibility that this could happen. It could just be a case of mistaken identity, which is most likely, or Jane Doe may have been Amanda Jenkins."

The encounter concerned Catherine very much. If it became a problem, she would be the one with the most to lose. With a sigh she said, "Well, Helen, what do we do now?"

Helen thought for a moment. "This could be very serious for the project. Did she follow you from the store?"

Catherine tried to recall the woman but couldn't remember a thing about her after she left the jewelry counter. "I don't know. I just left the store as quickly as I could. I didn't think to look back to see if I were followed."

Helen knew that they had to do something about this. "This has to be reported to Dr. Weston first thing in the morning."

Catherine had started to feel better after speaking with Helen, she said, "Okay, I'll report it to Dr. Weston first thing in the morning."

Helen said starting to get up to check the dinner on the range. "I'll go with you. Oh, by the way, Sam called. He wants to know if you are

MICHAEL O. GREGORY

free for dinner tomorrow."

Catherine went to the phone to call Sam to make a dinner date, then talked with him until dinner was ready.

CHAPTER FOURTEEN

The doorbell rang and Elisabeth Jenkins, a well-dressed woman of forty-nine years with black hair crossed the entry hall to answer the door. Beth opened the door to find her good friend Peggy, a middle-aged woman of stout build and reddish-brown hair. Beth noticed right off that Peggy had dressed elegantly in a white with pink polka dot cotton dress, with a white purse and white high-heel shoes. Beth also noticed the attention that Peggy had given to her make-up and jewelry and figured that she had a lunch date with a man, and this would be just a short visit. Beth held open the door for Peggy to enter. "Good-morning, Peggy, it's so good to see you. Please come in."

"Thank you, Beth."

Peggy stepped into the entry hall and Beth closed the door behind her. "Well, Peggy, what brings you over so early in the day?" Beth could tell right away by her demeanor that Peggy had something exciting to tell.

Peggy was quick to say, "Beth, I have some very important news for you. So important that I had to come over right away, it can't wait."

Beth wondered what it could be that would have Peggy so excited, but she wasn't the hostess to keep a guest standing in the entry hall. Beth replied, "Okay, but first I have a fresh cheese Danish in the kitchen. Let me make you a cup of coffee, then I'll split the Danish with you."

Peggy followed Beth back to the kitchen and took a seat at the kitchen table. All the while Peggy kept carrying on about how hot it was going to be today, and how she would like to see some rain to cool things down. Beth nodded and made comments of agreement while

93

she made the coffee and served it with the cheese Danish. When Beth had taken a seat across the table from Peggy she sipped her coffee, then looked at Peggy. "Now, what is this important news of yours?"

Peggy took a bite of cheese Danish and washed it down with coffee before she spoke. "Well, I went to Atlanta to visit my sister. You know how hard it is to find everything that you're looking for here in Gadsden. I went shopping at the Lenox Square Mall. It's so huge, if you can't find what you're looking for there, you won't find it anywhere in the southeast. Well, I happened to be in the lady's sportswear department of Macy's when I spotted a young woman who looked familiar. I followed her all over the store. Her hair is styled differently, but I'm certain that it was Amanda."

Beth flinched, almost dropping her cup as she had a sharp intake of breath. Her palms started to sweat and her hands trembled. Her heart pounded in her chest and her breathing became rapid. When she answered she could only manage a whisper. "Are you sure?"

Peggy could see the effect on Beth and quickly reassured her. She remembered how it had been on Beth when her daughter Amanda had vanished years ago. "As I said, the hair and clothes were different, but the face and voice were the same. If it wasn't her, then she has a twin sister."

Peggy took Beth's hand and squeezed it to reassure her. "She looked just fine and in good health. When I went up and spoke to her, she denied being Amanda, but I know she was." Peggy paused for a moment before she went on. "There's something strange about her."

Beth became concerned about Amanda's well-being. "What's that?"

"Well, she must have seen me several times in the store, but she seemed not to know me. Even when I called her Amanda, she gave no sign that she knew me, but she became upset and left the store immediately."

Beth sat motionless on the edge of her chair, so excited that she dared hardly to draw a breath. Peggy continued, "There's one last thing. She was wearing that silver and turquoise cross on a silver chain that you and Ted gave her for graduation."

WOMAN IN THE MIRROR

Beth could no longer control her tears. They flowed freely down her cheeks. "Oh, my God, It's her! It must be Amanda! You say that she gave no sign that she knew you. Could that have just been an act on her part to deny that she was Amanda?"

Peggy took a few seconds to recall in her mind the encounter with Amanda and the exact feelings that she got from her. "Listen, Beth, I don't think that she was trying to deceive me. I looked right into her eyes and saw no recognition in them, only surprise and alarm."

Beth started to be frightened by what Peggy had said about Amanda's behavior. "What are you trying to tell me Peggy?"

Peggy had to admit to herself that she too had been baffled by it and caught off guard, so much that she didn't follow up on her inquiry with Amanda. "I don't know, all I can say is what I've observed. There's one more thing." Peggy went into her purse and brought out a piece of paper. "I followed her to the parking lot. She drove away in a red Ford Taurus. I got the tag number; it is Georgia 9781 AEK." Peggy handed the paper with the tag number to Beth.

With trembling hands Beth took it and held it to her breast as though it were a precious jewel. "Thank you, Peggy. Thank you very much, you're a true friend. We won't forget what you've done for us today." Beth took a napkin and dabbed the tears from her eyes.

Peggy got up from the table. Beth got up with her. Peggy said, "I've must go now. I have an appointment downtown."

Beth started to get her emotions under control and had once more become the gracious hostess, "Yes, thank you again. Finally, after more than six years, we know that our Amanda is alive and well and where to find her. Please come again soon when you can. You're always welcome in our house."

Peggy started for the front door. She had taken the time to bring the news about Amanda to Beth. Now she had to get going to make her luncheon date. "Thanks, I will."

As soon as Beth showed Peggy out, she got her purse and car keys and went to her car. She had to see her husband Ted right away, this

95

MICHAEL O. GREGORY

couldn't wait. She drove to the building site where her husband was framing a new house with one of his construction crews.

Ted saw Beth drive up and get out of the car. It wasn't Beth's habit to show up at the construction site, and she seemed to be very excited about something. He climbed down the ladder to the first floor and walked out to see what she wanted.

When Beth saw Ted come out of the house, she rushed to him exclaiming, "Ted, we've found her!"

Ted caught her in his arms. "What?"

Beth was so excited that she could barely control herself. "We found Amanda!"

Beth's exclamation took Ted by surprise. "Where?"

Beth now had the piece of paper with the license number on it in her hand. "She's in Atlanta. Peggy saw her there in Macy's yesterday afternoon."

For a moment Ted was shocked, then disbelieving, then he became excited. "Then you know where she lives?"

Beth shook her head. "No, we don't know where she lives. When Peggy encountered her in Macy's yesterday afternoon, she denied that she was Amanda, but Peggy is certain that she is. I'm certain that Peggy is right on this. Peggy got her car tag number. It's Georgia 9781 AEK, a red Ford Taurus."

Ted took the paper with Catherine's tag number from Beth. "I know a man in Anniston who's a retired policeman. He's now a private investigator and a good one. I built a house for him about three years ago, and he told me that if I ever needed his help to let him know. I'll call him and get him on this right away."

Beth felt better now that Ted would be taking care of it. She gave him a hug and a kiss. "Oh, Ted, it feels so good that we may at last be getting our Amanda back. Now I must go home and fix your lunch."

Smiling, Beth hugged and kissed Ted again and left for home.

Chapter Fifteen

Catherine kept on seeing Sam as before. She tried to pretend that the relationship hadn't changed, that it was still platonic. Sam no longer wanted a platonic relationship; he felt that the relationship should progress to one of romantic interest. Sam didn't insist on having his way, but it had become clear to Catherine that he now expected more. Catherine on the other hand had been careful to not get in a situation again where she couldn't control the relationship. This had the effect of causing tension in the relationship. Sam had become desperate and looked for an idea to get the relationship moving forward.

Sam and Fred were at Burger King for lunch. Sam needed to talk to someone, and Fred could be counted on to be a good listener. "I don't understand her Fred."

Fred looked up at Sam. "I assume that you're speaking of Catherine. I thought that you two were a real item."

Sam scowled at Fred. "You know that it's Catherine that I'm talking about. Who else is there?" Sam's scowl died. "As for us being a real item, that's what I can't figure out. She likes me. We see each other often. In fact, neither one of us sees anyone else. We're at ease with each other and really enjoy each other's company, but each time I try to take our relationship beyond the point of just being friends, she backs off and the barriers go up. I know that she has a problem with her memory loss. I also know that she's a normal female. The other night on impulse, I swept her into my arms and gave her a long and passionate kiss and felt her respond to me. She enjoyed it as much as

MICHAEL O. GREGORY

I did. I just don't know what to do."

Fred continued to eat his Whopper and fries as he listened to Sam. He had proved to be a good friend of Sam's and was always ready to give advice. "As I see it you started out by letting her set the rules and control the relationship. Now you want to change it and take control, but you're not sure how you can do it. Maybe if you stop seeing her for a while and let her think about it, she may come around."

Sam thought Fred's response to be too severe a step to take. "What a dumb idea. No wonder you can't keep a girlfriend." Sam got a rise from Fred.

"What do you mean can't keep a girlfriend!" Fred said with indignation.

Sam burst out with laughter. When it subsided, he said, "As for not seeing her, that's no good. I want to be with her too much to do a dumb thing like that. In fact, from the time that I met her I can think of no one else."

Fred put his Coke down and grinned at Sam. "Then I say old buddy, you have a problem. You can't go forward, and you can't go back."

Sam shook his head in resignation. "I have to do something to break this impasse it's driving me crazy."

Fred tried to think of something as he swallowed the last of his Whopper. "I know what you mean. I'm glad that it's your problem and not mine." Fred checked his watch. "Time to go. We have court this afternoon."

Sam and Fred were in the car in the parking lot. Sam was ready to back out of the parking space when he got an idea. "I know what I'm going to do."

Fred looked at Sam. "What's that?"

Sam said, "On our next date, instead of going out to some restaurant, I'll make dinner for her at my place. That way I'll have her alone. There will be no distractions, we can talk this out."

With a nod, Fred replied, "That sounds good. For one, you're a good cook, and two, you'll have her undivided attention."

Sam smiled, pleased that he now had a plan. "I'm going to give this relationship a nudge, hopefully in the right direction."

Sam picked Catherine up at seven and took her to his apartment for dinner. He served roast chicken with brown rice stuffing, early peas, tomato and cucumber salad, muscadine wine and fresh strawberries with cream.

The meal started off with light conversation. They related to each other what they had done at work that day. Catherine had been surprised at Sam's expertise as a gourmet cook and complimented him on it. "Oh, Sam, the dinner was just great. You're a much better cook than I am."

It pleased, Sam that Catherine had enjoyed the meal. He wanted for her to be in a good mood. With a smile, he said, "Thank you Catherine, I wanted everything to be special this evening."

Catherine looked at Sam over the rim of her wine glass, "Everything is, especially the wine. What is it anyway?"

Sam took a sip from his own glass and held it in front of his face. "That's muscadine wine. My dad makes it each year from scuppernongs that he gets from his vineyard in the backyard. He gives me some each year, but not much, so I must hoard it and use it only for special occasions."

Catherine continued to regard Sam over the rim of her wine glass as she wondered what he had in mind. "Oh, is this a special occasion?"

Sam put his wine glass down and smiled at Catherine, "Yes, it's the first time for you in my home."

Catherine smiled back at Sam as she put her wine glass down, "And I'm enjoying it. I think that you have a nice place."

Sam looked into Catherine's eyes. He felt the time was right to bring up the subject of their relationship. Sam cleared his throat and began. "Catherine, there's a reason that I brought you here this evening. I wanted a private place to talk to you about our relationship."

Catherine hadn't been expecting this and it had taken her by surprise. To buy time to collect her thoughts, she asked a question. "What about our relationship? I thought that it was doing just fine."

Sam had been expecting this question and had a ready answer for her, "There's a saying that my dad likes to use that applies to us. 'If you're not doing better, you're doing worse'. In other words, I believe we've reached a point in our relationship where we'll start to grow closer together or start to pull apart."

Catherine realized that the relationship she had with Sam had to change, it needed to grow. She also wanted it to change. She really wanted, Sam in her life, and she felt ready to be romantically involved with a man. She also wanted to maintain control of the relationship, so she would have to seem to be reluctant to maintain control. "We're having such a good time. Why do you have to bring this up now?"

Their eyes were now locked together across the table. The conversation had grown serious, and their faces reflected it. Sam replied, "Because it needs to be brought up now. You must know by now how I feel about you."

Catherine had become well aware of how Sam felt about her. She felt the same about him, "Yes, I know how you feel about me. I'd have to be blind not to see it." She said in an imploring voice, "Oh, Sam, I don't need a lover now, just a friend. I've enough to deal with now without that." She kept watching, Sam's face, trying to read his thoughts. She wondered if she had played it right.

Sam had to think fast. He didn't want to lose Catherine, "Hay, I'm not saying that we start playing house. I just want to see if perhaps we have a future together."

Catherine averted her eyes from Sam's, looking down. "Oh, Sam, I thought that we were doing quite well as friends. You are a very dear friend to me, and even though I'm not ready to start sleeping together yet, I still very much want to keep you as a friend." Catherine hoped that she had sent the signal that even if she wasn't ready for a sexual encounter yet, she was still open to a closer, more affectionate relationship.

Sam thought that he saw a small opening and took it. "I'm sorry Catherine, but I can no longer be just friends. I can't see you as just my friend anymore. I see you as a very desirable woman, whom I have grown very fond of."

Catherine worked to take the conversation in the direction that she wanted it to go. "Then what you are saying is that we can no longer go on as just friends. That we become more than just friends, or the relationship dies."

Sam felt it the right time to give his ultimatum. "As much as I hate to say it, that's how I see it. I want to be not only your friend, but the man in your life." Sam hoped that he hadn't over done it and tried to push farther than Catherine would be willing to go.

Catherine looked down at the table and slowly turned the wine glass in her hand. She let the tension build for well over a minute before she answered. "Oh, Sam, you're a true friend and I don't want to lose you. Yes, I agree with you. We mustn't put limits on our relationship. We must let it go where it will. However, I'm still not ready to go all the way and as you say, play house."

Sam felt that he had won. "That's just great! I can go along with that."

Instantly the tension was gone from the room. They were both all smiles. Sam got up from the table, Took Catherine in his arms and gave her a long and passionate kiss that she returned with equal passion. Their bodies came together, and Catherine felt his gentle strength as she pressed her body hard against his. She had that warm feeling deep down in her loins again. As they pressed up against each other Catherine could feel his manhood pressing against her belly through their clothing, and fires of passion were kindled within her. Catherine realized that if she wanted to maintain limits in their relationship, she would have to control not only his passions, but hers also.

When the kiss had finally ended, Sam said, "I believe this to be the beginning of a long and beautiful relationship."

Catherine put her head on his shoulder. "So do I Sam, so do I."

After coffee they went out to the sofa in the living room, where they talked and watched television for a while before Sam took Catherine home."

MICHAEL O. GREGORY

Sam pulled into the parking space in front of Catherine's apartment. They sat in Sam's car for a few minutes talking before they got out of the car and Sam escorted Catherine to her door. At the door they tarried, not yet ready to part. They embraced and kissed then; Catherine let herself into her apartment. Sam turned and returned to his car and left for home.

Neither Sam nor Catherine had noticed a man sitting in a car parked at the end of the apartment block with a camera.

CHAPTER SIXTEEN

atherine sat at the kitchen table with her hands wrapped around her coffee cup with a far-away look in her eyes. Helen sat across from her drinking her coffee. "Why the dreamy look?" Helen said.

Catherine's eyes focused on Helen. "What?"

Helen chuckled. "I said, why the dreamy look? You've been sitting there unmoving for five minutes with that far-away look in your eyes. Is it someone that I know?"

Catherine laughed. "You know darn well it's Sam."

Helen laughed with her, then said, "Well, it takes no great leap of logic, unless you're seeing someone that I don't know about."

Catherine fretted a hurt look. "Oh, Helen, you know that there could be no one but Sam." Her hurt look vanished as she brushed a lock of hair out of her eyes with her hand. "We had a talk last night, rather he did most of the talking, while I did most of the listening."

"And." Helen said.

"He told me that he no longer considered our relationship a platonic one. That it must grow or die."

Helen laughed and slapped the table with her hand. "It's about time! I've wondered when he would have enough of your platonic crap and make his move. So, now what?"

Catherine looked pleased with herself, "I couldn't stop him, and I really didn't want to. I reluctantly let him talk me into letting the relationship take its course. That way I can still set some limits and

103

keep control of things."

Helen patted Catherine's forearm and said in a conspiratorial tone. "Smart girl. Men always want things their way. We must keep them from getting it all the time."

Catherine smiled at Helen, "I really like Sam a lot, and I can't think of anyone else that I'd rather have as my first love interest."

Helen had been about to ask another question of Catherine about her date with Sam when the phone rang. Helen got up from the table and went to answer it, "Hello." Helen turned her head to call out to Catherine. "It's, Sam."

Catherine got up to take the phone. "Hi, Sam."

"Hi, Catherine. Would you like to take a ride with me somewhere today?"

Catherine decided to be coy with him. "Well, I don't know. It depends on where this someplace is."

"It's to Augusta to see my folks."

Catherine didn't know if she was ready to meet Sam's parents. She would rather have had more warning so that she could be better prepared to meet them. "Isn't this a little fast. I let you have your way last night, and today you want to take me home to mother. Do I see an ulterior motive here?"

Sam laughed. "I may be fast, but not that fast. Believe me, there's no ulterior motive in it. I already had plans to visit and have lunch with them today. I thought that you might like to come along. I promise you an interesting time. Will you come?"

Catherine thought. *Sam might make light of it, but this is a most important occasion. First impressions are very important, and I only have one chance to get it right. Should I go with him on such short notice?* Catherine made up her mind. "Okay, because you want me to, I'll go with you to Augusta to meet your parents."

It pleased and relieved Sam that Catherine had accepted his invitation to visit his parents. Since last night he had become convinced that she would someday be his wife. The time had come for his parents to get to know her. He felt certain that they would grow to love her as he did. "That's great, then I'll be there to pick you up in say forty-five minutes. We can be at my parents' home before one. That's if you can be ready by the time I get there."

Catherine thought for a moment, forty-five minutes wasn't much time to get ready. She would have to hurry, but she could be ready. "I'll be ready. See you soon."

When Catherine hung up the phone Helen was at her elbow. "Well, girl, don't keep me in suspense. What did Sam want?"

Looking at Helen, Catherine said, "Sam had already made plans to visit his parents and have lunch with them today. He wants me to come along with him."

With a grin Helen exclaimed, "Wow! I say that he's serious about you to be taking you home to meet mother."

Catherine said with a thoughtful tone to her voice. "I don't know how serious he is, but first impressions are very important, and I don't want to blow this one. What am I going to wear?"

Helen put her hand on Catherine's shoulder. "You just leave that to me. I'll see that you look your best."

Catherine, with Helen's help, had managed to be ready by the time Sam arrived. She had decided on a light-blue dress with white polka dots and white lace collar, white purse and white high-heel shoes. She had just the right amount of make-up to look like the proper southern lady who had just come from church. When Sam saw her, he beamed with pleasure, certain that Catherine would really make a hit with his parents.

The trip to Augusta took a little over two and one-half hours. The only point of interest during the trip had been Lake Oconee halfway between Atlanta and Augusta. They took exit 196 off of Interstate 20 onto Bobby Jones Expressway and were at Sam's parents' house in twenty minutes.

Sam pulled into the driveway to his parents' house and parked. They got out of the car and went to the front door. Sam rang the doorbell.

MICHAEL O. GREGORY

A middle-aged woman of age fifty-three years, with dark-brown hair streaked with gray and blue eyes opened the door. She embraced Sam immediately. "Oh, it's so good to see you Sammy. I'm so glad that you could come." She let go of Sam and turned her head to face back into the house. "They're here Daddy."

Sam, taking Catherine by the arm, said, "Mom, this is Catherine."

Catherine expected to get a handshake. Instead, Sam's mother gave her a hug. "I'm so glad to finally meet you, Catherine. You're the only thing that Sammy talks about anymore. Please, both of you, come in and take it easy. Lunch will be ready in a few minutes, and please Catherine calls me Mom. Everyone else does."

Sam's father came into the hallway to greet them. He gave Sam a friendly slap on the back. He then shook Catherine's hand and welcomed her to their home. Catherine found him to be just as charming and pleasant as Sam's mother. He was fifty-six years old, with thinning gray hair, blue eyes and a little heavier than Sam. No doubt that Sam was his father's son, they were so much alike.

Sam's mother had the meal ready. They had just been waiting for Sam and Catherine to arrive. It took Sam's mother only a couple of minutes to get everything on the table. Everyone then went into the dining room and took their seats at the table.

For lunch they had pork pot roast with garlic and onions, boiled red potatoes, carrots and a garden salad. The conversation keeps Catherine busy during the meal. San's parents wanted to know everything about her work, and what she liked to do in her leisure time. Sam must have briefed his parents ahead of time, as there were no questions about her family or past.

After the meal Sam's mother got up from the table. "I have some coffee and red velvet cake in the kitchen. Catherine, dear, would you like to help me serve?"

Catherine started to get up from the table. "Why yes, I would." Catherine followed Sam's mother into the kitchen to serve the coffee and cake.

WOMAN IN THE MIRROR

Sam's father took the opportunity of the women's absence from the dining room to speak to his son. "So, this is the girl that you told us about? The one with the amnesia?"

With a nod, Sam replied, "Yes, Dad, she's the one."

"I would not have known it. She seems so normal."

Sam had to correct his father. "That's because she is normal. Amnesia isn't a mental illness. It's a mental condition, a loss of memory due to a trauma to the brain. She was in a coma. When she woke up she had no memory of her past life."

Sam's father could understand what Sam said, he still wanted to know more about her condition. "What do the doctors say of her chances of getting her memory back?"

Sam knew of his father's concern about his relationship with Catherine. His main concern being that she was a person without a past. "Well, Dad, the doctors don't know. She was in a coma for a long time. She may get some of it back, all of it back, or none at all. The fact that she woke up at all is miraculous. The coma was thought to be irreversible. The doctors didn't expect her to wake up ever. Even if she never gets her memory back, she's still beaten the odds. She's had one miracle already, and maybe one per customer is all you get."

Sam's father still felt some concern about Catherine not having a past, but she seemed to be a polite and lovely young woman, and what he had seen so far of her he liked. "Then you like this girl?"

Sam sensed that his father had started to like Catherine and smiled. "Yes, Dad, I do."

With an intent look, Sam's father said. "Then you're not concerned of any problems that may come up? You don't know anything about this girl."

Sam knew what his father meant, but it didn't matter. "I know enough about her to know that I love her. Any problems that may come up, I'm sure that we'll be able to deal with."

Sam's father let out a sigh. "Well, we hope you're right." He looked up to see Catherine and his wife coming back from the kitchen with the

107

coffee and cake. "Oh, here come the ladies with our coffee and cake."

After the coffee and cake, Sam's parents gave Catherine a tour of their place. Their house was a sand hill cottage style and sat on four acres of land. A mix of pine, oak, sweetgum and elm shaded the front yard. Azaleas were planted around the house and in clusters around the bases of some of the trees. Most of the back yard had been cleared for a vegetable garden and the vineyard. Sam's father ended the tour by showing Catherine his vineyard of scuppernong vines. Catherine fell in love with the place. She wished that someday she could have a place like this. Perhaps she could have it with Sam.

After the tour they went back into the family room where they relaxed and talked. Since Sam and Catherine would be driving back to Atlanta, Sam's father served only soft drinks. Sam's mother brought out the family photo albums to show Catherine photos of the whole family, to include Sam's baby photos. Catherine saw them with more excitement than Sam did.

By the time that they had gone through the family photo albums and Sam's mother had told Catherine some stories of Sam's childhood, it had started to get late. Sam's mother put the coffee maker on and made more coffee for everyone. Sam and Catherine were offered more cake but declined. Undeterred Sam's mother wrapped some cake for them to take with them.

They were finally away a little after five. They arrived back at Catherine's apartment just before eight. Helen had seen them drive up and met them at the door. Catherine invited Sam in for a sandwich and Coke.

After the sandwich and Coke, Sam kissed Catherine good night at the door then left.

Helen could hardly wait for the door to close. "I'm dying to know. How did it go?"

Catherine had a pleased look as she leaned back against the door. "I think that it went well, but I'm not sure. I'll have to wait to get a report from Sam. I really loved Sam's parents and their home."

"Do you think that they like you?" Helen said with an inquisitive look.

Catherine thought for a moment before she answered. "You know, I believe they do. I was a little nervous at first, but they were nice to me. They went out of their way to make me feel at home and get to know me."

Helen thought that Catherine and Sam were the perfect couple. "Even if he hasn't said it yet, I believe that Sam loves you."

Catherine nodded. "Yes, I'm sure that you're right. There's no other man that I'd rather be with."

Helen smiled. "That's good to hear you say that. You and Sam were made for each other."

Chapter Seventeen

Ted and Beth found the office that turned out to be a single room in an older office building in Anniston, Alabama. The sign on the door read.

> DAVID GRAY-INVESTIGATIONS
> Divorce Photographs
> Child Custody Etc.
> Licensed in Alabama and Georgia

Ted knocked on the door and a male voice called out. "Come in!"

Ted opened the door and entered with Beth. The office was small with a gray-metal desk in front of the window in the wall across from the door. Next to the door stood a coat tree with a maroon blazer and raincoat hanging on it. There were two wooden office chairs in front of the desk. In one corner stood two gray-metal filling cabinets. In the other corner were a table with personal computer, television and video tape recorder. David Gray stood as they entered the room. Ted and Beth shook hands with David. David then directed them to have a seat in the two office chairs in front of the desk.

Once everyone had settled into his or her chairs, David reached into the center drawer of his desk and withdrew a file-folder. He then opened it on his desk and looked at Ted. "Ted, I checked up on that Georgia tag number for you. The auto is registered in Fulton County to a Miss Catherine White of Atlanta. She works for the Evans Clinic as a nurse's aide. She lives with a Miss Helen Schofield, a registered nurse who also works at the Evans Clinic. Miss White has been seeing a man, an attorney a Mr. Samuel Tankersley, also of Atlanta."

David pulled out a stack of eight by ten photos from the folder and handed them to Ted and Beth. The photos were of Catherine coming and going from her apartment in her nurse's aide uniform, in shorts and polo shirt and in a light-blue polka dot dress, being escorted by Sam.

Ted and Beth started to look through the photos. Ted then asked David. "You said that her name is Catherine White?"

David nodded. "Yes."

Ted kept looking at the photos as he spoke. "She may call herself Catherine White, but she looks just like our Amanda. Right Beth?"

Beth kept looking down at the photos as she spoke; she just couldn't take her eyes off them. "She could really be our Amanda. She looks just like her." Beth was so emotionally charged that she could barely control her voice.

David reached into his desk, withdrew a video cassette and put it into the video cassette recorder. "I also have this. I was able to pick up the voices by using a directional mike." He pressed the play button. The video showed Catherine coming and going from her apartment in the company, and speaking with Helen or Sam.

Beth couldn't take her eyes from the television as tears ran down her cheeks. That had to be her daughter Amanda on the television screen in front of her, she was absolutely certain of that. She could feel her heart pounding in her chest. "It's Amanda for sure. She may call herself Catherine White, but I'd know that face and voice anywhere. She must be Amanda!"

Ted put his arm around Beth's shoulder to comfort her. He knew how she felt. Even though he didn't show it as much, his heart was also pounding in his chest, and his palms were sweating. "You're right, Beth, she can be no one else but, Amanda."

David hit the off button, removed the cassette, and turned off the television. He then turned back to face Ted and Beth. "There's something

MICHAEL O. GREGORY

else that I must tell you. I did a background check and found that before March of this year Catherine White didn't exist." David paused for a moment to let the information sink in then continued. "I have made discrete inquiries with some of the clinic personnel. Catherine White is a Jane Doe who was found in a coma from an overdose of sleeping pills in a Nashville motel room. She had no identification and had registered under a false name. All attempts to identify her were fruitless. The doctors at the hospital in Nashville declared her to be in an irreversible coma. To save themselves the trouble of getting a court order to pull the plug, they had her transferred to the long-term care facility of the Evans Clinic, where against all odds she woke up three weeks later. Now she is completely recovered except for one thing, she has complete amnesia. She has taken the name Catherine White."

Beth tried hard not to break down into a fit of sobbing. "You say that she has amnesia?" Beth asked with a quaking voice.

David could see that Beth had really taken it hard. He wished that there were a better way to present this, but there wasn't. It had started out just being a simple job of finding the person that belonged to an auto tag, but had revealed some strange twists. He spoke to Beth. "Yes, according to my sources, she can remember nothing from before the time before she woke up from the coma at the Evans Clinic."

"That explains it." Beth said.

Ted gave Beth a puzzled look. "Explains what?"

Beth responded, "Why, Peggy was able to follow her through Macy's and speak to her and not be recognized." Beth looked imploringly at her husband, "Ted, I must see her. She's my child and she needs me, I know she does. Without knowing who she is, she must feel all alone and frightened."

Ted continued to comfort Beth. "I want to see her too, but I believe that we will need help." Ted turned to David. "David, what should we do?"

David leaned forward and put his elbows on the desk, then spoke to Ted. "Well, for one thing, I doubt that you can just step up and

WOMAN IN THE MIRROR

expect her to fall into your arms. That's if this amnesia thing's for real, and I believe it to be."

Ted understood David's reasoning so far and agreed with him. "Then what do you recommend that we do?"

David sat back in his chair and thought for a few seconds before he answered. "Look, I'm just a retired cop, not a shrink. I just find them. I can't say what to do afterwards. However, I do have one question."

"Yes, what's that?" Ted asked.

David looked at both Ted and Beth. "How was your relationship with your daughter before she disappeared?"

Beth sat back in her chair and looked at David for a while before answering his question. All that had transpired between her and her daughter Amanda raced through her mind. She found it hard to talk about such unpleasantness to a stranger, but she knew that she had to. She steeled herself and began to relate the story. "The relationship was bad, very bad. In fact, I don't see how it could've been worse than it was. Amanda was a head strong and rebellious child. She wanted everything her own way. It was like every time we said go right, she went left just to spite us. Despite the problems at home she was always a good student at school. She had a natural ability to learn.

"After graduation from high school we decided to send her to college. She had been accepted at the University of Alabama so we let her go there. We figured that away from home she would settle down and make something of herself. Well, for six months all she majored in was boys and extracurricular activities, so we brought her back home.

"We were going to let her attend a junior college close to home and live with us. There was a terrible fight and she ran away, just vanished. We haven't been able to locate her until now."

David looked at both Ted and Beth again before he spoke, "Well. I have done all that I can do. The rest is up to you. Just one thing to keep in mind. Be honest with her. Don't try to con her into believing that everything before was hearts and flowers. If she asks questions, give her truthful answers."

113

MICHAEL O. GREGORY

Ted nodded agreement. "All right, and a point well taken."

David had another point to make, "Oh, one last thing, she's what… twenty-five years old"

"She'll be twenty-five years old on the third of December." Beth said.

David nodded. "Well, whatever, she's an adult. You can't just go up there and bring her back home. The fact that she has amnesia doesn't matter. If she doesn't like what's happening and tells you to get lost, you must respect her wishes."

David took a large envelope from his desk. In the envelope he put a copy of his report, the photographs and the video cassette. He handed the envelope to Ted. "One last thing. We're almost certain that she's Amanda, but not positive. There's that outside chance that maybe she's someone else."

Ted nodded. "We'll keep that in mind."

David asked, "Is there anything else that I can do for you?"

Ted handed him a check. "No, that's about it. Your investigation and report is very thorough. You've done more than enough already."

David wished them all the luck at reconciliation with their daughter. Ted and Beth thanked him for everything that he had done for them. He again offered his help if they had any further need of it. Everyone got up and shook hands. Ted and Beth then left the office.

Ted and Beth got into their car and started for home. They got on US highway 431 north to Gadsden and drove in silence for a few minutes, each one alone with their thoughts. Finally Ted said, "What are we going to do? We can't just drive to Atlanta, put her in the car, then drive back home."

Beth didn't have a plan yet, but that wouldn't be for long. She was determined to do whatever she had to do to get her daughter back. "I know that, but we must do something. Our little girl's out there in the world, not knowing who she is. She needs our help."

Ted also wanted Amanda back. He also knew how determined Beth could be when it came to something that really mattered to her. "You know that we can't make her do anything that she doesn't want to do. There's still a remote chance that she's not Amanda."

Beth started to cry. "It's Amanda, I tell you. Any mother can tell her own daughter. I can't just sit back and do nothing. I want my daughter back. We must do something."

Ted agreed with Beth. "We will Beth. I want Amanda back as much as you do."

CHAPTER EIGHTEEN

Catherine had come to Maryanne's office for her weekly session. They were sitting on the sofa drinking coffee. Maryanne put her cup down on the coffee table and looked at Catherine. "How did it go last week? Anything that you would like to talk to me about?"

Catherine put her cup down on the coffee table, sat back comfortably in the sofa and faced Maryanne. "I started classes at the business college last week. I've finally taken the first step to my new carrier."

It pleased Maryanne to hear this from Catherine. It showed that she looked forward to her future and wanted to make the best of it. "That's good. Nurse's aide is a dead-end job anyway."

Catherine felt good about herself. Everything had been going well up to now. She now felt that everything would turn out right, her carrier moves and her relationship with Sam. She also wanted to tell Maryanne what she and Sam had been doing. "That's not all that I've been doing. Sam's been teaching me to play tennis."

Maryanne found this interesting. Anything new that Catherine did with Sam she wanted to hear about. "How are you doing?"

Catherine reached for her cup and took a sip of coffee before she answered. "As I said, we just got started, so you need to ask me that question later. When I was in high school I thought that tennis was just a game for wimps. Was I wrong! I'm running my ass off chasing that little ball. It's really hard work. I do have a cute little tennis outfit, so at least I look the part."

Maryanne got a good laugh from that. "Oh, I'm sure that you do. By the way, how are you and Sam getting along?"

Catherine took her time in answering, taking another sip of coffee and putting her cup back down on the coffee table before she spoke. "Our relationship has changed, it's no longer platonic. I'm no longer going to try to set limits. He had a romantic interest in me, and I in him. We agreed to let the relationship go where it will."

Maryanne and the rest of the staff had known all along that for 'Trade In' to be successful Catherine would have to become a complete person, not just physicality, but also mentality and emotionality. It now looked like they were close to declaring 'Trade In' a success. With a nod, Maryanne said, "I say, it sounds like you have changed."

Catherine leaned closer to Maryanne, putting her hand on the sofa between them. As she spoke her cheeks reddened with a blush. "Yes, I've developed a sexual interest in men. Sam in particular."

Maryanne took Catherine's hand in hers and gave it a pat. She would like to ask Catherine more direct questions about her newfound sexuality, but she felt that it might be too early for that. "Oh, that's great! I'm glad to hear that you now have a normal interest in men."

Catherine corrected, "I have a normal interest in Sam. All other men are irrelevant.' Catherine's face took on a contented look of pleasure as she thought of Sam and their relationship. "When he asked me to go with him to meet his parents, he tried to make believe that it was just a last minute decision to invite me, but I believe that he had it all planned in advance, so that when he did ask me and I accepted, I wouldn't have time to get cold feet and back out. Sam took me to Augusta with him to meet his parents. We had lunch with his parents, visited with them for over four hours, then drove back home."

Maryanne wanted to hear more about the trip to see Sam's parents. "How did it go?"

Catherine thought for a few moments of the trip to Augusta, of the visit with Sam's parents, and what Sam had told her later. "It went well. I was nervous at first, but they're really nice people, and we got along just fine. Sam got a call from them after he got home that evening. They told him that they really enjoyed having me, and to bring me again soon."

Maryanne smiled, pleased that Catherine had done so well with the visit to Sam's parents, "Taking you home to mother sounds like Sam has plans for you. I would say that he's in love with you."

A smile lit Catherine's face as she thought of Sam and their relationship, "Yes, it seems so. He has indicated often enough to me that he loves me. I even think that someday he will propose marriage to me."

Maryanne looked at Catherine. "Are you in love with him?"

Catherine took a minute before she answered. The answer to that question had been in her mind for some time, but she had yet to voice it. "I've tried to avoid the question, even in my own mind, but I know that I must now answer it. I'd rather be with him than anyone else. I can't bear the thought of losing him. Yes, I do love him."

Maryanne now asked the next, most obvious, question. "If he asked you to marry him, would you accept and become his wife?"

Catherine found the idea new to her that she could be a wife and mother. "Oh, Maryanne, I've not given it any thought. I've never thought of myself as being a wife and mother, but if I marry I will be the wife and mother. If Sam asked me I will most likely accept, but not now. I need some time to get use to the idea."

Maryanne took pleasure in Catherine's progress. "That's good, I'm so happy for you. Is there anything else?"

Catherine shook her head. "No, not much."

Maryanne changed the subject. "What about your dreams? Are you still having the dream about the clothes?"

Catherine nodded. "Yes, sometimes. I did have a dream the other night, but I don't remember much about it, except for one thing."

"What's that?" Maryanne said showing interest.

Catherine recalled the dream in her mind. "Well, in my dream I'm getting ready to go someplace. I look at myself in the mirror, and I'm the woman in the mirror. So, Maryanne, what do you think about that?"

Maryanne took a few moments to consider Catherine's dream as she sipped her coffee. She put the cup back down on the coffee table and looked at Catherine. "I would say that you're finally starting to see yourself as you really are. Right after the surgery you could say that you were out of sync. Your mind was living in the body of a stranger. Over the past months the mind had adapted to the new body, and now looks at it as its own. Ever since the surgery a new mix of hormones has been rewiring your conscious brain, changing it. You are now mentally a female and in tune with your gender."

Catherine thought for a moment about what Maryanne had just said. "I understand what you mean. For a long time I was somewhat confused in my sexual feelings for men. Then one morning I woke up and everything was as it naturally should be, and seemed to have been that way for a long time. There's no more gender confusion."

Maryanne had decided that they had covered enough for today. She smiled, pleased that Catherine had made good progress, "Is there anything else?"

Catherine said as she started to get up from the sofa. "No, that's it."

The session over Maryanne got up from the sofa with Catherine. Maryanne praised Catherine on the progress that she had made, and reminded her of her next appointment for the same time next week. They then shook hands and Catherine left to get back to her duties.

That evening Sam made dinner for Catherine again in his apartment. A simple meal of steak with, baked potato, broccoli, salad and a little burgundy wine to make everything just right. After dinner they had orange sherbet and coffee. Afterwards they went out to the living room, put on some music and talked. Catherine said, "That was a very good dinner. You're a really good cook."

Sam smiled at Catherine's praise and tried to make little of his accomplishments. "Thank you. I do manage to get by in the kitchen."

Catherine looked at him. "You do more than just manage. I just manage; you're a much better cook than I am. Besides, all one has to do is look at your kitchen. It's a well-appointed kitchen that belongs to someone who knows what to do in it."

Sam reached out for Catherine, she moved closer to him on the sofa and cuddled into his shoulder. He said, "My mother taught me how to cook when I was growing up. She said that a man living on his own had better know how to cook if he didn't intend to starve."

Catherine kissed Sam on the cheek. "I'm glad that your mother taught you how to cook. I can see that you like it. It's a pity that she didn't teach you anything about decoration."

Sam sat up straight on the sofa "What do you mean by that?"

Catherine waved a hand about the room. "Well, look at your place."

Sam looked about. "So, I'm looking at it. What's wrong with it?"

Catherine tried to hide her pleasure at having fun with Sam with a concerned look. "Oh, it's a really nice place, big rooms, plenty of space. But!"

Sam looked at Catherine. "Now what does that, but, mean?"

Catherine waved her arm about the room again. "Just look at this place. Where did you get your ideas from? Contemporary dorm room one-o-one? This is just a place to keep your things and sleep."

Sam looked around his apartment again with a more critical eye, then looked at Catherine. "So I'm not a decorator. Maybe someday I'll let you help me to do it over."

Catherine smiled. "I'd be glad to do it for you."

Sam leaned back into the sofa. Catherine leaned back up against his shoulder, snuggling in close. Sam put his arm around her, "How would you like to go back to Stone Mountain again this Saturday?"

Catherine wiggled up even closer to Sam and put her arm about him. "I'd love to."

Looking into Catherine's eyes, and giving her a smile, Sam said, "Then I'll pick you up at eight on Saturday morning."

Catherine kissed Sam. "I love you, Sam."

Sam replied, "And I love you too Catherine." They kissed again passionately.

CHAPTER NINETEEN

When Sam arrived back at the office after lunch he found Fred waiting for him. Fred said, "I thought you were going to go to lunch with me today. What happened?"

Sam gave Fred an apologetic look. "I was, but I had a special errand to run."

Fred gave Sam a quizzical look. "Special errand?"

Sam reached into his coat pocket and took out a small jeweler's gift box. He opened it and showed it to Fred. "I got this for, Catherine. Do you think that she will like it?" Sam proudly displayed the box for Fred's inspection. The jeweler's box contained a gold heart-shaped pendant set with an opal on a gold chain.

Fred took a look at the pendant inside the box and made a soft whistle. "Hay, that's really something you have there. It must have set you back a bit. If she doesn't like it, she's crazy. I'm sure that she will love it."

Sam had a satisfied smile on his face. "I just happened to see it and thought that she would like to have it."

Fred laughed. "Sure, and you just happened to be in a jewelry store browsing."

With humor, Sam said, "Of course, what else?" They both had a good laugh.

Sam put the jeweler's box back in his coat pocket and had a seat at his desk. Fred pulled up a chair and sat across the desk from Sam. Fred looked at Sam and shook his head, "Boy, Catherine has really got you hooked. Now she's reeling you in."

Sam laughed again. He then thought of Catherine and everything that she meant to him. "She didn't have to do anything. I was hooked from the first day I met her."

Having met Catherine, Fred could understand why Sam had been so smitten by her. If he had been lucky enough to meet her first, he would feel the same as Sam about her. "Well then, when do you plan to give it to her?"

Sam took the pendant out of his pocket and looked at it again, "I'm taking her to Stone Mountain on Saturday. I plan to give it to her there."

Fred shifted forward, leaning over the desk to get another look at the pendant, "I know that she'll love it, and I'm glad for you that you've found the woman of your dreams. I've just one question."

Sam looked at Fred. "Yes, what's that?"

With a smile, Fred said, "Can I be best man?"

With a smirk, Sam said, "I don't know. I'll have to think about that." They both laughed again.

Saturday the week after Labor Day dawned partly cloudy with an expected high of ninety-six degrees and a thirty- percent chance of afternoon thunder storms. Sam picked up Catherine at her apartment at eight in the morning and drove to Stone Mountain.

In the park a group of Civil War reenactors had a bivouac set up that was open to the public. The male reenactors were all dressed in an assortment of confederate uniforms. The female reenactors were dressed in clothing of the Civil War period. Sam and Catherine found it interesting how people lived back then. Catherine thought, comparing how everything had been back then with what she had now, that there wasn't much good about the good old days.

After the Civil War bivouac they toured the antebellum homes on display in the park. They were authentic antebellum homes moved from all over the state of Georgia to the Stone Mountain Park. Catherine enjoyed the tour. She thought of how great it must have been to live in such a house and tried to imagine herself living in one of them. However, she found it a little too much of a stretch of the imagination to see herself as Scarlet O'Hara coming down the grand staircase in her ball gown.

After the tour of the antebellum homes it was time for lunch. They had fried chicken at the restaurant next to the train depot.

After lunch they took the train around the mountain, to the base of the hiking trail to the top of the mountain. They wanted to climb the mountain on foot this time, rather than take the cable car. The heat and humidity hadn't as yet become so oppressive, and they only had one and three-tenth of a mile to hike to the top.

Catherine found the view from the top even more spectacular than when they had taken the cable car. Perhaps because they had worked harder for it this time. From the top Catherine could see that some of the trees were just starting to show their fall colors.

Sam chose a secluded spot next to some pine trees with a view to the west from where they could see the downtown Atlanta skyline. After taking in the view, Catherine exclaimed, "Oh, it's so beautiful from up here! Even more than the last time! I just love it!"

Sam had been sure that Catherine would be impressed by the view. He had been on top of Stone Mountain several times, and this had become his favorite spot. "So it is, but the best is yet to come. Peak fall colors will occur around the first week of November, or about nine weeks from now. How about we make a date to come back to this same spot on the first Saturday of November to view nature in all her glory?"

Catherine wouldn't miss a chance to come back. "Oh, Sam, I'd love that."

Sam smiled. "All right then the first Saturday of November we have a date to come back to this very spot."

Sam then took Catherine's hands into his own and stood there face to face looking into each-other's eyes. "Catherine, your company these last months has been a joy to me. Since I met you, I've thought of no other woman but you."

MICHAEL O. GREGORY

Catherine started to blush and cast her eyes down. She could tell that Sam was building up to something big. "Oh, Sam."

"Please, Catherine, let me continue. You mean more to me than I have words to convey. I want only you."

Catherine could feel that Sam had something in mind to be acting like this, but what? "What can I say?"

Sam gave a reassuring squeeze of the hands, "Just say what you feel."

Catherine looked back up into Sam's eyes. "Oh, Sam, I'm sure that you know how I feel about you, but you must know that I can't make any commitments now. It's too soon to be making permanent plans for the future."

Sam could feel that despite the fact that they had agreed to let the relationship take its course, she had started to put up the barriers again. He wasn't trying to push too much. "I'm not asking you to commit to anything now. I just want you to know how I feel about you."

Catherine knew well by now how Sam felt about her. "But you don't know anything about me. I can't even remember anything from my own past."

Sam wanted to be reassuring to her, "I don't care about not knowing about your past. I feel that I know you and what I know I like. You're a considerate and caring person. If your past is the same as your present there's nothing to be concerned about."

Catherine wanted to make a commitment to Sam. She now felt certain that she loved him, but for some reason she had a feeling that she shouldn't make any commitments just yet. "Thank you for your confidence in me and I do love you. I just need time to work things out. I still have some unresolved issues to deal with first. Now this I'll promise you. I'll have these issues resolved before too long. Then I'll be able to make a full and permanent commitment. When the time comes I'll make it so obvious that you won't have to ask."

Sam figured that now would be a good time to give Catherine her present. He took the jeweler's box from his pocket and offered it to her. "I saw this the other day and I knew that it would look right only on

124

you. Please accept this as a token of my affection for you."

Catherine took the box and opened it. She was surprised and pleased to see the pendant and chain in the box. She removed the pendant and chain from the box and looked at it in the sunlight. A smile of pleasure lit her face in appreciation of Sam's gift. She could see the fire in the stone as the sun reflected the colors. She threw her arms around Sam's neck and kissed him. "Oh, thank you, Sam, it's so lovely. Here, put it on for me." Catherine handed Sam the chain, then turned around and lifted her hair off the back of her neck so that he could put it on for her.

After Sam had the chain in place they embraced and kissed again, "Thank you again Sam. It's the loveliest thing that anyone has ever given me. I'll cherish it forever."

Sam felt very pleased that Catherine had loved her gift. It had been a real pleasure to give it to her. He wanted to give her the world if he could. "I'm glad that you like it Catherine. When I first saw it in the store I could see some of the same green fire in the stone that's in your eyes. I knew right then that you must have it."

Catherine hugged Sam and kissed him again intensely. She felt the fires of passion rekindle within her. When the kiss ended she remained within his embrace with her head on his shoulder. "Oh, Sam, you're so good to me. Sometimes your compliments just overwhelm me."

Sam tightened his embrace on Catherine so that their bodies made more firm contact. "My compliments shouldn't seem so overwhelming to you, I mean every one of them and they're well deserved. Today I have given you an opal. Someday I'll make it a diamond."

Catherine kissed Sam again. "That would be nice, but not now. Let's give our relationship time to mature."

The sun reached its zenith and the day had turned hot. A large cloud to the northwest had gotten larger and now started to turn dark. Sam looked at the cloud. "I think that we should start back down now."

Catherine looked at the cloud and nodded. "Yes, you're right. It looks like we may get some rain soon."

They hiked back down the mountain to the train stop. By the time they got there the cloud looked even more threatening. They took the train back to the depot. They then went to the parking lot to get their car.

After leaving Stone Mountain, they went back to Sam's apartment. They put on some music and talked for a while. When it came time for dinner they decided to go out to Red Lobster, then after dinner take in a movie. Sam changed, then drove Catherine back to her apartment so that she could change into a dress for the evening. They had dinner at Red lobster. After dinner they went to the theatre. Sam had Catherine back home just before midnight. They kissed good-night, then Sam left.

When Catherine let herself in, she found Helen still up watching television. Helen immediately spotted the pendant and chain. "Did Sam give that to you today?"

Catherine smiling went over to Helen's chair and bent forward so that she could get a close look at the pendant. "Why, yes, Sam gave it to me. How do you like it?"

Helen made a quick appraisal of the pendant. "It's really beautiful Catherine. The opal is of good quality."

Catherine took a seat in the chair next to Helen, kicked off her shoes and scrunched her toes in the carpet. "Yes, Sam said that it had some of the same green fire in the stone that's in my eyes. He also said that someday he plans to make it a diamond."

Helen considered Sam to be a wonderful man, and felt that Catherine had been very lucky to find him. She believed that Sam would be the one to make Catherine's life complete. "I can see why Sam wants to give you a diamond. You and Sam are destined for each other. You both know that it's true."

Catherine leaned back in her chair and looked dreamily at the ceiling, "Yes, I want Sam badly. My life has been on hold for too long. I want to settle down and have the good things that life has to offer."

Helen gave Catherine an inquisitive look. "Then I assume that Sam is the one that you want to have all these things with. Then I've a question for you. When do you think that you'll give in and sleep with him?"

Helen's question took Catherine by surprise, but didn't shock her. "That's my own business, but I'll tell you anyway. I'm waiting to make sure that everything is going as planned and my future is secure. It's my first time and I want it to be special."

Helen looked into her friend's face to see if she had been kidding her. "Do you mean the first time since after the operation, or the first time ever?"

Catherine replied, "As for Karl, he was a shy boy and felt so insecure with the girls. He was never able to make it with any of the girls."

Helen had a curious smile on her face. "So you're a virgin?"

Catherine blushed. "In my memory I am. As for Jane Doe, Well, who knows? Although I doubt it very much."

Helen gave Catherine a wink of the eye. "Well, as they say, sex is in the mind, so technically you're still a virgin."

Catherine nodded agreement. "Yes, that's how I see it too."

Helen understood Catherine. "I see that you want to save it for the right man. That's noble of you. We would all like to do that. Don't let anyone push you; when the time comes you'll know it."

Catherine sighed. "The time isn't right yet, but not for the reason that you think. I'm ready and would like to do it. I really love Sam."

"Well then, why not?" Helen asked with an inquisitive look.

Catherine shook her head. "I don't know. I guess that everything seems to have gone too easy. I still have an uneasy feeling that the other shoe is about to drop. I can't explain it. It's just a feeling I have, and until I can resolve it I can't feel totally free to go on with my life. One other thing, what about that woman that spoke to me at Macy's?"

Helen thought for a moment of Catherine's encounter with the mystery woman at the mall. It had been a cause for concern for everyone at the clinic for a while. However it seemed to have been a false alarm. "Oh, that was quite a while ago and nothing has come of it. It must have been a case of mistaken identity, so don't worry about it."

MICHAEL O. GREGORY

Catherine nodded. "Ok, I'll try not to."

CHAPTER TWENTY

Ted and Beth were having lunch in their home after church. Their son Bill a sophomore at the University of Alabama had come home for the weekend. Beth was speaking to Ted. "Have you decided what to do yet?"

Ted shook his head. "Not yet. I don't want to move too fast. We don't want her to just take off and disappear. If that happened we may never find her again."

Beth stopped eating and put her fork on her plate, her breakfast forgotten for now. "I know that, Amanda is in trouble. She's lost and all alone in the world. She needs our help."

Ted had been expecting this discussion. He knew what Beth would want to do. However, he didn't feel so sure that it would be the right thing to do. "All right, what if we just show up at her door, to her a couple of strangers. Then she panics and runs. What then?"

Beth wasn't going to be put off any longer. "So we just sit here and do nothing! That's not good enough! I know where my daughter is and I want her back! If you don't know what to do, I do!"

Ted now stopped eating and put his fork down. "What do you plan to do?"

Beth looked at Ted. Ted could tell by the look on her face that Beth had a plan and was determined to carry it out. "I want to see my daughter. I'm going to Atlanta."

Ted wasn't so sure that Beth's way would be the right way. "Are you going to just walk up and ring the doorbell and say hello Amanda,

I'm your mother."

Beth was determined to get her way. She had been patient for a few days at her husband's request, while he tried to come up with a plan of his own, but now her patience was at an end. She didn't want any more foot dragging. "It might just come to that. First I just want to look at her, to see how she's doing. Then and if the time is right and I can get her alone, that's just what I might do. Just walk up and ring the doorbell. She might run again, but I have to take that chance."

Bill had been listening to his parent's conversation. He also wanted to have his sister back. He had to take his mother's side in this. "Dad, I think Mom's right. At some time we must come face to face with her and make contact."

Ted looked at his wife. "Is this really what you want to do? Once you have made contact there's no going back."

Beth nodded. "Yes, that's what I want to do."

Ted still had some doubts that this would be the best course of action, but he usually let Beth have her way. "Okay, do you want me to do anything? I can go with you if you want me to."

Beth shook her head. "No, I'll go by myself. I think it should be that way at first. It will be traumatic enough for her with me alone. So I must go alone. There will be plenty for you to do later on."

"When are you going?" Ted asked.

Beth thought. "Tomorrow morning, I want to see where she lives first, and get a look at her. Then I'll pick the best time to make contact with her."

Bill had been listening to every word and wanted to help. "Is there anything that I can do to help?"

Beth smiled at her son. "Later, but not now. The first move is mine."

After church Sam and Catherine went back to Sam's apartment for lunch. Sam and Catherine were sitting at the kitchen table. Catherine said, "It's such a beautiful day. What should we do after lunch?"

Sam and Catherine hadn't planned anything for the day other than going to church together. Sam, however had been thinking of a

WOMAN IN THE MIRROR

conversation that they had the other day, and had an idea as to what they should do with the afternoon. "I have an idea. Let's drive up to Commerce."

Catherine looked into, Sam's eyes, and wondered what he had in mind. "To Commerce, what for?"

"They have a factory outlet mall there." Sam said with a sly smile starting to show. "I've been planning on fixing up my apartment. I know that you don't think much of the way that I have it decorated now."

Catherine glanced about the kitchen in a somewhat critical manner. "I would say that it could use a woman's touch."

Sam had a broad grin and that amused look in his eye. "Then how would you like to be my decorator?"

Catherine had been a little taken back by Sam's sudden proposal. "You want me to do your decorating? I really don't have much experience at it."

Sam, still smiling, said, "Well, if you can see what's wrong with it, you're better at it than I am." Catherine felt pleased that Sam wanted her to decorate his apartment and smiled. "Okay, I'll be your decorator, but you have to tell me what you have in mind so that I can do it right."

Sam smiled back at Catherine and waved his hand about to indicate the apartment. "Why don't you just fix it up the way you would like it."

Catherine wasn't sure that he really meant that she could have a free hand. "How will I know if you'll like it?"

Sam wanted Catherine to know that he trusted her judgement, and that she could be free to do whatever she wanted. "If you like it I will. I want you to be comfortable, to feel at home here."

With a playful voice, Catherin said, "Do I see an agenda here? Are you thinking that someday I'll be living here with you?"

Sam, still grinning, said, "Why yes, I do."

Catherine reached across the table and patted Sam's hand. "Okay, I'm your decorator. As for my moving in, let's just say that I'm thinking about it."

Sam took Catherine's hand and kissed it lightly on the back, "Okay, that's all that I ask for. Now, let's finish lunch so that we can get going."

Catherine decided to have some sport with Sam. "All right, but one thing first. That picture that you have on the wall over the sofa in the living room. The English bulldog with a red jersey with a large 'G' on it. What is it?"

"Oh, that's Uga." Sam replied.

Catherine pretended ignorance of who Uga was. "Who's, Uga?"

Sam pretended shock that there could be someone in the state of Georgia who didn't know who Uga was. "Well, Uga is the mascot for the University of Georgia."

Catherine said to Sam in a stern voice, while trying to keep a straight face and to stifle a laugh. "Well, you may keep him in your office if you want, but Uga must go."

With a nod, Sam said, "Okay, you're the boss. I'll take Uga to the office."

Catherine had tested Sam to see if he meant what he said. She knew that if he let her get rid of Uga, she could do anything.

They drove up to and spent the afternoon at the factory outlet mall in Commerce. Catherine picked out some pillows for the sofa and some place mats. She then found some curtains and three lamps. They left only when they had no more room in the car for anything else.

By the time they got back to Sam's apartment and unloaded, it was after seven. They decided to go to Captain D's for takeout and bring it back to Sam's apartment for dinner.

On the way to Captain D's they talked. "I had a good time today." Catherine said, "I believe that we got a good start on decorating your apartment."

Sam responded, "I'd say that we have. By the way, you haven't told me just how you plan to decorate it yet."

Catherine recalled a mental picture of Sam's apartment, of what he had and what he needed, "For one thing we'll keep all your furniture. It's all good. In fact we'll have to get some more pieces. You have a sofa, two chairs and a coffee table, but you also need a couple of end tables.

WOMAN IN THE MIRROR

We'll look for some to match what you already have."

Sam smiled, pleased that Catherine wouldn't be making such drastic changes. "Good, that won't set me back much."

Catherine continued, "Also two night tables to go in the bedroom."

Sam nodded agreement, "Okay, two night tables."

"We will also need a nice bookcase for the living room."

Sam hadn't anticipated this. "But I also have a bookcase in the bedroom."

Catherine held firm on that point. "That has to go."

Sam replied, "I thought that you said that we didn't need to get rid of anything?"

Catherine gave Sam a serious look. "That home-built thing that you call a bookcase, that looks like it's leaning into a strong wind. That's not furniture, that's an eyesore."

Sam gave in. "Okay, I said that you're the boss, it goes."

Catherine kissed Sam on the cheek. "Thank you Sam. I promise not to spend too much of your money. Now, can you come with me to the art gallery after work tomorrow? I saw some pictures that I'd like to get for your place."

With a nod, Sam said, "All right, I'll pick you up at your apartment as soon as I can get away from the office."

Catherine gave Sam another kiss on the cheek, "I'll be ready when you get there."

CHAPTER TWENTY-ONE

Beth didn't leave for Atlanta before she had made lunch for Ted. Arriving in Atlanta she found, Catherine's apartment just before four. A red Ford Taurus with license 9781 AEK stood in the parking space in front of the apartment, but no one was home. Beth parked at the end of the apartment block and waited.

Just after 4:30 a dark-blue Ford Mustang pulled into the parking space next to the Ford Taurus. Two women got out of the Mustang and walked to the apartment door. One a petite blond woman in green hospital scrubs. The other a taller woman with shoulder-length black hair, dressed in the white short-sleeve blouse and red jumper of a nurse's aide. Beth watched as they let themselves into their apartment. It took all of her self-control to keep from jumping out of her car and running up to them. That had to be Amanda. Beth was sure of it. Beth knew that she must see and talk to her, but now wasn't a good time. She must wait until she could get Amanda alone. She believed it best that they have their first meeting with no one else around.

After they let themselves in Catherine went to the kitchen to put coffee on, while Helen went to her bedroom to change. After she started the coffee, Catherine went to her bedroom and changed into a bathrobe, then came back out for her coffee. Helen had already poured herself a cup of coffee, and then taken a seat at the kitchen table. Catherine made her coffee, then had a seat at the able across from Helen. Helen asked, "Do you want to eat in this evening?"

Catherine shook her head. "No thanks. Sam will be picking me up soon. We're going shopping at the art gallery. There are some things that I saw there that I want to get for his apartment. We'll then be eating out."

Helen took a sip of coffee, then put the cup back down on the table. "Then I think I'll call James and have him come over. I can cook for him. Oh, by the way, James and I are going out to hit the nightclubs and go dancing this Friday. How would you and Sam like to come with us? We could make it a foursome."

Catherine had never been a great dancer, and she didn't know how well of a dancer Sam was, having never gone dancing with him. But it would be fun to go out together with Helen and James. "Okay, I'll ask Sam. I'm sure that he will want to."

It pleased Helen that Catherine had accepted. Now Helen had to bring up the fact that Catherine didn't have a suitable party dress. "Now, we need to start thinking about getting you a nice dress."

Catherine put her coffee cup down on the table and looked at Helen. "I already have some nice dresses."

Helen knew that Catherine had a lot to learn about buying a party dress. "Yes, I know that you have some nice dresses, but they aren't the right kind of nice."

Catherine's brow wrinkled, "Oh, what do you mean by that?"

Helen knew that Catherine had no clue as to what she meant, "Well, everything that you have makes you look like you're going to church, or to tea with the ladies garden club. For night clubbing you need something more revealing. Something with more flash."

Catherine knew what Helen meant. She would have to look for something. "Okay, I'll look for something tomorrow at the mall."

Helen knew Catherine's likes and dislikes, and knew that if she were left on her own, she would never make the right choice. She would have to go to the mall with Catherine to help her choose the right dress. "Alright, after work tomorrow we go to the mall to look for a dress."

Catherine finished her coffee. She then took a bath, and got ready for Sam to pick her up. Helen called James and asked him to come over

MICHAEL O. GREGORY

for dinner. Sam showed up at a quarter to six, and they left for the mall.

Beth saw the white Honda pull up in front of the apartment. A man in a light-gray suit, with a red and gold-striped tie got out and went into the apartment. About ten minutes later he came out with Amanda on his arm. Amanda wore a blue dress, and through the binoculars, Beth could see that she wore a silver and turquoise cross on a silver chain. They got into the car and drove off. Beth followed them out of the parking lot.

Sam and, Catherine drove to the mall, then headed for the art gallery. At the art gallery Catherine picked out two framed prints, one showing children in late nineteenth century costume playing in the surf at the beach with a Saint Bernard dog. The other of someone walking a country road through the woods in the rain with a red umbrella. She then found an oil painting of a young girl in a walled garden, barefoot and dressed in early nineteenth century peasant costume, standing on tiptoes drinking from a fountain. Before leaving the store she found one more picture that she liked, a water color of blue irises. From the art gallery they went to another store where they bought a bedspread with dust ruffle and pillow covers. They also got curtains to match.

After their shopping, they left the mall for Sam's place to drop everything off. From there they went to Red lobster for dinner. After dinner Sam drove Catherine back home.

Just as Catherine and Sam left the mall parking lot, Beth left the mall. She got into her car and started home. She had been able to get close and observe without being seen. She now knew for certain that it was Amanda. Today hadn't been a good time to try to make contact. She would try again tomorrow.

Beth arrived back at the apartment the next day right at four in the afternoon. Catherine's car still occupied the parking space in front of the Apartment, but as the day before she found no one home. She took up her position the same as the day before and waited.

At 4:45 Catherine and Helen arrived and went into the apartment. Twenty minutes later they left the apartment, got into the blue Mustang

WOMAN IN THE MIRROR

and left for the mall. Beth followed them to the mall where they entered a ladies boutique and started to look at party dresses.

After a couple of minutes looking Catherine choose a dress off the rack, a dark-blue satin with the hem at mid-calf length. She went into the dressing room to change, then came out to check herself in the mirror. "What do you think of it Helen?"

Helen, shaking her head, said, "Do you want the truth?"

Catherine gave Helen a hard look, knowing that she would be critical of her choice. "Of course I do."

Helen grinned at Catherine. "Okay, you look like a teenager on her way to her high school prom."

Catherine tried to ignore Helen's remarks as she looked at herself again in the mirror. "Well, I think that it looks good on me."

Helen could see that it wouldn't be easy to get Catherine to be bold and try on something rally revealing. "Yes, but you're going night clubbing, not to a school dance. That just won't do."

Helen took a short metallic-gold sleeveless dress from the rack and held it out for Catherine, "Here, this is your size. Try it on."

Catherine took one look at the dress and rejected it. The very idea of wearing that dress was appalling to her. To her it would be like raising a flag and shouting 'I'm here, look at me'. Shaking her head, Catherine said, "I can't wear that, it's too short."

Helen wasn't going to take no for an answer. "No, it's not too short! You have really attractive legs. This will show them off to your best advantage."

Catherine took another look at the dress. She could swear that she had seen T-shirts with more fabric in them than this dress had. "But it's so short."

Helen was determined to have Catherine try on the dress and tried to reason with her. "So, you show your legs when you wear shorts don't you?"

Catherine, still looking at the dress, said, "Well, yes, but that's shorts. This is a dress, what there is of it."

MICHAEL O. GREGORY

Helen felt that Catherine needed to get over her shyness about wearing really short skirts and dresses of revealing styles. "So, what's the problem? Are you afraid that someone may get a peek at something that they shouldn't?"

Catherine blushed. "Oh, Helen, you're terrible!"

Helen laughed at Catherine's embarrassment. "All right, so I am. If that's what's worrying you just wear something with lots of lace, preferably black, or a color that matches the dress. Besides, even if someone sees something, they still don't see anything."

Catherine just had to laugh at Helen's remark. Helen laughed with her. The levity of Helen's remark put Catherine in a mood to be bold and try the dress on. Catherine took the dress from Helen. "Okay, I'll try it on."

Catherine went into the dressing room, changed and came back out to the mirror. Helen thought that the dress looked really great on Catherine. "Now, that looks a lot better."

Catherine turned to get a good look at herself in the mirror. The dress was really short, but well cut and flattering to her figure. She had been pleasantly surprised that instead of making her look cheap, it had an overall effect of elegance. "I must agree with you, but it's not really me, though I do like the fashion."

Helen went back to the rack and found a short blue-sequined dress. "Here, this is your size. Try it on."

Catherine went back to change and came back to the mirror. As she turned to get a good look at the dress, Helen said, "Oh, that's really pretty."

Catherine made two more turns in front of the mirror. "Yes, it's nice, but it just won't do either."

They looked and found a short sleeveless dress of white satin. This dress wasn't suitable either. Catherine went back to the racks and soon found a sleeveless dress of mid-thigh length made of emerald-green silk that when the light hit it at a certain angle seemed to flash blue-green. When Catherine came out of the dressing room to stand in front of

WOMAN IN THE MIRROR

the mirror she smiled. Helen said, "Oh, that's you. It's perfect."

Catherine took a few more turns in front of the mirror. "Okay, I'm going to take it."

After Catherine made her purchase they went to the shoe store. There Catherine found a pair of green high-heel shoes that went well with her dress and bought them. They continued to look until they found a small green-sequined handbag to complete the ensemble.

After completing their shopping, they went to their car and started for home. They stopped at Bojangles Chicken for takeout.

Beth had followed them from the apartment to the mall, and had stayed close to them as they did their shopping. She watched Amanda as she tried on the dresses and thought at how beautiful she had become. Beth had to use all of her self-control to keep from going up and speaking with her. When they left the mall, Beth drove home determined to come back tomorrow and make contact with Amanda.

The next morning Catherine and Helen drove their own cars to work. Catherine planned to come straight home from work. Helen planned to stop at the market on the way home to do some shopping.

Beth arrived at four and observed that both cars were absent. She took up her position at the end of the apartment block and waited. At 4:30 Catherine pulled into her parking space, got out of her car, and let herself into the apartment.

Beth watched Amanda enter the apartment alone. Beth sat in her car for a minute to calm her nerves as much as possible. She then got out of her car and walked to the apartment door.

Catherine had put the coffee on, and was about to change when the doorbell rang. Catherine thought. *That's Helen. She must have her arms full of grocery bags and can't get to her key. She wants me to open the door for her.* Catherine opened the door expecting Helen. Instead a middle-aged woman of about fifty stood at the door. One look at her face with those green eyes and black hair and Catherine felt certain who this woman must be. Catherine blanched and her blood ran cold. It took a few moments for her to get her composure back and speak.

139

MICHAEL O. GREGORY

Her effort to seem casual fell flat. "Yes, may I help you?"

Finally Beth stood face to face with her daughter. The emotion of the moment almost overcame her. "You're Miss Catherine White?" Beth managed to say.

Catherine nodded. "Yes, I am."

Beth would have liked to have said, 'Hello, Amanda, I'm your mother', but she knew that that would be wrong, instead she said, "I'm Mrs. Elisabeth Jenkins. I must speak with you. May I come in?"

Catherine wished that this woman would just go away, but she knew that she wouldn't. She would have to invite her in and speak to her. "Yes, please do." Catherine held open the door for Beth, and directed her to a seat on the sofa. "I'm just making coffee for myself. Would you like to have a cup?"

Beth nodded, glad for the momentary distraction. "Why, yes, thank you. I'll take it with milk and one level teaspoon of sugar."

Catherine took the time that it took to make the coffee to get over the shock, and try to calm down. Beth was also glad of the time to plan how she would be able to explain herself.

Catherine came back into the living room and placed Beth's coffee in front of her on the coffee table. She then took a seat in a chair across from, Beth and sipped her coffee as she watched her. Beth sipped her coffee, taking time to study Catherine before she spoke. Finally, Beth said, "I'm sorry if I seem to be prying into your personal affairs, but I must ask you these questions."

Catherine put her cup down on the coffee table and looked at Beth. "I'm not sure what this is all about, but go ahead."

Beth started out with a fact that they both knew to be true. "You were found in a Nashville motel room in a coma?"

Catherine nodded. "Yes, that's what they told me."

Beth took another sip of her coffee, then put her cup back down on the coffee table. "When you woke up from the coma you had no memory of who you are, or any memory of your past life?"

Catherine again nodded. "Yes, that's true."

WOMAN IN THE MIRROR

The answer to the next question would be very important to Beth. "And you haven't been able to regain any of your memory?"

Catherine shook her head. "No, I haven't."

Beth cleared her throat, picked up her cup, took a sip, then put the cup back down. She was very nervous, but resisted whipping her sweaty palms on her thighs. "Well, I guess that the only way to say this is to just come out and say it. We, that's my husband and I believe you to be our daughter Amanda."

Catherine and Beth sat there for a few seconds just looking at each other before Catherine spoke. "I must ask. What makes you think that I'm your daughter?"

Beth reached into her purse and took out a high school yearbook photo of their daughter Amanda and handed it to Catherine. Catherine looked at the photo. She found herself looking at a younger version of herself. Beth said, "And that's not all. You have the same build as Amanda. You're the same height, and you have the same voice."

Catherine sat there looking at the photo. It would be hard to deny this woman, but she had to do something. She needed time to think. "I'd like to believe you, but I have no memory of you. You're a stranger to me. I could be your daughter Amanda, and then it could just be a coincidence. I need to know for sure."

Beth nodded. "Well, that's okay, I can understand your anxiety in this matter. There's one other thing. When my good friend Peggy spotted you in Macy's you were wearing a silver and turquoise cross on a silver chain. It's just like the one that we gave Amanda when she graduated from high school."

Catherine handed the photo back to Beth. "Please forgive me, but this is all very sudden. I'd like the time to sort it all out. May I have your name, address and phone number? I'd like the chance to talk to my doctor at work first before doing anything else. I hope that you understand."

Beth had made her case. Now all she could do was let events take their course. "Yes, I do understand Miss White."

MICHAEL O. GREGORY

"You may call me Catherine." Catherine replied.

"Thank you, my friends call me Beth." Beth took a card and pen from her purse, wrote on the back of it, then handed it to Catherine. "Here, this is my husband's business card. I have written our home address and phone number on the back."

Catherine took the card from Beth. "Thank you, I'll be in touch with you really soon. You have my word on that."

They both stood and Catherine showed Beth to the door. Beth left to start back home. As soon as she closed the door Catherine collapsed into the chair. Her mind was in turmoil. She felt so nervous that she shook all over.

When Helen got back home a few minutes later, Catherine still sat in the chair in the living room in shock. One look and Helen knew that something very wrong had occurred. "What's wrong? You look like you're about to have teeth pulled."

Catherine said with a trembling voice. "Oh, Helen, it's worse than that. We have a big problem."

Helen sat the groceries on the coffee table, then took a seat on the sofa. "Now, tell me, what's the problem?"

With a shaking hand Catherine reached up to push a lock of hair out of her eyes before she spoke. "Well, I had just put the coffee on, and was about to change when the doorbell rang. I thought that it was you wanting me to open the door for you. When I opened the door there was a stranger, a woman at the door. The moment that I saw her I knew who she must be. She was Jane Doe's mother. She believes me to be her daughter Amanda."

The news shocked Helen. This had to be the worst thing that could have happened. "Did you get her name and address?"

Catherine held up the business card. "Yes, it's right here on her husband's card. He's a general contractor in Gadsden Alabama. They're Theodore and Elisabeth Jenkins."

Helen took the card from Catherine. "We must notify the clinic right away." Helen went to the phone and dialed the clinic.

142

After Helen phoned the clinic, they went there without delay for a meeting with Dr. Evans. The meeting had been called in the conference room. Present for the meeting were Dr. Evans, Dr. Weston, Dr. Prater, Nurse Schofield and Nurse's Aide White. Dr. Evans opened the meeting. "Ladies, everyone knows why we're here, so let's get started." Dr. Evans turned to Catherine. "Now, Catherine, how valid do you believe this woman's claim to be?"

Catherine had had time to get over the shock and regain her composure. She remained calm as she spoke. "There could be a chance that she's wrong, but I doubt it. The family resemblance is strong and her evidence is undeniable. She is Jane Doe's mother."

Dr. Evans asked, "Did she say anything about how she had been able to find you?"

Catherine recalled what Beth had told her about the woman at Macy's being her friend. "Yes, the woman that spoke to me at Macy's is a friend of hers. She must have gotten the license number from my car and given it to her. That must have been how they found me. One other thing, when she showed up at my door she already knew about the amnesia."

Dr. Evans rubbed his chin with his thumb and index finger. "That must have been the way that they did it. They got a private investigator to check you out. Well, we can't go back and undo it, so let's just deal with it the best way that we can. After all we knew that this was a possibility. We must handle it in such a way as to maintain the confidentiality of 'Trade In'. Grace, do you have the address and phone number of the Jenkins?"

Dr. Weston showed him the card that she had gotten from Catherine. "Yes, I do."

Dr. Evans nodded. "Good, then write them a letter and follow it up with a phone call. Invite them to meet with us here at the clinic to determine if Catherine is their daughter Amanda. The best plan isn't to try to stall or stonewall them. When they ask a question they get an answer. That way we can be sure that they get the answers that we want

MICHAEL O. GREGORY

them to have. It'll be up to you to see that they have what they want."

Dr. Weston made a note in her notebook. "Okay, I'll take care of it. By the way, there's one way that we can buy time. We can have a DNA test conducted before we confirm that Catherine is their daughter."

Dr. Evans liked the idea. "Good idea, have it done."

Dr. Weston made another entry in her notebook.

Dr. Evans now turned his attention to Dr. Prater. "Now, Maryanne, your job is to make it clear to them that Catherine's amnesia is complete, and most likely permanent."

Dr. Prater nodded. "Is that all that you need me to do?"

Dr. Evans replied, "That's all for now, but keep on your toes. We may have to make changes. Also I want you with Grace for the first meeting with the Jenkins."

Dr. Evans now turned to Catherine. "Catherine, you're going to have the hardest time of it. You're the eye of the storm, so to speak. You will have to meet with them, at least here at the clinic. They will likely want to make contact with you outside the clinic, like at home so be prepared for it. They will try to spark your memory with photos, momentous, or stories. Don't ever try to fake it, you will be caught at it. If at any time you feel that you may be losing control get in touch with us."

Catherine could see that the burden would be on her, but there wasn't anything that she could do about it. "All right, I'll get with Maryanne anytime I need her."

Dr. Evans now turned to Helen. "Now, Nurse Schofield, you will be close support for Catherine. To back her up when needed. I don't want Catherine to think that we have left her out there all alone. Be close to her and give her support as much as you can."

Helen nodded. "Yes, Dr. Evans."

Dr. Evans looked at everyone. "Any questions?" No one had anything to add. "Good, then meeting adjourned. Let's get to it."

He next morning, Ted and, Beth were having coffee and breakfast at the kitchen table. "Well, Beth, did you make contact with her? What do you think, is she Amanda?"

Beth had been so exhausted last night after three trips to Atlanta in three days that she went right to bed and slept. She had been so physicality and emotionally exhausted that she didn't even speak with Ted. Beth took a sip of coffee, then said, "After meeting with her face to face and talking with her, I'm one-hundred percent certain that she's Amanda. Oh, I wanted so much to embrace her, kiss her and tell her how much I missed her, but I had to restrain myself. She was so close, but I dare not even touch her."

Ted looked at his wife. He could tell that she was still very tired from all the travel and excitement of the last three days. "Are you going back again today?"

Beth shook her head. "No, not after three trips to Atlanta in three days. I'm going to just rest up today. I may go again tomorrow, or this weekend."

They talked a while longer until Ted finished his breakfast and left for work. Alone at the kitchen table Beth reflected on the meeting with Amanda the day before. Peggy had said that she looked different, that she may have changed in some way. Beth had been close to her the first two days as she followed her through the stores. She had watched her interact with other people. Then her impression of Amanda during the meeting yesterday, Beth had noticed that she had changed, matured in some way. Perhaps now there could be a chance of a good relationship between them.

At 9:30 the phone rang and Beth went to answer it. "Hello."

Dr. Weston was on the other end. "Hello, is this, Mrs. Elizabeth Jenkins?"

"Yes, I'm Mrs. Jenkins."

"I'm Dr. Grace Weston, Assistant Director of the Evan's Clinic in Atlanta Georgia. You met with one of our nurse's aides Miss Catherine White yesterday."

Beth started to get excited and her hands started to perspire. "Yes, I was at her apartment. We're sure that she's our daughter Amanda."

"Well, that's what I'm calling about. You know that you really shocked Catherine, just showing up like that. She's still upset over it. She called us as soon as you left. She's anxious to find out if your claim that she's your daughter is true. I know that it's short notice, but can you and your husband come to the Evans Clinic Monday morning at eleven. We would like to run some tests."

Beth was elated. She would go right now if asked. "Yes, we'll be there."

"Good. Do you need directions?"

"No," Beth said shaking her head, "we know where the clinic is."

"Then we will see you Monday morning. Thank you for your time and good-bye."

Beth hung up the phone. She could hardly wait for Ted to get home for lunch so that she could tell him the news.

When, Ted got home for lunch Beth waited for him at the door to tell him about the call from Dr. Weston. They made plans to drive to Atlanta Monday morning. Now all Beth had to do would be to endure the wait until Monday.

Friday evening at 7:30 Sam and James picked up Catherine and Helen for an evening of dancing. Catherine wore her new dress and looked ravishing. However on the inside her nerves had her all in knots. Catherine didn't feel in the mood for dancing, but didn't want to spoil it for Sam. Sam had been able to pick up her mood a little by how she reacted to an enthusiastic compliment by him of how marvelous she looked in her new dress. Catherine tried to keep her true feelings from Sam, but he knew her too well. It didn't take Sam long to notice that something was really troubling her. She claimed a headache and had Sam take her home.

At home they talked and Catherine told Sam about Beth. Sam had been pleased for Catherine that she may have found her family. He could also see that it had been a very confusing development for her. He pledged to her his steadfast support.

Chapter Twenty-Two

When Catherine got to work Monday morning the head nurse directed her to report to Dr. Prater's office right away. Catherine went to Maryanne's office and knocked on the door. Maryanne called out, "Come in!"

After they exchanged greetings, Maryanne directed Catherine to have a seat on the sofa. Maryanne said, "Would you like to have a cup of coffee?"

"No, thank you." Catherine said as she took her seat on the sofa.

Maryanne continued, "Okay, we need to talk about what has happened, and what is likely to happen in the future."

Catherine had wanted to talk to Maryanne about this. She had been in turmoil since Beth had shown up at her door. "Yes, I do need to talk to you about this. I've spoken to Sam about it, but I can't tell him the whole truth ever. All I told him is that I may have found my family." Catherine paused to give her words emphasis. "I don't mind telling you that this whole thing frightens me. I don't want my life turned upside down, and I don't want to lose Sam."

Maryanne felt that even though Sam would have to be kept ignorant of some facts, he could be of help to Catherine. "I can understand your concern. You really love Sam, I can see that. If he loves you, as I suspect he does, he can be a big help to you in this crisis. I know that you can't tell him everything, but lean on him, he'll want to help."

With a nod, Catherine replied, "I know that I can count on Sam. Now what are we to do about the Jenkins?"

147

MICHAEL O. GREGORY

Maryanne had just come from a meeting with Dr. Evans and Dr. Weston and knew what had to be done. She just wondered how willing Catherine would be to go along with it. "All right, Catherine, this is what you're going to have to do. You are going to have to meet with them and spend some time with them. What relationship you develop with the Jenkins is up to you. They will try to get you to accept them as your family, but we will not push you to accept them. You may accept them, or you can remain estrange, that's up to you. You may even actually take their daughter's name, or keep the one you have, that's up to you. When asked we can and will advise, but we will not direct you to do anything that you don't want to do. Now, are you straight on these facts?"

Catherine could see that even though the people at the clinic meant well, there wasn't much that they could do to make this thing go away. Their main concern would be the confidentially of 'Trade In'. "Yes, I understand. You're saying that I must deal with the Jenkins, but I've a free hand as to how I do it. Also that when it is proven that I am their daughter, and it will, what relationship I have with them is up to me."

Maryanne could see that even if Catherine didn't want to accept the inevitable yet, she at least had not balked at its mention. "Good, now I have some precautions for you. At first they will just be happy to have you back again, but soon they will want to try to revive your memory. They will have you meet family members and friends. They will show you family photographs and personal items. They will prepare your favorite foods for you. Now you may recall things after they have been shone to you, but only as they were shone to you. Don't try to fake any recollections or they will find you out. Any questions?"

Catherine shook her head. "No questions I've had this briefing already."

Maryanne now started to go over the day's itinerary with Catherine. "All right, now for what will happen today. The Jenkins will arrive here at the clinic at eleven this morning. They will first be briefed in Dr. Weston's office. After the briefing they will be brought to the clinic's

WOMAN IN THE MIRROR

lab for their blood to be drawn for testing. You will be in the lab when they get there. We will first type everyone's blood, both theirs and yours. Now, if there's no match it's all over and they go back home. If there is a match we will then draw blood and send it out for testing. As you know we can do the DNA testing here at the clinic, but will send it out to another lab to buy you some time to decide what you need to do. Any questions?"

Catherine already knew the answer to the question, but she had to ask it anyway. "Yes, one, is there any chance that the surgery altered Jane Doe's DNA in any way?"

Maryanne could see that Catherine was grasping at straws. "There's no chance for that. For sure you have Jane Doe's, or as we know her now, Amanda Jenkins DNA."

Catherine nodded. "Yes, I know, but I had to ask anyway."

Maryanne asked, "Is there anything else?"

Catherine shook her head. "No, I got all of it."

Maryanne raised one hand with a finger extended to emphasize the next subject. "Now, one other thing. They will want to meet with you after the blood has been taken. We would like for you to go to lunch with them. You will be given the afternoon off for that."

Catherine would have preferred not to become involved with the Jenkins, but she knew that it was inevitable. "Okay, if I have to spend time with them I may as well start today."

Catherine's willingness to do her part and meet with the Jenkins reassured Maryanne that they just might have a successful resolution to the matter. "Good, now what I want you to do is go back home and change out of your uniform into street clothes. We want you to look good for them, but not too dressed up, keep it casual. Everything has already been cleared with your shift supervisor. Just leave now, go home, change and be back by eleven."

Catherine and Maryanne got to their feet. Maryanne shook, Catherine's hand and wished her luck, and again told Catherine that her door would always be open to her. Catherine then thanked Maryanne

149

MICHAEL O. GREGORY

for her help and left for home.

On arriving at home, Catherine went to her closet to decide what to wear. A dress seemed a little too much for the occasion. She set out a short-sleeve orchid color silk blouse, plumb color pleated skirt, black pumps and black purse. She bathed, fixed her hair and make-up, dressed and arrived back at the clinic by 11:00.

Ted and Beth left home a little after seven. They arrived at the Evans clinic at eleven. They were met by a receptionist and shown into Dr. Weston's office. As they entered Dr. Weston stood up and stepped from behind her desk, extending her hand. "Mr. and Mrs. Jenkins, good-morning and welcome to the Evans Clinic. I'm Dr. Grace Weston." Ted and Beth introduced themselves and shook hands with Dr. Weston. Indicating Maryanne, Dr. Weston continued, "This is my colleague Dr. Maryanne Prater." Ted and Beth shook hands with Dr. Prater. Everyone then took their seats.

Dr. Weston then said, "It's a long drive from Gadsden. Would you like some coffee, or perhaps a Coke?" Ted and Beth said that they would like a cup of coffee. Dr. Weston served them from a coffee maker on a table behind her desk.

After every one had made themselves comfortable, Dr. Weston said, "Mr. and Mrs. Jenkins, or might I call you something other than Jenkins?"

Ted indicated Beth and himself. "You may call us, Ted and Beth."

Dr. Weston replied, "You may call me Grace. Now, Ted Beth, thank you for coming in today on short notice. I'm sure that we all want this resolved as soon as possible. Now, Beth, you made contact with, Catherine last week. During this meeting you expressed your belief that she's your daughter."

For Beth it had to be more than just a possibility, she had no doubt that she was Amanda. "Yes you're right. I'm certain that she's Amanda."

Dr. Weston took a sip of coffee, put the cup back down on her desk then continued, "You know that you shocked Catherine when you just showed up at her door like that?"

150

WOMAN IN THE MIRROR

Beth could understand, it had been just as stressful for her, but she had to do it. "I didn't mean to cause her so much distress, but I couldn't think of any other way to do it."

Dr. Weston nodded. "Well I guess that there isn't any easy way, but if she hadn't noticed the remarkable physical resemblance between the two of you she may have slammed the door in your face. As it is she wants to know who she is so she let you in. After you mentioned a silver cross and how you gave it to your daughter she realized that you're most likely her parents. That's why we are here today. Physical appearances can be a coincidence, but blood will tell the truth. After we are through here, we will go to the lab where Catherine will meet us. We will draw blood from the both of you and Catherine for testing."

Ted had been drinking coffee, and now put his cup down on the end table next to his chair. "How long will it take to test the blood?"

Dr. Weston answered, "Well, there are many test. Some take longer than others do. The first test that we will do is to type for blood group. This is a very quick and easy test. It only takes a few minutes. We just prick your finger and get a couple of drops of blood. We then type it to see what blood group each person is in. We will do this test here in our lab. Now a child must have the same blood group as either the father, or mother. If we get a match we will draw blood from each of you and Catherine and send it out to the lab that specializes in DNA testing to be tested."

Beth already knew the answer to the question, but she had to ask it anyway. "What if you don't get a match?"

Dr. Weston answered, "Then it's all over. Catherine can't be your daughter."

Beth asked, anxious to know how long all this testing would take. "If you get a match how long will the other tests take?"

Dr. Weston answered, "From six to eight weeks."

Beth said, wanting everything to go much quicker. "That long?"

Dr. Weston responded, "Some of the test can come back quicker, but the more definitive tests will take that long." Dr. Weston now

151

paused before she went to the next subject. "Now, Catherine, by the way, that's the name she still wants to go by for now. You know that she was in a coma when she came to us. Then when she woke up she had amnesia."

Ted and Beth nodded that they understood. Beth said, "Yes, we know that."

Dr. Weston after meeting with Ted and Beth knew for sure that they were Jane Doe's parents. She couldn't say Catherine's parents because Catherine's consciousness wasn't Amanda's consciousness. She would have to make it clear to them that they couldn't have the old Amanda back without revealing anything about 'Trade In'. That way Catherine would be free to build whatever relationship with the Jenkins that she wanted to. Dr. Weston said, "The fact that she woke up at all can only be seen as a miracle. When we received her from the hospital in Nashville she was thought to be in an irreversible coma, there being no detectable higher brain functions. We never expected her to come out of the coma ever. We were really amazed when she woke up. Now she seems normal and she is, except for her memory. You may be tempted to push her to remember, but please don't. You will only frustrate her and cause her anxiety. Just accept her as she is and let her get to know you again in her own way. She's been awake for about five months now with no recall. We believe the amnesia to be complete and permanent. I know that if she is Amanda that you can't have the old Amanda back, but you can still have a future with her."

Ted and Beth looked at each other. Dr. Weston had just confirmed what they had already been told. Ted said, "Thank you Grace. We will do our best to make her feel comfortable with us."

Dr. Weston got to her feet and everyone else stood up with her. "Now if you will follow me I will take you to the lab."

Ted and Beth followed Dr. Weston through the clinic until they got to the entrance to the lab. Dr. Weston opened the door for them and they entered. Catherine had been waiting just inside the door for them. Dr. Weston looked at Catherine. "Catherine, you already know

Elizabeth. This is her husband Theodore."

Ted saw her standing there and was amazed at how lovely his daughter had become. He wanted to take her in his arms and give her a hug, but he settled for a handshake. "Please call me Ted."

As, Catherine took his hand to shake it she took a good look at him and could see a little of herself in his face. She smiled. "All right Ted, I'm Catherine."

Ted had also studied Catherine. He now felt certain that she had to be his daughter Amanda. "Hello, Catherine."

Catherine shook hands with Beth. "Good-morning, Beth."

"Good-morning, Catherine."

The lab technician typed Catherine's blood first. Catherine typed 'B' positive. The technician next typed Beth's blood. She typed 'O' positive. Beth had expected this. She and Amanda were of different blood types anyway. Ted was the last to be typed. He typed 'B' positive.

Dr. Weston checked the results. "Okay, Ted, you and Catherine are a match. We will now draw blood from each of you. Then everyone can go to lunch."

As the lab technician drew the blood, Dr. Weston wondered how this would all turn out. She wasn't worried that anyone would notice that surgery had been done on Catherine. Their surgery technique had been so flawless that no visible sign of it remained. She didn't worry about the Jenkins. They were so glad to have their daughter back that they would accept her as she was. The only person that she need worry about was Catherine. Right now Catherine was trying to find a way to just get these people out of her life, but that wasn't going to happen. Dr. Weston could tell that the Jenkins were her biological parents and that they wouldn't be going away. Dr. Weston and the others in 'Trade In' would like to see Catherine accept the Jenkins as her family, but that would depend on Catherine's sense of morality and decency. She might not think it right that she take Amanda Jenkins identity and live her life.

After the lab technician drew blood, Catherine took Ted and, Beth

153

out to the parking lot where she got her car. Ted and Beth followed her back to her apartment. From there Catherine went with Ted and Beth for lunch at Red Lobster.

After ordering, Beth started the conversation, "Well, Catherine, how do you like working at the Evans Clinic?"

Catherine being in the neutral setting of the restaurant started to relax with the Jenkins, "Oh, it's a good job. I get along with everyone there and I'm treated well. However, I don't want to make it my life's work. I'm going to Business College. I'm taking administrative office management."

Beth smiled at Catherine, "That sounds good. You were always an exceptional student, you learned very quickly. We're sure that you will do well in your studies."

It felt strange to Catherine that Beth talked about her as if she already knew her.

Beth continued, "You also have a nice apartment. It's roomy and well decorated and in a good area."

"Yes, I like it." Catherine said, "The apartment is Helen's. She invited me to live there with her as her roommate. So I'm living there and sharing the rent and expenses with her."

Catherine now turned her attention to Ted. "Ted, if you don't mind me asking, what you do for a living?" She already knew the answer, but it was a way to begin an exchange with him.

Ted's answer was short and to the point, "I'm a building contractor. I build homes for people."

Catherine figured that Ted must be as much or more nervous as she was. "It must make you feel proud to be able to put together buildings like that. It must take a lot of skill."

Ted relaxed a little and warmed to Catherine "It's a rewarding carrier, and it provides well. You say that you have a roommate Helen?"

Catherine could see that Ted felt content to let Beth do most of the talking while he just listened. She was glad that he had started to talk to her, "Yes, Helen Schofield, she's a nurse at the clinic. We're good friends, and we sometime double date together."

Ted knew all of this, but was just making conversation. "So, you have a boyfriend?"

Catherine smiled as she thought of Sam. "Yes, his name is Samuel Tankersley. He's an attorney here in Atlanta. He calls me his mystery lady because of my amnesia. He puts up with all my moods and bad manners and is very patient with me. We met by accident. I bumped into the back of his car with mine."

Beth exclaimed, "Oh, you didn't!"

Catherine laughed at the recollection of it. "Yes I did, and was he angry. Three days later he called insisting on a dinner date, so that he could apologize for being so angry with me. There has been no one else since then."

Beth had been about to ask something else, when the waitress arrived with their orders and everyone started to eat. After a couple of minutes Catherine had a question for Beth, "Is Amanda your only child, or do you have others?"

Beth looked up from her plate. It had been an unexpected question, but considering Amanda's amnesia not an unreasonable one, "No, Amanda wasn't our only child. We have two others Audrey and William, we call him Bill. You, I mean, Amanda is the oldest. She will be twenty-five on the third of December. Audrey is the next oldest. She turned twenty-three last month, the twenty first of August. Bill is the youngest. He was nineteen this last May the eighth."

Catherine wondered if there had been a reason for the names of both of her daughter's to start with an 'A'. She could also use it as a way to learn more about Beth's children. "Beth, both of the girl's names start with an 'A' and the boy's name is William. Is there any reason why the girl's names start with an 'A'?"

Beth responded, "Yes, I wanted them to have names with meaning. For the first I chose Amanda. It means worthy to be loved. For the second I chose Audrey. It means noble strength. Bill is named for both of his grandfathers, William Sherman."

MICHAEL O. GREGORY

Catherine nodded. "That's interesting. It seems that there can be a lot to a name. By the way, what does Audrey and Bill do?"

Beth answered, "Audrey's a graduate of the University of Alabama. She's now the personnel manager for an auto dealership in Birmingham. Bill's a sophomore at the University of Alabama. He wants to be a doctor."

The rest of the meal Catherine asked questions. Ted and Beth talked a lot about family and friends. At Catherine's urging, Ted and Beth showed her pitchers of Audrey and Bill. Catherine paid close attention to what they had to say; any information on the family may prove useful to her later on.

After lunch Beth said that she wanted to go shopping before they left Atlanta. They all went to the Lenox Square Mall to shop. Beth wanted to get something for Catherine, but Catherine kept resisting. Catherine didn't feel it appropriate that she accept gifts from the Jenkins at this time.

They finally arrived back at Catherine's apartment at five. Catherine had been about to get out of the car when Beth spoke to her, "Oh, Catherine, we've had such a good time today. How would you like to come to our house for lunch on Saturday?"

Catherine had been expecting something like this and knew that she couldn't say no. "That would be nice. What time should I be there?"

Beth said, "How about one O'clock? If you leave Atlanta at eleven your time, you can be at our house by one our time. Ted will tell you how to get there."

Catherine turned to Ted as he started to speak, "Now you leave Atlanta on Interstate 20 West. After you cross the Alabama state line and pass through the Talladega National Forest you will come to the exit for US Highway 431 North. Don't take this exit. Go two more exits to the exit for Alabama State Highway 21 at Oxford. Go north on highway 21 for no more than one mile and you will run into US Highway 431. Go straight through the light and you will be on US Highway 431 North. Just stay on US Highway 431 North through Anniston and on to Gadsden."

156

WOMAN IN THE MIRROR

Ted took a note pad from the glove box and drew a map, then handed it to Catherine. They said their good-byes. Catherine then got out of the car. Ted and Beth drove out of the parking lot on their way back to Gadsden.

CHAPTER TWENTY-THREE

Ted and Beth took Interstate 285 west then south to Interstate 20. They drove in silence until they were west of Douglasville and away from the Atlanta metro traffic. Finally Beth spoke, "Well, what do you think about her?"

Ted took a few seconds to put his thoughts in order before he spoke. He reviewed in his mind his experience that day with Amanda, or as she now calls herself Catherine, "Well, everything about her the face, eyes, hair, hands, voice, everything about her is Amanda, yet there's something different about her."

Beth nodded agreement. "So you've noticed it too?"

Ted said, taking his eyes off the road for just a second to glance at his wife. "Of course I have. The Amanda that I remember was rude, ill mannered, short-tempered and disrespectful. This girl who calls herself Catherine is a courteous, well-mannered and apparently well-adjusted young woman. It's not at all what I expected from Amanda. It's like she's a whole different person."

Beth had also observed Amanda as they spent the day with her and had to agree with Ted, "Yes, that's the same impression that I have. The transformation is startling. How do you account for it?"

Ted shook his head baffled by the unexpected changes in Amanda, "I don't know. I don't think that I can explain it. She's been on her own for over six years now, close to seven. That might be part of it."

Nodding, Beth said, "Yes, part of it, but not all. I can't see anyone changing this much in just six years."

WOMAN IN THE MIRROR

Ted wondered if Amanda's mental condition could have something to do with it, "Do you think that her amnesia could have something to do with it?"

Before Beth answered she took a minute or so to think about it. It would be a strange question for her to try to answer. This girl calling herself Catherine was Amanda and yet she wasn't. It seemed to be more than just a maturing through experience. Perhaps it did have something to do with her amnesia, "Well, perhaps that's the reason for the new personality. Could be that when she lost her memory, she lost the demons that were driving her."

Ted couldn't think of anything different so nodded in agreement. "Yes, that might be the reason for it. Whatever the cause the results are dramatic. I know that the old Amanda was the daughter that we knew and loved despite the problems, but this new Amanda. I still have a hard time calling her Catherine. She's now the daughter that we always wanted her to be."

It didn't matter to Beth how much she had changed, she was still Amanda, "I don't care if it's the old Amanda or the new Amanda. I'm just glad to have her back. I don't ever want to lose her again. She may call herself Catherine now and not know us, but just give it time. I know that she's Amanda, and I believe that soon she'll come to know us as her family again."

Ted changed the subject to the up-coming lunch on Saturday. "Do you have a plan for lunch Saturday?"

Beth had been thinking of how she would handle Amanda's first homecoming, "Yes, we must call Bill and see if he can come home for Saturday. I'll also get in touch with Audrey and see if she will come. I think that immediate family is all that we should have over. There will be plenty of time later on for her to get to know the rest of the family."

Ted took another glance at Beth. "Have you thought of what you're going to serve for lunch?"

Beth had already given it some thought, and would be making some of Amanda's favorites, "Yes, I'll make Dairyland Confetti Chicken.

159

MICHAEL O. GREGORY

She used to love that. I'll also make a coconut cake, which is also one of her favorites. I want this homecoming to be perfect."

"I'm sure that it will be." Ted said patting Beth on the hand.

The next morning Catherine knocked and entered Maryanne's office. "Maryanne, are you busy?"

Maryanne, from behind her desk looked at Catherine. "No. In fact I expected that you would want to see me." Getting up from behind her desk she indicated the sofa, "Please have a seat."

Catherine and Maryanne took a seat on the sofa. Maryanne said, "Well' how are you today?"

Catherine's shoulders drooped as she sighed. "Oh, I feel just lousy."

Maryanne could see that Catherine was distraught. "Oh, tell me about it."

Catherine turned toward Maryanne and threw up her hands in a sign of frustration. "I'm a fraud. I don't like what I'm doing to Ted and Beth. They're good and trusting people who believe me to be their daughter. I'm misrepresenting myself as their daughter when I know that they no longer have a daughter."

Maryanne could see Catherine's desperation and tried to reassure her. "I know that you're having a hard time."

Catherine pounded her fist on the arm of the sofa. "You're damn right that I'm having a hard time! I don't know if I can keep this up!"

Maryanne reached out to put her hand on Catherine's shoulder and looked her in the eyes. "You must go along with it, at least for a while. Then you can find a way to end it, or at least maintain a distant relationship. After all, their relationship before she left home may not have been good."

Remembering how eager Ted and Beth were to have her recognize them as her parents, Catherine said, "Oh, I know that, but I still don't like to build up their hopes, then dash them."

Maryanne could see that Catherine had started to get to know the Jenkins as decent people. As a caring person herself, Catherine felt bad about having to deceive them as to the true status of their daughter. "I know that you don't like it, but keep in mind what's at stake." Maryanne would like to see Catherine eventuality accept the Jenkins in some way as her parents. What relationship she would have with them would be up to her.

Catherine knew all too well what was at stake for her personally. "Yes, I know that. I've just as much at stake as anyone, maybe more."

Maryanne tried her very best to be reassuring to Catherine. "Just remember, you're the one who will call the shots. We will assist you in whatever you want to do. If you need time off for anything you'll have it. Whatever you need just ask for it."

Catherine nodded, and pushed back a lock of hair that had fallen in front of her eyes. She wondered that with everyone telling her that they were behind her. Then why did she feel so alone. "Well, I don't feel much better, but at least it's good to talk to someone about it."

Maryanne patted Catherine's forearm. "Just hang in there. Give us a chance to work it out."

Catherine let out a sigh. "All right. I'm not going to panic. I'm sure that we can find a way to get out of this thing gracefully. There's one other thing. I have a date with them for lunch at their home on Saturday. Is there anything that I should do?"

Maryanne thought for a moment if they had overlooked any instructions. "Just keep doing as you have been doing and you'll be okay."

Catherine felt confident that she could get through the dinner without tripping herself up. For now she could still call herself Catherine, but eventually she would have to acknowledge being Amanda, at least in body, and it weighted heavy on her soul, "And what do we do when the blood tests come back? You know that it'll show me as their daughter. After all it's their daughter's body that I have, we know that now. They'll think it odd that after we make the link that I try to break it."

Maryanne smiled at Catherine, trying to show confidence. "We have time to work it out. Just keep the faith."

Catherine had tired of everyone telling her that everything would be just fine, but what could she do about it. She had no choice, but to go along with it. "Okay, but I don't like it."

Maryanne knew that Catherine had started to get to know the Jenkins and had an idea of what she must be feeling. "Well, it's good to know that you have feelings for them. I know that you don't want to hurt them and that you find yourself in a quandary. By the way, we don't like it either."

Catherine started to get up from the sofa. "I guess that's all that I have for now. I should be getting back to work."

Maryanne got up from the sofa with Catherine. Maryanne said, while giving Catherine a hug. "Whenever you need me, I'm here for you anytime day or night."

"Thank you." Catherine said. She then turned to the door and left the office.

That evening Catherine had dinner with Sam at his apartment. She tried to make it a good evening, but her problems hung heavy on her. They had just finished dinner and were having coffee, "You look like you've lost your best friend." Sam said.

Catherine put her coffee cup down on the table. "I'm sorry Sam. I don't mean to be a drag on you." Catherine had been trying to hide her feelings from Sam, to keep her problems to herself, but wasn't good at it.

Sam could see how it had really been eating away at her. "It's the Jenkins that you're worried about?"

Catherine cast her eyes down and her shoulders seemed to slump. "Yes, I'm concerned as to how all this will change my life."

Sam wanted to help Catherine through all this, but didn't really know what to do. "You did say that they seemed to be really nice people, didn't you?"

Catherine nodded. "Well, yes, I did."

Sam reached across the table and took Catherine's hands into his and gently stroked the back of her hand. "Then don't worry about it. You're no longer a little girl. You're a grown woman. So you recognize them as your parents. You don't have to go back home and live with them. All you do is change your name and live your life as before. That

WOMAN IN THE MIRROR

shouldn't be too hard for you since you don't monogram anything anyway." Catherine broke into a smile, giving a little chuckle at Sam's wit. Sam continued, "Now that's better. You look much better when you smile."

Catherine looked up into Sam's eyes, and said with a voice made soft by her feelings for Sam's concern. "Oh, Sam, you always have a way to make me feel better. I don't want to ever lose you."

Sam gave her hand a gentle squeeze. "You can't lose me. I'll never let you go."

Sam got up from the table, pulled Catherine to her feet and kissed her fervently. After the kiss Catherine lay her head on Sam's shoulder. She then said into Sam's ear. "I feel much better now. Let's go to the store and rent a movie. I would like to get something really funny. I need something to laugh at for a change."

Sam responded, "All right, we're finished with dinner. Just grab your purse and let's go."

Catherine got her purse and they left to rent a movie.

163

CHAPTER TWENTY-FOUR

Saturday turned out to be a clear day with low humidity. A fine day for a trip. Catherine left her apartment by eleven AM. She took Interstate 285 West then South to Interstate 20, then West to Oxford Alabama. There she picked up US Highway 431 North to Gadsden, arriving at the Jenkins home just before one PM.

Catherine pulled into the driveway and parked. As she got out of the car Ted and Beth came out of the front door of the house, followed by a young woman and a young man. As they approached, Ted said, "Hello, Catherine, how was your trip?"

Catherine closed the door of her car and turned to Ted, "I had a pleasant trip and managed not to get lost, thanks to GPS navigation. The drive on the Interstate was pleasant, once I got out of the Atlanta metro area. Even US 431 wasn't all that bad. The hardest part was getting through Anniston with all those traffic lights and heavy traffic. Am I on time?"

Beth, taking Catherine's hand and shaking it said, "Yes, you're right on time." Beth indicated her other two children, "Catherine, I would like to introduce my other two children. They're Audrey and William." Catherine exchanged greetings with Audrey and William. Audrey to Catherine seemed to be cold and distant. William, on the other hand, gave her a very warm greeting. He not only shook her hand, but also gave her a tentative hug. William asked that he be called Bill.

After the introductions were done with, Beth said, "All right, now that we have the introductions done, lunch is ready." Beth then turned

164

WOMAN IN THE MIRROR

to Audrey, "Audrey, will you give me a hand with the tea and glasses?"

Audrey answered, "Yes, Mom."

Everyone went into the house. Beth and Audrey made the last minute preparations, then everyone took their places at the table. Ted gave the blessing, then everyone started to serve him or herself. After everyone had been served, Beth said to Catherine, "It's so good to have you here with us. I fixed one of, Amanda's favorites, Dairyland Confetti Chicken with fresh garden salad and coconut cake."

Catherine complimented Beth on the dinner, "Everything looks really good. I'm sure that I'll really like it."

The conversation started out with topics of current events and the weather. Once everyone started to get comfortable with Catherine, Audrey and Bill started asking questions. They wanted to know how Catherine liked living in Atlanta. Then Audrey started asking Catherine about herself. "I hear that you work for a medical clinic."

Catherine nodded. "Yes, I work for the Evans Clinic in Atlanta."

Audrey had stopped eating to give her full attention to Catherine. "That sounds interesting. What do you do there?"

Catherine started to get a feeling that Audrey had some motive to her questioning and started to guard her words "I'm a nurse's aide."

Audrey said, in a slightly patronizing tone. "So, you are in nursing?"

Catherine put her fork down to devote more attention to Audrey. She thought that she detected hostility in Audrey and wondered why, "No, not really. A nurse's aide does all the mundane jobs that need to be done, so the nurses have more time to do what they're trained for. There's no advancement into nursing from nurse's aide, it's a dead end job."

In a casual tone, Audrey said, "What were you doing before?"

Catherine hadn't been expecting a question like that. It made her feel uncomfortable. She wasn't sure if the question had just been a casual one, or was Audrey up to something.

When Catherine gave no answer to the question, Audrey said, "Oh, excuse me. I didn't mean to ask that."

MICHAEL O. GREGORY

Catherine managed to respond in a casual voice, "That's all right, it's a natural question to ask." She could see that Audrey had been trying to trip her up, and would have to be more on guard not to make a slip.

Audrey fretted embarrassment for asking an inappropriate question. Having not being able to trip Catherine up on this so-called amnesia act, she changed to another subject, "How about friends? Do you have any friends in Atlanta?"

Catherine now listened more closely to Audrey, expecting more traps. "Yes, there's Helen Schofield. She's a nurse at the clinic. We're best friends and we share an apartment. Then there's Sam Tankersley. He's a special friend."

Audrey became intrigued and wanted to know more about Sam, "So, Sam's your boyfriend. What does he do?"

Catherine said, "He's a criminal defense attorney in Atlanta."

Audrey raised her eyebrows. "Hey, a lawyer. That's not bad. Do you love him?"

Catherine didn't like this direct questioning by Audrey. It may seem like just curious interest, but she sensed an ulterior motive to Audrey's questions. Catherine wondered what there could be between, Audrey and her sister Amanda to make her act like this, "Yes, I do love Sam. By the way, what do you do?"

Audrey said, "I'm a personnel manager at an auto dealership in Birmingham."

Catherine took a bite of food before she continued, "Are you seeing anyone Audrey?"

"Yes," Audrey said, "his name is Henry Cleveland. He's a manager for a jewelry store in Birmingham."

Catherine wanted to get away from Audrey's questioning. She didn't want to risk a prolonged dialogue with her. She knew for sure that Audrey would try to trip her up again. She directed her next question to Bill. "Bill, Beth tells me that you're attending college at the University of Alabama."

Bill put his fork down and looked at Catherine. "Yes, I'm a

sophomore there in pre-med."

Catherine spent some time asking Bill about his studies and how he liked going to the University of Alabama. Bill seemed eager to tell her about his experiences at school. She could tell that Bill's attitude towards her was very different than Audrey's. After Bill finished telling Catherine about his studies she said, "It sounds like you're doing really well at the university. Now what about your social life, are you seeing anyone?"

Bill shook his head. "No, I'm just playing the field."

Everyone had finished the main course, so Beth got up from her chair, "If everyone is ready, I'll now serve the cake and coffee. Audrey, will you give me a hand?"

Starting to get up from the table, Audrey replied, "Yes, Mom."

Beth and Audrey went into the kitchen, where Beth started to cut the cake and put it on plates. Audrey started the coffee maker. Audrey's behavior towards her sister angered Beth and she spoke sharply to her. "All right, Audrey, what's the meaning of that question?"

Audrey expected this from her mother. She knew that her mother would defend Amada, she always had. She didn't want to get into an argument with her mother and answered with an appeasing voice. "Oh, Mon, I just wanted to know if this amnesia is for real."

Beth made eye contact with her daughter. "Just back off it, Audrey, I mean it! Amanda's not faking it, she does have amnesia." Beth wasn't about to let Audrey, or anyone else spoil Amanda's homecoming.

Audrey had been put on the defensive now. "Mom, I just don't want her coming back here again and turn the family upside down like she did before."

Beth looked hard at Audrey. "Now, listen to me. Amanda's also my daughter and I want her back in our lives again. Please give her a chance."

Audrey put her head down to avoid eye contact with her mother. "Okay, Mom, for you I'll keep the peace, but I still don't trust her."

Beth, having made her point, hugged her daughter to let her know

167

that the matter had been settled and put behind them. Beth said, "Good, that's all that I ask. Now, let's go back and serve the cake and coffee."

After lunch everyone went to the family room to relax and talk. Beth got out the family photo albums and showed Catherine all the family photos. Catherine got to see all the photos of Amanda from the time that she was an infant, till the time that she left home at eighteen. It felt strange to see how Amanda grew up, knowing that these photos were of her, but were not her. Beth knew that it wouldn't do much good to push her to remember, but she couldn't help it. She wanted to show Catherine how she had been before leaving home.

After a while Catherine excused herself and went to the kitchen for some water. Audrey followed her into the kitchen. As soon as they were in the kitchen, Audrey said, "I'm leaving now. It's getting late, and I have a date this evening." Catherine offered her hand, but Audrey ignored it saying, "For my parent's sake I hope that this works out, but listen to me Amanda. You almost ripped this family apart the last time, then you left. Mother went through hell. I don't want that to happen again. Now they say that you have lost your memory, and that you've changed. Ok, I'll go along with that and give you the benefit of the doubt, but if it's going to be the same old Amanda, just leave now. Just vanish and never come back again."

Catherine could see that Amanda had really hurt Audrey. Catherine felt that she had to start to bridge the gap between them. "I'm very sorry to hear this. Amanda must have really hurt you."

Audrey said with forcefulness. "You don't know the half of it! She hurt everyone."

Catherine wanted to be reassuring. "Believe me, it won't happen again."

Audrey, without any feeling of affection, said, "I hope not Catherine."

Catherine said with sincerity. "Good-bye, Audrey. Please believe me when I tell you, I mean no ill-will to anyone."

Audrey went back into the family room to say good-bye to the rest of the family. Catherine followed her back into the family room. Audrey

WOMAN IN THE MIRROR

said good-bye to the family, then left for her drive back to Birmingham.

It was getting close to four. If Catherine expected to get back to Atlanta before eight she needed to start back soon. Catherine approached Beth to thank her for the afternoon, and to express her need to leave now so as to get back to Atlanta at a reasonable hour. "Beth, thank you for a wonderful afternoon. I must be going now. I need to get back to Atlanta before it's too late."

Beth had been enjoying Catherine's visit and hadn't been keeping track of time. She wished that she could have more time with Catherine. "You're going already. It seems like you just got here. I wish that you could stay longer. In fact your room, I mean Amanda's room is just as she left it. Everything still's there, the Barbie Doll collection, the pictures and posters. Even the clothes and shoes that she left behind. I put fresh sheets on the bed. You could stay the night with us and go to church with us in the morning.

Catherine didn't want to stay. She wanted to get back to Atlanta as soon as she could. She knew that, Beth would do anything to get her to stay overnight, but she just couldn't. Catherine started to make her excuses for not being able to stay the night. One look into Beth's eyes and Catherine couldn't bring herself to say no. "I'm tempted to say yes, but I brought nothing with me. I've no nightgown, or robe, or slippers, or toothbrush. I don't even have a dress to wear to church tomorrow."

Beth could see Amanda start to waver and smiled. She now felt certain that she could get her to spend the night, "If that's all that's bothering you we've everything you need here. If we don't we can get it."

Catherine had become trapped. She couldn't say no. She would have to stay the night. "Okay, you talked me into it. I'll stay the night, and attend church with you in the morning."

Overjoyed, Beth gave Catherine a hug, "Oh, thank you. Now let me show you your room."

Ted had been standing close by and also gave Catherine a hug, expressing his joy at having her stay the night. Catherine felt trapped, the more she wanted to keep her distance from them, the closer they

169

drew her to them. Her relationship with the Jenkins had become more involved.

Beth took Catherine through the kitchen and down the hall to a bedroom that on first sight belonged to a teenage girl. Although judging from the posters and pictures, was dated by over six years. Beth said, "This is Amanda's room. You'll sleep here tonight. Feel free to make yourself at home."

Catherine took a look at the room. It gave her an uneasy feeling to be occupying this room. It seemed to her like by accepting the room she had admitted something about herself. That she was their daughter Amanda. Despite uneasy feelings about the room she accepted it with good grace, "Thank you, this will be just fine."

Beth smiled, being so happy to have Amanda home again. "We have just about everything that you need, even a new toothbrush. The only thing we need to get is a dress. We can go out now and I'll get you one. We have some very good shops here in Gadsden."

Catherine didn't want to feel any more in their debt by allowing them to buy things for her. "We can go out, but you don't have to get the dress for me. I can pay for it myself."

Beth had no intention of letting Catherine pay for the dress, "I asked you to stay so I owe you something. Besides I won't take no for an answer." Catherine just gave in to Beth.

They went shopping that afternoon. They found a beautiful raspberry-red dress that would go with the black pumps and purse that Catherine had with her. Catherine had worn pants with knee-highs, so she also needed a pair of pantyhose. Catherine tried to pay for it herself, but Beth wouldn't let her.

After they got back home, Ted took everyone out to dinner. They went to a nice family restaurant that Ted and Beth liked. The food was very good and at a very reasonable price. Catherine had a wonderful time. Despite her intention not to become emotionally involved with this family, she couldn't help feeling a connection to them. The more involved she became with them, the harder it would be to pull away,

WOMAN IN THE MIRROR

and she would eventually have to pull away if she wanted her life to be her own.

After dinner they went back home, watched television and talked for a while until it was time for bed. At first it felt disquieting to be in Amanda's room with all the ghosts of the past. However eventually Catherine became drowsy and fell to sleep.

Catherine got up early the next morning before anyone else. She put on robe and slippers, then went to the kitchen. She found a jar of instant coffee and put some water on the stove for coffee. She had her coffee and sat at the table sipping it when Bill came in dressed in T-shirt, denim cut-off shorts and shower shoes. Catherine said, "Good-morning, Bill."

Bill smiled at her and replied, "Good-morning, Catherine. I heard you get up and come into the kitchen. Is there hot water left for coffee?"

Catherine pointed to the pan on the stove, "Yes, on the stove, help yourself."

Bill made himself a cup of coffee, and had a seat at the table across from Catherine. Bill looked at Catherine. "It's hard to remember to call you Catherine. To me you're my sister Amanda."

Catherine looked at him over her coffee cup. "Well, perhaps I am, but we don't know that for sure yet. So rather than build up hope and find out that we're wrong later, I'd rather keep it as it is for now."

They continued to drink their coffee for a while, then Catherine said, "I have a question for you."

Putting down his cup, Bill replied, "Yes, what is it?"

Catherine took a sip of coffee then continued, "Why is Audrey so angry with me? She acts like she doesn't even want me here."

Bill put his coffee cup down and looked at Catherine. "So you don't even remember anything?"

Catherine shook her head. "No, nothing."

"It's a long story." Bill said, as if reluctant to tell it.

Catherine put her cup down on the table. "There's just the two of us here now. We've plenty of time."

171

MICHAEL O. GREGORY

Bill took a moment before he said, "Okay, Mom told me that if you asked any questions to be truthful with you. So here's the story. You're my oldest and big sister. You were always looking out for me. When I got into trouble, you were always on my side. If bigger kids wanted to beat me up, you were there to defend me. We were the best of friends.

"Now with the rest of the family it was like war. You wanted things your own way. When Mom or Dad would tell you to do, or not to do something you would disobey. They would try to ground you, and you would sneak out in defiance of them. You took most of Mom's and Dad's attention and Audrey resented it. She blamed you for all the troubles in the family. She felt that you were getting all the attention."

Catherine had been holding her coffee cup on the table in front of her listening to Bill, she said, "All right, now I see why Audrey feels like she does toward me. Now Amanda just disappeared. What's the story behind hat?"

Bill took another sip of coffee and put the cup back down on the table. "Well, you, I mean Amanda went off to college at the University of Alabama and was failing at everything. Mom and Dad took her out of the University and brought her back home. They were going to make her go to Gadsden State College and live at home. There was a really ugly fight, and the next morning you, I mean Amanda was gone. She just packed up and left in the night. Mom and Dad tried to find her. First they checked with all of her friends. When they couldn't locate her that way they filed a missing person report with the police. Since Amanda was eighteen, there wasn't much that the police could do. They tried a private detective, but they could never find a trace of Amanda."

Catherine took a sip of coffee and put the cup back down on the table. "That must have been hard on Ted and Beth."

Bill nodded. "Yes, Mom cried a lot at first, then everything seemed to get back to normal, but something had gone out of Mom. She has never been quite the same again. It's like when Amanda left she took something from all of us.

You don't know how much Mom wanted her back. You should've

WOMAN IN THE MIRROR

seen her when you told her that you were coming for a visit. She started planning to cook your favorites. She worked to clean the whole house. She wanted everything to be perfect. Yesterday when it got close to the time for your arrival she couldn't sit still. She was out of her chair every five minutes to look out the window at the driveway and up the road. She's trying so hard to please you."

Catherine nodded "Yes, I know, it's embarrassing how she had doted on me."

Bill gave Catherine a look of affection, "She just wants you to know that she loves you. I love you too. After all you're my big sister."

Catherine gave Bill a mirthful look. "If I am we'll have to rethink that. It seems that you've done a lot more growing than I have." They both broke into laughter.

When they settled down, Bill said, "Yes, you're right. Seems that it's my turn to look out after you and be your defender."

Catherine was touched by Bill's concern for her. She leaned across the table and kissed him on the forehead, "You're so sweet Bill. Anyone would be proud to have you as a brother."

They heard someone coming down the hall. Beth came into the kitchen followed by Ted. Beth said, "Good-morning. How does sausage and eggs for breakfast sound." Everyone nodded. Beth cooked breakfast while Catherine helped out by setting the table and making toast.

After breakfast everyone got dressed, and they left for church. At church Catherine met some of, Beth's friends, including Peggy Watson, the woman who had spoken to her in Macy's. Amanda's grandparents were also there.

After church they all went to Beth's parent's home for lunch. Everyone was there, all the grandparents and some of her aunts, uncles and cousins. Catherine tried her best to remember every face and name. It seemed that Beth hadn't been the only one making plans. Beth's parents had put all this together as soon as they found out that Catherine would be at church that day.

After lunch they went back to Ted and Beth's home. Catherine

173

changed into her traveling clothes. She got away heading back to Atlanta by 3:00 PM, arriving back home just before seven.

CHAPTER TWENTY-FIVE

Catherine had just finished changing clothes, and had put coffee on, when Helen got home. As soon as Helen came through the door, she called out, "Welcome home, I was about to call out the National Guard. You were to be back home yesterday."

Catherine came out from the kitchen into the living room. She said, "Beth asked me to stay the night. As much as I wanted to say no, I couldn't refuse her."

Helen stepped out of her shoes and put her purse down on the coffee table. "I figured that it was something like that."

The coffee had finished making, so Catherine said, "I have coffee ready. Do you want some?"

Following Catherine into the kitchen, Helen said, "Yes, thanks."

Once in the kitchen they made their coffee, and sat at the kitchen table. Helen as usual wanted to know everything, "Okay, how did it go?"

Catherine sipped her coffee, then put her cup down on the table. "I'd say that overall it went very well. There were some problems with Amanda's younger sister Audrey, but nothing that I need be concerned about now."

Helen had been looking at Catherine over the rim of her coffee cup. She took a sip, then put the cup back down on the table. "You can tell me all about the sister later on if you like. Now, how did it go with the rest of the family?"

Catherine showed concern on her face as she turned her coffee cup in her hands. "There's no problems with the rest of the family. The

175

grandparents, other family members and family friends that I met, they all accepted me as Amanda Jenkins without reservations. However I'm concerned about, Beth. She's trying so hard to have her daughter back. No matter how much she's been hurt she won't give up."

Helen nodded in understanding. "I guess that's what being a mother is about."

Catherine took another sip of coffee, and continued to look at Helen over the rim of her cup. "Yes, I'm sure that we'll know the feeling ourselves someday. When she asked me to stay over I needed a dress for church. I tried to pay for it myself, but she wouldn't have it. She said that she had created the need for the dress when she asked me to stay over and insisted on paying for it herself."

"What about, Amanda's father?" Helen asked.

Catherine took another sip of coffee. "Ted's a good man, and I'm sure a loving husband and father. He even showed a father's affection to me. He also wants Amanda back, but foremost he doesn't want Beth hurt again."

Helen took a sip of coffee, "It seems that they are all nice people."

Putting her cup back down on the table, Catherine said, "Yes, they are. After church this morning, we went to Beth's parent's house for lunch. All the grandparents and a lot of other family members and friends were there. I have gotten to like them."

Helen looked at Catherine, trying to read what had been unsaid in her eyes. "Well, what are you going to do?"

Catherine fidgeted for a few seconds before she answered. "I don't know. I hoped them to be the kind of family that you could get to know, then say thanks, but no thanks and keep my distance. They're a warm and loving family and wouldn't understand my acting that way, especial Beth. She would really be hurt. How can I have a relationship with this family, knowing that the real Amanda is no more? I'm taking their gifts like a thief. I'm living a lie."

Helen looked Catherine in the eyes. "Okay, then what are you going to do?"

176

WOMAN IN THE MIRROR

Catherine thought about it. Time was running out. The test would be back soon. She would have to acknowledge them as family and be daughter, sister, cousin and niece to them. Catherine didn't feel that she could do that, but what other choice did she have? Everyone had given her encouragement, and told her that they would work it all out, but she could see that she would be on her own. With a sigh, she said, "I don't want to think about it anymore right now. I just want Sam."

Catherine went to the phone to call Sam. "Hello, Sam."

"Hello, Catherine, I missed you. I thought we had a date last night?"

"Oh, I'm sorry Sam. Beth asked me to stay over last night and go to church with them this morning. I just couldn't say no. I hope that you understand."

"I understand. I figured it was something like that."

Catherine needed to see him now. "Oh, Sam, can I come over? I need to be with you now."

Sam had been about to go out for dinner. He would pick Catherine up and take her with him. "I was about to go out for dinner. I'll come over to pick you up. We can then go out together."

"I'll be ready. I love you Sam, bye."

"I love you too."

Catherine hung up the phone and turned to Helen. "I'm going out with Sam. He's on his way over now. Oh, by the way, this coming Saturday, Beth is coming here to take me to lunch and go shopping. I just thought that I'd let you know, so that you can decide if you want to be here when she gets here."

Helen responded, "Thanks, I'll think about it."

Sam arrived at the apartment twenty minutes later and took Catherine to Ryan's Steak House for dinner. Catherine felt relieved to be with him again. She knew that whatever happened she could never leave him.

Sam and Fred took their Whoppers, fries and cold drinks, then got a table. After they were seated and had started to eat, Sam said, "Have you decided what new car that you're going to get yet?"

MICHAEL O. GREGORY

Fred put down his Whopper, "I'd like to get a Beamer, but unfortunately or fortunately, depending on your point of view, I also know what I can afford. I'm going to get a Toyota Camry."

Sam swallowed a French fry and said, "Toyota's a good car."

Fred took another bite of his Whopper, then continued, "Yes, I'm getting a good deal on this one. It was kept by the factory for testing and has almost ten-thousand miles on it. I'm getting a four-thousand two-hundred dollar discount. It's never been registered, so it's being sold as a new car with full warranty."

Sam put down his Coke, "I say, that sounds like a great deal."

Fred felt pleased with himself that he had gotten such a good deal on the car, "Yes, it is. The dealer has four cars, three white and one light-blue. I'm getting the blue one. I'll pick it up this afternoon."

Sam gave Fred a friendly slap on the shoulder and grinned. "You'll have to give me a test drive."

Fred, grinning back at Sam, said, "Okay, you got it. By the way, how are you and Catherine doing?"

Sam took a bite of his Whopper and chewed as he thought. "Our relationship is going great. However, there is one problem."

Fred's eyebrows went up. "Oh, what's the problem?"

Sam stopped eating, put down his Whopper, and said, "The good part is that in her present crisis she wants to lean on me for comfort and support. It has brought us closer together. The not so good part is that I can't understand why she's reacting as she has to her finding out about her family, and who she is. She's often moody and depressed lately. She acts as if she expects her world to come crashing down around her at any time. You'd expect that even if she can't remember, she'd at least be relieved to have her family back, and to have a connection to the past. She seemed to be afraid of something, and I don't know what."

Fred swallowed a couple of French fries and washed them down with Coke before he spoke, "To you and me, what seems normal may not seem normal to her. With her anything new and unexpected may seem threatening until she has had time to work it out."

WOMAN IN THE MIRROR

Sam considered what Fred had said. "So you think that's what it is?"

With a nod, Fred replied, "Yes, I do."

Sam decided to get an opinion from Fred. "Okay, then what do you think that I should do?"

Fred finished the last of his French fries, washed them down with more Coke, then looked at Sam. "Just support her and give her the space to work it out."

Sam nodded understanding. "Yes, I know that. I just want to be more helpful, but I don't know what to do."

Fred gave Sam a friendly pat on the shoulder. "Just be patient with her and everything will come out all right in the end."

Sam knew that it was all up to Catherine. "I hope so. I want to do more, but I guess that it's all in her hands."

Fred looked at his watch. "Hey, we have to go if we don't want to be late for court."

That evening Catherine had gone to Sam's apartment for dinner. They had finished dinner and were on the sofa having an after dinner liqueur while listening to music. Sam said, "We must talk. I can't just stand by and watch you go through all this agony and not want to help."

Catherine had been aware of how Sam felt. She wished that she could unburden herself to him, but that she could never do. "Oh, Sam, I know that you want to help me, and I'd let you if I thought you could, but there's nothing that you can do."

Sam put his glass on the coffee table, then put his arm around her shoulders. Catherine placed her glass on the coffee table and looked at Sam with those lovely green eyes. Sam looked into her eyes and it struck him how incredibly desirable she had become. He wanted to always hold her close and protect her. He said, "Catherine, I love you, and when you have a problem it's my problem too. I always want to be close to you, to protect you and care for you."

Catherine put her arm around Sam and lay her head on his shoulder. She loved Sam dearly. His gentle strength and selfless love gave her solace. She hoped that she could always have him to lean on.

179

"Thank you for your concern, but I must work this out for myself. The one thing that you can do for me is to always be here to comfort me."

Sam started to stroke Catherine's hair as he spoke, "I don't understand The Jenkins are almost certainly your family. You should be relieved that you have them back, that you have a link to your past."

Catherine had to think of something to tell Sam. "I wish that it were easy. My intellect tells me that they're family, and that I should love them, but they're still strangers. I know that everything seems just fine now, but that could just be because everyone is on his or her best behavior. Remember Amanda was estranged from her family for a reason. Right now it seems that the problem was Amanda, but I still don't know much about these people. I don't want to go headfirst into a relationship with my guard down and get blindsided. I need to know what I'm getting into."

Sam tried to understand Catherine's reservations, but as he understood it they were good people. "I hope you can get things worked out soon. It hurts me to see you like this."

Catherine let out a sigh. "Oh, I don't know what's going to happen, or what I'm going to do yet. Let me assure you that whatever happens, I don't want to lose you."

Sam looked again into those lovely green eyes. "You won't lose me. I won't let you go." They embraced and kissed fervently.

All that week Catherine went to work and came home. Wen to class and saw Sam, or talked to him on the phone, but the joy had gone out of living. The only time that she felt good was when she had Sam at her side. Try as she could, she couldn't think of any way out of her dilemma. She had become so depressed that it had started to show in her work, and in her relationships.

One evening Catherine and Helen were in the kitchen having a cup of coffee. "Why the somber mood. You thinking of the Jenkins?" Helen said.

Catherine nodded. "Yes, why?"

Helen took a sip of coffee, then said, "Well, I'd like to know what you think about them. Say to start with, what about Beth?"

Catherine thought of Beth. "I really like Beth. We get along well together, and she tries so hard to please me. I'd like to love her back as much as she loves me."

"Then why not love them back?" Helen remarked.

Helen's remark caught Catherine off guard, and it took her a moment to recover her poise. "I can't! It's not her, it's me. Every time I see her looking at me, I know that she believes that she is looking at her daughter Amanda. I can't help it, I know that the daughter that she loved and raised from an infant ended her own existence in a motel room. I'm her daughter's physical self, but I'm not her. How can I pretend that I'm someone that I'm not?"

Helen could see that Catherine hadn't yet come to terms with her relationship with Beth. She decided to move on. "What about Ted?"

Catherine breathed a little easier, not to have to talk about Beth anymore. "I have much the same feelings about Ted as I do about Beth."

Helen wanted to know about Amanda's siblings. "Okay, what about the others, say Bill?"

Catherine recalled Bill, especially their talk Sunday morning. "Bill is easy to like. We were friends right off."

Helen took a sip of coffee and continued, "And Audrey?"

Catherine thought of Audrey. "The relationship between Audrey and I is cold now, but I believe that deep down she loves her sister Amanda. It's just that she loves her mother more. She doesn't want to see her mother hurt again."

Helen put her cup back down on the table. "Yes, I know that you like them, and that you don't want to hurt them either."

Catherine shook her head. "No, I don't."

Helen had witnessed how Catherine had changed since her trip to visit the Jenkins at Gadsden. It seemed that she had been overcome by an air of hopelessness, and had even heard her cry a couple of times late at night. She had started to worry about Catherine. "So, I guess that's part of the reason for the tears at night when you think that

I'm sleeping."

Catherine hadn't been aware that Helen could overhear her at night, she said, "I don't want to do anything drastic, but I might have to leave and go someplace else. Get a new identity, and just let Amanda disappear for good."

With concern in her voice, Helen said, "Isn't that sort of a last resort?"

Catherine nodded. "Yes, it is, and I really don't want to have to do it. That would mean losing Sam, and I just couldn't take that."

Helen got up, came around the table, and put her arm around Catherine's shoulder, "Just hold out for a little while longer, and don't do anything dumb. I think that we may be able to help you."

Catherine was grateful to have Helen as a friend. It felt better just to have someone show concern for her. "I don't know. It seems that I'm out on a limb alone on this."

CHAPTER TWENTY-SIX

S unday morning dawned with an overcast sky. One of those days that looked like it was about to rain all day long, but never did. Beth had hoped for better weather for this day of travel and shopping, but you didn't always get to choose your weather. Beth and her daughter Audrey left Gadsden at 7:15 AM, arriving at Catherine's apartment at eleven.

Audrey had driven up from Birmingham and spent the night with her parents. She had agreed to come with Beth partly because Beth had pleaded, then insisted that she come. Beth wanted Audrey to be with and start to trust Amanda. Audrey also figured that she might find something new in Atlanta that she couldn't find in Birmingham.

They pulled up in front of Catherine's apartment, parked and walked to the door Catherine had seen them pull up and met them at the door. She was glad to see that Beth had brought Audrey with her. It had been disquieting to Catherine to learn of the animosity between Amanda and Audrey. For some reason she felt the need to do something to try to heal the rift between them. Catherine exchanged greetings and hugged Beth and Audrey.

Catherine invited them into her apartment. Helen stood as they entered the living room. Catherine introduced Beth and Audrey to Helen. Helen shook hands with Beth and Audrey and exchanged greetings with them. Catherine made an offer of hospitality so that Beth and Audrey could refresh themselves before they went out to have lunch and shop. "We have some iced tea, or I can make us some coffee if you want before we go."

Beth considered Amanda's, or as she wanted to be called Catherine's offer, but was anxious to have lunch, then have as much time as they could for shopping at the mall. "I think we can go now. Where would you like to go for lunch?"

Catherine had already decided where she would like to take them for lunch. "How about the Cracker Barrel? Is that all right with you and Audrey?"

Audrey nodded to Beth. Beth said, "The Cracker Barrel sounds just fine."

Catherine got her purse and they left for the Cracker Barrel.

After lunch they went to the mall. At the mall they had a good time looking through the shops, but that had been secondary to Beth. She had been pleased to have her two daughters with her for the afternoon, and to spend time with Catherine. She noticed that Catherine had been making an effort to reach out to Audrey, to try to bridge the rift between them. After a while Beth also felt that Audrey had started to lose some of her hostility toward her sister.

They looked through all the shops at the mall and found many things that interested them. Beth ended up buying a natural-color knit-wool pullover sweater and a dark-blue plaid-wool pleated skirt for, Audrey. Catherine finally let Beth get her a red and gold silk scarf and a pair of amethyst ear studs.

They arrived back at Catherine's apartment at 3:30. Helen had left on a date, so they had the apartment to themselves. They took coffee in the kitchen, then Catherine showed them her apartment. Audrey paid close attention, taking particular interest in everything that belonged to Catherine. She looked into Catherine's closet and a couple of drawers. Catherine noticed this, but decided to not say anything about it.

After the tour of the apartment, they settled in the living room where Catherine served Cokes, and they talked until five. Catherine asked Audrey about her apartment, and if she had a roommate, or lived alone. Catherine felt that her attempt to gain Audrey's trust and respect had started to have some effect. Beth felt pleased to see that Catherine's effort at trying to win Audrey over was having some effect.

At five Beth and Audrey started back to Gadsden. They didn't talk much until they were away from the Atlanta metro traffic, and on Interstate 20 West back to Alabama. Finally, Beth said, "Well, are you glad that I asked you to come along today?"

Audrey had been thinking of the day's events, "Yes, I am. It turned out better than I thought it would. One thing that you can't help but notice is how much she's changed."

Beth nodded, "Yes, I've talked to Dr. Prater about that. She believes that the amnesia has something to do with it. Also six years is a long time. A person can change."

Audrey had also noticed the change. It looks to me that it's more than a change. I'd say that it's more like a complete transformation. It seems like Amanda, or Catherine, or whatever she wants to call herself has reinvented herself. I watched her, the way she acts with other people, the way she talks, the things that she's interested in, all different. And did you see her closet. That closet belongs to a woman of conservative taste in dress. I looked and except for a green party dress she has nothing above the knee, and as much as I could see, she has nothing cut as low as to show a lot of cleavage. She likes color, but nothing wild like Amanda did. Amanda was a tease. She wanted to show off, to be the center of attention. Now this Catherine, she wants to be inconspicuous, to blend in with the crowd. It's like two different people."

Beth thought for a few moments before she spoke, "Yes, that's true that she could be someone else, but Dr. Prater called me yesterday. They got back the first test results from the lab. The test results are an almost absolute certainty that she can be no one else but Amanda. The odds of it not being her is one in thousands. For sure she's Amanda."

Audrey thought for a moment about what her mother had just said before she spoke. It all seemed so strange to her. "Okay, then why does she keep calling herself Catherine? She also must have gotten the same information on the test."

MICHAEL O. GREGORY

Beth shook her head. "I don't know. Could be that since she woke up with amnesia she worked to build a new identity for herself that she's comfortable with. Then we come along saying that we're family, but to her we're strangers. We just need to give her the time that she needs to adjust. It's confusing to us. Just think how it must be for her. For her there's no past, just these last few months."

Audrey looked at her mother. "Well, at least one good thing has come of this."

Beth took her eyes off the road for a second to glance at Audrey. "What's that?"

A contented smile lit Audrey's face. "I like this Amanda a lot more than the old one."

After Beth and Audrey left, Catherine called Sam. He came over and they went to the Olive Garden. After dinner they took in a movie. Afterwards Sam took her back home.

When Catherine got home she found Helen sitting in the living room reading a book. Helen remarked, "I see that you've been out with Sam."

Catherine took a seat in a chair next to her, "Yes, we went to the Olive Garden, then took in a movie."

Helen put down the book. "That's good, but what I want to ask you is, how did it go with Beth and Audrey?"

Catherine kicked off her shoes and wiggled her toes in the carpet. She gave it a moment's thought before she answered, "As well as could be expected, I guess. Beth brought Audrey along with her today to see if she could start repairing the bad relationship between her and Amanda."

Helen had a very attentive look. "And how did it go?"

Catherine thought for a moment of the events of the day. "I think that I could get along well with Audrey. Her problems were with Amanda, not me. With me there's no history between us, so if need be I could bring her around."

Helen's next question was meant to get a response from Catherine. To see how well she had adjusted to the Jenkins. "Then you're saying

186

WOMAN IN THE MIRROR

that you'll be maintaining a relationship with them?"

Catherine rejected the idea out of hand. "No, I didn't say that! How can I? I'm not who they think I am!"

Helen looked straight into Catherine's eyes. "Don't be too quick to judge Catherine. You may be more of that person than you think you are."

What Helen had suggested shocked Catherine? "Oh, cut it out Helen. I'm not Amanda. You know that." Catherine leaned forward and put her head in her hands, "What am I going to do? Everything I can do is wrong for one reason or the other."

Helen wanted to help Catherine, but she had no answers either. She got out of her chair, and went over to sit on the arm of Catherine's chair. She leaned over and put her arm around Catherine's shoulders to try and comfort her. After a minute Catherine got up from the chair and went to get ready for bed.

CHAPTER TWENTY-SEVEN

By Monday the weather had improved, but not Catherine's mood. She had become depressed and withdrawn. She felt trapped in a no-win situation, and each day brought her closer to the precipice.

By midweek she had reached the end of her endurance with no place to go. She needed to talk to someone about it. She went to see Maryanne. When Catherine entered Maryanne's office, Maryanne immediately saw that she was distraught and had puffy eyes from crying. Maryanne directed Catherine to have a seat on the sofa where she joined her. When they were both settled on the sofa, Maryanne turned to Catherine and said, "Okay, now you said that you needed to see me?"

Catherine turned a long face with sad eyes to Maryanne, and with a sniffle said, "Oh, Maryanne, I don't know what to do. I need help."

Maryanne had been receiving regular reports from Helen, as to Catherine's state of mind, and had been expecting a visit from her. "I was wondering when you would be in to see me. I've been talking with Helen. She's very concerned about you. I take it that you want to talk about the Jenkins?"

Catherine did want to talk about the Jenkins, but she also wanted to talk about the DNA tests. "Yes, but first, how long before the rest of the test come back?"

Maryanne put a finger to her cheek as she tried to determine when the test would be back. "Oh, I would say, three weeks at the most."

188

WOMAN IN THE MIRROR

Catherine nodded in resignation. "And then there will be no doubt that I'm Amanda?"

Maryanne knew that Catherine was looking for a miracle, but she didn't have one for her. "Let me put it this way. These last tests are so precise that it will exclude all of humanity except you."

There came an audible release of breath from Catherine. She looked defeated. "Yes, that's what I figured. It means that I have decisions to make, and I have to make them now." Catherine's voice trembled, and tears ran down her cheeks. She took an already damp handkerchief from her pocket and dabbed her eyes.

Maryanne went to her desk, got a pack of tissue, and put it on the coffee table in front of Catherine. Then sat back down on the sofa.

Catherine looked at her imploringly. "Oh, Maryanne, I still don't know what to do."

Maryanne knew that to make any progress she had to get Catherine to look at her problem logically instead of emotionally. Maryanne sat back in the sofa trying to show an air of confidence. "All right then, let's talk it out. You may see something that you missed before."

Catherine took a tissue and dabbed her eyes. Maryanne's show of confidence had started to have a calming effect on Catherine, she said, "Okay, the problem is that Beth is sure that I'm Amanda, and the DNA results will show that I'm Amanda, but you and I know that's a lie. Amanda was only the donor. Everything that was really Amanda is no more. That died in the motel room in Nashville."

Maryanne nodded to Catherine that she had followed her so far. "Okay, I follow you so far, go on."

Catherine drew a deep breath and continued, "At first I figured that even after it was proven that I was Amanda, I could just maintain a distant relationship with them. Maybe visit once a year or so, send Mother's Day and Christmas cards. Well, I can see now that Beth wouldn't be satisfied with a distant relationship. If I didn't go to her, she would find some pretext to show up on my doorstep."

Maryanne understood what Catherine had tried to say, "Yes, I see

189

MICHAEL O. GREGORY

what you mean. Beth is a person that wants to be close to her children."

The tears kept running down Catherine's cheeks. She had gone through a lot of tissue, but the talking seemed to be having a calming effect on her. "When I first met them I in a way hoped that they were a terribly dysfunctional family. As it turns out they're a wonderfully warm and loving family that most people would be proud to belong to. They're a lot better than my own family was. The only one dysfunctional was Amanda. So you can see my problem."

Maryanne decided to ask a question to evoke a response, "So what you're saying is that you're not Amanda?"

Catherine didn't like the way that Maryanne had asked that question. "Now you know I'm not, Amanda!"

Maryanne now asked a question that would be sure to provoke Catherine. "Are you sure?"

Catherine shot up straight in her seat startled by Maryanne's question. "Yes, I'm sure! Why are you asking me that question?"

Maryanne had expected that response. "I just felt that it needed to be asked, that's all. I needed to know more before I can help you."

Catherine, still dabbing her eyes with a tissue, said, "The problem is me. I could say that I'm Amanda and no one would know the difference. There's no way that anyone could say that I'm not. I can fool other people, but I can't fool myself. If I pass myself off as Amanda, every time that I come face to face with Beth, I'll know that I'm living a lie. I have gotten to know Beth well, and I really like and respect her. How can I keep up a relationship with her believing that she has found her daughter, but my knowing that she hasn't and never will?"

Maryanne got up from the sofa and walked around behind her desk and looked out the window. After a couple of minutes she went back to take her seat on the sofa. She then said, "Okay, it's good that you have principals and are considerate of others feelings. It shows that you are a good person. If you were not you would just think of yourself, and might end up hurting the people around you even more." Maryanne put her hand on, Catherine's shoulder and said, "All right, you know the problem. Now what do you think the answer is?"

Maryanne's frankness caught Catherine off guard. She looked down at the tissue in her hands before she answered, "I'd say that one answer to my problem would be to just leave Atlanta. To go someplace else and change my name and identity so they can't find me, but that's no good for three reasons. One, Beth loves her daughter and it would break her heart. I couldn't do that to her. She's been through enough already. Two, I love Sam and can't bear the thought of losing him. Three, if I left and started my life over again, could I ever feel free or safe? Could I ever fall in love again, knowing that someday someone may show up on my doorstep again?"

Maryanne responded, "Well, what are you going to do leave"

Catherine's voice tremble as she answered, "Oh, I don't know what to do. I can't run and I can't stay. What should I do? I'm running out of time."

Maryanne patted Catherine on the shoulder and said, "I can help you with the problem, but I can't give you the answer. You must find the answer for yourself."

Catherine started to cry. "I don't have any good answers. Maybe it would've been better if the operation hadn't worked. I just can't live like this."

Catherine was still crying. Maryanne had to think of something, and fast. It had become clear to her that Catherine was desperate. Maryanne said, "Just hold it, and don't give up yet. I might have an idea."

Maryanne got up and paced in front of her desk for a couple of minutes, then sat back down beside Catherine. After another minute she said, "I don't know the answer to your problem, but I do believe that part of it is that you are too close to it. You are trying to please everyone and yourself. You are so busy dealing with everyone that you can't see the answer. I think that you have to back off, just get away from everybody and everything for a while. Instead of trying to please everyone else, just look to your own needs and how to meet them. I have to go someplace now. Just make yourself comfortable. There's

MICHAEL O. GREGORY

coffee in the coffee maker. You can freshen-up in the washroom. Just stay here until I get back."

Maryanne left the office. Catherine went into the washroom and splashed some water on her face. She then made herself a cup of coffee and waited for Maryanne to return.

Maryanne returned in about thirty minutes with a folder in her hand. She took a seat on the sofa beside Catherine, and opened the folder on the coffee table. Maryanne then turned to Catherine. "Listen to me, I have a proposal for you."

Catherine, looking at the folder, said, "Okay, I'm listening."

Maryanne continued, "Okay, here's the deal. I want you to take some time off. Take as much time as you need. We will make it an administrative leave with pay. I want you to go home, pack your bags, and get away from everybody and everything. Don't tell anyone where you are going. Don't even let them know that you are leaving. I want you to be alone to work this out. When you are ready, come back and tell me what you have decided. We will help you to do whatever you want to do. Do we have a deal?"

Catherine and Maryanne shook hands. "Okay, it's a deal." Catherine said.

Maryanne took a brochure from the folder and handed it to Catherine. "One of our staff members owns a condo at the Hilton Head Island Beach and Tennis Resort on Hilton Head Island, South Carolina. There's a map of the resort in the brochure. The condo is in block 'C' of the ocean front villas, over-looking the bar and swimming pool, with a clear view of the ocean." Maryanne handed her a key. "This is the key to the condo." Maryanne handed her a sheet of paper. "Keep this in your car at all times. This is the authorization from the owner to use the condo. You must show this to the security guard at the gate each time you enter the resort, so don't lose it. The condo number and location is on the authorization form. You can locate it on the map." Maryanne handed her a last sheet of paper. "This is the directions for you to get there from Atlanta. You go South on Interstate 75 to Macon,

WOMAN IN THE MIRROR

then take Interstate 16 to Savannah. When you reach Interstate 95, go north to the South Carolina state line. About ten miles inside South Carolina you will come to the Interstate connector for Hilton Head Island. Take it and stay on it until you are there. The trip will take you about five hours, more or less, depending on how fast you drive. After you cross the bridge onto the island and pass the visitor's center don't take the cross island expressway. Take US 287 to the fifth traffic light. That will be Folly Field Road, take a left. The entrance to the resort will be one block on the right. Any questions?"

Catherine shook her head. "No questions. I have it all."

Maryanne gave Catherine a smile. "Now get going. I will see you when you get back. And Catherine."

Catherine managed a faint smile in return. "Yes."

Maryanne again cautioned Catherine. "Remember, no one must know where you are."

Catherine got up from the sofa and left to go home to pack.

CHAPTER TWENTY-EIGHT

Catherine got away from her apartment by 11:30. She took Interstate 75 South through downtown Atlanta toward Macon. When she got to McDonough and away from the Atlanta metro traffic, she stopped for gas and a quick lunch.

After lunch she got back on the interstate and headed south. At Macon she picked up Interstate 16 to Savannah. She had never been in this part of Georgia before, so she took an interest in the scenery. Around Macon it was much the same as Atlanta; rolling hills with forests of pine with oak, sweetgum, elm and other varieties. By the time she reached the intersection with Interstate 95 the land had become flat, and she had started to see live oak, cypress and palmetto trees, with Spanish moss draped on the trees. She crossed the Savannah River into South Carolina, then took the Interstate connector. A few miles before she reached the island, she started to see tidal marshes. She passed over the bridge onto Hilton Head Island just before five.

US Highway 278, a four-land divided roadway with a broad median planted with palmetto trees, oleander, azalea, dogwood and other ornamental plants ran the length of Hilton Head Island. The businesses were set well back from the roadway, with a green belt on pine and shrubbery in between. The overall effect had been to give a person the idea that nature took precedence over commerce.

Catherine missed the turnoff to the resort, and had driven as far as Shelter Cove before she turned back. She found Folly Field Road and the entrance to the Hilton Head Island Beach and Tennis Resort.

194

The guard at the gate checked her authorization and directed her to the condo, or as they called it a villa. It was a one-bedroom condo, with the bedroom just inside the front door to the right. The second door to the right opened into the bathroom. To the left side of the hallway that led to the rear of the condo were two sets of double bunk beds, built into the wall. The hallway opened into the living room and small kitchen at the back of the condo. At the far end of the living room a sliding glass door opened onto a deck that over looked the bar and swimming pool. From the deck she had a grand view of the beach and ocean. Catherine put her bags in the bedroom, then decided to go shopping for groceries and have dinner.

Catherine got back on the highway and continued down US Highway 278 until she came to the Shelter Cove Plaza. She stopped first at Fuddruckers, a sports bar and restaurant for a hamburger and Coke. She found the food very good, but she had to fend off the advances of two want-to-be jocks who were sitting at the bar watching a baseball game on television.

After dinner she went to the Piggly Wiggly and bought groceries to last her for at least a week. After leaving the Piggly Wiggly she returned to the condo and put everything away.

That evening she went for a walk on the beach. It seemed so peaceful alone on the beach at night, with just the sound of the waves and the lights in the distance to keep her company. Far to the south, almost over the horizon, she could see the lights of a ship leaving Savannah for the open ocean. She watched the lights for a while, wondering where the ship was bound. After her walk she took a bath and turned in early.

Friday morning Catherine went for a run on the beach, then had breakfast. When it warmed up enough, she put on her bikini and went out to a lounge chair beside the swimming pool to work on her tan. She avoided being with other people' preferring to be alone. She stayed close to the condo all that day. She took another walk on the beach that evening before going to bed.

Saturday morning after her run on the beach and breakfast,

195

MICHAEL O. GREGORY

Catherine decided that she wanted to get out and go somewhere. She didn't want to meet anyone, but she needed to do something. She decided to look at some of the shops on Hilton Head Island.

She started out at the Shelter Cove Plaza. At the plaza she found a lot of great shops and a Sax Fifth Avenue. At Sax Fifth Avenue she found a lot of fashions that looked really great on her, but was a little too much for her pocketbook.

After leaving Shelter Cove Plaza, Catherine drove down to Harbor Town to see what they had in the shops there. She saw a lot of lovely things, but she wasn't there to buy anything. She just wanted to shop to relax and think.

That evening Catherine decided to go out for dinner. She went out toward the visitor's center to the Crazy Crab Restaurant and had lobster for dinner. After getting back to the condo, Catherine went for her evening walk on the beach.

Sunday morning Catherine went for her run on the beach. Then she took a shower, had breakfast, then coffee on the deck. She then got dressed, asked the security guard at the gate for directions, and went to church.

After church she went off island to the factory outlet malls on the mainland. She took her time looking through the shops. At one shop she bought two Hilton Head Island souvenir T-shirts, one for herself and one for Sam. At another shop she bought two brass candlesticks. For the candlestick she also got two upright miniature brass enameled garlands of purple irises with green leaves. The garlands fit around the top of the candlesticks and surrounded the base of the candles. Catherine also got some green candles to go with the candle sticks.

The rest of the afternoon Catherine sunned herself by the swimming pool. She had dinner in the condo that evening. She then went for her walk on the beach.

Monday through Wednesday Catherine followed much the same routine. A run on the beach in the morning, a shower, then breakfast, with coffee on the deck looking out at the ocean. After coffee she would

WOMAN IN THE MIRROR

clean the condo. She would then sun herself by the pool, or go for a walk on the beach; picking up sand dollars or other seashells. Since the summer vacation season had ended there weren't so many people on the beach. That way Catherine didn't have to talk much to other people. During this time she didn't leave the resort.

Thursday morning Catherine went for her run on the beach, then took her shower. She had breakfast, then took her coffee on the deck as usual.

As she sat on the deck looking out at the ocean and drinking her coffee, Catherine put her hand to her throat and felt the heart shaped pendant and cross that hung there. They each had been given to her with love by three people who loved her each in their own way without reservation. This had been just a reactive gesture as she was deep in thought about her problem. Touching the pendant and cross reminded her of how she had acquired them, and how important they were for her. Suddenly everything had become very clear for her. She had made her decision. She got up and started to move with purpose. Instead of the quick cleanup as usual, Catherine washed and put away all the pans and dishes. After the dishes she changed the sheets on the bed and cleaned the whole place.

By then it was lunch time. She went to Fuddruckers for a hamburger and Coke. After lunch she came back to the condo, got her soiled clothes, found a laundromat and did her laundry.

After doing her laundry she came back to the condo and packed her bags. She then loaded her bags into the car. She gave the condo one last check, and started off on her way back to Atlanta.

Catherine crossed over the bridge to the mainland a little after four in the afternoon. She drove back to Atlanta, stopping only for gas and coffee. She arrived back at her apartment at 9:15 PM. Helen wasn't at home when Catherine let herself in. She went straight to the phone and called Sam. Catherine reveled at the sound of Sam's voice when he answered the phone, she said, "Sam."

Sam was startled to hear Catherine's voice. "Oh, Catherine, it's so good to hear your voice."

Catherine had really missed the sound of Sam's voice and was comforted by it. "Oh, Sam, I've missed you so much."

"I've missed you too Catherine. Where were you? No one would tell me anything."

"I'm sorry that I didn't tell you. Dr. Prater told me not to tell anyone that I was going, or where."

"Well your back now. Where were you?"

"I've been staying in a condo at the Hilton Head Island Beach and Tennis Resort on Hilton Head Island."

"Did you have a good time?"

"Not as good a time as I could have if you had been there."

Sam paused before he asked the all-important question. "Are you back to stay?"

"Yes, this is my home, and I'm not going anywhere."

"That's good. That's what I wanted to hear."

"Sam."

"Yes."

"I've just gotten back, and I haven't had dinner yet. If I came over to your place, could you fix me something?"

Sam would like to see Catherine now, but he worried about her being out so late at night, "I'd love to see you now, and it would be no problem to fix you dinner. However, by the time that you're finished it would be close to midnight. I don't want you driving the streets alone at that hour."

Catherine realizing the late hour had anticipated that no matter how much Sam would want to see her, he wouldn't want her driving the streets alone late at night. She had an answer for that. She had had it since that morning. When she spoke it was with a soft-alluring voice that held the promise of passion. "Sam, what would you say if I told you that once I get there, I have no intention of driving home tonight?"

Sam took a couple of seconds to grasp the meaning of Catherine's words. "In that case, what are you waiting for?"

WOMAN IN THE MIRROR

"I'm on my way." Catherine hung up the phone and headed for the door.

Twenty minutes later Catherine stood at Sam's door. She rang the doorbell and Sam let her in. As soon as the door was closed she threw herself into his arms kissing him tempestuously. The kiss was long and fiery as she pressed her body up hard against his body. When the kiss had ended, Sam said, "Oh, how I've missed you."

Catherine, while rubbing her body against Sam, said, "I've missed you too, and I want you, now."

Catherine kissed Sam again and started to unbutton and remove his shirt. Sam reached behind her, unbuttoned and unzipped her skirt. Her skirt fell to the floor and she stepped out of it. By then she had gotten his shirt off. As they continued to kiss, she undid his trousers and let them fall down around his ankles where he stepped out of them. He unbuttoned and removed her blouse and unhooked her bra.

He picked her up in his arms, and carried her into the bedroom and placed her on the bed. Catherine was eager to have Sam, but he tried to resist his urges and go slow, as much for her pleasure as for his own. Their hands were all over each other. His hands and lips were exploring her erogenous zone. Every place that his fingertips or tongue touched caused a spark of pleasure. The caress of her breast brought excitement that increased as his fingertips scribed softly down her belly. When his hand touched her inner thigh, electric pulses of ecstasy throbbed through her body. When finally he found her special spot of ultimate pleasure, her senses went wild. She couldn't imagine anything more gratifying until he entered her, then she did. Locked in passionate embrace they moved with an urgency of mutual need. Their passions slowly built to a culmination of ecstasy. They were both engulfed in a wave of passion. They lay unmoving until the wave passed before they uncoupled and lay resting in each-others' arms.

Finally Catherine said, "Oh, Sam that was the most marvelously wonderful experience of my whole life. It was so beautiful."

Sam looked into her eyes as he slowly ran his fingers down her back "Then what you're saying is that this is your first time? That you're a virgin?"

Catherine in response to Sam's attention snuggled up closer to him. "What I'm saying is that in my memory you're the first, the only man that I've ever known. So I guess that you could say that I'm a virgin. I'm glad that I was able to give the gift to you. I told you that when I was ready I would make it so obvious that you wouldn't have to ask."

Sam grinned. "Yes, I remember, and it was worth the wait."

They kissed and she lay with her head on his shoulder with his arm around her. She said, "Sam, I have an announcement to make, and you are the first to hear it. Catherine is no more. I know now that I am, and have always been, Amanda Jenkins."

Sam now had the reason for the sudden turn in their relationship. "So, that's the reason that you're suddenly so willing to make love to me. You've come to know yourself for who you are, and are at ease with yourself. Have you regained any of your memory?"

Amanda shook her head. "No, I haven't, but the Jenkins are my family, that can't be denied, and I want and need them in my life."

Sam stroked her hair. "I'm so happy for you Amanda. It's so strange to be calling you Amanda. If I lapse and call you Catherine, please forgive me for it."

Amanda giggled. "You'll get used to it fast enough. By the way, how much space do you have in your closets?"

"Why is that?" Sam replied.

Amanda giggled again. "You now have a roommate, me. My bags are in the car. I need space to hang my clothes."

Although he had guessed her intentions, the suddenness of it all still took him by surprise. "Are you saying that you want to move in with me?"

Amanda looked into Sam's eyes. "Yes, I do. It's like the stray kitten that you find on your doorstep. Once you take it in it's yours; you have to keep it. Well, you've taken me in. I'm here to stay."

A smile spread across Sam's face. "Oh, that's wonderful. I'll take care of it right away."

Sam started to get up, but Amanda pulled him back down. "Not now, we have plenty of time. Oh, by the way, can you take a day off?"

Sam wondered what Amanda had in mind. "Why yes. I just have to call Fred first thing in the morning. What do you have in mind?"

Amanda responded, "I have to go into the clinic for a few minutes in the morning. When I get back I'm going to call mother and tell her that I'm coming for the weekend, and that I'll be bringing a friend with me."

Sam said, starting to get up, "All right, I'll call Fred first thing in the morning. Now you haven't had dinner yet."

Amanda said pulling Sam back down again, "There's also plenty of time for that." Amanda snuggled up close to Sam and started to rub herself against his thigh. He took her in his arms and kissed her. She took him in her hand and felt him respond to her touch.

Chapter Twenty-Nine

Friday morning Sam and Amanda had breakfast together. After breakfast Amanda dressed and drove to the clinic. She went straight to Dr. Prater's office and knocked on the door.

Dr. Prater called out, "Come in."

Amanda opened the door and entered. Maryanne got up from her desk and stepped around to greet her, 'Good-morning Catherine. When did you get back? Helen said nothing about you being back." Maryanne noticed immediately Amanda's jovial mood and figured that she had come to a decision obviously pleasing to her.

As Amanda shook hands with Maryanne, she said, "I got back last night, and spent the night with Sam. Helen didn't know that I was back."

Maryanne's eyebrows came up in surprise at Amanda's statement. She then gave her an appraising look. "No wonder you're so radiant and all smiles this morning. I can assume Catherine, or is it now Amanda, that you found your answer?"

A smile lit Amanda's face. "Yes, I have, and it's Amanda. Catherine is no more."

Maryanne directed Amanda to the sofa, and they both took a seat. As soon as they both were settled on the sofa, Maryanne said, "All right, now you said that you have found your answer. Would you like to talk about it?"

Amanda having made her decision, was eager to talk about it with Maryanne, "Yes, I would. This last week I've thought of nothing but this. I tried to view it from every perspective. I had to search the

202

WOMAN IN THE MIRROR

depths of my soul, and I had to ask and answer the question. Who really am I? For a long time I've thought of myself as, still at the core of my consciousness, still being Karl Boyle. In the end I realized that I wasn't, and could no longer be Karl Boyle. Karl Boyle is no more. He's dead. Not just in body, but totally."

Maryanne had to think about Amanda's statement tor a few seconds before she spoke to her. Finally she said, "That's quite a statement. What do you mean by it?"

Amanda settled into a more comfortable position on the sofa, as she tried to put words to the thoughts in her mind. "Well, I have it straight in my own mind. I'll try to find the words to explain it to you. It's like for a long time I was two persons. The public me was Catherine. She eventually became the dominant personality. I was Catherine, however there was still deep inside of me that private voice, even though weaker, was still saying, 'you're still Karl Boyle'. I finally realized that little voice was nothing but a ghost from the past, an echo of my former self. Am I making myself clear? Do you understand what I'm saying so far?"

Maryanne had been able to follow Amanda's reasoning so far. She wanted a couple of minutes to plan as to how she would test Amanda's conclusions. She got up and went to the coffee maker to get a cup of Coffee. She said, "Would you like a cup of coffee?"

Amanda shook her head. "No thank you. I've just had breakfast and coffee."

Maryanne finished making her coffee, took her seat on the sofa, and put her cup on the coffee table. She then turned to Amanda and said, "That's nice that you now believe yourself to be Amanda. What I would like to know is what led you to this conclusion, and that Karl Boyle is dead"

Amanda took her time before answering. She wanted to be sure that she could put into words, what she felt in her mind and heart. "Well, I remember Karl. When I woke up after surgery, despite the new body I was still Karl. I had his memories, but there was nothing more. So, it's just as I said. Karl Boyle no longer exists. I'm who you see me as now.

203

My memories from the time of the surgery are mine only, not Karl's."

Maryanne had no trouble following Amanda's reasoning so far. She decided to play the devil's advocate to test Amanda. "Now, just wait, Jane Doe was just a donor. When her upper brain functions ceased she was no longer a person."

Amanda had expected to have to explain herself to Maryanne and was ready. "I can see what you're trying to say, but she was still a person, just an incomplete one. When the brain was transplanted she became a complete person again. Different in a way, but still the same person. At first she was known as Jane Doe. Then I started to call myself, and thinking of myself as Catherine. There was just one person, the woman in the mirror, and I was that person."

Maryanne liked Amanda's responses so far. "That sounds good, but what about Karl? Isn't he still in there somewhere?"

Amanda thought about Karl. It no longer felt strange to her to think of Karl in the third person. "Yes, he was, but there can be only one, so he's nothing more than a memory. I now see him as just an old-close friend that I knew a long time ago, but had since passed away. When this all begin Karl was asked what he would be willing to sacrifice to have a normal life again. He didn't know it at the time that he would be sacrificing everything. That he would have to become part of someone else. It had been a long time in coming. I had to search my inner self for the answers. I can now say that I am, and have always been Amanda. I feel it in the core of my being. As long as I was still Catherine there was still a tie to what no longer existed. I came to realize that I had to move on. To break the tie to the past. I had to become Amanda."

Maryanne took a sip of coffee and put the cup back down on the coffee table. She then looked at, Amanda. "But it was just Amanda's body, it was Karl's consciousness."

Amanda nodded in the affirmative. "Yes, I know that, but who is a person anyway? Is he or she their physical selves, or are they who they see themselves in their own mind, or are they both? Amanda paused for a moment for emphasis, "I've a question for you."

"Yes, what is it?" Maryanne replied with a curious look.

Amanda looked as if she had knowledge of some great secret. "Tell me, of Amanda and Karl, who really was the donor, and who the recipient?"

Maryanne found it an unusual and unexpected question. She took a minute to think about it before she answered Amanda's question. "I would say that it depends on your point of view. Perhaps you can say a little of each."

Amanda sat back in the sofa with her hands in front of her with her fingers forming a tent, as she looked at Maryanne. "I believe that I know how to put it. There's a progression. The candidate takes possession of the donor, becoming the recipient. The recipient merges with the donor. Finally the donor becomes the recipient. Have I been able to make it clear for you? Perhaps there's another way to put it. When Karl and Amanda merged a third personality was created, different from the old Amanda, but still Amanda. You can say that I'm an amalgamation of both Karl and Amanda. For Karl and Amanda this is a second life. By a rash show of bravado Karl ruined his life. Amanda, for as yet some unknown reason, tried to end hers. For both Karl and Amanda this is a second chance to get it right."

Smiling at Amanda, Maryanne reached out and took Amanda's hand in hers, "Yes you have convinced me. I now know that you are Amanda. So what are your plans now?"

Amanda had already thought out the answer to that question, "Well, life alone is no life. I want to belong to someone. I've a family now, a good family whom anyone would be proud of. They're prepared to take me as I am and love me, and I'm willing and want to love them in return. After all, as Mom said, Amanda means worthy to be loved, and I believe that I'm worthy to be loved." Amanda realized that she had just referred to Beth as Mom for the first time, and it had seemed natural to do so. After all she was Amanda, and Beth was her mother."

Still holding Amanda's hand, Maryanne said, "I can see that everything is going well with Sam."

MICHAEL O. GREGORY

Amanda recalled Sam when she had left the apartment and smiled. "Yes, we're doing just great. When I left he was making space in his closet and dresser for my things. I'm going to be living with Sam now."

The suddenness of Amanda's decision took Maryanne by surprise. "I say, when you make up your mind you don't waste any time."

Amanda chuckled. "Sam had his mind made up a long time ago. I'm just getting caught up with him."

Maryanne let go of Amanda's hand and sat back in the sofa. She felt pleased with Amanda, "I wish you and Sam all the happiness, and you deserve it."

With a smile, Amanda responded, "Thank you, Maryanne."

Maryanne now changed the subject. "Oh, you haven't told me how your trip was yet. How did you like Hilton Head Island?"

Amanda took a moment to recall her trip to Helton Head Island. "It's a really beautiful place, and I'm sure a fun place to be. However, it was really lonely without Sam. I'd like to go back some day with Sam. One other thing, am I still on leave? There's something that I need to do today."

With a nod, Maryanne said, "Yes, you don't have to be back at work until Monday morning. Just one other thing. We know that you are planning another carrier and will be leaving us some day. We would like for you to return as needed as a consultant. We will pay you a fee for your services."

Amanda didn't know what to think about Maryanne's offer, "I don't know. I'm no expert on anything."

Maryanne put her hand on Amanda's forearm and said with feeling, "Oh, but you are. You are the first to go through this procedure, so that makes you the expert. You have been down that road and know where all the bumps and potholes are."

Amanda thought for a few seconds. "All right, you can count on me. So, when will you do it again?"

Maryanne picked up her cup, took a sip of coffee, and put her cup back down on the coffee table before she spoke, "I don't know. There is a

WOMAN IN THE MIRROR

lot to look at first. We answered the question whether it could be done. Now we have many more questions to answer before we do it again."

Amanda felt that it was time to go. She got up to leave, and Maryanne got up with her. They shook hands. "Thank you for everything that you've done for me." Amanda said.

Maryanne felt really pleased at how everything had turned out. She thought that if anyone deserved a happy ending, it had to be Amanda, "No thanks needed. It has been a pleasure to serve you my door will always be open, but I don't think that we need to schedule any more sessions."

Amanda thanked Maryanne again and left her office. As, Amanda made her way to the parking lot she ran into Helen. "Oh, Catherine, you're back!"

Amanda gave Helen a hug. "Yes, I got back last night."

Helen was at a loss for a moment. Then a look of comprehension showed on her face, to be replaced by a playful smile knowing what the answer would be. "Last night. Then where were you?"

Amanda was all-aglow with a flush of well-being. "I spent the night with Sam. And please call me Amanda."

Helen gave a squeal of delight and hugged Amanda about the neck. "You did it!" Laughing she repeated, "You did it!" Helen held Amanda at arm's length and gave her an appraising look, "I'm so happy for you. Well, I must say that you're really full of surprises today. I take it the trip was what you needed?"

Amanda nodded agreement. "Yes, I really needed to get away from everyone and everything. To just think about myself, and what I needed to do."

Helen released her grip on Amanda, "I'm glad that you're back. Dr. Prater told me why you were gone, but not where. Sam called me constantly wanting to know where you were. All I could tell him was that I had no idea where you were. I don't know rather he believed me, or not."

Amanda reached out and took Helen's hand, "There's one other

207

MICHAEL O. GREGORY

thing. You're losing a roommate. I'm moving in with Sam."

Helen gave Amanda another hug. "Good for you. This is so sudden, but not unexpected. I figured that the only thing holding you back was the uncertainty about your future. If ever two people were meant for each other, it's you and Sam."

Amanda searched Helen's face for a reaction, "Then you're not disappointed that I'm moving out?"

Helen put her arm around Amanda's shoulder, "No, 'm not disappointed. I'm happy for you, and glad that you and Sam found each other; and envious that I'm still looking. It seemed so easy for you. How did you do it?"

Amanda shrugged her shoulders. "I don't know, lucky I guess." They both shared a bit of laughter.

After the laughter subsided, Helen said, "Promise me one thing."

Amanda said, looking at Helen. "Yes, what's that?"

Helen said, with a touch of levity, "That I can be one of your bridesmaids."

Amanda looked surprised. "But Sam hasn't asked me to marry him."

Helen, still smiling, said, "Not yet, but I know Sam. He will. I bet that he can't wait to get a ring on your finger."

Smiling, Amanda said, "I hope so. By the way, I hope that you will forgive me for moving out on you without notice. I know that it'll be a hardship on you."

Helen reassured Amanda. "Don't worry about that. The clinic subsidized my getting a large apartment so that I could invite you to be my roommate. It was my duty to shepherd you through these first few months until you got your feet on the ground. Amanda, I want to tell you that I've come to regard you as a dear and close friend."

Hearing this gave Amanda a rush of emotion. She also had a warm regard for Helen. "Thank you, and you'll always be a very special friend to me. And, yes, you can be a bridesmaid. I wouldn't have it any other way. I have to go now. We can talk more Monday." Amanda hugged Helen again, said good-bye, then continued out to the parking lot.

WOMAN IN THE MIRROR

When Amanda got back home, Sam had most of her things put away, and had packed a weekend bag for himself. She repacked a bag for herself, then went to the phone to call her mother.

The phone rang and Beth picked it up. "Hello."

"Hello, Mom, it's, Amanda."

When, Beth heard, Amanda call her Mom and use her name Amanda, she was so overcome with emotion that she had to swallow the lump in her throat before she could speak. She struggled to hold back the tears. "Oh, Amanda, you're back. You can remember."

Amanda also had to struggle to control her emotions, "No, Mother, I still don't remember, and doubt that I ever will, but this I do know, I'm your daughter. That's undeniable, and I know it in my heart. I want us to be a family again."

Beth could no longer hold back the tears. She started to weep openly. "Oh, Amanda, I've waited so long to hear you say that. We're family, and we'll always be family."

Amanda also had to dab tears from her eyes, "Mom, I'd like to see you. Do you mind if I come now for the weekend?"

Beth was overjoyed that Amanda wanted to come to visit, "I want to see you too. Anytime you want to come you're welcome. When can you be here?"

Amanda looked at her watch, "Say three hours. It's ten-thirty here. That's nine-thirty your time. We'll be there by twelve-thirty your time."

Beth said a little surprised, "You said we?"

"Yes, Mom, I'm bringing a friend, I'm bringing Sam. It's time that you and Dad got to know him. I must run now. We need to get on the road. Good-bye." Amanda hung up the phone and went to load her bag into the car.

CHAPTER THIRTY

They had a pleasant trip to Gadsden. This time Amanda was going home, and she looked forward to it. Sam did the driving while Amanda gave directions. Amanda talked a lot, telling Sam what she knew about her parents and their home. Sam made good time on the road, and they arrived at Amanda's parent's home at 12:15 PM.

Beth had been watching the road for their car, and had seen it as Sam slowed to turn into the drive. She was out of the house as soon as Sam had stopped the car in the drive, with Ted right behind her. He had taken the rest of the day off to be with Amanda. As soon as Amanda got out of the car, Beth embraced her and kissed her on the cheek. Ted followed with a hug and kiss on the cheek. Amanda now welcomed the familiarity, being that they were her family now. When she had a chance she turned to Sam. "Sam, these are my parents Ted and Beth." turning back to her parents she said, "Mom Dad, this is Sam." Sam shook hands with Ted and Beth. They were both impressed by Sam right off. Beth liked his smart appearance and manner. Ted liked his forthright manner and strong handshake.

They went to the family room where Beth served everyone Cokes. The table had already been set, and the meal ready. Beth just had to heat some items in the microwave, and put them on the table.

They talked for a few minutes, then Beth went to put the meal on the table. Amanda got up to give her a hand. When they were in the kitchen, Amanda turned to her mother, "Well, Mom, what do you think of Sam?"

Beth had just turned on the microwave. She turned to Amanda. "We're glad that you brought Sam. We wanted the chance to meet him. He seems to be such a nice man."

Amanda had been anxious for her parent's approval, especially her mother. "It makes me feel good that you like him, and that Dad likes him also. There's a reason that I brought him here with me today. I figured that you and Dad needed to get to know him, since I'm now living with him."

This revelation took Beth by surprise. "What! When did this happen?"

Amanda hadn't expected such a strong reaction from her mother, but she was committed now and had to continue. "Yesterday, as soon as I got back from Hilton Head Island."

Beth started to say, "You know my," She caught herself before she completed the sentence, "But you don't know, do you?" Beth realized that this could be a delicate time in her relationship with Amanda, and she didn't want to spoil it with an argument. She had to find a way around this. "I'm sorry Amanda. You're a grown woman now, and I've no right to interfere in your life. I just think that a woman shouldn't commit herself to a man until she's married."

Now it would be Amanda's turn to be embarrassed by the conversation, "Oh, Mom, I'm sorry if I have offended you, but I love Sam. I want to be with him as much as possible. He's the only man that I've known, and the only man that I ever want to know."

The food in the microwave was ready. Nothing more would be said of it while they finished putting everything on the table. By the time that they had the table ready, Beth had made up her mind about Amanda and Sam. "Okay, I'm willing to keep an open mind. If that's what you want, then it's all right with me. Just one question, if you don't mind answering. How long have you been sleeping with him?"

Amanda gave Beth a sheepish look, still embarrassed by it. "Last night was the first time. I wanted to before then, but I wasn't ready to make the commitment."

Beth being eager to please Amanda would be willing to let her have whatever she wanted. "Okay, I'm a modern woman. I can be liberal about this. Do you want to share a bedroom with Sam?"

With a cry of delight, Amanda hugged Beth and kissed her on the cheek. "Oh, thank you, Mom, I love you."

Beth put her arm around Amanda's shoulder. "All right then, Sam can sleep in your room with you. I just want you to be happy. Now all I have to do is explain it to your father. Just leave your bags in the car for now. I'll take care of them myself later. Now, let's call our men to lunch." Reflecting on what had just happened, Beth felt sure that she had made the right decision about Amanda and Sam. She knew that if she had insisted, Amanda would have agreed to separate rooms for herself and Sam, but Amanda was her own person, and had a right to have it her way.

After lunch they went into the family room and talked some more. Sam and Ted got to talking about football. They ended up making a bet as to who would win the Alabama/Georgia game this year. Beth and Amanda decided to go shopping for the afternoon, and leave the men to talk sports, or whatever else they wanted to talk about.

Ted took everyone out to dinner that evening. After dinner they came back home and watched television. By the time that Beth explained the sleeping arrangements to Ted, he had been quite reasonable about it.

Saturday Bill came home for the weekend. Sam and Bill hit it off right away. Amanda was glad to see Bill, and to start the bonding process as brother and sister. She also hoped that Audrey could make it home for the weekend. Amanda wanted so much to start to repair the rift between them, and start the bonding process as sisters.

Audrey couldn't make it home for the weekend due to previous commitments that she didn't want to break. Beth did call her on the phone and let Amanda talk to her for a while. Amanda hung up the phone feeling that she had started to mend some of the ill feelings between Audrey and herself.

WOMAN IN THE MIRROR

Sunday everyone went to church. Ted and Beth introduced Sam to other members of the family and friends. After church they had lunch at Amanda's parent's home. Sam and Amanda left at 3:00 PM, arriving back home just before 7:00 PM.

The next weekend Sam and Amanda drove to Helen, Georgia for Oktoberfest. Hey stayed overnight at the Hofbrauhaus Inn. Amanda found Helen to be a charming alpine-style village in the north Georgia mountains, with cobblestone streets, a multitude of shops and wall to wall polka music. There were all kinds of activity and merriment. Sam and Amanda both had a wonderful time.

The first Saturday in November Sam and Amanda got up and dressed for their date. It being a cold morning, they dressed in matching red sweat suits with University of Georgia on the front of Amanda's sweat shirt. Sam had the head and face of an English bulldog, with a small red and black cap with the letter 'G' on the front of his sweat shirt.

They drove to Stone Mountain Park, arriving after 9:00 AM. They took the first cable car to the top of the Mountain at 10:00 AM. At the top of the mountain they went to their special place, looking west toward the Atlanta skyline. The fall colors were at their peak. They stood there together Sam with his arm around Amanda, he said, "How do you like it?"

Amanda enjoyed the panoramic view spread out before her, "Oh, it's wonderful. The colors are so beautiful."

Sam sensed that now would be just the right time. He took from his pocket a jeweler's ring box and opened it to reveal a diamond ring. Amanda had been expecting this, but it was still a very pleasant surprise. Sam had been rehearsing his proposal all week for just this moment. As he faced Amanda he felt so nervous that he was sure that she could see him shaking. "Amanda, the last time we were up here I gave you an opal. This time it's a diamond. You're a precious bright shining light in my life. I love you dearly. You are the woman whom I wish to spend all eternity. Will you honor me by becoming my wife?"

Sam's eloquent proposal carried Amanda away. Obviously he had put a lot of thought into it. She would have been satisfied with a simple, 'Will you marry me?' This had been an unexpected treat for her. She put her arms around Sam, and rested her head on his shoulder, "Oh, Sam, you know that I will. I want us to be together forever." They embraced and kissed ardently. Sam placed the ring on Amanda's finger, and they kissed again. "Besides," Amanda said, "how could a girl say no to such an eloquent proposal?"

Sam felt pleased, and had a broad smile. "Did you like it?"

Amanda cuddled up close to him. "Oh, it was so beautiful. You must have worked on it for a long time."

Sam kissed her again, then said, "Oh, just ever since I first met you."

Amanda turned and leaned back against Sam's chest and rested her head on his shoulder. Sam put his arms around her waist. She said, "I need to call mother as soon as we get back home. I'm sure that she'll be thrilled with the news. She has been after me to know when we're going to be married; ever since I took you to meet with them. You know how old-fashioned Mother is."

Sam said with a mocking voice, "Old-fashioned! Look who's talking!"

Amanda poked Sam in the ribs with her elbow playfully, "I'm not old-fashioned. I'm just what you call, conservative. Besides, you like me that way. Admit it!"

Sam laughed. "Okay, I wouldn't have you any other way." Sam paused for a moment, "Let's wait until after the weekend before we tell the folks. By then we may have a date for the wedding. I want to have it here in Atlanta. If we leave it up to my parent's, we'll have to have it in Augusta. And I'm sure that your parent's would like to have it in Gadsden."

Amanda considered Sam's request that they wait through the weekend before notifying their parent's, "I'd say that you're right on that. We'll wait to call our folks. I also have to tell Helen. I promised her that she could be a bridesmaid. The Maid of Honor will have to be Audrey.

"Sam, this is our special place. I want to come back here each year at the same time."

Sam tightened his grip around, Amanda's waist and breathed into her ear, "Okay, that's a date."

Amanda reveled in the wonderful feeling of security in Sam's arms, and looked out at the vista spread out before her. Amanda's world was complete.

CHAPTER THIRTY-ONE

During the drive home from Stone Mountain, Amanda kept looking at the diamond ring that now encircled her left ring finger. She loved how it sparkled when it caught the sunlight. She loved Sam, and wanted very much to be a good wife to him. She had been living with Sam for a few weeks now. Ever since her mother had found out that she and Sam had been living together she had, in her own words wanted to now, 'when he planned to make an honest woman of her'. Her mother would be thrilled to hear that they were to be married.

As they drove back home, Amanda thought back over the last year. Her transformation over the last several months had sometimes been exciting and sometimes difficult, but always interesting. Now the transformation to her feminine self had been fully realized. She now had a wonderful and supporting family, and the love of a wonderful man. What more could she ask for.

Amanda and Sam were in the car leaving Stone Mountain Park. As Sam drove Amanda lay her left hand on his thigh, and he took it in his right hand. She looked at him. "Sam, I feel wonderful and would like to celebrate."

Sam gave her hand a squeeze. "Okay, how about this evening we go out to a fancy restaurant where I have to wear a tie, and you have to wear a dress. Afterwards we can take in a movie. We can even see a 'chick flick' if you want."

Amanda gave a little chuckle, then gave him a warm smile. "That

WOMAN IN THE MIRROR

sounds good, and I'll hold you to that 'chick flick', but I would also like to go to lunch at the Captain D's where we first met."

Sam gave her a quick glance and rolled his eyes. "You're not ever going to let me forget that day. Are you?"

"No, I'm not." Amanda had to laugh at how Sam had been embarrassed by their disastrous first meeting.

Sam laughed with her. "Okay, then its Captain D's for lunch."

They had lunch at Captain D's. That evening they had dinner at a nice restaurant, then went to a movie.

The first thing that they needed to do would be to set the date for the wedding. After church services the next morning, they checked with the pastor of their church and found out that the last Saturday of January had been open. They reserved this date for their wedding. Having now reserved the date at their church for the wedding, there would be no chance for Sam's parents to try to have the wedding in Augusta, Georgia. Or for Amanda's parents to plan for it in Gadsden, Alabama.

Sam and Amanda had in mind a small-intimate wedding ceremony, with just the family and a few close friends. Nothing big or elaborate, just keep it simple. That impossible dream lasted only till they called their parents Sunday evening. Amanda's mother had been dreaming of this day ever since Amanda's birth, and she wouldn't be denied. Beth could already visualize the church packed with guests, with all the flowers and candles. The wedding march would be played and Amanda would come down the aisle on Ted's arm, the most beautiful bride, in the most elaborate gown that anyone had ever seen. She wanted this wedding to be an event to be remembered for a lifetime.

Sam's parents were also in favor of a big wedding. They saw it to be the family social event of the year. Sam and Amanda became resigned to the fact that they were going to have a big wedding.

The first, after their parents, to learn of Sam and Amanda's engagement had been Fred and Helen. Sam told Fred as soon as they met in the office Monday morning.

MICHAEL O. GREGORY

Fred had been expecting it, and brought out from a drawer in his desk a bottle of Jack Daniel Bourbon. Holding up the bottle, Fred said, "We have to drink to this. Get the cups." Sam grabbed his and Fred's coffee cups, and washed them out in the wash room. Fred poured a little Jack Daniel into each cup, and they clicked them together. "Lahime!" Fred said.

"Lahime!" Sam responded. They drank the toast. As they put the cups down, Sam said, "Do you still want to be my best man?"

"I'd feel slighted if you didn't ask me." Fred said smiling, as he poured another shot of Jack Daniel into the cups.

With a short laugh Sam slapped Fred playfully on the shoulder, "Okay, then you're my best man. Now drink up and let's get to work."

When, Amanda got to work Monday morning Helen had already arrived. Amanda caught up with her at the nurse's station. Helen had been getting the medication tray ready for the long-term care patients under her care. Amanda held her left hand in a manner to attract Helen's attention. Helen noticed the radiant smile on Amanda's face and immediately spotted the sparkle on her ring finger. With a squeal of delight, Helen gave Amanda a hug, "Congratulations Amanda. I see that Sam did it."

Amanda felt so excited to be telling her friend the news, "Yes, it was up on Stone Mountain Saturday. Even though I had been expected it, the thrill of it wasn't diminished. He swept my off my feet, figuratively speaking."

By now the other nurse's and nurse's aides within ear shot had gathered to give their congratulations to Amanda. While looking at the ring, Helen said, "Have you and Sam set a date yet?"

Amanda felt pride in showing off her ring to Helen and her other friends. She wanted Helen to share her happiness, "Yes, we have. We made a reservation at our church for the last Saturday of January. Do you still want to be my bridesmaid?"

Helen hugged Amanda again, then said, "Why you know I do. I've been looking forward to it."

218

The other nurse's and nurse's aides gave Amanda hugs, congratulated her again on her betrothal to Sam, and wished her happiness.

Amanda would have liked to talk more, but she had work to do. It would have to wait until later when they took their midmorning break together, "Thank you for agreeing to be my bridesmaid Helen. Now I must be getting to work. I'll see you at the break." Amanda turned and started to walk away in the direction of the linen room.

During the midmorning break Amanda and Helen talked about the upcoming wedding. Helen offered her help for any of the planning or preparation for the wedding. She also told Amanda about the best place in Atlanta to get a bargain price on bridal and bridesmaid gowns and other wedding supplies.

Once Amanda got into the planning and preparation for the wedding, she was amazed to see what all had to be done. All of this did however have a bonus. Beth had started to spend a lot of time with her, to help her with the preparations. Beth had to come to Atlanta at least two to three days a week to go shopping with Amanda for whatever she needed for the wedding, or to help in whatever way that she could. Beth had been glad to have Amanda back as her daughter, after all the years that she had been gone from them. She looked for every opportunity to be with Amanda, and cherished every moment.

With all the time spent together, Amanda had also been developing a genuine affection for Beth. It now seemed natural for her to address Beth as Mother or Mom, and seek her advice on any matter. Amanda could now believe in her own mind that she was in fact Beth's true daughter. It had proved to be a real benefit for Amanda to have the love and support of a family again.

Amanda's sister Audrey would be the Maid of Honor. Amanda wanting to mend the past bitter feelings had been working hard on her relations with Audrey, and it had started to bear fruit. Audrey may not completely trust her yet, but at least they were trying to become good friends. Amanda's cousins Joyce, Pricilla, Helen and Sam's cousin Silvia were the other Bridesmaids.

MICHAEL O. GREGORY

With the guest list, invitations, music, flowers, gowns, catering and many other details they barely had time to get ready. Beth's friend Peggy would be the coordinator, and her granddaughter Sonya would be the flower girl. Amanda's brother Bill would be one of the ushers. The rest of the ushers were Sam's brother Jeffery and his cousins Brian and Wayne. At times it seemed that they wouldn't make it, but with her mother and Helen's help everything had been ready on time.

Friday afternoon, the day before the wedding, a cold front moved into Georgia and collided with warm-moist air coming up from the Gulf of Mexico, and it snowed in Atlanta. There were the usual finder benders and traffic jams, but everyone managed to get to the church in time for the rehearsal. They went through the ceremony so that everyone would know what to do. Peggy got together with everyone to make sure that they would understand her instructions and signals tomorrow. There had been a lot of levity and joking, with everyone in a jovial mood.

They held the rehearsal dinner in the church hall. Sam's father had more than enough pizza delivered from Pizza Hut. There was also plenty of Coke, 7up and beer for everyone, and there were chocolate éclairs for dessert. The dinner had been very informal, and everyone had a wonderful time.

After dinner Sam with Fred and the other men went out for a bachelor party that Fred had arranged. After the party, Sam went home to the apartment.

Amanda had her bachelorette party at Helen's apartment, with Helen and the rest of the girls in the wedding party. After the party, Amanda spent the night with Helen. The rest of the wedding party had rooms at a nearby Motel 6.

Sunday morning all the ladies in the bridal party were at the church early so that they could have their hair and make-up done. Afterwards they all got dressed for the ceremony. Amanda had chosen red for the bridesmaid's gowns in keeping with the season. Amanda wore the traditional white bridal gown of satin with high collar, long sleeves,

220

WOMAN IN THE MIRROR

fitted bodice and full skirt with train. The gown had liberal amounts of embroidery and seed pearls. Being a heavy gown unlike anything that she had ever worn before, Amanda had worn it often enough ahead of time to get used to it. A garland of white-silk roses crowned her vail. Something old had been her white high-heel shoes. Something borrowed a pair of pearl earrings from Helen. Something blue was a garter. The bride's bouquet had been made up of white and pink roses. The bridesmaids had smaller bouquets of red and white roses. Flowers and candles were in abundance in the church for the ceremony.

The men arrived shortly before the time for the ceremony to begin. They had all dressed for the ceremony in black tuxedos before arriving at the church. Upon arrival they received their boutonnieres from Peggy. Everyone was now ready.

When Ted entered Beth and Amanda were standing in the center of the room facing the door. Amanda in her wedding gown. Beth wore a dark-green silk dress, with matching green high-heel shoes and handbag. She also wore a double strand of pearls. Ted took a few seconds to just stand inside the door and look at Amanda before he spoke. The sight of her took his breath away. Arrayed in her wedding gown, she looked to him to be as radiant and lovely as any goddess ever imagined by man. When he finally found his voice he said, "I see that my ladies are ready to go."

Ted stepped up and kissed Amanda and Beth on the cheek. He then looked at Beth to receive a nod, then took a long jeweler's box from his pocket. "Amanda, your mother and I have this gift for you to remember us on this your special day." Ted opened the jeweler's box. Inside Amanda saw a single strand of pearls. Beth took the strand of pearls and put them on Amanda. Ted and Beth admired and complemented Amanda on how wonderful the pearls looked on her. They had just a couple of minutes to wait before the ceremony started. Amanda felt content to spend this time alone with her parents.

A knock came at the door, then it opened. Bill had come to escort Beth to her seat for the ceremony. After Beth left with Bill, Ted and

MICHAEL O. GREGORY

Amanda waited for a while. Then came another knock at the door. Ted turned to Amanda, "It's time now. Are you ready?"

Amanda smiled at her father and nodded, "Yes, Dad, let's do it." Ted took Amanda's arm, and they started for the door. Before they left the room, Amanda said, "Oh, Dad, I want to thank you and Mom for everything. You've really been wonderful to me." Ted didn't say anything. He just patted Amanda's hand. She got the message.

Peggy insured that everything went flawlessly. The flower girl, bridesmaids, and ushers went down the aisle on cue and took their places. The music changed and Amanda on her Father's arm, walked down the aisle to join Sam at the altar. No one could tell Beth that Amanda wasn't the most beautiful bride to ever walk down the aisle. Amanda and Sam only had eyes for each other. They gave their vows, exchanged rings and they were husband and wife.

They held the reception in the church hall. After the photograph session, the wedding party joined their guests in the church hall. Sam and Amanda cut the cake. They danced together. Then Amanda danced with her Dad. After the dancing they opened their gifts. When Amanda threw the bouquet, Helen caught it. One of Sam's cousins caught the garter. Sam and Amanda changed and left in a limousine to start their honeymoon.

Sam and Amanda honeymooned for a week in Honolulu, Hawaii. It became a week of sun, sandy beaches and ocean. They did some shopping for aloha shirts, muumuus, swim trunks and bikini in matching bright-floral print fabric. They also took some time to do some sightseeing.

One of the paces that they saw was the Iolani Palace. They were amazed that the lifestyle of the Hawaiian Royal Family matched that of other royal families of the period. The Polynesian Cultural Center showed Sam and Amanda that the Polynesians had a very advanced culture. The one thing that they couldn't leave Hawaii without seeing was the USS Arizona. It proved to be a very moving experience.

On the last day they went to buy souvenirs for family and friends.

WOMAN IN THE MIRROR

Sam also bought a gold neckless and earrings for Amanda. At last with reluctance they had to leave the warm sun of Hawaii for the winter of Atlanta.

Helen met them at the airport and drove them back to their apartment. During the drive Helen kept asking them about their trip to Hawaii. Amanda promised to tell her all about it later.

CHAPTER THIRTY-TWO

When Amanda came to work Monday morning, Helen had been waiting for her. Helen said, "What you told me last night was great, but you must now tell me everything. Don't leave anything out."

Amanda responded with a mirthful tone to her voice, "Do you mean, EVERYTHING?"

They both broke into laughter. With a blush, Helen said, "Oh, you know what I mean. You can leave that out, just tell me all the rest."

Amanda started walking toward the linen room, "Okay, but you're going to have to keep up with me. I've some beds to make."

Helen followed Amanda to the linen room. Amanda picked up some sheets and pillowcases, then walked with Helen to the first room, and started to make the beds. Helen gave her a hand. "Okay, don't keep me waiting."

Amanda glanced up at Helen as she made the bed. "You just have to go there someday. You have to see it for yourself. It's the most beautiful place that I've ever seen. Our week ended too soon. I didn't want to leave." Amanda started to tell Helen about their trip to Hawaii. About how beautiful the islands were, and all the sights.

They finished making the beds in the first room and went on to the second room. They finished the beds in the second room and had started on the first bed in the third room. Helen finally said, "I'm sorry, but I've other things that I must do now. You can tell me the rest at lunch." Helen left the room to go about her own duties. Amanda

224

continued to make the beds.

At lunch Amanda and Helen talked more about Hawaii. Amanda told Helen all about Waikiki and the ride in the canoe. She also told her about Honolulu, Iolani Palace, Pearl Harbor and the trip around the island. Helen was thrilled by it all.

After work Amanda went to Helen's apartment. They had coffee and talked for a while. Amanda left in time to be home to greet Sam, when he got home.

The month of February went by fast. Sam had work to catch up on. Amanda kept busy with her classes. They continued to fix up their apartment. They even started to talk about getting a larger place. Amanda kept busy writing thank-you notes for the gifts that they had received.

The second Saturday after they got back from Hawaii, they drove to Augusta to visit Sam's parents. They had a long visit, and arrived back home after 10:00 PM. The next day they drove up to Commerce to shop at the factory outlet mall.

By the end of February Amanda started to notice something by its absence. It was the second Monday of March, and she sat having lunch with Helen, in the clinic cafeteria. Amanda said with a half-smile, "Something that's supposed to happen hasn't."

Helen asked with just a hint of curiosity in her voice, "What's that?"

With a hint of mystery in her voice Amanda said, "I'm late."

Helen put down her fork. She no longer had any thought of her lunch. "You are! How many days?"

Amanda started to count silently on her fingers, "This is the eleventh of March, I'm twenty-two days late."

Helen regarded Amanda for a couple of seconds with open mouth amazement, then regained her poise. "You're not late, you've missed!"

Amanda had to put down her fork as she beamed with pleasure. "Yes, I know, and I've been losing my breakfast the last couple of days."

Helen bounced in her chair, and clapped her hands together in front of her face, "You mean that you're...?"

Amanda's eyes now sparkled, and a broad smile lit her face, "Yes,

MICHAEL O. GREGORY

I'm almost sure that I am."

Helen became ecstatic. She reached across the table and took Amanda's hands in hers, Oh, this is great news, congratulations."

Amanda was in a great mood now. She could barely contain her joy. Helen felt happy for her friend. Amanda said, "Thank you, but I want to be sure before I start to celebrate. I want to stop at the drugstore after work to get a pregnancy test kit; then come to your apartment. If it's all right with you?"

Helen's curiosity was piqued, and she wanted to know as much as Amanda did what the results of a home pregnancy test would be. "Yes, of course you can. If you want I can go to the drugstore with you."

With a nod, Amanda said, "Okay, I'll follow you home after work today. We'll stop off at the drugstore on the way," They continued to talk as they ate lunch, then went back to work.

After work Amanda followed Helen home; stopping off at the drugstore to get a pregnancy test kit. When they got to Helen's apartment, Helen put the coffee on. They read the instructions on the package. Helen continued to make the coffee, while Amanda went into the bathroom and took the test.

Helen had the coffee ready when Amanda returned from the bathroom. Beaming with joy, Amanda said, "Well, I have a plus. The test is positive, I'm with child."

Thrilled, Helen hugged Amanda, "Oh, that's just great Amanda! How do you feel?"

Bringing her hand up in front of her mouth, Amanda giggled. "I guess I feel pregnant."

Helen laughed. "Oh, you know what I mean!"

Amanda, still smiling, said, "Yes, I do, and I feel great. Like this is the best moment of my life."

Helen had already made cups of coffee for herself and Amanda. Amanda turned down the coffee, saying that she needed to start watching what she ate and drank. She finally settled for a glass of orange juice. When they were both sitting at the table, Helen said, "When are you

226

going to tell Sam?"

Amanda took a swallow of orange juice, and put the glass down on the table, "I'm going to tell him as soon as he gets home this evening. This is too good to keep to myself. Oh, by the way, since you're my best friend; I want you to be my baby's Aunt Helen."

Helen was very moved by Amanda's gesture, "Thank you Amanda, I'm honored. By the way, do you have a gynecologist?"

Amanda shook her head. "No, not yet."

Helen knew that Amanda had never been to a gynecologist before, and needed someone that she could be comfortable with and trust, "I have a good one. If you want, I can make an appointment for you with her?"

Amanda nodded, grateful for Helen's offer. "Yes, please do. I've never been to a gynecologist before. I don't know the first thing about getting a good one."

The talk now turned to preparing for the arrival of the baby. Amanda realized that she and Sam would be busy getting everything that they needed well before the baby got there. Amanda and Helen talked for a while longer. Then Amanda left to be home when Sam arrived.

When Sam arrived home, Amanda was dressed and ready to go out. She fell into his arms and kissed him as soon as he came through the door. Amanda said, "Are you ready to go to dinner?"

Sam had been taken by surprise. He hadn't been aware that they were to go out to dinner this evening. "Gong out to dinner?" He said with his forehead wrinkling to show his amazement.

Still in Sam's arms with her head on his shoulder, she said, "I thought that we'd go out to celebrate."

Sam pulled back and gave her an inquisitive look. "And what are we to be celebrating."

Amanda, with a cryptic smile, said, "Oh, just that we've decided to get a bigger apartment."

Amanda's behavior puzzled Sam. What was she up to? Sam responded, "I know that we've talked about it, but when did we

MICHAEL O. GREGORY

decide this?"

Amanda kissed Sam passionately, then said, "Oh, Sam, we must have a bigger apartment. We need a room for the baby."

Sam's mouth fell open in surprise. He then swept Amanda into his arms, lifted her off the floor and spun her about. He then set her feet back on the floor, and gave her a long fervent kiss. He ended the kiss with an exclamation, "Wow, a baby!"

Amanda put her head back on Sam's shoulder "Yes, Sam, it's for certain, I'm with child. You're going to be a father."

Sam was so overcome with joy that he could hardly keep still. He had to resist the urge to go dancing about the room with Amanda in his arms, "When did you find out?"

Amanda replied, "I've suspected it for a few days now. I took a home-pregnancy test today. It was positive."

Sam kissed Amanda again ardently, then said, "Yes we do need to celebrate. We can start looking for a bigger apartment tomorrow. Now, this is your night. Whatever you want it's yours."

Amanda said, starting to break her embrace with Sam, "I feel like Italian this evening. Let's start out with dinner at the Olive Garden. After dinner, if there's time, we can take in a movie." Amanda got her purse and they were off to the Olive Garden.

Chapter Thirty-Three

When Amanda arrived at work Wednesday morning, Helen had already arrived, and had been waiting for her. "I made an appointment for you with my gynecologist. She's, Dr. Lisa Pittman, OB/GYN. Your appointment is on Tuesday the nineteenth at two forty-five PM." Helen handed Amanda a slip of paper. "This is your appointment with, Dr. Pittman and her address."

Amanda took the slip of paper and put it in her purse. "Thank you, Helen."

Helen patted Amanda on the wrist. "My pleasure, and by the way, how's Sam reacting to the news?"

Amanda smiled with pleasure, thinking of how Sam had reacted to the news. "He's just thrilled. He's been catering to my every whim. He acts like he can't do enough for me." Amanda's expression now turned serious, "Helen, as you know, I've never been to a gynecologist before. Can you tell me what to expect?"

Helen took Amanda by the arm and started to advise her as an older sister would. "Okay, since this is your first visit you need to come, say twenty to twenty-five minutes early. Before you are seen, you will have to fill out a medical history form. Then they will take your blood pressure and other vitals. Dr. Pittman will then examine you. She'll also examine your breasts, and give you a pelvic examination."

The words 'pelvic examination' invoked uneasy feelings in Amanda. With a grimace, she said, "Yes, I've heard about pelvic examinations."

Helen tried to keep a straight face, and not laugh at Amanda's discomfort. She understood, having been through it herself, but first had to smile over Amanda's concern, she replied, "I'm sure that you, have, and they're as uncomfortable as you've imagined. Don't worry though, Dr. Pittman's an excellent gynecologist. She'll take good care of you."

Amanda trusted Helen's judgement, and felt reassured by her endorsement. With a nod, Amanda said, "All right, I trust your judgement. I know that I'll be all right with her."

Helen said as an afterthought, "Oh, one other thing, they'll want blood and urine for laboratory examination."

Amanda nodded in understanding. Getting stuck with a needle for a blood sample had to be one of her least pleasurable experiences, "Okay, I get the picture. Now, let's talk about something else, something more pleasant."

Helen changed the subject. "Have you told your parents yet?"

Amanda shook her head. "No, Sam and I decided to wait until after my first appointment with the doctor."

Helen looked at her watch. "I have to get to work now. I'll see you at lunch."

On Tuesday, the day of the appointment, Amanda left work at noon. She went home to change clothes, and arrived at the doctor's office by 2:20 PM.

The receptionist checked her against the appointment schedule, then handed her a clipboard with a medical history form to fill out. There were other women in the office, but everyone kept to themselves. Amanda filled out the form, then handed it back to the desk.

After a few minutes a nurse called her, handed her a sample cup for a urine sample, and directed her to the lavatory. After the urine sample had been collected, the nurse took Amanda back to an exam room. The nurse took her vitals, weight and drew blood. The nurse then gave Amanda a hospital gown that opened at the back, and instructed her to remove all of her clothing, put on the gown, and sit on the exam table. After the nurse left the exam room, Amanda changed into the hospital gown, thinking that it had been deliberately designed to

WOMAN IN THE MIRROR

be uncomfortable, so as to put the patient at a disadvantage before the doctor.

In a few minutes Dr. Pittman entered the exam room. She was a woman of about forty years of age, petite, of trim figure, with red hair. She wore a white lab coat over a navy-blue dress. "Good afternoon, Mrs. Tankersley. I'm Dr. Pittman. How are you today?"

Amanda felt nervous, but tried to appear calm before Dr. Pittman. "Just fine doctor."

Dr. Pittman looked at Amanda's chart to try to get an idea of her new patient. "I see here that you have missed a period."

Amanda started to describe her symptoms to Dr. Pittman, trying to be as comprehensive as she could, "Yes, the next period should have started Sunday, but it hasn't, and I know it won't come. And one other thing, I've been having morning sickness. It has been a few days now. I also took a home pregnancy test that tested positive."

Dr. Pittman, while still looking at Amanda's chart, nodded. "Okay, it sounds like you're pregnant, but that's what we're here to determine for sure. Have you ever been pregnant before?"

Amanda shook her head. "No, this is my first time."

Dr. Pittman gave Amanda a big smile. "So, your first time. I imagine that you're really excited about it?"

Amanda managed a smile back at Dr. Pittman, although she still felt nervous inside. "Yes, I am."

Dr. Pittman looked at the medical form. "I see that you haven't given the date of your last pelvic examination. When was it?"

Amanda felt the nervousness welt up inside of her, and looked down at the floor to avoid eye contact with, Dr. Pittman. "I don't know. I don't know if I have ever had one."

Dr. Pittman hadn't been expecting that answer, and gave Amanda a puzzling look. She wondered how a woman could ever forget her last pelvic examination. "What do you mean by that?"

Amanda looked at Dr. Pittman. Once again she had to rely on the cover story. "Well, to make a long story short, I was in a coma. I

231

MICHAEL O. GREGORY

woke up about this time last year. I have no memory of anything before I woke up last year."

Dr. Pittman looked at Amanda with renewed interest. "That's interesting. Do you have any other medical condition that I should know about?"

Amanda shook her head, relieved that the cover story had seemed to work. "No, that's it."

Dr. Pittman put the chart aside. "Okay, now I'd like to check you out." Dr. Pittman looked at Amanda's eyes, ears nose and throat. She then listened to Amanda's heart and lungs. Dr. Pittman checked Amanda's breasts, and had her lie down on the exam table so that she could probe her abdomen. "Now, Mrs. Tankersley, if you will slide down to the end of the table and put your feet in the stirrups, we can get the pelvic examination."

Amanda scooted down to the end of the table, and put her feet into the stirrups. After having Amanda adjust her position, Dr. Pittman put on rubber gloves and conducted the pelvic examination.

After the completion of the examination, Dr. Pittman had Amanda get out of the stirrups, and sit on the edge of the table. Something troubled Dr. Pittman about this examination, and she had to get to the bottom of it. "Mrs. Tankersley, you say that this is your first pregnancy?"

Amanda thought the question a bit odd, and started to become concerned that something could be wrong. She nodded. "Yes, it's my first."

Dr. Pittman just looked at Amanda for a few seconds, unsure of how to continue before she finally spoke, "Well, Mrs. Tankersley, there's only one way to say this. According to my examination this isn't your first time."

Amanda sat stunned for a few seconds before she spoke. "But doctor that just can't be."

Dr. Pittman replied, "Oh, it can and it is. You have an episiotomy scar. You haven't just been pregnant before, you've given birth."

Amanda just couldn't believe what she had just heard. This had to

232

be a bad dream, a nightmare. Amanda was too shocked by this revelation to do anything for a couple of minutes. Finally she managed to speak, "But that can't be! It just can't!"

Dr. Pittman could clearly see the stress in Amanda's posture and speech. She had never had a patient like this before. "You really don't know, do you?"

Amanda shook her head, still barley able to grasp what was happening. "No, I don't. I left home at eighteen years of age. When I woke up from the coma I was twenty-four years old. The six years in between are the dead years. I have absolutely no knowledge of them."

Dr. Pittman could only imagine what Amanda was going through and had sympathy for her. "Well, Mrs. Tankersley, even if you don't remember, you still have a child out there somewhere. I can see that this has been a terrible shock for you. Is there anyone that I can call for you? Can I be of any help?"

Amanda just sat on the edge of the exam table still in shock. "Thank you doctor, but no. I just want to go now."

Dr. Pittman could see that even though Amanda had been shocked and distraught from the news, she could see no reason that she needed help if she didn't want it. She said, "Okay, you can get dressed now. Everything looks good." Dr. Pittman wrote out some prescriptions and handed them to Amanda, "Have these filled and take them. They're vitamins and other supplements."

Amanda took the prescriptions from Dr. Pitman. "Yes, and thank you doctor."

Dr. Pittman wanted to be reassuring to Amanda, to give her confidence. "Mrs. Tankersley, with my help you should get through this pregnancy just fine. As for your other problem, I'm sorry that I can't be of any help to you. You'll have to get help from someone else on that."

Amanda said, putting out her right hand, "Thank you, I'll manage somehow."

Dr. Pittman shook Amanda's hand. "I wish you luck. You can see the receptionist on your way out for your next appointment. And,

MICHAEL O. GREGORY

Mrs. Tankersley."

Amanda replied, "Yes doctor?"

With sincerity in her voice, Dr. Pittman said, "I can only imagine what you're going through. I wish you a happy resolution to your problem."

Amanda released Dr. Pittman's hand, and said, "Thank you doctor,"

Dr. Pittman left the room to let Amanda get dressed.

Amanda just had to get out of there. She got dressed as quickly as she could. She hurried to the receptionist and made her appointment. She had to get away from everyone; she needed to be alone. She got into her car in the parking lot, and started to put the key in the ignition. She shook so much from her pent up emotions that she couldn't get the key in the ignition. In frustration she started to cry uncontrollability. Great sobs racked her body as the tears flowed freely. It took several minutes before she could get herself under control enough to be able to start her car and leave the parking lot.

When Helen got home, Amanda stood in the parking lot waiting for her. She could see immediately that Amanda was distraught and had been crying. She immediately felt concern for Amanda. She hoped that nothing had gone wrong with the pregnancy, or with Amanda. She tried to get Amanda to tell her what had gone wrong, but Amanda didn't want to talk in the parking lot.

Helen invited Amanda in and they went to the kitchen. Amanda took a seat at the table as Helen put the coffee on. Helen then got Amanda a glass of orange juice, then sat down at the table across from her. Helen then said, "Do you want to talk about it now?"

Amanda started to cry. Helen became very concerned for her. There must be something terribly wrong for Amanda to be acting like this. Before she could ask, Amanda said, "Oh, I don't know what to do. I still can't believe it."

Helen moved around the table and put her arm around Amanda. "Now, tell me. What is it?"

Amanda could hardly bring herself to speak. "This isn't my

first time."

Helen was really perplexed and looked closely at Amanda. "What are you trying to say?"

When Amanda spoke again, it all came out at once. "I have another child."

This revelation took Helen by surprise. "You what?" It was as much of an exclamation as a question.

Amanda had her handkerchief out dabbing her eyes. She responded, "Well, Helen, during the examination Dr. Pittman told me that this wasn't my first pregnancy. That I've given birth before."

Helen left Amanda sitting at the table while she made herself a cup of coffee. She needed the time to assimilate Amanda's statement. Amanda could also use the time to get herself back under control. After Helen had her coffee, she sat back down at the table across from Amanda. She took a sip of coffee, then looked at Amanda. "Now, just what did Dr. Pittman say?"

Amanda dabbed her eyes again and looked at Helen. "She said that I've an episiotomy scar. What's that?"

Helen took a moment to recall what she had learned on the subject in nursing school before she spoke. "An episiotomy is an incision of the margin of the vulva. It's done just before the baby's head distends. It's done to prevent birth injuries. The obstetrician closes it after delivery."

Amanda looked at Helen. "Then there's no doubt that I've had a baby before? What should I do? How do I tell, Sam?"

Helen considered Amanda's questions for a few moments before she spoke. She knew Amanda's history, and the problems that she faced. "All right, now this baby had to be born sometime during those six lost years. Can you really do anything about it? We know nothing about those six lost years. If we can't do anything about it, do you really need to tell Sam?"

Helen's reasoning, although well intentioned, wasn't what Amanda had been looking for. "Oh, Helen, how could you even think of that? Out there somewhere is a part of me. I don't know if it's a boy or girl.

235

MICHAEL O. GREGORY

I don't know how old it is. I don't know where it was born, or where it is now, but this I do know. I must find it, so I have to tell Sam."

Helen thought that she knew why Amanda had reacted as she had. "Yes, I see you do. I guess that you owe it to, Amanda."

Amanda corrected Helen. "I'm, Amanda! It's my child!"

Helen just sat for a minute in thought while drinking her coffee. She came to the conclusion that Amanda had been right. It was her child, and she did have an obligation to do whatever she could to try to find her child. Helen nodded. "Okay, let's look at what we do know. When you left home at age eighteen you weren't pregnant. When we got you at age twenty-four you didn't seem to have recently given birth. So we can say that the child, whatever it is, is from two to six years of age. Now that's not much to go on."

Amanda had listened to Helen outline the futile effort of trying to find the child. When Helen had finished, Amanda said, "Yes, I know what you're saying, but I don't care. If there's any chance at all, I must take it. There's only one thing that I'm afraid of. I don't know how Sam will take it."

Despite her misgivings as to Amanda's chance of ever finding her child, Helen wanted to show support. She reached out and took Amanda's hand. "Yes, I understand what you must do. Would you like for me to be with you when you tell Sam?"

Amanda shook her head. "Thank you, but this is something that I must do myself. I just needed a sympathetic ear to dump on before I tell Sam."

Helen and Amanda talked for a few minutes more. They kicked the problem around, but couldn't come up with any worthwhile ideas. At least it did have the effect of calming Amanda down. Then, Amanda had to leave to be at home before Sam.

When Sam arrived home, Amanda met him at the door. Sam put down his briefcase, took her in his arms and kissed her. He could tell right away that Amanda was really nervous about something. He became very concerned. "Did something go wrong with the exam today?"

236

WOMAN IN THE MIRROR

Amanda reassured him that everything was well with her pregnancy. "Don't worry, Sam, there's nothing wrong with my baby. There is however something that we must talk about." Visibility now upset, Amanda took a seat on the sofa. Sam took a seat beside her. Amanda continued, "Sam, please don't be angry about what I'm going to tell you." Sam didn't know what to make of this. Amanda could hardly make the words come out. He started to speak, but she held up her hand as she continued, "During my examination today I learned from the doctor said that this isn't my first pregnancy." Sam again tried to speak, but she went on, "And that's not all. I've given birth before."

Sam had been taken completely by surprise. He tried to speak, but could only say, "What?" Sam was dumbfounded. He tried to speak again, but couldn't. Amanda started to cry.

Sam got up and paced the floor a couple of times. Amanda's revelation had overwhelmed him, and he needed time to think. He left the apartment, got into his car and drove off. He wasn't driving anywhere. He just drove aimlessly about as he thought of what Amanda had told him.

Two hours later Sam arrived back home. When he entered the apartment Amanda stood in the middle of the living room looking forlorn and vulnerable. Sam could see that she had been crying. He knew then that no matter what his love for her was absolute. When she spoke, it was with a pensive voice. "Oh, Sam, you have a right to be angry with me. I know that I have let you down. I deceived and shamed you."

Sam gently reached out and took her by the shoulders. Looking into her eyes, he said, "Just listen, and don't talk. I'm not angry with you. How can I be angry with someone who's a part of me? I was just taken by surprise. And how could you deceive me if you had no knowledge of the child."

Tears started to run down Amanda's cheeks, Sam took her in his arms and kissed her. He could feel her tremble under his touch. She had been physicality and mentality drained, and close to collapse. With a

237

MICHAEL O. GREGORY

motion of his head toward the sofa, Sam said, "Now, let's just sit here on the sofa, and you can me all about it."

They took a seat next to each other on the sofa. With a sigh, Amanda said, "Well, there's not much to say. It happened sometime between the time that I left home at eighteen, and the time that I woke up from the coma here in Atlanta. So I have a child between two to six years old, boy or girl unknown. I don't know where it was born, or where it is now. I only know that it exist."

Sam thought for a while. He knew that he had to do something to help her. "Okay, since there's almost no chance of ever finding this child; you didn't have to tell me about it. Why did you?"

Amanda appealed to Sam. "I know that it's almost impossible to find my child, but a part of me is out there somewhere. If I didn't try my best to find my child, what kind of a mother would I be? I must know. Oh, Sam, please help me."

Sam looked into Amanda's eyes and saw the determination there. He knew that she would do anything to succeed. "You know that I can't say no to you." Sam said to her, giving her a smile.

Amanda threw her arms around Sam's neck and started kissing him. "Oh, thank you, Sam."

Putting his arms around her, Sam said, "Okay, but we need a professional investigator. I know a really good one who has done some work for us before. I'll get in touch with her first thing in the morning. Now, have you had anything to eat since breakfast?" Amanda shook her head. He said, "It's too late to start cooking. Get your purse, and we'll go out for dinner." Amanda went to the bathroom to fix her make-up.

CHAPTER THIRTY-FOUR

Amanda pulled up in front of the office and parked in one of the empty parking spaces. She was right on time for her appointment with the private investigator. She got out of her car, took a bag from the back seat of the car and walked to the door. The sign on the door read.

IDA MAY WAMMOCK
Private Investigator
Confidential Discreet
Reasonable/Bonded

She knocked on the door and a woman's voice called out from within. "Come in!" Amanda opened the door and walked in.

A woman stood just inside the door waiting for her. The woman put out her right hand to Amanda. "Mrs. Tankersley, I'm Ida May Wammock. I've been expecting you."

Amanda shook hands with her. "Hello, I'm Mrs. Amanda Tankersley. Sam's told me a lot about you." Amanda noticed Ida's firm hand shake warm smile and friendly manner. Amanda warmed to her immediately.

"You don't mind if I call you Amanda? I'm Ida to all my friends, just call me Ida."

Amanda responded. "Okay, you can call me Amanda."

Ida's office had a large window in the front. On the right side as you walked in stood her desk, with two metal filling cabinets and

239

MICHAEL O. GREGORY

folding chairs. There was also a table in the corner with a television and a video player/recorder. On the left side of the room were a sofa, two easy chairs and a coffee table. Another door gave access to a back room that Amanda figured to be a utility room and lavatory. Ida looked to be in her early to mid-fifties, five foot six inches, with graying brown hair and brown eyes. in her present dress she had the look of a grandmother/homemaker type. Ida motioned to the sofa. "Please, Amanda, have a seat on the sofa. You can put the bag on the coffee table. Would you like a Coke?"

Amanda, turning to the sofa, said. "Yes, a Coke would be fine." Amanda took a seat on the sofa and put the overnight bag that she had been carrying on the coffee table.

Ida got two Cokes from a small refrigerator behind her desk and brought them to the coffee table. Ida said. "I hope that you don't mind diet soda?"

Amanda responded. "No, I don't mind."

Ida took her seat on the sofa and came right to the point. "I checked out Nashville and Columbia, South Carolina. The police had already checked them out. I had no better luck. Nashville and Columbia are dead ends."

Amanda had been sure that Nashville and Columbia would be dead ends. With a nod, Amanda replied. "Yes, I expected that. I don't think that I have ever lived in either of those two cities."

Ida pointed to the bag. "Is that everything that was with you when they found you in the motel room in Nashville?"

Amanda gave a little shrug of the shoulders as a show of regret, knowing that very little remained from what had been in the motel room. "Well, it's everything that I kept. Most of it I wouldn't be caught on the street in. Some of the things I wouldn't even wear in the privacy of my own bedroom."

Ida smiled, trying to imagine what Amanda referred to and gave a little chuckle. "Yes, I think I know what you mean. Tell me, just what did these items look like?"

240

WOMAN IN THE MIRROR

Amanda took a few seconds to recall everything that she had received after she had woken up after the surgery. "Let's see now, there were some very short skirts and dresses. Some in my opinion as to be indecent. There were some other revealing items like halter tops, low cut blouses that displayed my breasts that I felt uncomfortable with. Then there were some items that looked like costumes for an exotic dancer or a stripper. They were of bright color material covered with sequins and so brief that they barely covered the genitals. They were even scantier than a thong."

Ida noticed Amanda's discomfort at recalling these items. She wondered if these items had belonged to her at some time, then why she felt so uncomfortable about it now.

Ida opened the bag to inspect the contents. Inside she found a green wool knit sweater, a polyester knit navy blue cardigan sweater, a black leather belt, a blue denim skirt and a black leather coat. "Okay, let's see what we have here." Ida took the items out of the bag one at a time and examined them closely. The first sweater had come from Sears. It could have been purchased anywhere. The same for the cardigan sweater and the denim skirt. They both had labels that showed that they had come from J. C. Pennies. There would be no help from these items. The belt also proved to be useless. If there had even been a label on it, it would have been worn off by use. The leather coat turned out to be an expensive designer fashion with a store label from an exclusive fashion boutique in New Orleans. Ida held up the coat. "We have something here." Amanda looked at the coat. Ida pointed to the label. "Look at the label. This coat is from an exclusive shop in New Orleans."

Amanda looked at the label. "Yes, I see. Is that a good clue?"

Looking at Amanda, Ida answered. "Yes, it is. I believe that this will put us on the right track. I'm glad that you saved this coat. It's the only thing we have to go on."

Amanda looked again at the coat label, relieved that she had decided to keep it. "So, you think that it will lead us somewhere?"

Ida wanted to reassure Amanda. It was a slim lead, but it could

241

possibility lead somewhere. "I hope so. Of course, you could have gotten it at a secondhand shop or a yard sale anywhere, but I doubt it. I can't see anyone getting rid of such a fine coat that's still in an almost new condition.

"I have a contact in New Orleans. It's Mr. Hugh Desormeaux, he can do the leg work for us there. I have the photos that you gave me of yourself. I'll take some photos of the coat and its label. Then send the photos along with any other information that may be helpful to him. Maybe he can get lucky." Ida put everything except the coat back into the bag. "All I need to keep for now is the coat. I'll let you know as soon as I have something from Hugh."

Amanda and Ida got to their feet and shook hands. Ida spoke. "I'll keep in touch."

Amanda now started to feel good for the first time since she had found out that she already had a child. She now felt that her situation wasn't so hopeless. "Oh, thank you, Ida. I sincerely hope that this bears fruit."

Ida said, while escorting Amanda to the door. "Don't you worry now. If there is a trail, we'll pick it up."

After Amanda left for home, Ida got out her camera and flash unit. She then hung the coat against a light background and started to photograph it.

Hugh Desormeaux a former policeman had retired from the New Orleans Police department following a long carrier as a detective. He now worked as a private investigator in New Orleans. A heavy-set man of sixty-seven with thinning gray hair. With his open collar shirt, loose fitted trousers that bagged at the knees, scuffed loafers and sweat stained fedora he looked like a refugee from a retirement home. He had the flushed face of a bourbon drinker, but he still had the discipline not to touch it before noon.

He had been on this assignment for Ida May Wammack for four days now. The designer boutique had been of some help. The address had proved to be of no use, but at least he now had a name to go with

WOMAN IN THE MIRROR

the photo, Miss Victoria Bujold. The information about the stripper costumes suggested that she might have worked in the clubs. He got out of his car and went into the Lucky 7 Club. It was still early in the day, so the dancers were not working yet. He noticed five women who must be the club dancers relaxing at the bar. The bartenders were behind the bar getting ready for the evening crowd. He took Amanda's photo out and started to show it around. Everyone took a quick glance and denied knowing her. However, he felt sure that one of the girls, a tall platinum blonde with large breasts knew Victoria Bujold. He asked her again if she knew Victoria Bujold. She denied it again, but he now felt sure that she did.

A check of the rest of the clubs turned up nothing. He could find no police record or any other parish record of Victoria Bujold. He wrote up his report and sent it to Ida.

Sam and Amanda entered the office and were greeted by Ida. She motioned them to the sofa. Sam and Amanda took seats on the sofa. Ida then asked if they wanted a Coke. They both accepted her offer. Ida got a Coke from the refrigerator for everyone. She then took a seat in one of the easy chairs and opened a file folder that she had on the coffee table. "Now, here's the report from Hugh Desormeaux. He checked out the coat and it proved to be a limited item, very exclusive, so it wasn't too hard to match up to a sales receipt. The address on the sales receipt turned out to be a dead in. However, we now know that you, Amanda, were going by the name of Victoria Bujold."

Sam started to laugh. "Wow, you have had more names than the phone book."

Amanda gave Sam an elbow to the ribs. "Cut it out, Sam, be serious."

Stifling another laugh, Sam said. "Yes, Dear. Excuse me, Ida."

Ida also stifled a laugh, trying to keep a straight face at Sam's and Amanda's antics and continued. "Hugh also believes that you worked the clubs in New Orleans. He showed your picture around all the clubs and bars in and around New Orleans, but no one would admit to knowing you."

243

MICHAEL O. GREGORY

Amanda felt let down. She had been hoping that they would turn up something. Now it seemed to be just another dead end. "So, you are saying that New Orleans is another dead end."

Ida took a drink from her Coke and put the can back down on the coffee table before she answered Amanda. "No, Amanda, I'm not saying that. We still have a chance. In his report Hugh said that he found a woman that even though she denied it, he's sure that she knows you."

Amanda's mood suddenly brightened at the prospect. "Then why doesn't she say so?"

Ida had encountered the same problem before and knew the answer. "Well, people are suspicious of strangers coming around asking questions. She must be a friend of Victoria Bujold. She thinks that to say anything could get you in trouble."

Amanda thought for a few moments, then had an idea. "You say that she won't talk to strangers. I bet that she will talk to Victoria Bujold." She glanced at Ida and Sam, knowing what she had to do. "Sam, Ida, I must go to New Orleans to meet with her."

The idea of Amanda going to New Orleans didn't sit well with Sam. He had no problem having an investigator looking into it, but to have Amanda get directly involved made him feel uneasy. He got up and paced the room a couple of times. He felt protective towards her and wanted to shield her from any risk. He also knew that whatever he said, in the end, Amanda was a strong-willed person and would have her own way. He didn't like it, but he knew that Amanda was right. She had to go to New Orleans. "I don't like it, but you are right. It's the only way. You must go to New Orleans yourself. So, when do you want to leave?"

Amanda smiled, relieved that she would have her own way. She had known that as much as Sam would have wanted to object on the grounds that he didn't want her to take any risks, he wouldn't stand in her way. "Tomorrow, Ida, can you call Mr. Desormeaux and tell him that I'm coming."

Ida made a note to call Hugh Desormeaux. "Yes, I will. Call me

244

WOMAN IN THE MIRROR

as soon as you have your flight time. Then I can let him know when to expect you. Oh, by the way, the woman's name is Gloria Franklin. She works at the Lucky 7 Club."

Amanda's plane touched down at New Orleans international Airport at two-forty-eight PM. Amanda went first to a motel close to the airport to check in. She then took a taxi downtown to Dumaine Street in the French Quarter to the office of Mr. Hugh Desormeaux. She found Hugh waiting for her when she arrived. His office looked like a set from an old Sam Spade movie with two exceptions. He had a personal computer with a printer on his desk and a television with a video recorder/player on a table behind his desk. "Amanda said, while offering her hand. "Good-afternoon Mr. Desormeaux, I'm Mrs. Tankersley. I presume that you have been expecting me."

Hugh took Amanda's hand and shook it. "Yes, Mrs. Tankersley, I've been expecting you. We can go now. Miss. Franklin should be at the club by the time we get there."

Eager to get going, Amanda replied. "Okay, that's what I came for. Let's get going."

Hugh had one caution for Amanda before they left. "Mrs. Tankersley, I believe it best that you do not use your real name, just use Victoria Bujold."

Amanda nodded. "Okay, whatever you say."

They arrived at the Lucky 7 Club a little before six. They went into the club and sat at the bar. Amanda noticed a girl on the runway dancing, and asked Hugh if it could be Gloria Franklin. He shook his head, indicating that it wasn't Gloria. The bartender came over and took their order. Hugh ordered a bourbon on the rocks, and a Coke for Amand. After the bartender took the orders, Amanda motioned to the bartender. "Oh, bartender."

The bartender looked at her. "Yes, Ma'am."

Amanda replied. "Is Miss. Gloria franklin in now?"

In a disinterested manner, he said, not bothering to interrupt his work. "She may be, what do you want with her?"

245

MICHAEL O. GREGORY

Amanda spoke. "Would you please tell her that miss. Victoria Bujold would like to see her."

Hugh slipped the bartended a bill to make sure that they had his attention. The bartender stuck the bill in his pocket and nodded. "Okay, I'll see if she's in."

The bartender went back, knocked on the dressing room door and was admitted. The dressing room was a long-narrow room, with a long dressing table cluttered with make-up and other beauty items, with mirrors and lights on one wall, and metal lockers on the other wall. There were two other women in the room besides Gloria Franklin, sitting at the dressing table, or adjusting their costumes. The bartender indicated that it was Gloria that he wanted to talk to. Gloria was sitting in front of a mirror checking her make-up. The Bartender said. "Gloria, that old geezer that was here the other day with the photo. Well, he's back, and he has a lady with him. She wants to see you."

Gloria turned her head to look at him. "Well, does she have a name?"

At the mention of the name, Victoria Bujold, Gloria suddenly became interested. "About twenty-five, cute, black hair and green eyes."

The bartender nodded. "Yes, that's her."

"Bring her back now!" Gloria exclaimed.

The bartender went back out to the bar and brought Amanda back to the dressing room. As soon as Amanda entered the dressing room Gloria embraced her. "Oh, Vicki, it's so good to see you again. It's been a long time."

It became immediately obvious to Amanda that Gloria and Victoria had been close friends. She decided that it would be best to play on that friendship. She returned the greeting with equal affection. "Hi, Gloria, it's good to see you again too."

Gloria stepped back to look at Amanda. "I say, you've really changed."

Gloria spotted the rings on Amanda's finger. "Hay, you're married! What does he do?"

Amanda spoke. "He's an attorney."

'Wow!" Gloria exclaimed with enthusiasm. "You really have

WOMAN IN THE MIRROR

done well!"

Amanda's tone got serious. "Gloria, do you have the time? I must talk with you."

Gloria took Amanda to the back of the room away from the other women where there were a couple of chairs. When they were seated, Gloria said. "Okay, now what's on your mind?"

Amanda leaned forward in her chair, so that she could speak with ease without being overheard by the other women. "Well, Gloria, I need to tell you a story first."

Gloria wondered what her friend had to say. "Okay, go ahead."

Amanda cleared her throat nervously, then began. "March of last year I awoke from a coma. I beat the odds. The doctors didn't expect me to wake-up ever."

Gloria had a concerned look on her face. "Oh, I hope that you are all right now."

Amanda assured Gloria that she had recovered. She then started to tell her the rest of the story. "Well, I do have amnesia. It's complete and permanent."

Gloria took her hand with a show of concern on her face. "Oh, I'm sorry to hear that." It hadn't dawned on her yet that if Vicki had amnesia, then how did she get here.

Amanda wondered how Gloria would react to her next statement. "Thanks, Gloria. To be truthful with you, I've no memory of you or New Orleans, or anything before March of last year."

Gloria regarded Amanda with wonder. "You don't remember me? Then how did you get here?"

Amanda now told Gloria how they found her. "I have a coat that had been purchased here in New Orleans. From the boutique my man got the name Victoria Bujold. Mr. Desormeaux took my photo around asking if anyone knew me. He found you."

Gloria recalled the old man with the photo from the other day. "So, he's your man. I guess that I should have said something sooner, but I didn't want to cause you any trouble."

247

MICHAEL O. GREGORY

Amanda now gave Gloria more information about herself without revealing her identity, or where she lived. "Yes, he's, my man. I've also found my parents and family. I've filled in my life up to the age of eighteen when I left home. I was twenty-four when I woke up from the coma. As you can see, I have six blank years. I call them the lost years. I got married in January and am now expecting."

Gloria let out a squeal of delight and hugged Amanda. "Oh, that's great, congratulations!"

Amanda smiled at Gloria's best wishes. "Thank you, Gloria, there's more. When I went for my first appointment with my gynecologist, she told me that this wasn't my first pregnancy, and that I had given birth before. Gloria, I have a child that I can't remember. I don't know what sex it is, its age, where it was born, where it is now, or how it's doing. I need help."

Gloria had been on the edge of her chair listening to Amanda's story. She now sat back in her chair regarding Amanda with a look of caring on her face. "I say, you do need help. What can I do?"

With a pleading look, Amanda said. "I need to know what happened to me while I was here in New Orleans. But first, did I have a baby with me, or did I give birth while I was here?"

Gloria shook her head. "No, you had no baby while you were here."

Amanda now at least knew that the child had been born some place other than New Orleans. "Okay, then can you tell me what happened while I was here?"

Gloria took some time to try to recall what had happened when she and Vicki had worked together before. "I'll try. We were working at another club together then, the Buccaneer. You were a good dancer." Amanda smiled at the compliment; Gloria continued. "You were a free spirit, but not into drugs or prostitution like some girls. However, you did like men. You were a sucker for every good-looking man with a smooth line. You told me that you had come from Dallas, but that was only your word on it. You were here for about five or six months. During that time, you met a man."

WOMAN IN THE MIRROR

At the mention of a Man Amanda's interest piqued. "I did, tell me about him."

Gloria tried her best to recall the man. "He was an older man about twenty-nine or thirty at the time. A real smart dresser, with lots of money. You fell for him right off."

Amanda was anxious to hear more about this man. "Well, what happened then?"

Gloria continued. "You left New Orleans with him."

Amanda just had to know where they had gone. "Do you know where to?"

Gloria put her index finger to the side of her head as she thought. "Let's see now, oh yes, Kentucky. I remember thinking at the time what can a person do in Kentucky to make so much money."

Amanda just had to know more. "Gloria, do you know where in Kentucky?"

Gloria thought for a few moments. "I believe that the name of the city started with an 'L'. that's all that I can remember."

Amanda tried to think of cities in Kentucky that started with an 'L'. "Please think, was it Louisville?"

Gloria shook her head. "No."

Amanda thought for a moment more. "Let's see now, Lexington, was it Lexington?"

Gloria thought for a moment. "Yes, that's it! It was Lexington!"

Amanda hugged Gloria. 'Oh, thank you, Gloria. Now, one more question. Do you know his name?"

Gloria thought. "It's hard to remember. I believe that the first name was a regular American name. The last name was Spanish, but he didn't look much like a Latin. Now the first name I draw a blank. The last name started with a 'Z'. Oh, let's see, Zerilli or Zamora, something like that. Is that of any help to you?"

Amanda was really thrilled. She now had a name and a place. "Now, how long ago was it that I left?"

Gloria replied. "I would say six, no, six and a half years ago now."

249

MICHAEL O. GREGORY

They talked for a few minutes more. Gloria then took her turn at dancing. Hugh took Amanda back to the motel. The next morning Amanda flew back to Atlanta.

CHAPTER THIRTY-FIVE

Amanda had called Sam to give him her arrival time. Sam had come to the airport to pick her up. When Amanda appeared they embraced and kissed. "How was your trip?" Sam asked. Amanda having gathered useful information in New Orleans, was eager to tell Sam about her trip. "Very fruitful. I learned a lot from Gloria."

Sam still holding Amanda in a loose embrace said. "Good, now let's get out of here first. We can talk later." Sam picked up Amanda's carry-on bag, and they walked to the bus stop to wait for the parking lot shuttle bus.

After getting their car from the parking lot, and getting on the road, they felt free to talk. Sam said, "What did you find out?"

Amanda looked at Sam. "Not everything, but a lot more than we knew before. Gloria proved to be very helpful. She told me that I had lived and worked in New Orleans for about six or seven months. That I had met, and later on left New Orleans with a man about thirty years old. She didn't remember his given name, but he had a Spanish surname. Something like, Zorrilla, or Zamora. She also told me that I had no child in New Orleans."

Sam, not wanting to take his eyes off the road, just nodded. "That's good. We have something to work with now."

Amanda was eager to relate the information to Ida, "I can hardly wait to relate what I found out to Ida

Sam patted her gently on the thigh smiling. "Well, you don't have

251

MICHAEL O. GREGORY

to wait for very long. I told her when you were getting in. She said to bring you over from the airport."

Ida had been waiting for them when they arrived at her office. She greeted Sam and Amanda as they entered the office, and had them take a seat on the sofa. Ida served Cokes, then took a seat in one of the easy chairs. Ida then had Amanda relate everything that she had learned from Gloria to her as she took notes. When Amanda had finished her report, Ida sat back in her chair, and gave a nod of approval. "You did really good Amanda. We now have something to work with. We now know where to look, and who to look for."

Amanda had been impatient to know what they were to do next. "What are you going to do now?"

Ida knew that Amanda would be impatient to find her child, and would want results. If she were in her place she would most likely feel the same, she said, "First off, we can make some inquires on the internet. I can check birth records of the counties in and around Lexington for a birth certificate with the name of Victoria Bujold as the birth mother. If I can't find anything on the internet, we get an investigator in Lexington to look for us."

Curious as to what Ida would do next, Amanda said, "What if you find a birth certificate?"

Ida replied, "If I find a birth certificate, then I can go up there, and follow up on my own."

Amanda knew what she had to do and turned to Sam. "Sam, If Ida goes to Lexington, I want to go with her."

Sam wasn't sure if Amanda should be running around the country like this. "I don't know. Ida can do her job without our help."

Amanda wouldn't be put off. She wanted to have her child back as soon as possible, and intended to go to Lexington with Ida. "But I need to go! What if there's someone who will only talk to me. Oh, Sam, I must go."

Sam objected to Amanda getting so involved in the investigation, and had been prepared to argue it with her, but he saw the look in

WOMAN IN THE MIRROR

her eyes, and knew that it would be one argument that he couldn't win. He knew that it wouldn't do any good to say no to Amanda. She would have her own way anyway. Looking at Ida, Sam said, "Ida, do you mind if Amanda comes along?"

It was outside of normal procedure, but Ida would allow it. "No, I don't mind, as long as she follows instructions. Can you do that Amanda?"

With a smile of satisfaction, Amanda nodded, "Yes I can. Whatever you say."

With everything settled, Ida said, "Okay, if I have to go to Lexington you can come with me. Now that should be all for now. I'll get to work on this, and let you know what I come up with." As Sam and Amanda started to get up to go, Ida said, "I should have something by tomorrow I'll give you a call."

Sam and Amanda said good-bye, then left the office. They got into their car and started home. After they were on the road, Amanda looked at Sam, "Are you disappointed in me for what you're finding out?"

Sam glanced at her, giving her a reassuring smile. "No, not disappointed, just surprised that you could be as completely different then as you are now. It's like we're finding out about a whole different person. You're the Amanda that I love and married, and I still love you."

Amanda put her hand on Sam's arm. She knew that she was indeed fortunate that she had such an understanding and supportive man as Sam. "Thank you, Sam. I seem to be needing a lot of reassurance these days."

Sam changed the subject. "Do you want to eat out tonight?"

At the mention of eating out, Amanda had an idea. "Yes, I feel like going where we first met, Captain D's"

Sam, recalling the awkwardness of their first meeting, had to laugh at how embarrassed he had been afterwards at his behavior. "Okay, then Captain D's it is. I'll be home from work about six. Be ready to go." Sam drove Amanda home, then went on to the office.

When Amanda got home from work the next day, she checked

253

MICHAEL O. GREGORY

the messages on her answering machine, and found a message to call Ida. Amanda picked up the phone and called Ida's number. Ida soon answered. "Good-afternoon, Wammock investigations."

"Ida, this is Amanda."

"Yes, Amanda, I've got news for you. Are you sitting down?"

"Yes, go ahead." Amanda said, noticing a certain cheerfulness in Ida's voice.

"I found a birth certificate in Fayette County, Kentucky, that's Lexington. The birth mother is listed as Victoria Bujold, age twenty years. The Child's name is Cheryl Bujold. Amanda, the age of the mother matches the age that you would've been at that time. Everything matches up. This must be you. Your daughter was five years old the ninth of January this year." After hearing this, Amanda had to sit down. Ida continued, "That's not all. The father is listed as unknown, but there's an address for the birth mother."

Amanda's eyes were brimming with tears of joy. She had a daughter. Questions about her were running through her head. How is she doing? Is she being well cared for? What does she look like? She had to know more. "Oh, thank you, Ida, this is really wonderful news. Are you going to Lexington now?"

"Yes, I'm leaving in the morning."

Amanda now knew for certain that she just had to go to Lexington with Ida. She had a daughter that she had to find. "I still want to come along."

"All right, I'll make reservations with the airline, then get back with you. You need to pack a carry-on, for say, two or three days. Keep in mind that it's colder in Lexington, than here in Atlanta."

"Okay, I'll do that, and Ida, thank you."

When Sam got home, Amanda stood at the door waiting for him as usual. As soon as he came through the door, she had her arms around his neck kissing him. She had been waiting for him to get home to give him the news. When finally she broke her embrace, she said, "Ida called. She had information from Lexington."

Sam dropped his briefcase down next to the door, and focused his full attention on Amanda. She literally beamed with excitement. He said, "This must be really good news. I can see it in your face." Sam now held Amanda with one arm around her waist in a loose embrace. He could feel the quiver of excitement from her, through his arm.

Amanda couldn't hold the good news in another second. "Sam, I have a daughter! She's five years old. Her name is Cheryl Bujold. There's no father listed. There's an address for the birth mother in Lexington. That's all that we know for now."

Sam was thrilled for Amanda's sake. He gathered her closer to him, and kissed her again ardently. When the embrace had ended, Sam said, "That's great, I'm really happy for you. It's not just an unknown anymore, it's a girl. You have a daughter." It pleased, Sam, that Amanda now had some information on her daughter. She hadn't been able to think of anything else but her lost child since the appointment with the gynecologist.

Amanda relaxed, and leaned into Sam's shoulder. "Yes, but I still don't know what she looks like, or where she is. Ida is going to Lexington to check out an address that's on the birth certificate. I'm going with her as planned. We'll be leaving tomorrow morning."

Sam still had misgivings about Amanda getting so directly involved in the search. He wished that she would stay home and let Ida do her job, but he also knew that it would be impossible to talk her out of it. He would just have to support her as much as he could, and do his best to protect her. With a nod, he said, "All right, I'll drive the both of you to the airport, and pick you up when you get back. About how long will you and Ida be gone?"

Knowing that Ida had told her to pack for two to three days, Amanda said, "About three days." Amanda, still in Sam's embrace, again put her arms around his neck. "I want you to know that I know a lot of this has been unpleasant for you. I'm truly sorry if I hurt you, and I thank you for being so understanding."

Sam looked into Amanda's eyes, and could see the plea for

MICHAEL O. GREGORY

understanding. Loving her as much as he did, he was determined to do everything that he could to help her get her daughter back. "We took a vow for better, or for worse. That means that we support each other no matter what. Besides, the past is gone. We can only take credit for it, or apologize for it, we can't change it. So the only thing that we have is the now, and the future."

Sam and Amanda got to Ida's office early the next morning, and found Ida waiting for them. On seeing Ida, Amanda had been amazed that she no longer had that grandmother/homemaker look. She had changed her hairdo and make-up, and had gotten rid of the bulky clothing that had made her look heavy. In its place she wore a navy-blue pin-stripe suit of skirt and jacket, peach color silk blouse, black pumps and black purse. She now had that business executive look. She also had a figure that Amanda had failed to notice before. A fullness and beauty of form that in a snug evening dress, could still turn heads. Ida seemed to be able to change her appearance at will, like a chameleon. She seemed to be able to be anyone that she wanted to be. Amanda wouldn't be surprised that if needed, Ida had a nurse's uniform and a nun's habit in her closet. She had proved to be an amazing woman.

Ida and Amanda took an early flight out of Hartsfield-Jackson International, arriving at Lexington at 9:20 AM. They went to the National car rental to pick up their car. They made sure that it had a GPS navigating system. Next they checked in at Motel 6. First they got settled into their motel room. Next they went to the Department of Vital Statistics for a notarized copy of Cheryl's birth certificate.

They drove out to the address listed on the birth certificate. During the drive Amanda wondered what they would find. Would they find Cheryl there? If not, would they find someone there to tell her where she could find Cheryl? Would she and Ida be welcome there? The closer they got the more nervous and jittery Amanda became, in anticipation of what they would find.

When they found the address it turned out to be a large Colonial-style two-story home of white brick, with six large fluted columns on

WOMAN IN THE MIRROR

the front. The house sat on about four to five acres. A high chain-link fence ran around the sides and back, with a wrought-iron fence and gate across the front. The property turned out to be vacant, with a for-sale sign in front.

They were sitting in the car, in front of the house. Amanda looked at Ida. "What do we do now?"

Ida could see the disappointment in Amanda's face, and understood her anxiety, "This is just a minor setback. I'll take the agents phone number. We'll then start by going next door."

Next door turned out to be a large Tudor-style two-story home on a large tract of land, with a brick wall and wrought-iron gate. They were admitted through the front gate to the front door. Ida rang the doorbell. A middle-aged black woman in a maid's uniform answered the door. "May I ask who is calling?" The woman got a good look at Amanda. Before Ida could answer, there was a spark of recognition by the maid, and a quick intake of breath. "Oh my God, it's you!" The maid said, pointing at Amanda, "You're the woman who used to live next door!" The woman kept carrying on excitedly about Amanda, "Oh my God, it's really you! We all thought that you were dead!"

Amanda and Ida wondered what had happened in the house next door to get such a response from this woman. Ida interrupted, "Excuse me. Is there anyone home? We're here on important business." Ida handed the woman her card.

The woman regained her composer and accepted the card, "Please excuse me. You may come in, and have a seat in the hall. I'll see if Mrs. Mitchell will see you."

Ida and Amanda entered the home, and took a seat on chairs in the hallway. The maid disappeared into the interior of the house. While the maid was gone, Ida and Amanda speculated about the reason for the maid's behavior. They also wondered what had gone on in the house next door, and why Amanda, or as she was known then as Victoria, had left without her daughter.

Five minutes later the maid returned. "Please come with me. Mrs.

257

MICHAEL O. GREGORY

Mitchell will see you now."

The maid led them back to a small library, with dark paneling, shelves filled with books and a single window. The room had been well furnished with light-blue leather-upholstered chairs and lamp tables. Mrs. Mitchell was a woman of small stature, but someone who commanded respect. She looked to be of about sixty years, with gray hair and hazel eyes. She wore a light-green dress and a single strand of pearls. She sat in one of the chairs holding Ida's card in front of her. "Please have a seat. My maid will bring us some coffee and shortbread." Ida and Amanda took chairs facing Mrs. Mitchell. Mrs. Mitchell looked at Ida. "Now, you are, Ms. Ida Mae Wammock private investigator?"

Ida nodded. "Yes, I am."

Mrs. Mitchell looked at Amanda. "And you are?"

Amanda responded, "I'm Mrs. Amanda Tankersley of Atlanta, Georgia."

Mrs. Mitchell continued to look at Amanda, studying her features, "My maid tells me that you're the woman who used to live next door. You do look a lot like her."

Amanda judged the character of Mrs. Mitchell, and knew that the truth, no matter how strange it seemed, would be the best. With a nod, Amanda replied, "Yes, I am that woman. At least I'm almost certain that I am."

Mrs. Mitchell had a somewhat puzzled look on her face. She had noticed the odd statement and wondered what Amanda had been trying to say. "And what do you mean by that Mrs. Tankersley?"

Amanda could tell that Mrs. Mitchell would want to hear everything. "Well, if you have time, it's a long story."

Mrs. Mitchell sat back in her chair and got comfortable. "I have as much time as you need. Please begin."

Amanda started to tell her story. The maid came in with a tray of coffee and shortbread, then left. After Mrs. Mitchell had served the coffee and shortbread, Amanda continued to tell her story. Mrs. Mitchell would ask a question from time to time, but mostly she just

WOMAN IN THE MIRROR

sat back in her chair and listened. When Amanda had finished, she sat back in her chair and watched for Mrs. Mitchell's reaction.

Mrs. Mitchell had been touched by Amanda's story, and wanted as much as she could to help her. "I say Mrs. Tankersley, that's a most incredible and tragic story. I want to help you as much as I can. What can I do for you?"

Ida said, "We do have some questions. First, the house next door, who was living there?"

After all the excitement and scandal, Mrs. Mitchell, or anyone else in the neighborhood, had no problem recalling who had lived in the house in question, "That was Mr. David Zamora, and other people from time to time, mostly men."

As Mrs. Mitchell spoke, Ida had her notebook out, and had started to take notes. She asked, "When did they move out?"

Mrs. Mitchell thought for a moment, mentality counting the time back to when the people next door had moved out. "They moved out seven months ago. After they moved out, we had some federal agents come around. You know, the FBI and those drug people. It appears that they were looking for him to arrest him.

Ida said, referring to the other agency that Mrs. Mitchell had referred to. "You mean the DEA?"

Mrs. Mitchell snapped her fingers, and pointed to Ida. "Yes, that's it. They were looking for Mr. Zamora."

Ida looked at Amanda before she went on. She had begun to get a bad feeling about this. Ida said, "Do you know where they went?"

Mrs. Mitchell shook her head. "No, I don't have any idea."

Ida made a note about the FBI and DEA being after David Zamora. Looking back at Mrs. Mitchell, she said, "What about the domestic help?"

Mrs. Mitchell said, "They're all gone, found new employment. My maid knew their cook. That may be of some help." Mrs. Mitchell pressed a button and the maid entered the room.

"Yes, Ma'am." The maid said.

259

MICHAEL O. GREGORY

Mrs. Mitchell said, "Betty, you knew the cook who used to work next door?"

The maid nodded. "Yes, Ma'am."

Mrs. Mitchell asked, "What was her name?"

The maid replied, "Her names Roberta Johnson, Ma'am."

Mrs. Mitchell now asked, "Do you know where she lives or works now?"

The maid shook her head. "No, Ma'am, I don't."

Mrs. Mitchell asked, "Do you know anyone else who worked there?"

The maid shook her head again. "No, Ma'am."

Mrs. Mitchell said, "Thank you, Betty, that's all." The maid turned and left the room. Mrs. Mitchell turned to. Ida. "Is that of any help to you?"

Taking more notes, Ida said, "Oh, yes, you can get a lot with a name. If she's still working in this area we may be able to locate her."

Mrs. Mitchell felt apologetic that she didn't have more to give to Amanda. "I'm sorry that I couldn't give you more help than I did."

Ida was pleased with the information that they had received from Mrs. Mitchell. "Thank you, Mrs. Mitchell, you've been a great help to us."

Ida and Amanda got up to leave. Before they left, Mrs. Mitchell wrote her address and phone number on the back of Ida's card, and handed it to Amanda. "Mrs. Tankersley, I would really like to know if you get your daughter back. Please write and let me know."

Amanda looked at Mrs. Mitchell. "Okay, I'll write and let you know." Mrs. Mitchell rang for the maid to show them out.

Ida and Amanda called at two other nearby homes, but could get mothing more than they had already gotten from Mrs. Mitchell. They then went to lunch at McDonald's. After lunch they called the Reality Company, then went to see the agent. Ida and Amanda found out that the house was owned by an offshore holding company.

They then returned to the motel. They started to call all the Johnson's in the phone book. They were not able to find Roberta

260

WOMAN IN THE MIRROR

Johnson the first day.

The next morning after breakfast, they started calling the numbers that had not answered the day before. On the forth call they got Roberta's family. Her family gave them Roberta's work number. Roberta had taken employment as a live-in cook for a family in Frankfort. She could see them after one that afternoon.

After lunch they drove to Frankfort, and located the house where Roberta worked. It was a large Georgian-style of red brick, with down-stairs wings on each side. It sat well back from the road, with a privacy hedge, and brick driveway. They rang the front doorbell. A maid answered and directed them to the rear entrance. At the rear entrance, Ida rang the doorbell. A black woman of about fifty years answered the door. As soon as she saw Amanda, she recognized her. "Vicki!" She exclaimed as she hugged Amanda around the neck, "Oh, Vicki, it's so good to see you. I thought that I'd never see you again." After the embrace had been broken, Roberta stepped back and held the door open, "Please, come in."

Roberta took them into the kitchen, and seated them at the table. She then said, "Oh, Vicki, after that terrible night, I thought that I would never see you again. I worried so much about you. What happened?"

Amanda told her story again to Roberta. She left out details such as where she had been found, where she now lived, or her real name. Ida felt that they should start using more caution. "Well, Roberta, that's the story. I'm trying to find Cheryl, and I need your help."

Roberta looked at Amanda with sympathy. "You know that I will help you all I can, but I don't know how much it can help you. Mr. Zamora, he's an evil man. The night that he threw you out, he threatened to kill you if you ever came back."

Amanda had to know what happened. "Roberta, please, tell me what happened."

Roberta nodded. "Okay, I'll try to make it brief. When he first brought you home you were really in love with him. He can be a very charming man when he wants to be. Well, anyway, the romance lasted

261

MICHAEL O. GREGORY

for a while, then you got pregnant. He wasn't interested in a child at the time, especially after you found out that it wouldn't be a boy, but a girl. He wanted you to get an abortion, but you wouldn't. He started to lose interest in you. When the child was born, he kept you and Cheryl on. He didn't care much about Cheryl, since she was just a girl. You wanted to take Cheryl and leave, but he wouldn't let you. You and Cheryl were like property to him. He wanted to keep you there so that he could make your life miserable for defying him. He let you have credit cards, but no cash. If you went out Cheryl had to stay home. If you had to take her anywhere, one of his men would take you, and bring you back home. You wanted to leave, so I helped you to hide away some cash. I even skimmed the grocery accounts to help you.

"The evening that you chose to leave they were out. You packed a bag for Cheryl, and one for yourself. You had the use of one of the cars, and were going to take it. Just as you were leaving they came back. They blocked you in the driveway. I watched from the house. Mr. Zamora flew into a rage. You had the doors of your car locked. He broke the window, and yanked the door open. He dragged you from the car by your hair, down the driveway, and out the gate. It was cold and raining, and you and Cheryl were crying. The whole time he shouted curses at you. He called you a bitch, a whoring slut, and many other vile things. He then had Cheryl taken back to the house. He took your wallet with your driver's license and credit cards from your purse. He then threw your purse and suitcase out the front gate. He said, 'You came to me with nothing. You leave with nothing'. He took his gun out, and fired a shot over your head. He then put the gun to the back of your head and said, 'If I ever see you back here again, the next bullet is going here'. He then closed and locked the gate, with you outside in the rain. We never saw you again after that."

Roberta's story had been very emotional and sad for Amanda. It had also started to answer questions that had been with her since she had woke up from the surgery. She now began to understand why the old Amanda had been in the motel room in a coma. When Roberta

262

WOMAN IN THE MIRROR

had finished, Amanda asked, "What about Cheryl?"

Roberta said, "He still has her with him."

Amanda looked imploringly at Roberta, "Where did they go? I just have to know!"

Roberta took a moment to recall what she had overheard from David Zamora's conversations. "They were trying to keep it a secret, but I did overhear two of his men talking about a place in Mexico. A Caz something or the other."

Amanda and Ida thought for a while, then Ida had an idea. "Was it, Cozumel?"

Roberta thought for a moment, then nodded. "Yes, that's it. That's where they said that they were going."

Amanda reached out and took Roberta's hand. "Oh, thank you, Roberta! Now I know where to look for her."

Roberta said, "Vicki."

Amanda replied, "Yes, Roberta?"

Roberta's demeanor became serious as she looked into Amanda's eyes, "Mr. Zamora is an evil man. If you try to get Cheryl back and he catches you, he will kill you."

Amanda was moved by Roberta's concern for her. "Thank you, Roberta. Now tell me, what does Cheryl look like?"

Roberta smiled, as she patted Amanda on the forearm. "I'll do better than that. I'll show you." Roberta went back to her room, and returned with a photo album. She looked through the album, then took out two photos, and handed them to, Amanda. "Here's one is of Cheryl on her forth birthday, just weeks before you left. The other is of you and Cheryl in the garden."

Amanda took the photos from Roberta as if they were precious treasures. "Oh, thank you, Roberta." She looked at the photos. One showed Cheryl at her birthday party, with cake and ice cream all over her face and bib. She had long-black hair and green eyes just like Amanda's. The second photo showed, Amanda and Cheryl in the garden, with Cheryl holding a bunch of blue irises in her arms. Amanda fell instantly

263

MICHAEL O. GREGORY

in love with her. Her heart ached to hold Cheryl in her arms.

Roberta noticed how Amanda regarded the photos and said, "You can keep them if you want."

Amanda was overjoyed. "Oh, thank you very much Roberta. You don't know how much this means to me. I love them." Amanda continued to look at the photos.

Ida questioned Roberta, "About David Zamora, do you have a photo of him?"

Roberta shook her head. "No, I don't, Mr. Zamora doesn't like cameras."

Ida suspected that David Zamora, being in the business that he was in, wouldn't want his photo taken. "Then you can tell me how he looks."

Roberta took a moment to get her facts together. "Yes, he's about five-foot ten-inch tall, black hair, dark-brown eyes, with dark complexion and about one-hundred seventy pounds. He has an athletic build, slender face and a little mustache. He's a very sharp dresser. His father was half Mexican and his mother Anglo."

Ida, writing everything down, said, "That helps. Is there anything else that you want to add?"

Roberta said, "Yes, he's a very charming man most of the time, but he's truly evil."

Ida talked to Roberta for a while longer to learn as much as she could about David Zamora. Ida and Amanda said their good-byes, and started back to Lexington. Amanda had become depressed. Being the kind of person that David Zamora was, she didn't know what they could do next. She hadn't expected to run into difficulties like this. For a few minute she just looked at Cheryl's photos and thought. *Is this all that I will ever have of Cheryl, just a couple of photos. Who is this David Zamora? Can I ever get Cheryl back from him? Oh, Amanda, what did you get yourself into?* Amanda finally spoke, "What do we do now Ida?"

Ida glanced quickly in Amanda's direction as she drove, "Now listed to me. We've learned a lot. We now know where to look for Cheryl.

264

However, this is as far as I can go on my own. Fortunately I know just the man to help you."

Amanda gave a questioning look at Ida, "What are you telling me?"

"What I'm saying is that you need more than just an investigator. You need a mercenary. As I said, I know a man. He's retired from the army, and lives in Columbus, Georgia, just outside of Fort Benning. He has an investigation and security company, and he also accepts special jobs from time to time. One other thing."

"Yes." Amanda replied.

"From now on we must be careful to cover our tracks."

On the way back, Ida called the airline to make reservations for the return flight to Atlanta. When they got to the motel, they packed their bags, checked out and headed to the airport. At the airport they called, Sam to let him know their flight number and arrival time. When they arrived in Atlanta, Sam was waiting for them.

When Ida got back home, she put on coffee and changed. She then went to the freezer, got out a meal of Budget Grommet Swedish meatballs, and put them in the microwave. She then went to the hall closet, and took out a card file box. After she was at the table with her coffee and Swedish meatballs, she opened the box and removed a business card and read it.

PATRICK J. FITZGERALD
Command Sergeant Major
United States Army Retired

She picked up the phone and dialed the number.

CHAPTER THIRTY-SIX

Two days later Amanda got a call from Ida. She wanted to see her and Sam in her office at two in the afternoon. Sam had to be in court so Amanda made the appointment on her own. When Amanda entered Ida's office, she found Ida sitting on the sofa with a man talking. They both stood when Amanda entered the office. The man looked to be in his mid-fifties, six- foot three-inch tall, two-hundred thirty pounds, short-cut gray hair and blue eyes. He wore a light-weight navy-blue blazer, white shirt, dark-gray trousers, black oxford shoes and red and blue striped tie. On his lapel were three pins. A silver with blue enamel miniature Combat Infantryman's Badge, a silver miniature Parachutist Badge and a red white and blue enamel Silver Star pin. Ida said, "Amanda, this is Sergeant Major Patrick Fitzgerald, United States Army Retired. Pat, this is Mrs. Amanda Tankersley."

Patrick offered his hand and Amanda took it. He had a firm, but not too hard a handshake, a pleasant smile and deep-blue eyes that seemed to look into her very soul. He projected a feeling of authority and confidence. There was a commanding presence about him, and a harness that she felt as much as seen. As they shook hands, Patrick said, "It's a pleasure to meet you Mrs. Tankersley. Everyone calls me Pat. You may call me, Pat"

Amanda said, "It's a pleasure to meet you Pat. You may call me Amanda."

Ida had Amanda and Patrick sit down. She then asked if they wanted a Coke. Amanda and Patrick said yes. Ida got three cans of

WOMAN IN THE MIRROR

Coke from the refrigerator and put them on the coffee table, then sat on the sofa next to Patrick, and said, "Amanda, Pat's here to help you, but before I turn it over to him, I have some information for you. I did some checking on David Zamora. The reason for his departure is that there's a federal arrest warrant out for him for drug trafficking. He had fled to Mexico to avoid arrest. Although he's now in Mexico, he still controls a large drug trafficking organization here in the United States. The government would like to get him in Mexico, but that's easier said than done. He isn't just a dangerous man, he can be lethal. If you do something to deliberately provoke him, he will definitely come looking for you. I just wanted you to know this before we went any farther."

Amanda found this information disconcerting, but she had no choice. She was a mother, and as a mother she was bound by the responsibility to do whatever she had to do to get Cheryl back. Nodding, she said, "Okay, I understand that there can be danger for me, but I still want to find Cheryl."

Ida had gotten to know Amanda well since she had started to work on her case, and knew that she wouldn't back down. "All right then. Pat, you have the floor." Having made her statement, Ida sat back in the sofa.

Patrick took a drink of Coke, put the can on the coffee table, then faced Amanda, "Okay, Amanda, Ida brought me up to speed on what has happened so far. Now what you would like me to do is to find your daughter in Mexico. Is this right?"

Amanda nodded in the affirmative. "Yes, that's what I'd like for you to do, to locate Cheryl for me."

Patrick continued, "After I find her, if I can, then what?" Patrick looked closely at Amanda to gage her response. A lot would depend on her resolve. If she had any doubts or insincerity he had to know about it now.

Amanda responded with firm determination. "I want my daughter back!"

Patrick could hear the passion in her voice, and see the determination

267

MICHAEL O. GREGORY

in her expression and posture. "You know what this means? We can't just knock on the door and ask for her back. We'll have to kidnap her and bring her back."

Amanda had expected that it might take something as drastic as that. If that were what it would take, then she would be willing, "Yes, I know. Even if it comes to that, I still want my daughter back."

Patrick, still looking hard at Amanda, said, "And do you know that even though you're the only parent on record, down there it means nothing?"

Amanda shook her head. "Okay, so I didn't know that."

Patrick wanted to gage Amanda's response. He wanted to know if she would be willing to put herself in jeopardy for her child. "Do you know that an enterprise like this will involve some personal risk?"

Amanda didn't hesitate, and her expression didn't change, "Yes, I do."

Patrick looked straight into Amanda's eyes to see if there would be any vacillation. "How willing are you to put yourself in harm's way to get your daughter back?"

Amanda didn't hesitate. She looked straight back into Patrick's eyes with an unflagging will. "I will willingly do whatever I must to get my daughter back."

Patrick probed the depths of Amanda's eyes, and studied her expression. He could see her resolve. He felt that she would be willing to take any risk for the sake of her daughter. He sat back smiling and slapped his hands on his knees. "Okay, I'll help you to get your daughter back."

Amanda's feeling of anxiety drained away, to be replaced by a feeling of relief. She reached out and put her hand on Patrick's hand. "Oh, thank you, Pat. I do need your help." She then sat back in her chair and tried to relax a little.

Patrick now lost some of his formality and became more congenial. "Now, Ida tells me that you have two photos of your daughter."

Amanda smiled at the thought of the two photos of Cheryl in her purse. "Yes, I do." Amanda took the two photos from her purse, and

268

handed them to Patrick.

Patrick took a pair of gold wire-rimmed glasses from the inside coat pocket, and put them on to look at the photos. He looked at both of them, then chose the one with Amanda and Cheryl, "Ida, you have a color printer. Can you make a copy of this?"

Nodding, Ida said, "Yes, I can do it."

Patrick held out the photo for Ida. "Good, and crop out Amanda. I just want the girl, and enlarge it as much as you can." Ida took the photograph and went to make the copy. Patrick spoke to Amanda, "We need to find her first. Then we can come up with a plan to get her back. I have a friend that lives not far from Cozumel. He's a retired Senior Chief Petty Officer. He was a navy seal. He entered service a little after the Vietnam War. If she's down there, he can find her."?"

Amanda said, "You say that he lives down there?"

Patrick smiled at the recollection of Petrozello. "Yes, he likes the warm climate; and he claims that his retirement goes farther down there. He's also an archaeology buff, and likes to hang out around the Mayan ruins. I'll FAX him the information so that he can get to work."

Amanda felt that now would be the time to bring up the subject of money. "I know that this will cost a lot. We'll be good for it."

Patrick reached out and patted Amanda on the forearm. "Don't worry about it, my rates are very flexible. I never charge any more than my client is able to pay."

Ida came back with the copy of the photo. She handed the copy to Patrick, and the photo back to Amanda.

Patrick turned back to Amanda. "I don't know David Zamora personally, but I do know what kind of a man he is. He has a very big macho ego. He puts a very low value on women. As far as he's concerned, the only purpose in life for women, is to serve and give pleasure to men, and to make sons. He took your daughter, not because he loves her, but because you defied him. He wanted to terrify, degrade, humiliate, and take from you the most important thing in your life. He wanted you to feel powerless to do anything about it. That was more of a victory for him than just killing you. Now as long as he has your daughter, he couldn't care less about you. When he finds out that you've taken your daughter back from him, he will be enraged. It will be an intolerable affront to his perverted sense of honor that you, an inferior female, beat him. His macho ego will force him to avenge this affront to his honor. He will use every resource he has to find you and kill you. He won't care about the girl; he'll just want you dead. He may even want to kill you himself. Now, knowing this, do you still want to go through with it?"

Without hesitation, and with a firmness of voice, Amanda said, "How can I not go through with it? I must have my daughter back!"

Patrick could see the determination, the quite resolve in her face and eyes. With a nod, Patrick said, "Okay, I believe that you are willing to go all the way with is. If you were not willing, knowing all the risks, I would have had to withdraw my offer to help. If I couldn't rely on you to do your part, we would be beaten before we started. Now I'm sure that we can get her back." Patrick's words filled, Amanda with hope. She could almost cry with relief. Her plight no longer seemed so hopeless. The chances were good that she would have Cheryl back. Patrick continued, "There's something else that you must consider. Right now you are safe, but once we have your daughter, that will change. That won't be the end of it, just the beginning. David will be looking for you. We will keep our eye on him, but we can't anticipate everything. There may come a time when you will have to defend yourself. Do you know how to use a firearm?"

Amanda shook her head. "No, I have no experience with guns."

Patrick knew that a lot of people had no experience with firearms and said, "That's okay, we all have to start somewhere. Now you need to get a handgun and learn how to use it. You also need to get a permit to carry it concealed. When you go to get the gun, don't let the gun dealer sell you some little pea shooter that he calls a ladies gun; and don't buy a big hand canon like Dirty Harry, that's too much gun for you. You need to get a .38 special or a 9mm, depending on rather you prefer a revolver or automatic. Ida can help you get the right handgun for you. She can also hook you up with a good gun club where you can learn how to use it."

Amanda replied, "Okay, I'll get with Ida on this."

Patrick now mentioned one other advantage that they had. "We do have one advantage. If he comes after you, we can notify the FBI and DEA. They may be able to arrest him before he gets to you. I believe that I have all I need for now. Give me about one to two weeks. I should have something for you."

The meeting over, Amanda got up, thanked Patrick again, and left to go back to work.

After Amanda left the office, Ida turned to Patrick. "Well, Pat, what do you think of her?"

Patrick thought for a moment, then said, "I like her. There's something about her, a special quality that appeals to me. I want to help her, and I've got the time now. I just finished a big assignment in Indiana."

Ida gave Patrick an inquiring look. "Oh, what was that?"

Patrick responded, "Industrial espionage. We were called in when the CEO of the company suspected that some of the company secrets were being compromised. We found the target to be a forty-seven year-old engineer. He had met a twenty-three year-old French beauty, a real seductress, with a honey-sweet heavily-accented voice and alluring eyes. The poor sap didn't have a chance. She let him believe that he was the love of her life. She was interested in everything about him, to include his job. She soon had him doing all his thinking with the wrong head."

Ida just had to laugh at that one. "Oh, Pat, you do have a way with words."

Patrick continued, "As I was saying. We picked up Mademoiselle Hot Pants for interrogation. We got all the details of the conspiracy, and put the fear of God in her. We then put her on a plane to France, with a warning 'stay home'. Her handler was a Mr. Jean Mandel; a career diplomat from the French Consulate in Chicago. We informed the State Department. He's being recalled by the French government."

Ida nodded. "Sounds like an interesting case."

Patrick said smiling, "Yes, interesting and profitable. To change the subject; you did say that if I came to Atlanta to talk to Amanda, you would let me take you out to dinner."

Ida smiled. "So I Will, you can follow me home. I can change, then we can go out."

Still smiling, Patrick remarked, "If you wear that Prussian blue dress of yours, I'll take you to dinner where ever you want to go."

When Sam got home, Amanda went over everything that had been said in the meeting with him. Sam felt concern for Amanda's safety. They talked it over, and Sam realized that Amanda just had to go through with it. He told her that whatever the risk, he would always be there for her. Amanda was in a mood to celebrate; so Sam took her out to dinner.

Chapter Thirty-Seven

The sun hung low on the sea to the east, with the sunlight sparkling off the water. The sea was almost calm, with very small waves lapping the shore. The morning had starting to warm up with the arrival of the sun. Henry Petrozello liked to get out in the morning, and run along the beach before it got too hot. At sixty-four Henry still remained a fit man. He had spent thirty years in the United States Navy, mostly as a seal, or diver. As a young man he had started his military carrier shortly after the Vietnam War. He believed in physical fitness, and liked to run and swim. He was bald, except for a gray fringe of hair around the sides and back of his head, so he shaved his head. He thought that it made him look younger and more virile. He had been living in Mexico for sixteen years now, and loved it, especially the Yucatan. He thought of himself as an amateur archaeologist, and this was the place to be. Henry spoke fluent Spanish; and had been there for so long that no one paid attention to him anymore.

He had received the FAX from Fitz yesterday afternoon, and studied it last night. Fitz had said that David Zamora could be in Cozumel, but he thought that Cozumel might be a little off the mark. More than likely, someone not wanting to be easily found wouldn't be there, but somewhere close by on the mainland. One thing helpful, he would be looking for a little girl with green eyes. Green eyes were very rare around here.

He started to make contact with his friends, and asked an occasional question. On the third day his queries bore fruit. He heard of a little girl who came to the market at Tulum each day between 9:00 and 11:00 AM, with a woman who cooked at a villa nine kilometers north of Tulum. It was an oceanfront villa off of Highway 307, in the direction of Puerto Morelos.

The next morning he arrived at the market in Tulum. At 9:30. At 10:05 he spotted the girl in the company of a Mexican woman of about forty years of age. The girl looked older that the photo, but he knew that it had to be the same girl. He observed them as the woman did her shopping. He snapped a photo from time to time with his cell phone camera, being careful not to be observed. When they left fifty minutes later, Henry had been able to follow them back to the place where they had parked their car.

He then got his car and drove north on Highway 307, past the villa that belonged to David Zamora. As he drove past he could see the car that the cook had been driving parked next to the villa.

The following morning at 7:00 Henry had his boat anchored off the beach within one-quarter mile of the villa, with his dive flag up. He would make a dive for a few minutes, then check the villa. At about 7:45 three men came out to the patio table for breakfast. Henry went into the cabin of the boat. With a camera and telephoto lens, he took some photos through the cabin window. He then made another dive, took down the dive flag, raised the anchor, and left.

The next five days Henry observed the routine of the cook and household. The cook's routine didn't vary, except on Sunday. On Sunday she didn't come to the market. As for the men in the villa, on four of the five days that Henry observed then, they left the villa by midmorning, and didn't return until after six in the afternoon. A young woman also lived in the villa, a light-skinned Mexican woman in her mid-twenties with Anglo features. She didn't seem to have a regular schedule. After five days Henry FAXed his first report to Patrick.

Two weeks after the first meeting, Ida called Sam and Amanda and asked them to come in at 4:00 PM for a meeting at her office.

At 4:00 PM Sam and Amanda arrived and entered Ida's office.

WOMAN IN THE MIRROR

Patrick had also come, and was waiting there with Ida. Ida made the introductions. "Sam, this is Sergeant Major Patrick Fitzgerald. Pat, this is Mr. Sam Tankersley." Sam and Patrick shook hands.

Patrick liked the way that Sam met his eyes, and had a firm handshake. "My friends call me Pat. You can call me Pat."

Ida directed everyone to sit around the coffee table, and got Cokes for everyone. She then took a seat and started the proceedings. "Sam, Amanda, Pat received a report from his friend in Cozumel. Pat, you have the floor."

Everyone looked at Patrick. "I'll start off by answering Amanda's first question. Yes, we found your daughter, and yes, I do have photos of her." Patrick pulled out some 8X10 photos from a folder in front of him on the coffee table, and handed them to Amanda, "These were taken at the market the first day. Now this is what we know. They aren't in Cozumel. They're in a seaside villa nine kilometers, about five miles north of Tulum, on the road to Puerto Morelos. The villa isn't far from one of the ferry landings for Cozumel. In the villa are David Zamora, and two of his bodyguards. There's a young Mexican woman; most likely David's latest mistress. There's also a live in cook and your daughter, Cheryl. They have a maid who comes in at least two times a week, maybe three. The cook takes Cheryl with her to the market in Tulum each day, except Sunday. We assume that that's her day off."

Patrick paused for a few seconds to take a drink of Coke, and to order his thoughts. "Okay, here's the plan as it is now. It's still being worked out, but we already have the basics fixed. To begin with we have the element of surprise. They feel safe enough to let the cook take her to the market alone. So we'll take her when they go to the market. I'll need a team of at least three, no more than four. I can't use my man there. He's known, and he's an Anglo. I already have the team members in mind. Now, Amanda, you're in this too."

Sam had to speak up, "Do you have to use Amanda? I don't want her to be in any danger."

Amanda placed a hand on Sam's forearm. "Sam, I can do it. I can't

275

ask other people to take risks if I won't. Besides, I don't think that Pat will make me do anything that I can't handle."

Patrick could understand how Sam felt; he had felt the same way about his wife. All there married life he had tried to protect her from any harm. When the end came it had been from cancer, something that he had been powerless to protect her from. Now he had to alleviate Sam's fears for Amanda. "She's right. I won't let her to get in over her head. She won't even be close to where we will kidnap Cheryl. She'll be miles away. What we need her there for is to take custody of Cheryl after we get her. Amanda's really important to the plan. We really need her."

Sam thought about it for a minute. He was torn between his desire to protect Amanda; and to help her to get Cheryl back. In the end he knew that Amanda would do whatever she needed to do despite his protest. Sam nodded. "All right, if you really need her, she can go."

Amanda gave Sam a kiss of appreciation on his cheek.

Patrick breathed easy now that they had put that behind them. "Good, now Amanda, here's what you will do. You are going to take a cruise on Norwegian Cruise Line. You'll be booked as Miss Victoria Bujold and daughter Cheryl. I'll provide the documents that you'll need. Cheryl won't board with you in Miami, but her name will stay on the manifest; I've made sure of that.

You will arrived in Cozumel on a Wednesday at 7:00 AM. You can go ashore and see the shops. At 1:00 PM you will go to the Maya Cozumel Hotel. You will take a table at the pool and wait there. Someone will come in and address you saying, 'Miss Bujold, I have that souvenir that you have been asking for'. You will go with him and be united with Cheryl. She'll be sedated to a point where she'll be barely awake. She'll stay that way until you get her back to the ship and in bed. She'll then sleep it off. By the time she wakes up you will be far out to sea. Now the ship leaves at 5:00 PM, so we'll have the time to time your going back on board. That way you'll be in with a lot of returning passengers." Patrick paused to give the point that he wanted to make more significance. He looked hard into Amanda's eyes. "We

WOMAN IN THE MIRROR

have just one chance to get it right. If everything isn't right we just walk away. So, Amanda, if no one makes contact with you, just go back to the ship. We'll try it again later. Ida, do you have any more Cokes? We can take a break now."

Ida got everyone a Coke, then they begin again. Patrick said, "Okay, let's get back to it. Amanda, you'll be traveling as a single woman. You need to remove your rings now, and not wear them again until this is over with. If you wait until the day before you leave there will be a mark around your finger where the rings were. You don't want to draw attention to them by their absence." Amanda removed her rings and put them in her purse. Patrick continued, "When aboard the ship you can't hide in your cabin. You'll attract attention that way. You must get out and move around the ship. Just don't form any friendships. Stay aloof from everyone. You can stay in your cabin as much as you want to after you have your daughter safely aboard. If everything goes as it should, you'll be safe in international waters before David Zamora knows that Cheryl is missing.

"Now the ship departs Cozumel at 5:00 PM Wednesday, arriving at Key West, Florida at 3:00 PM Thursday. You will leave the ship there. We'll have reservations for you and Cheryl to fly to Charlotte, North Carolina. Sam, you'll meet her at the airport at Charlotte. I will let you know the flight number and arrival time. Now, the both of you listen to me. Leave your credit cards at home on this enterprise; pay only in cash. Don't put your real name on receipts, and don't give your real name to anyone. Oh, Sam, don't drive up to Charlotte the day before and stay overnight. Drive up and back the same day. We don't want your tag number on any motel register"

Sam nodded in understanding, "You can count on me. We won't leave ant paper trail."

Patrick could see that Sam had taken it seriously and wouldn't make any mistakes. "Good, we'll be getting together again as the plan comes together in its final form." Patrick looked at Ida, "Did you get with Hugh Desormeaux and have him get rid of any reference to you

277

or Amanda in his files?"

Ida had already gotten in touch with Hugh about this, "Yes, I have; and I also warned him about David Zamora."

Patrick now looked at Sam. "That's good, Ida. Now, Sam, what kind of gun do you have?"

Sam responded, "I have a twelve gage Remmington auto loader. Amanda and I now have 9mm Glock model 17's, and permits to carry them concealed. We have joined a gun club. Amanda's getting to be a real expert with the Glock."

Patrick smiled at Sam. "That's fine. Now get some 00 buck for the twelve gage, and keep it a home. A shotgun is better for home defense than a pistol is anyway. You should also take Amanda out into the woods to let her get used to firing the twelve gage."

Sam nodded, thinking that Amanda might enjoy learning how to use the shotgun, "Okay, we'll do that too."

Patrick knew that there was a lot more about using a gun than just being able to hit a target. Sam and Amanda had to be mentally prepared to defend themselves. "Sam, Amanda, about the guns. It's one thing to learn to shoot them, and another thing to shoot someone with them. Now do this, every time that you handle the gun, shoot it, clean it, or whatever think of what it's for. It's a weapon to use in your, or someone else's defense. Mentally prepare yourself to use it. Now, if ever you must use it don't hesitate. Don't say 'I have a gun', or 'stop or I'll shoot', or any other dumb thing like that. Just aim the gun and fire as quickly as you can. Don't think about it, just do it. Your first priority is to stay alive. You can square it with your conscience later. Any questions?" Patrick gave them a few seconds to think about it. No one had any questions. Patrick continued, "That's all I have for now. We'll be getting together again soon."

Everyone got up and shook hands. Sam and Amanda went to their car and started home. After they were away from Ida's office and on the road, Amanda said, "This is really getting serious."

Not taking his eyes off the road, Sam nodded. "That's for sure!

WOMAN IN THE MIRROR

Are you having second thoughts?"

Amanda shook her head. "No, I still want to go through with it. I just feel that I'm asking you for more than I should."

Sam said in a firm-reassuring tone, "Nonsense, I want to do it."

Amanda put her hand on Sam's forearm, "Thank you, Sam."

Sam said, glancing quickly at Amanda, "I believe that we have to do one other thing. We need to see a judge to get a court order granting you full custody of Cheryl in Georgia. I believe that we have enough to convince a judge that you're Cheryl's mother, and one other thing."

Amanda looked at Sam. "Yes."

Sam continued, "When we get Cheryl back, I want to adopt her."

With a squeal Amanda threw her arms around Sam's neck, and started kissing him.

With a grin, Sam said, "Do you want me to wreck the car? Save it till we get home."

Chapter Thirty-Eight

It was a beautiful spring day in Columbus, Georgia; with the sky full of cumulus clouds, that paraded across the heavens in stately order. A gentle breeze blew, carrying the scent of fresh-spring blossoms, and a temperature perfect for people to want to spend time out-of-doors. Patrick Fitzgerald and his guests were out on the patio. Patrick had ribeye steaks on the grill, along with grilled corn on the cob. A large bowl of German potato salad and rolls sat on the table. Seated at the table were Juan Salazar, age forty-seven, retired Army First Sergeant. Hernandez Pinzon, age thirty-six, former Marine paratrooper, now a security consultant. Then Bonita Valazquez, age thirty-three, former Dallas, Texas police officer, now private investigator. This was the team that Patrick would send to Mexico to retrieve Cheryl. They had been chosen not just for their reliability and expertise, but also they were Mexican Americans that spoke Spanish like Mexicans; not Texmex, or any other Spanish dialects spoken in the United States. Patrick called out, "Okay, the steaks are ready. There's plenty of cold beer in the cooler. Just help yourself." Everyone got up from the table to be served a steak and corn on the cob by Patrick, then got their beer.

After everyone had taken their places at the table and filled their plated, Patrick got down to business. "All right Gentlemen and lady, you have studied the operation, now let's talk about it. Salazar, you'll be the team leader. Pinzon, you'll be second in command. Now the chain of command is set. Salazar, you have seen the reports from Petrozello. Where do you think we should take the child?"

Salazar put down the ear of corn that he had been gnawing at, and looked at Patrick. "For starters, to take her at the villa is out. We could take her on the road to or from the market. We can do it if need be, but I don't like it. We wouldn't have complete control. There's too much risk involved. It'll have to be in Tulum."

Patrick nodded approval. He could see that he and Salazar were thinking the same. "That sounds good. Now, Pinzon, what do you think?"

Pinzon looked up swallowing the piece of steak that he had been chewing on, and said, "I also studied the reports. I agree with, Salazar."

Patrick then said, "Bonita, what about you?"

Valazquez, while buttering a roll, said, "I also agree with Salazar. To take her on the road is too risky."

Patrick nodded, pleased that everyone agreed with him. He had already started to make plans for taking the girl in Tulum. "Okay, then I agree with all of you. We'll take the girl in town. I'm open for comments."

Valazquez spoke first, "We can't do it right in the market place; there are too many people about. We need to do it to or from the car, or at the car."

Patrick had already decided that it would have to be at the car. "Very good Bonita. Now, Salazar?"

Salazar, after studying everything, had to agree with Valazquez. "Agreed, at the car."

Patrick said, "Pinzon?"

Pinzon, starting to chew on a piece of steak nodded. "I agree with Salazar and Valazquez."

Salazar said, "I've been reading Petrozello's reports. He reports that the cook parks her car at the same place every time. It's a north/south running street, more like an alleyway. She parks on the east side next to a high wall, to keep the car in the shade. There are no windows close by, just a couple of double doors for autos and trucks."

Patrick could see that Salazar had much the same idea as he had. "Okay, are there any objections to taking the girl at the car?" Patrick

MICHAEL O. GREGORY

looked around the table. There were no objections. He continued, "Okay, we take her at the car. We do it when they return from the market. All right, now what do we need, Salazar?"

Salazar had started to consider what they would need for the operation. "Well, the first thing that we'll need is transportation. I say two cars, one for the island of Cozumel, and one for the mainland."

Patrick nodded agreement. "Okay then, two cars. What else?"

Salazar knew that they would have to knock the cook out, and keep her out until the operation was over with. "We will need something to take care of the cook. Like a hypodermic syringe filled with sodium pentothal, or something like that."

Patrick had already anticipated that. "I've already thought of that. You'll have an automatic injector, like the ones in the protective mask carriers that we had in the service. It'll be preloaded with the correct dosage. All you have to do is remove the safety cap, and press it to her neck. Everything is automatic. The injector's no larger than a tube of lipstick, easily concealed. You'll also need to be able to control the girl. You don't want her to panic and blow the whole operation. You'll have a sugar cube to give her. It will be coated with just enough tranquilizer to calm her and make her drowsy."

Salazar could see that Patrick already had a plan. He had just wanted to query everyone to see if anyone had seen anything that had been overlooked. Salazar nodded. "That's just what we need. It seems that you already have most of the plan worked out."

Patrick, putting down his beer, said, "Yes, I do. Once you take the girl, you'll need to get rid of her clothes. They'll know what she is wearing. You'll need one change of clothing to make her look like a Mexican girl: the daughter of Pinzon and Bonita. They have to be convincing as a family for the ride on the ferry to Cozumel. And a second change of clothing when you turn her over to her mother in Cozumel. She'll have to look like a middle-class American girl on holiday with her mother. You'll also have radios that can be concealed."

Salazar looked at Patrick. "It seems that you've thought of just

282

WOMAN IN THE MIRROR

about everything."

Patrick spoke to Salazar, but he intended it for everyone's benefit. "I do have a plan that's just about finalized. All the documents will be ready before you go. I have photos of everyone involved. I have photos of the street where the car is parked, and the car. I have maps of the area, and ferry schedules. Petrozello has driven the routes and recorded the times. Anything else you need, I'll get it for you. Now, there will be no weapons. No one is to be harmed. We don't want the police any more involved that they will already be. We have just one chance at this, so if it's not just right, just walk away. We can always try again. Any questions?" Patrick paused to give anyone who wanted time to ask a question, then continued, "On the day of the operation a power yacht will call at Tulum, at about eight AM. At ten AM they'll go shopping at the market. They'll have a large bag, like a duffle bag, and other items. After twelve noon they'll return to the yacht, and get underway, then turn south to Belize. If David Zamora and the police go for it, we'll have them looking the other way. I'm still working on the alternate plan. If for some reason we can't make contact with the mother after we have the girl, we'll have it. One last thing." Patrick removed a yellow and green scarf from a paper sack that had been sitting on the table near him, "You know the mother from her photo. She'll also be wearing this, so take a good look at it."

Patrick let everyone look at the scarf, then continued, "The Friday before the operation Salazar, you'll go by air from Dallas, Texas to Mexico City. From there you will go by bus to Merida. At Merida you'll pick up a rental car that will be reserved for you. From there you'll drive to Puerto Juarez, and make contact with Petrozello. Pinzon, you and Bonita will fly out Sunday before the operation from New Orleans. You'll be Juan and Marta Martinez, husband and wife on vacation. You'll fly directly to Cozumel. There will be a rental car reserved for you there. Any questions?" Patrick looked around the table. There were no questions. "Good, let's eat; then we can start our rehearsals."

283

MICHAEL O. GREGORY

One week later Amanda had come to Ida's office for another meeting with Patrick. They all had their Cokes, and were sitting around the coffee table. Patrick started the meeting. "Amanda, you'll be glad to know that everything's ready. You'll depart one week from this coming Monday. Sam will drive you up to Charlotte for you to get the morning flight to Miami. At Miami you'll board the Norwegian cruise line ship Majesty. You're booked along with your daughter Cheryl. You have stateroom four-sixty-eight on the baroness deck. It has two single beds, and isn't far from the after elevators. The ship departs from Miami at four PM. It arrives in Cozumel at seven AM Wednesday.

"After you go ashore at Cozumel, you may do whatever you want until one PM. At one PM you have to be at the pool area at the Maya Cozumel Hotel. If no one makes contact with you by three PM, you're to leave and get back to the ship."

Patrick now took the scarf from the sack and handed it to Amanda, "You're to wear this scarf. It doesn't matter how you wear it, as long as it's visible to someone entering the pool area. Now when someone enters the pool area and says to you, 'Miss Bujold, I have that souvenir that you have been asking for', he will have your daughter."

"After you have your daughter; both of you will be driven back to the ship. Then you'll board the ship with Cheryl, along with a large tour group. Go to your stateroom and put Cheryl to bed. She'll sleep off the tranquilizer in a couple of hours. Stay in your stateroom until the ship is well out to sea. The ship departs at five PM; arriving at Key West, Florida at three PM the next day. You know what to do from there."

With a nod, Amanda said, "Yes, I know. I take a flight with Cheryl to Charlotte, North Carolina, and meet Sam there."

Patrick took a packet from his briefcase, and handed it to Amanda. "This is all of your ID and other documents for you and Cheryl. You have her birth certificate. Take it with you."

Taking the packet from Patrick, Amanda replied, "Okay, I'll do that."

Patrick pointed at the packet. "Your cruise tickets are also in there, and also your airline reservations from Key West to Charlotte. Now,

284

WOMAN IN THE MIRROR

if we get her, but can't get her to you, we have a backup plan. It's to fly her out and meet you in Miami. If we need to use the backup plan, you'll get a radiogram saying 'Happy birthday, Vicki'. Understand?"

Amanda nodded. "Yes, I understand."

Patrick reached out and patted Amanda on the forearm. "Okay, that's good. We kick off the operation one week from Monday. Are you ready?"

Patrick's positive manner reassured Amanda, she nodded. "Yes, as much as I can be."

Patrick gave a reassuring smile to Amanda. "Well, don't worry about a thing. Before you know it, you'll have your daughter back in your arms."

The meeting over, Amanda got to her feet, shook hands with Patrick and Ida, then left for home.

After Amanda had left, Patrick turned to Ida and said, "We're ready to go. Tell me, what do you think of Amanda? How will she react under pressure?"

Ida responded, "I've gotten to know her really well. She's tougher than she looks. She'll be okay."

Patrick nodded. "That's good to know."

CHAPTER THIRTY-NINE

Saturday Sam and Amanda drove to Gadsden. Amanda needed to have some time with her mother before going to Cozumel. The closer that she got to the date of the operation to take back Cheryl, the more nervous she became. She very much wanted to feel the closeness of her mother for the support that it would convey. She also had the photos of Cheryl that had been taken at the market in Tulum to show her mother. Ever since Amanda had told her mother about Cheryl, Beth had insisted on knowing everything as soon as possible.

When they arrived at her parent's home, Ted and Beth met them at the car. They first went to the family room where Beth served Cokes. Amanda then went into the kitchen with her mother, while Sam stayed in the family room with her father. A soon as they were in the kitchen, Amanda took the photos of Cheryl from her purse, and handed them to her mother. "Here, Mom, these are the photos that they recently took of Cheryl at the market in Tulum. I made this copy for you so that you could have them."

Taking the photos from Amanda, Beth leaned back against the counter top and started to look at the photos. "Oh, she's such a lovely child. I can hardly wait to meet her."

Amanda knew that ever since her mother had found out that she was a Grandmother; all that she could think of had been Cheryl. Amanda said, "Well, Mom, if everything goes as planned I'll have her home safe with me in thirteen days."

Beth was glad that she would soon be seeing her Granddaughter.

However, she had concerns about Amanda's welfare. She knew that there could be a risk to Amanda in this enterprise. "Tell me, what do you know about these men who are going to get Cheryl back for you?"

Amanda looked at her mother. "I don't know much about them, but Ida does. She's done work for Sam before, and he trusts her, and so do I. Sergeant Major Fitzgerald seems to know his business. This isn't the first time that he's done something like this."

Beth had heard Amanda mention Patrick Fitzgerald, but she knew almost nothing about him. "Amanda, this person Patrick Fitzgerald that you keep mentioning; what kind of business does he have?"

Amanda could see that she needed to tell her mother more about Patrick Fitzgerald. "Well, Mom, he has a security and investigating company, but that's not all he has. The organization that's doing the job is different. It's an organization that isn't supposed to be well known. He has on call any people with any specialty that you may need. If you need a jet or helicopter pilot, he has them. He has experts on any boat or ship, to include submarines. He also has engineers, divers, both hard hat and scuba, demolition experts, communication experts, computer experts, document specialist, accountants, or any other specialty that you may need. He can tailor a team to fit any mission. He does work in the private sector, and sometimes for government agencies when they want a barrier between themselves and the operation, so that they can deny responsibility if need be. He also from time to time does a job for an individual like myself. Ida said that I was lucky to get him."

To Beth this all sounded like mission impossible, or something else like that. "What's the name of his organization?"

Amanda shrugged. "There's no name. Pat said that the first step in finding out about something is to know its name."

Beth couldn't help being very concerned about Amanda's safety, and it showed in her voice. She took Amanda's hands into her own, and gave them a squeeze. "Amanda, I wish that you didn't have to do it this way, but I know that you must. Just be careful."

Amanda knew that her mother worried for her. She tried to be

MICHAEL O. GREGORY

reassuring. "I will, Mom. I'll call you as soon as I get back."

Beth smiled. "Good, I can't wait to meet my Granddaughter."

The Friday before the operation Juan Salazar, traveling as Angel Gomez boarded a plane at Dallas/Fort Worth International airport for Mexico City. From Mexico City he took a bus to Merida, Yucatan, arriving early Saturday afternoon. At Merida he picked up a rental car, and drove to Puerto Juarez in Quintana Roo. There he met up with Henry Petrozello.

They went for an initial reconnaissance of Tulum, and the routes. He then checked with Petrozello to make sure that they had everything needed for the operation.

Sunday, Pinzon and Velazquez traveling as husband and wife boarded a plane in New Orleans for a flight to Cozumel. On arrival in Cozumel, they picked up the rental car that had been reserved for them. They then checked in at the Flores Hotel in San Miguel De Cozumel. They made sure to convey the impression on everyone that they were a married couple on vacation.

The next day they took the ferry to Playa De Carmen. At Playa De Carmen they met Salazar at the restaurant in the Cabanas Tucan for breakfast.

After breakfast, Salazar took them on a reconnaissance of Tulum and the route. They then went back to, Salazar's hotel room, where they went over the plan one more time. Salazar started the meeting. 'First thing, if the cook and Cheryl don't get back to the car by eleven- 0 five, or eleven-ten at the latest, we call it off. We have fifty kilometers, that's thirty-one miles to drive, and we must make the twelve-fifteen ferry to Cozumel. Velazquez, you'll have a radio with you. Your long hair will hide the wire coming up out of your collar. I'll have the other radio with me. I'll be around the corner from the car. When they pass me I'll key the mike two times. That will be the signal for you and Pinzon to go into your act. Do you need any more rehearsal?"

Velazquez and, Pinzon shook their heads. They already had everything memorized.

WOMAN IN THE MIRROR

Salazar continued. "Good, now as they near the car their attention will be focused on your act; they won't see me coming up behind them. When the moment is right, I'll stick her with the automatic injector, and she'll be out like a light. Now, Velazquez, the girl is your responsibility. You make sure that she gets in the car, and that she stays quite."

Velazquez nodded. "Okay."

Salazar said, "Pinzon, you and I will get the woman in the back seat of the car as soon as she drops. You take the back seat with her. Velazquez, you take the right front seat with the girl. I'll drive the car. The first change of clothing for the girl will be in my car. Her second change of clothing will be in your car at the ferry landing at Cozumel. You'll leave my car at the ferry landing on this side. I'll show you where to park the car, and where to hide the key in it. Now remember, we're on a tight timetable, so every minute counts."

Salazar looked at Pinzon and Velazquez in turn. "Okay, we've rehearsed this many times. Now, let's talk about it. If there are any flaws, we need to take care of them now."

On Monday before the operation, Amanda traveling as Victoria Bujold took the morning flight from Charlotte, North Carolina to Miami, Florida, arriving at Miami International Airport at 12:10 PM. From the airport Amanda took a taxi to the pier to board the Norwegian Cruise Line ship Majesty.

The first sight of the ship took her breath away. She wondered how something so big could float. Despite the size, she found the appearance of the ship to be pleasing to the eye. She boarded the ship and was shone to her stateroom. The stateroom seemed a bit small, but efficiently laid out, and tastefully decorated. It had everything that she needed. She felt sure that she could be very comfortable there. She stayed in her stateroom until the ship got underway. Now that the operation had finally started to happen; she started to get nervous and wanted to be by herself.

Once the ship had gotten underway, Amanda went up on deck and watched Miami and the coastline fall away astern. She then looked ahead

289

out to sea. She was committed now. Things were automatically going to happen; she couldn't stop them. The words of Julius Caesar again came to mind, 'the die is cast'. The words seemed to be appropriate for her. What will be will be, there would be no turning back. Now that she was irrevocably committed she started to feel calmer.

She had dinner in the Epicurean Restaurant. After dinner she played the one-armed bandits in the Winners Circle. She then went back to her stateroom and turned in early.

The next morning Amanda had breakfast in her stateroom. Her plan would be to spend some time in her stateroom, and the rest of the time out and about the ship; not spending too much time in any one place. She would try to discourage people from being overly friendly without being rude. If a man would come on to her, and she couldn't shake him off, she would excuse herself. She would say that she had to go to the lady's room, or to her stateroom for something, then leave. She managed to get through the day okay. She had dinner again in the Epicurean Restaurant.

After dinner she tried her luck again with the one-armed bandits. She now knew why they were called that.

She arrived back at her stateroom before 10:00 PM. She wanted to turn in early to get a good night's sleep, but had been so nervous that sleep wouldn't come. She tried every trick that she knew to fall to sleep, but nothing worked. After what seemed to be many fitful hours, exhaustion overtook her and she slept.

Wednesday 5:45 AM: Pinzon and Velazquez left their hotel for the ferry landing in Cozumel. They were dressed as a local working class couple.

6:30 AM: They took the ferry to Playa Del Carmen.

7:00 AM: The Norwegian Cruise Line ship Majesty arrived at Cozumel

7:15: The ferry docked at Playa Del Carmen. Salazar waited at the dock with his car for the rest of his team.

7:25 AM: David Zamora and his bodyguard sat down for breakfast

WOMAN IN THE MIRROR

on the patio.

8:00 AM: Cheryl and David's mistress Inez Sosa had breakfast in the kitchen. Inez had planned to ride into Tulum with the cook Rosa Segovia this morning. She wanted to visit her mother; then get a ride back with a neighbor in the afternoon.

8:02 AM: Salazar and his team arrived in Tulum. They parked the car at a secluded spot at the edge of town, and walked to the market.

8:20: Amanda ordered breakfast in her stateroom. When it arrived she felt too nervous to eat it. She at least managed to get down a little orange juice and coffee. Afterward she had a bout of morning sickness and had to throw up.

8:30 AM: The fifty-six foot power cruiser Aces Over out of Houston, Texas, dropped anchor at Tulum.

8:50 AM: David Zamora and his bodyguard departed on a business trip to Chelumal.

9:00 AM: Amanda left the ship with a tour group. She then took a taxi to the Maya Cozumel Hotel. After looking over the hotel and pool area, she went out and walked about the city. She just couldn't sit still. She had to keep moving. She counted every minute until she could have Cheryl in her arms. She passed the time by visiting the shops in town.

9:10 AM: Rosa Segovia with Inez Sosa and Cheryl left for Tulum.

9:21 AM: Rosa parked the car in her regular spot. Rosa and Cheryl then went to the market. Inez went to visit her mother.

9:37: Salazar and his team were sitting in a café having coffee when they saw Rosa and Cheryl. Salazar and his team kept them under surveillance, as Rosa did her shopping. After ten it appeared that Rosa had finished with her shopping. Salazar sent Pinzon and Velazquez to get in position.

10:00: Three men from the Aces Over came ashore to do some shopping in Tulum.

10:18 AM: Rosa with Cheryl started back to the car. Salazar moved quickly to get in position.

291

MICHAEL O. GREGORY

10:29 AM: As, Rosa and Cheryl approached the corner they passed a man standing in a doorway. When they were almost to the corner, Salazar pressed the transmit button on his radio two times. Velazquez heard the two bleeps in her ear. That was their cue to start the argument.

Rosa turned the corner. They were almost to the car. Rosa saw a couple just the other side of the car arguing. The woman had her back to the street. The man had his back against the wall. He turned to walk away. The Woman grabbed him by the arm. He threw her hand off. She tried to slap him. He caught her hand. Rosa had reached the car now. . She had been able to hear them very well. He had been seeing another woman. She was enraged. He didn't want to talk about it. Rosa opened the driver's door. Cheryl jumped in and climbed over to the right seat. The couple kept arguing. Rosa thought. *That's a man for you! Men are all pigs!*

Something stung her neck. Before she had the presence of mind to cry out, everything went black.

They had rehearsed this so much that everything was automatic. Velazquez moved quickly to the right-front door and got in with Cheryl, to control her and to keep her quite. Salazar and Pinzon had Rosa almost before she hit the ground. They picked her up and put her in the back seat, along with her purse and groceries. Salazar got into the driver's seat. Pinzon got in the back with Rosa. He took the keys from Rosa's purse and handed them to Salazar. The car started and they were away. It all took no more than a few seconds.

On their way out to Salazar's car, Velazquez reassured Cheryl that they were taking good care of Rosa. She gave Cheryl a sugar cube to suck on; the sugar cube coated with the tranquilizer.

10:38 AM: they arrived at Salazar's car. The tranquilizer had started to take effect. Cheryl, although confused and a little frightened, felt drowsy and sleepy. She could hardly keep her eyes open.

Pinzon and Velazquez transferred to Salazar's car with Cheryl, and started north on highway 307 to Playa Del Carmen. Salazar checked Rosa to make sure that she would be okay, then followed five minutes behind in Rosa's car. Velazquez changed Cheryl out of the dress that she had on, to a dress to make her look like a member of their family. Cheryl had a dark tan and black hair. As long as no one got too close she could pass as Mexican. She would look like a little girl who was tired and sleepy, and wanted to sleep in her mother's arms.

11:44 AM: Pinzon and Velazquez arrived at the ferry landing in Playa Del Carmen with Cheryl. They had thirty-one minutes before the ferry left for Cozumel.

12:03 PM: Salazar reached a secluded place where he would keep Rosa knocked out until after the ship departed Cozumel. He would then leave her to wake up on her own. He would walk down to the ferry landing, get onto his car, and start back to Merida, Yucatan.

12:15 PM: Pinzon and Velazquez with Cheryl took the ferry to Cozumel. Amanda stopped for lunch at a restaurant in Cozumel.

12:30 PM: Three men returned to the Aces Over. They were carrying a large duffle bag that they handled with care. The Aces Over stood out to sea; then turned south to Belize.

1:00 PM: The ferry arrived at Cozumel. Pinzon and Velazquez with Cheryl got into their car and headed for the Maya Cozumel Hotel. Velazquez changed Cheryl again to look like a middle-class American girl on holiday with her mother.

Amanda arrived at the pool area of the Maya Cozumel Hotel. She took a seat and ordered a Coke. She wore the scarf as a headband.

1:25 PM: Pinzon entered the pool area. He saw Amanda and stepped up to her table. "Miss Bujold, I have that souvenir that you've been asking for."

Amanda looked up. "Oh, thank God!"

Pinzon said, "Please come with me."

Amanda got up and followed Pinzon out to the car. Amanda got into the back seat, Velazquez then handed Cheryl over to her. Amanda bonded with Cheryl instantly. There was no way that she would ever lose her again.

Cheryl felt herself being passed to someone else. She felt the

MICHAEL O. GREGORY

warmth of the person's body. The beat of her heart, she smelled the scent of the hair, and heard the sound of the voice. From deep inside her consciousness memories stirred. She sensed something very familiar, comforting and reassuring about this person. All of Cheryl's anxieties and fears vanished. Cheryl uttered a single word, "Mommy."

She then laid her head on Amanda's shoulder and went to sleep.

3:00 PM: Amanda boarded the ship with Cheryl. She went right to her stateroom and put, Cheryl to bed, to sleep off the effects of the tranquilizer.

Pinzon and Velazquez had already checked out of their hotel. They drove straight to the airport for a chartered flight to the Grand Cayman Island.

5:00 PM: The Norwegian Cruise Line ship Majesty got underway from Cozumel. Salazar left Rosa sleeping off the drug in her car. He walked to the ferry landing, arriving at 5:45 PM. His car had been parked at the prearranged spot. He recovered the key from the hiding place, got in and started up. He left Playa Del Carmen, heading back to Merida, Yucatan.

CHAPTER FORTY

At 6:40 PM David Zamora and his men returned from Chelumal. They immediately noticed that Rosa's car wasn't in the driveway; something had to be wrong. Rosa should have already been at the villa preparing supper for everyone. David and his bodyguards got out of their car. Their guns were at the ready as they approached the villa. David cautiously opened the front door and looked inside. Everything looked okay. He stepped into the vestibule, followed by his men. He called out, "Rosa!" After receiving no answer he called out again, "Rosa!" There was still no answer. He motioned for his men to check the rest of the house.

At that time Inez Sosa came walking slowly out from the bedroom wing of the villa. She seemed to be fearful and submissive. When she had arrived back at the villa, and noticed that Rosa hadn't arrived, she knew that there would be trouble; and she didn't want to become the focus of David's wrath.

David turned to her. "Inez, where is Rosa?"

Inez responded with fear in her voice, "I don't know."

Seeing that there would be no threat from inside the villa, David and his men put their guns away. David then moved across the living room to where Inez stood. His cook wasn't where she should be. He didn't like it when things started to get out of control. David got angry when things were out of control. He was getting angry, and he could be very cruel when he got angry. Inez felt frightened that David in his anger, would take it out on her, and started to cry. David grabbed Inez by the shoulders and shook her hard. "Inez, damn you! You better tell me, where's Rosa?" A sudden realization dawned on him, "Where's Cheryl?"

Inez shook her head. "I don't know." She broke free from David, and cringed in the corner crying.

David wanted to strike someone, but he needed answers. He struggled hard to control himself. "Stop crying Woman! I want answers! When did you get back?"

Inez brought the tears under control enough to speak, "Almost one hour ago."

David realized that If Rosa and Cheryl hadn't come home from the market this morning, then the trail would be several hour's old and getting cold. "And Rosa wasn't here?"

Inez shook her head. "No, she wasn't here. She hasn't come back from the market today."

David said, "Do you know where her family lives?"

Inez nodded. "Yes, I do."

David motioned to one of his men, "You, take Inez and go into Tulum. I want you to question, Rosa's family, to see if they know where she is." He then turned to the other man, "We have friends in the police; it's time for them to earn their pay. You call them, give them a description of Rosa's car. Tell them that my cook and daughter is missing. I want them found."

His man went to the phone to call the police. David paced the floor nervously grumbling and swearing to himself under his breath as he thought. *How stupid could I have been not to have a bodyguard on, Cheryl? After all only her mother wanted her, and I took care of that sniveling-spineless bitch for good. I broke her spirit. If she hadn't killed herself; she most likely ended up an alcoholic, or drug addict. Who would dare to do this to me on my own turf?*

After a couple of minutes David went to the bar in the living room and made himself a strong drink. He then sat on the sofa; still grumbling and swearing to himself under his breath.

Sometime after seven-thirty Rosa started to wake up. She still lay

WOMAN IN THE MIRROR

in the back seat of her car. She had a dry mouth, felt nauseous and had a violent headache. She opened the door and got out of the car. As soon as she stood up she felt lightheaded and dizzy. She braced herself against the car, bent over at the waist and vomited beside the car. She had nothing on her stomach, so it was the dry heaves, with a little bitter-tasting yellow bile. After she had been able to get her stomach under control. Rosa got into the driver's seat. She could see that the keys were still in the ignition. She started the car, put it in drive and started off. She had to go very slowly. She still felt dizzy, and had a hard time controlling the car. She found it hard to see the road; and then she remembered to turn on the headlights.

In fifteen minutes she had reached Playa Del Carmen. When she reached Highway 307 she turned south. She had gone less than ten kilometers south on Highway 307 when a police car pulled up behind her, and turned on his lights.

The whole time that Cheryl slept, Amanda sat on the bed at her side. From the time that Amanda had brought Cheryl into the stateroom and put her to bed, she hadn't left her side. Amanda would touch her, stroke her hair, but mostly just look at her. It was such an incredible feeling for Amanda that this beautiful child belonged to her, that she could be her mother. Now that she had her, Amanda didn't want to let Cheryl out of her sight.

Just before 7:00 PM Cheryl woke up. The room lights were dim, and Cheryl at first was disoriented. As soon as she was fully awakened and recognized Amanda, Cheryl jumped up and threw her arms around Amanda's neck crying, "Mommy, Mommy!" Repeatedly.

Amanda took Cheryl into her arms and pressed her into her bosom. "Yes, Baby, Mommy's here."

Cheryl just hugged Amanda around the neck, not wanting to let go. "Mommy, are we in heaven?"

Amanda hadn't expected that question. She would have to start getting use to a child's logic. "No, Baby, we're on a ship."

Cheryl gave Amanda a questioning look. "But David said that

297

MICHAEL O. GREGORY

you are in heaven."

Amanda smiled, amused by Cheryl's logic, "No, Baby, I'm not in heaven. I was sick for a long time, but I'm well now. I came back for you." Amanda continued to hold Cheryl in her arms, "Are you hungry Baby?"

Cheryl nodded. "Yes, Mommy."

Amanda sat Cheryl on the edge of the bed, then turned on the lights. "Okay, let's go to eat, but first, I have something nice for you."

Amanda produced a package wrapped in bright gift wrapping paper, with a pink ribbon and bow. Cheryl smiled, and her eyes sparkled at the sight of the package. Amanda had relied upon her mother's advice when it came to choosing the right size for a girl of Cheryl's age. Amanda helped Cheryl to open her present. Inside were a new red dress and a red-velvet ribbon for her hair. Amanda handed, Cheryl another gift box. In it was a new pair of red shoes. Amanda dressed Cheryl in her new dress and shoes. The dress fit perfectly. The shoes were a little loose fitting, but she could wear them. Amanda then brushed Cheryl's hair, and tied it back with the new red-velvet ribbon. Amanda then changed into a red dress and shoes.

When they were both dressed, Amanda stood with Cheryl in front of the mirror. With pride, Amanda thought Cheryl to be the most beautiful child in the world. This would be Amanda's first chance to show her daughter off, and she wasn't going to miss it.

Amanda took Cheryl up to the Café Royale for a late dinner. She let Cheryl order anything she wanted. After dinner they went for a walk around the ship. Cheryl was amazed at everything that she saw.

After the walk, they went back to their stateroom for a good night's rest. Cheryl wanted to sleep in Amanda's bed with her. Amanda thought that to be just great.

At 9:30 PM David Zamora got the word from the police that they had his cook Rosa in Playa Del Carmen. The police had no word of his daughter. The police were sure that it had been a kidnapping. David was livid, the police were idiots; being that they had to question Rosa

WOMAN IN THE MIRROR

to be sure that it had been a kidnapping before they called him. He had known that it had been a kidnapping from the very beginning. He swore death and damnation to all his enemies. However, he didn't know who could be behind the kidnapping. The police were questioning Rosa, but she had very little useful information. The police were going to investigate, but there wasn't much that they could do until morning. Even then he didn't have much faith in the ability of the police to solve anything. The rest of the night David just sat in the living room drinking. Out of fear of David's wrath, no one wanted to get near him unless they were called.

The next morning at first light, David and his men were in Tulum looking for leads. The police were investigating, but he had more confidence in his own investigation. Several people recalled a power cruiser that had called at Tulum the day before. The power cruiser had arrived after 8:00 AM, and stayed until after noon. Some people also remembered three men carrying a duffle bag aboard, and they had handled it with care. They were the only Anglos in town that day. After noon the power cruiser got underway, and headed south toward Belize. The police were sure that there were others involved, but they had no leads. David, his men, and the police questioned everyone that they could think of, but no one had seen anything. That morning David fired Rosa.

Amanda ordered breakfast in her stateroom for Cheryl and herself. It surprised Amanda how hungry Cheryl seemed to be, after everything that she had eaten the night before. They took their time at breakfast; Amanda glad of the time alone to get to know her daughter. Cheryl was thrilled to be back with her mother and became very talkative. Amanda could tell that Cheryl was anxious about something. Perhaps she still feared that David would come and take her back. Amanda told her about her Grandparents, her Aunt Audrey, Uncle Bill and Sam.

After breakfast, Amanda packed her bags, and got ready to leave the ship. Afterwards Amanda took Cheryl on a stroll about the ship until they came in sight of Key West. They then went to the observation

299

deck to watch the approach to Key West.

Amanda and Cheryl left the ship as soon as they could, taking a taxi to the airport. They got their flight to Miami, then a connecting flight to Charlotte, North Carolina, arriving after 7:00 PM.

Sam had arrived at the airport to meet them. Amanda had been surprised to see that her mother had also come. Sam kissed Amanda. Cheryl stood next to Amanda holding her hand. Amanda took Cheryl in her arms. "Sam, Mom, I'd like you to meet Cheryl." Amanda pointed to Sam, "Cheryl, this is Sam."

Cheryl said, "Hi, Sam."

Sam couldn't help but notice how much Cheryl looked like Amanda. He said, "Hi, Cheryl, you're such a lovely little girl."

Amanda pointed to Beth, "Cheryl, this is your Grandmother."

Cheryl said, "Hi, Grand Mommy."

Beth's heart was filled with joy at finally being able to meet her granddaughter. She reached out and took Cheryl into her own arms. She hugged Cheryl and kissed her on the cheeks. Cheryl decided that she liked this woman that they called Grandmother. She hugged Beth back. Beth said, "Hi, Baby, I'm so glad to meet you. We're going to have a lot of fun together."

It pleased Amanda to see how Cheryl took to Beth. Amanda said, "Mom, I didn't expect you to be here."

Beth replied, "Did you expect me not to come? How could I wait one more day, or even one more hour to see my granddaughter? Sam let me come with him," Amanda smiled, knowing just how her mother felt.

Sam took Amanda's carry on, and they went to get the rest of her luggage. Amanda offered to help carry Cheryl, but Beth wouldn't hear of it. She wanted a chance to get to know Cheryl.

When they got to the car, Beth took the back seat with Cheryl. Amanda took the front seat next to, Sam.

After they got on the Interstate Highway, they stopped for gas and dinner. They ate at McDonald's so that Cheryl could have a happy meal and get a toy.

WOMAN IN THE MIRROR

They made good time, arriving back home in Atlanta a little after midnight. Sam had the sofa bed ready. Cheryl slept that night in the sofa bed with Beth.

The next morning, Sam went to work. Before he left he had a surprise for Amanda. He had signed a lease for a three-bedroom house. Sam figured that since they were now a family of three, and soon to be four, they needed the room. Amanda was thrilled that the house had been available for immediate occupancy. They could move in right away. Sam planned to take her to see it as soon as he got off work today.

After breakfast Amanda called the clinic and spoke to Dr. Weston. Dr. Weston congratulated her on getting her daughter back safely. Amanda asked for, and was granted an extended leave of absence.

The rest of the day Amanda and Beth spent shopping with Cheryl. Cheryl needed everything. Beth would have been willing to buy her the whole store, so Amanda had to set limits. Cheryl was so happy to be back with her mother. She also liked having a grandmother who spent time with her, played with her, and wanted to get her anything she wanted.

All day Thursday David and his men, along with the police, tried to develop clues and run down leads. The police were checking on the power cruiser that had called at Tulum Wednesday. It didn't turn up in Belize. It must have turned east to the Grand Caymen Islands, or Jamaica. There must've been an accomplice to take Rosa to Playa Del Carmen. The police were asking questions, but so far nothing had turned up. David was concerned that he had an enemy willing to go this far; and that he didn't know who it could be. This made him feel uneasy.

Friday the police continued to question people in Tulum and other towns along the coast. They also had a photograph of Cheryl that they were showing. No one could say that they had seen the girl.

Late that afternoon a policeman interviewed a man who had taken the 12:15 PM ferry from Playa Del Carmen to Cozumel. The only girl of that age he remembered had been the daughter of a Mexican family. He felt sure that the girl had been Mexican, not Anglo. He remembered

MICHAEL O. GREGORY

that the girl slept all the way over in her mother's arms. The policeman filled the report away with the rest.

CHAPTER FORTY-ONE

Sam and Amanda spent the weekend moving into their new home. Amanda had really been pleased with the house. Beth had gone along with them to have a look at the new home before leaving for Gadsden. Best of all Cheryl could have her own bedroom, and they could have a nursery for the baby. They also had a real kitchen, with dining room, family room, and a carport for the cars. There would also be a large backyard for Cheryl to play in. Behind the back fence they had woods, with a small stream about thirty yards from the fence. Between the fence and the stream ran a trail that was used for riding dirt bikes and all-terrain vehicles. Sam and Amanda liked not having neighbors behind them. It gave them more privacy, despite the occasional dirt bike or all-terrain vehicle.

Monday afternoon Amanda was still trying to get everything in order, when Helen came for a visit. Amanda introduced Helen to Cheryl as Aunt Helen. Helen squatted down to be at eye level with Cheryl, and gave her a big smile. Cheryl took to her right away. She liked Aunt Helen. Helen reached out and hugged Cheryl, and kissed her on the cheek. Cheryl hugged and kissed Helen on the cheek in turn. Helen was happy for Amanda, that she now had Cheryl, and envious of her. Seeing Cheryl had awakened feelings in her that something was missing in her life.

After she got finished getting acquainted with Cheryl; Helen went into the kitchen with Amanda, where they each got a Coke from the refrigerator, and had a seat at the kitchen table. Cheryl continued to

MICHAEL O. GREGORY

watch cartoons on the television in the family room. When they were seated at the table, Helen said, "Thank you for making me a part of your family with Cheryl."

Amanda smiled, recalling that from the time that she had awoken from the surgery, Helen had been there, a rock that she could lean on during her initial period of vulnerability. Through Helen's tutorage, Amanda had learned what it meant to be the person who she had become, and to enjoy being herself. This had led to a friendship with Helen, a special bond that she had with no one else. Amanda said, "You're my best friend, even more than a best friend. We have secrets that I can share with no one else, ever. We are as close as sisters are, maybe even closer. You are a part of the family."

Helen knew what Amanda meant, and felt pleased that Amanda cherished their friendship as much as she did. To change the subject, Helen looked around the kitchen. "It's amazing what has happened to you in the last fifteen months. You started out with almost nothing. Now look at you. You have a wonderful husband, a nice home, a beautiful five-year-old daughter and you're expecting. Well, I know that some of the circumstances are a bit unusual, but you've handled it well."

Putting her coke can down on the table, Amanda sighed. "You can say that again. I never dreamed that things would turn out as they did."

Helen replied, "I'll say it again, you've handled it well."

Amanda again sighed as she cast her eyes up at the ceiling. "Tell me that in a year from now. I have a five-year-old daughter, going on six, and I'm expecting a second child. I'm trying my best, but I have no experience with children. My daughter remembers me as her mother, but I have no memory of her. She's mine, a part of me, and at the same time a stranger, but I love her as if I've known her from the time she was in my womb. You know that I get up at night just to watch her sleep. She's such a beautiful child. I want so very much to be a good mother to her."

Helen took Amanda's hand into hers, and patted the back of her hand as she smiled at her. "Don't worry Amanda, just love her, care for

WOMAN IN THE MIRROR

her and always keep her best interest in mind. If you do that, you'll be a great mother. Circumstance thrust all of this on you all at once, but you're equal to it. You'll do just fine."

Amanda nodded. "Yes, my circumstance is very inconvenient at times, but I wouldn't have it any other way."

With a nod, Helen said, "Well, let's hope that all he surprises are behind you now."

Amanda sighed. "Yes, it seems that I've uncovered most of my life now. I don't think there can be many more surprises left."

Helen said with humor in her voice. "Well, you could have twins."

Amanda threw up her hands in mock supplication. "Please, Helen, don't even think it."

Helen laughed. "Oh, I'm just kidding."

Amanda, also laughing, said, "I know. By the way, Sam's going to adopt Cheryl"

Helen regarded Amanda with a look of affection. She was happy for Amanda, for her good fortune. "You know, you really got lucky with Sam. He's a really good man."

Amanda became introspective at the thought of her and Sam's love for each other. "Yes, he really loves me, and he really loves Cheryl also. He's going to get her a dog this week. We're going to the pound to get one."

"So you're going to get a puppy?" Helen said with glee.

Amanda shook her head. "No, Sam thanks that they're too much trouble. He said that they chew up everything, and they have to be house broken. He wants to get a mature dog. I told him that's okay, as long as it's not a bulldog."

Helen laughed again. "There you go about bulldogs again. What is it that you have against bulldogs anyway?"

Smiling, Amanda said, "Actuality nothing, it's just a private joke between Sam and myself. Sam can get a bulldog if he really wants one, I don't mind."

Helen dropped the humor as she again changed the subject. "To

305

be serious now, do you think that Cheryl's father can ever find you?"

Amanda became very serious. "I don't know. We took care to cover our tracks, but you never know. Mr. Fitzgerald is keeping an eye on him. If he makes a move to come back to the United States, Pat will alert me, the FBI and the DEA."

Helen, speaking of Patrick Fitzgerald, said, "Can you rely on him?"

Amanda responded, "He hasn't let me down yet, and he has an incentive. There's a reward for David Zamora. Pat has assured me that if David Zamora finds me, that he will be here to protect me.

"I hope it doesn't come to that. I hope that he never finds you."

Amanda put her hands on the table. "Enough of that. Would you like to see the rest of the house?"

With a smile, Helen responded, "Why, yes, I'd love to." They finished their Cokes; then Amanda took Helen to see the rest of the house.

David Zamora had been getting impatient with the police. They had been looking and found nothing. David even brought in additional men, but even this effort produced no leads. David thought. *This is really strange, no ransom, no threats, no anything. Whoever took her wants to keep her, but why? She's only a girl, nothing more.*

The power cruiser had proved to be a dead end. It had been traced down, and had turned out to be some businessmen on a cruise, nothing more. Whom-ever had taken Cheryl, had to have gotten her out some other way. She couldn't be found around here anywhere. There didn't seem to be any use in continuing to look around Tulum, there were no leads there. David would have to think of something else.

The next five days David Zamora spent going through police reports and interviews. He was particularity interested in the interviews. On the surface there wasn't anything out of the ordinary, but he knew that people's observations were notorious for being inaccurate. People would believe that they saw what they said that they saw; but David knew that people tend to see what they're expecting to see, so someone may have overlooked something.

WOMAN IN THE MIRROR

David now read an interview of a man who took the 12:15 ferry to Cozumel on the day of the kidnapping. He mentioned a Mexican couple with a daughter the same age as Cheryl. The man had said how the little girl had slept in her mother's arms all the way over on the ferry. David thought. *Maybe he saw a Mexican girl because that is what he expected to see. Perhaps they took her to Cozumel. I need to send some men over to Cozumel to start asking around. They may come up with something.*

The next day David sent two men over to Cozumel to ask questions, and show Cheryl's photograph around. They started by questioning the ferry crews and passengers. By the second day they had finished questioning the ferry crews and passengers. They learned some facts and made some conclusions. The family in question had been remembered by some of the crew and passengers. They were dressed as a local working-class family. They stayed apart from everyone as much as possible. The couple had been in their thirties, the child about four to five years old. No one had ever seen them before. By the end of the second day all of David's efforts were focused on Cozumel.

It didn't take David's men long to determine that they were not a local family. A check of the hotels turned up information on a Mexican-American couple in their thirties. They had spent four days vacationing in Cozumel. They had left by charted aircraft for the Grand Cayman Islands the afternoon of the kidnapping. They didn't have a child with them when they boarded the aircraft. This promising trail seemed to be a dead end.

Three days later one of David's men questioned a woman who sold souvenirs to the tourist from the cruise ships. She remembered a young woman with a little girl boarding the cruise ship the afternoon of the day of the kidnapping. The information seemed promising.

He took the ferry back to Playa Del Carmen. From there he got a ride back to the villa. He was shown into the living room to report to David. David stood at a window looking out to sea. David said, "Okay, what is it?"

The man responded, "The afternoon of the kidnapping a young

MICHAEL O. GREGORY

woman in her mid-twenties was seen boarding a cruise ship. She had a little girl with her, about four to five years old, who was asleep in her arms."

David half turned his head to look at the man that was giving the report. "Okay, what's so special about this one?"

The man continued, "The woman that I spoke to said that the woman with the little girl didn't come back in a taxi, or with a tour group. She came in a private car with an older Mexican couple."

David turned around to face the man. The man continued to give his report. "They waited until a tour group returned. The young woman then got out of the car and joined the tour group to board the ship."

Something started to click in David's mind. "Quick, tell me, what she looked like?"

The man replied, "She had a yellow and green scarf, shorts and..."

David yelled, "Damn it! I don't give a damn what she was wearing! What did she look like?"

The man was somewhat taken aback, and subdued by David's behavior, "Well, Boss, she was almost your height, about sixty kilos, black hair and blue or green eyes."

David exploded in a rage. He started knocking over furniture, breaking lamps and swearing, "Damn it! That bitch! That whoring slut! I'm going to kill her! I'm going to rip her heart out!" David kept up a steady stream of profanity. It took at least five minutes before he had been able to calm himself enough to talk to anyone. "I'm going to kill that bitch!"

The man asked, "Who's that, Boss?"

David spit out the words, "Vicki! That's whom it was that took Cheryl! I'm going to kill that whoring bitch! You!" David pointed at the man who gave the report, "You go back to Cozumel. You find out everything that you can about her. I want to know everywhere that she went, and everyone she talked to."

The man said, turning to leave, "Yes, Boss."

David waved him out of the room, "Go! Get out of here!" David turned to another man, "You get in touch with our people in the states. Tell them to start looking for Victoria Bujold, they know who she is. I don't care what it takes, I want her found. That stinking little whore. I should've killed her the first time."

David made himself a stiff drink, and sat on the sofa. "Find out what ship she was on. See if we can pick up her trail."

CHAPTER FORTY-TWO

Sam and Amanda took Cheryl to the animal control shelter to look for a dog. After looking over what was available, they settled on a friendly and well behaved two-year-old thereabouts, female, half German Shepard and half whatever. Cheryl and the dog took to each other right off. Sam and Amanda started to come up with a proper name for the dog. They settled on the dog's name when Cheryl decided to call her Lady. Not very original, but Sam and Amanda agreed that it suited her.

Cheryl now had someone to play with in the backyard. Lady followed Cheryl everywhere around the yard and house. Lady would lie on the floor next to Cheryl as she watched television. Cheryl even wanted Lady to sleep with her, but Amanda had to draw the line somewhere. Lady's bed would be in the laundry room, off the kitchen. With taking care of Sam, Cheryl and Lady, Amanda's home had quickly become a full-time job.

Amanda had entered into her second trimester now, and had started to show. She went for a sonogram to show to Sam. That evening when Sam got home, Amanda waited for him at the front door as usual. Cheryl had started to wait with Amanda for Sam. A strong bond had started to develop between Sam and Cheryl. When Sam came in the front door he embraced and kissed Amanda. He would then pick up Cheryl, hug her, and kiss her on the cheeks. With Amanda and Sam's love and affection, Cheryl had started to become a well-adjusted, happy and outgoing child.

WOMAN IN THE MIRROR

After Sam arrived, and the now familiar greetings had taken place; Cheryl couldn't wait to break the news to Sam. "Mommy has something for you. It's a picture."

Still holding Cheryl, Sam looked at her, and gave her a smile; knowing that Amanda had gone to the doctor for a sonogram that day. "Oh, she does, and what is this picture of?"

Cheryl said with pride, "Mommy said that it's a picture of her baby."

Amanda handed Sam the sonogram. Sam took the sonogram image in one hand, while still holding, Cheryl on his hip with the other arm. "Here, Sam, the first picture of our baby."

While still holding Cheryl, Sam looked at the image. He could make out the image of a fetus. Amanda pointed to a spot on the image. "See this."

Cheryl giggled, then said, "Mommy said that's his little boy thing."

Sam looked at Amanda with a broad grin on his face. "It's a boy?" It was as much of an exclamation as a question.

Smiling, Amanda put her arms around Sam and Cheryl, and kissed Sam. "Yes, Sam, you're going to have a son."

Cheryl, eager to express her joy, said, "And I'm going to have a little brother."

Sam kissed Cheryl on the cheek. "So you will, and you can help Mommy take care of him." Sam kissed Cheryl on the cheek again, then put her back down on the floor. He then embraced and kissed Amanda again, as Cheryl looked on. This outward show of affection thrilled, and reassured Cheryl. Such uninhibited show of affection was new to her, she liked it, and she liked Sam. He was unlike any other man that she had ever known. Sam looked at them. "Okay, I say that this calls for a celebration. What do you say that we eat out tonight?" Amanda and Cheryl agreed. Sam asked Cheryl where she wanted to eat. They went to KFC for dinner.

The next Sunday Sam and Amanda spent at the pistol range. Amanda had become a very good shot now. The Glock no longer seemed alien to her. She now felt comfortable with the feel of it in

311

MICHAEL O. GREGORY

her hand. The range where they shot had a regular known distance range, and a combat range. She could come to enjoy it, if she didn't always have to think of why she had to do this. She took seriously what Patrick Fitzgerald had said about every time you handle the weapon, or clean it, you think of what it's for. The idea of having to take a life had been repugnant to her at first, but after thinking about it often it no longer seemed so shocking to her. She now felt that if need be, she could shoot someone without hesitation. Sam had also taught Amanda how to use the shotgun.

Helen had offered to do the baby sitting for Amanda while they were at the range, or any other time that Amanda needed someone to look after Cheryl. Helen had been glad to do it for Amanda. Cheryl proved to be a delightful child that Helen enjoyed having around. Cheryl enjoyed the time spent with Aunt Helen. Tiger lived with Aunt Helen, and Cheryl wanted to play with Tiger. Tiger, however, wasn't use to having children around. He tried as much as he could to stay out of Cheryl's way.

David had gone to the home of, Arrio Jimenez, an associate of his in Chetumal. They had been discussing a shipment of heroin to be moved into the United States through Baltimore, Maryland. They had a working lunch where they had discussed the business of the heroin shipment. The maid had just brought the coffee. Arrio said, "Tell me, what the latest on this problem with Cheryl?"

David put down his coffee cup, and faced Arrio. "I know who's behind it now."

Arrio also knew who was behind it, but asked the question anyway, "Yes, who's that?"

David became enraged every time that he had to think or say the name Victoria Bujold. "It was that bitch Victoria Bujold, her mother."

Arrio knew that this had to be about the worst thing that could have happened to David. This went far beyond the custody of a child; it meant that their security could, and had been penetrated. "How could you have let this happen David?"

WOMAN IN THE MIRROR

David shrugged. "I just didn't think that it could happen. I got rid of that whore Vicki a long time ago. I hadn't heard of her since the night that I kicked her out. For all I knew, she could have been dead."

Arrio smiled, knowing that his remark would draw a sharp reaction from David. "Well, obliviously she's not dead. She did this to you."

David's rage started to welt up in him again. "The bitch isn't going to get away with it! I'm going to find her; then I'm going to kill her!" David started to get control of his rage. He didn't want to seem out of control in front of Arrio, "I know that she was down here. There had been a Miss Victoria Bujold and daughter Cheryl booked on the Norwegian Cruise Line ship Majesty. The ship had called at Cozumel at the time of the kidnapping. Of the crew members that we've been able to talk to, no one remembers seeing the girl until after the ship left Cozumel. They left the ship at Key West. From there they flew to Miami, then to Charlotte, North Carolina. That's where the trail ends."

Arrio nodded. He had been kept informed of David's efforts to locate Cheryl and her mother. "Well, David, you can stop looking for Victoria Bujold. That's not her real name, or she wouldn't be so open about it."

"Yes, I know that." David said nodding.

Arrio lit a cigar and got it going before he continued, "Look, David, I'm not as concerned about her, as I am about who helped her. Now the people who did this had to be watching you for a long time. They knew just when to strike. What I want to know is, who are they?"

David shook his head. "I don't know."

Arrio exhaled a cloud of smoke, and said, "Well, David, we have to know. This could hurt the business."

David slammed his fist down on the table, rattling the coffee cups. "Damn her, I should have killed her the first time."

Arrio looked at him. "Then why didn't you?"

David got a sadistic look on his face. 'It gave me more pleasure to completely destroy her without killing her. Besides, I figured that she would do that to herself."

MICHAEL O. GREGORY

Arrio blew out another cloud of smoke. "Well she didn't do what you thought that she would do. Now you need to take care of this mess before it starts to interfere with business. Understand David?"

David nodded. "Yes, I understand."

The doorbell rang. Amanda went to answer it. Patrick Fitzgerald stood at the door. Stepping back and holding the door open, Amanda said, "Hello, Pat, please come in."

"Good to see you Amanda." Patrick stepped through the door and saw Cheryl standing behind Amanda, holding on tightly to her skirt with both hands. He squatted down to be at eye level with her. "So you're Cheryl, I'm glad to finally meet you. You're a really pretty young lady. I'm Patrick Fitzgerald. You can call me Pat."

Still holding on tightly to Amanda's skirt, Cheryl gave Patrick a tentative smile, and said, "Hi, Pat."

Patrick gave Cheryl a broad-reassuring smile, and said, "Hi, Cheryl." He stood back up and said, "Amanda, we have to talk."

Amanda looked at Patrick, and wondered what could be so urgent to bring him here, she said, "Would you like to have some coffee, Coke, or iced tea?"

Patrick said, "It's warm today. The iced tea sounds good."

Patrick followed Amanda back to the kitchen, and took a seat at the table. Amanda made iced tea for Patrick and herself. She served Cheryl a glass of Coke in front of the television in the family room. Cheryl could watch her favorite television show, while Patrick and her mother talked in private. When Amanda finally sat down at the table with him, Patrick said, "You really look good."

Amanda smiled. "Thank you, Pat, I needed that. It's hard to feel that you look good when you can't fit into most of your clothes anymore."

Patrick smiled at Amanda's remarks about her figure. "How far along are you?"

"I'm in my fifth month." Amanda replied.

Patrick looked at Amanda with an appraising eye. "Well, I still say that you look good. Now for the reason that I've come. David knows

314

WOMAN IN THE MIRROR

of your involvement in Cheryl's abduction."

Amanda looked down at the tea glass in her hand. "Yes, well we can't say that we didn't expect him not to find out."

Patrick said, "He traced you as far as Charlotte."

Amanda sighed. "Yes, we expected that much also."

Patrick gave her a reassuring smile. "I just wanted to let you know that we're still looking out for you. We don't have anyone on the inside to feed us information. However if he leaves Mexico to come to the United States, we can assume that he has located you. We're keeping an eye on him. If he makes a move, we'll know about it."

Amanda looked up from her tea glass at Patrick. "That's good. Sam and I are very careful, and I hardly let Cheryl out of my sight."

Patrick gave Amanda a pat on the forearm. "Well, keep it up, it's not over with yet. We'll try to be quick enough to get the feds involved, and get him entering the country. If we can't intercept him before he gets to Atlanta, we need to have contingency plans ready. Also I'd like to make a security survey of your home. First off, do you have a security system?"

Amanda shook her head. "No, we don't."

"Okay, then I'll tell you the best one to get. Once you get it, you need to use it all the time. Now, when you moved did you leave a forwarding address?"

Amanda and Sam had taken the proper precautions. "Only with the post office."

Patrick smiled. "That's good, and you have an unlisted phone number?"

Amanda nodded. "Yes, we do."

Patrick said, "Okay, let's first talk about security. Then I want to look at your house, and check out the rest of your property."

CHAPTER FORTY-THREE

David had been able to trace Vicki as far as Charlotte, North Carolina, then nothing a dead end. They had checked the telephone book without results. David felt certain that wherever she was, Vicki would no longer be going by the name of Victoria Bujold. When he had thrown Vicki out, he had gotten rid of every memory of her. He didn't even have a photograph of her. He had put out a reward on the street with a description of Vicki and Cheryl. There were many leads, but none of them bore results. After a few days it became obvious that Vicki didn't live in Charlotte under any name. She didn't fly out of Charlotte, and no taxi driver remembered picking her up at the airport. It seemed that they just vanished without a trace.

David and his two companions were having breakfast on the patio. They were trying to decide what to do next. David looked around the table. "Okay, any ideas? What do we do next?"

The man sitting on his left said. "Well, Boss, I don't know."

In anger David slammed his fist on the table rattling the tableware. "Damn it, I don't want to hear 'I don't know'! I want ideas! Now think!"

After a minute of silence, the same man spoke again. "Well, Boss, Lexington is a dead end. She has no family or friends there that she could have gone to. She left Lexington when you kicked her out, but no one knows how or to where."

The other man asked. "Did she have family, Boss?"

David thought for a moment, then shook his head. "If she does, she never told me anything about them. I can now see how very little I

316

knew about her. I never knew what her real name was, if Victoria Bujold wasn't her real name." David sat thinking for a couple of minutes before he spoke again. His men just sat at the table their breakfast forgotten as they waited on David's pleasure. Finally, David said. "Okay, we can't find her any other way, let's go back to where I first met her. We'll get in touch with our people in New Orleans. I want them to put out a net. Let's see if we can catch anything in it."

David placed a call to his head man, Jack Monroe in New Orleans. He instructed Jack to make inquiries at the clubs, bars and any other place that he could think of, to see if anyone knew Vicki or her family.

Jack Monroe detailed four men to start checking the clubs, bars and any other place that they could think of to try to find out anything about Victoria Bujold. It soon became apparent that someone else had been making inquiries about Victoria Bujold earlier. They soon learned that the person making the inquires was a private investigator by the name of Hugh Desormeaux, with an office on Dumaine Street in the French Quarter. Jack relayed this information to David Zamora. Orders were given to pay Mr. Desormeaux a call to inquire as to why he had been looking for Victoria Bujold and who he had been working for.

The next morning at eight Hugh Desormeaux left his apartment. He walked to his favorite café for coffee and a crescent. Next, he stopped off for the morning paper, before going to his office. He entered the building and took the stairs to the second floor. He turned left, stopped at the first door and put his key into the lock. As he stepped into his office two men suddenly came up behind him. They shoved him through the door, up against the desk. The two men held him with his arms pinned behind his back, while a third man slapped duct tape over his mouth. They then rushed him downstairs to a waiting van and drove off.

The van took Interstate 10 East towards Slidell. Hugh had been bound, blindfolded and dumped on the floor of the van. The van crossed Lake Pontchartrain, then turned left on State Highway 433. After a few miles the van turned off onto an unimproved road. They

MICHAEL O. GREGORY

finally stopped in front of a barn deep in the woods. It was a ramshackle structure long out of use, with a leaky roof, sunlight showing through the board siding and a dirt floor.

When the van reached the barn there were two men standing next to a car smoking. As soon as the van stopped, they went over to it. The older of the two men said. "Take him inside and tie him to a post."

The driver of the van said. "Okay, Jack."

Everyone got out of the van, dragging Hugh with them. Two men dragged Hugh into the barn and tied him up to one of the posts that supported the roof of the barn. The two men from the car came into the barn and stood in front of Hugh. They were in no hurry to begin. They just stood in front of Hugh for about three minutes to let the tension build. Finally, Jack ordered Hugh's blindfold and gag removed. as soon as they were removed, he said. "Mr. Desormeaux, we would like a word with you."

Hugh blinked at the light, took a few seconds to get his bearings, then looked at Jack. When he answered it was with forced casualness. "You could have just come down to my office. You didn't have to go to all this trouble."

Jack could see that the old man had some spirit. He would have to use guile as much as force to get what he wanted from the old man. Jack addressed Hugh in a patronizing tone of voice. "Oh, but Mr. Desormeaux, we wanted to be sure that we had your full attention. It will soon be clear to you. Mr. Desormeaux, you were showing a picture of a young woman around about two months ago."

Hugh shot back. "So, I show a lot of pictures around."

Jack shook his head and said harshly. "Wrong answer, old man!"

Jack Monroe stepped back and gave the other man a nod. The other man stepped up and drove his fist into Hugh's solar plexus. The air exploded out of Hugh's lungs. Even knowing that the blow was coming and tightening his abdominal muscles in preparation for it, the pain was excruciating. He went double as much as he could. He tried to breathe again, but he had a hard time catching his breath. The man hit him again lower in the abdomen. Perspiration started to bead on his forehead. His breathing became ragged and labored.

Jack Monroe motioned his man away, then stepped up in front of Hugh. He said in a matter-of-fact voice. "Okay, Mr. Desormeaux, same question. The picture of the young woman that you were showing around. Why were you showing it around?" Hugh just looked at him saying nothing. Jack Monroe could see that the old man was being stubborn. He nodded to his man and stepped back.

Hugh's antagonist struck again. This time he went for the head. He hit Hugh on the jaw, and pain exploded in his head. The force of the blow broke Hugh's dentures, cutting his gums and the inside of his mouth. Hugh spit out his dentures to keep from incurring farther injury or swallowing them. One of the men cried out. "Hay, George, you just knocked the old man's teeth out." This was followed by loud guffaws.

Hugh had started to feel all the effects from the abuse on his body. His muscles ached from the beating that he had sustained and from the strain against his bindings. He wanted to vomit, and his head hurt. Hugh had no illusions as to who these people were. He knew for certain that regardless if he cooperated or not, he would soon be a dead man. All he had left was his dignity. He must hold out for as long as he could.

Jack Monroe stepped up again. He spoke to Hugh in a soft-reassuring tone of voice. "Okay, Mr. Desormeaux, it doesn't have to be this way. Just answer the questions and you can be back in your office in no time. Tell me, who are you working for?"

Jack looked hard at the old man. He had to respect his courage, but he would get the information that he wanted. "Well, Mr. Desormeaux, it seems that you need an attitude adjustment.'

Jack gave the signal and his man struck Hugh several more times, mostly body blows, but a couple in the face. One blow cracked two ribs. Another broke a cheek bone. The pain had become intense. Hugh even had a pain in his back. It had started to become hard for him to breathe. His knees were shaking so much that if he weren't tied to the post, he wouldn't be able to stand. He had bent forward as much as

MICHAEL O. GREGORY

his bindings would allow, trying to guard himself against the blows.

Jack waved his man aside, then stepped in front of Hugh. When he spoke his voice again had a consolatory tone. "Come now, Mr. Desormeaux, we don't have to do it this way. All we want to know is who you are working for, and why you were looking for Miss. Victoria Bujold?"

Hugh could barely speak now, but he was still defiant. He knew that if he didn't keep fighting, he would be lost. He spoke. "Go to hell!"

Jack had expected this response from Hugh. The old man had a lot of fight in him. It would take a while to break his spirit. "All right, Mr. Desormeaux, have it your own way." Jack nodded to his man and stepped back.

The blows came again. Hugh felt faint, and he still had trouble breathing. He felt pain throughout his body. His left arm had started to get numb.

After the beating stopped, Jack Monroe questioned Hugh again. His attitude switched from conciliatory to sharp admonishment. "Mr. Desormeaux, you better tell us, who are you working for? Why were you looking for Miss. Victoria Bujold?"

Hugh couldn't even speak. He just shook his head. Breathing had become extremely difficult. It felt like his chest was in a vise. Hugh Desormeaux lost consciousness and stopped breathing. He collapsed as much as his bindings would allow.

One of jack's men spoke. "Look, the old fool has passed out."

Another of the men checked Hugh. "Damn, hay he's stopped breathing! Quick, cut the ropes!"

One of the men took out a pocketknife, flipped open the blade and started to cut the ropes. The other men took hold of Hugh, lowered him to the floor and rolled him onto his back. They started CPR, but it was of no use. Hugh Desormeaux had died of a heart attack.

Jack Monroe, who had been kneeling next to Hugh's body jumped to his feet and started kicking the body. "Damn! Damn him to hell!' seeing it as a useless action, he stopped kicking the body and turned to the men from the van. He kicked the body one last time. "Take him out to the swamp and feed him to the gators. I don't want him found."

The men from the van picked up the body and carried it away. Jack Monroe and his man George were left in the barn alone. "Jack, I'm sorry. I didn't mean to kill him."

Jack put his hand on the man's shoulder to reassure him. "Don't worry, it couldn't be helped. You didn't know that he had such a frail heart. He was probably due to drop dead soon anyway."

Jack and his man paced the floor of the barn. George said. "What do we do now? He was our only lead."

Jack looked at him. "Not our only lead, only our first. He had been looking for something. If he found it, we can too. Just keep checking the clubs and other public places."

They left the barn, got into their car and drove back to New Orleans.

It was early afternoon. David Zamora had gone to Arrio Jimenez's home on business. They were seated on the veranda having drinks. The home sat on high ground behind Chetumal and had a splendid view of the city and bay. Arrio put his drink down on the side table and looking at David, said. "David, we need to talk."

David knew what Arrio wanted to talk about, the problem with Vicki and Cheryl. He had been expecting it. "Yes, what about?"

Arrio spoke. "This thing about Cheryl's kidnapping. What have you found out so far?"

David regarded the ice in his drink as he replied. "Her trail led to Charlotte, North Carolina. We know now that it was just a phony lead. We were meant to look there."

Arrio took his drink in hand and got up to pace about the veranda. He looked away from David toward the bay as he spoke. "I hear that you have a lead in New Orleans?"

David looked at Arrio. "I see that not much gets past you."

Arrio turned to face David and said with hubris. "If it did, I wouldn't be on top for very long. Now, what do you have from New Orleans?"

David responded. "New Orleans was where I first met Vicki. I

MICHAEL O. GREGORY

knew that she had no friends or family in Lexington where we lived and that she had left there when I threw her out. So, the only place to look was New Orleans. When we started to look something curious happened. We found that a private investigator had been looking for Vicki ahead of us."

Arrio nodded, already familiar with what had transpired in New Orleans. "Yes, I know about the detective, and I know that he died before you could get anything out of him."

David responded. "We're checking all the clubs, bars and other public places. Whatever he found we can find too." It didn't surprise David that Arrio had the information about New Orleans. What concerned him was who in his organization had been giving him his information.

Arrio knew that David had this thing about personal honor. Perhaps if it had happened to him, he would feel the same, but that wasn't important to him now. He had to know who could come down here and do this. "I know what you are doing, but I have a question for you."

"Yes, what's that?" David responded.

Arrio looked at David in a manner of a superior to a subordinate. "Have you found out anything about the people who helped her yet?"

David looked back at Arrio, not wanting to appear intimidated. "We know that there was a Mexican American couple that flew out of Cozumel the afternoon of the kidnapping. We later found that another Mexican American man was with them in Tulum that day. We know that he left by way of Merida to Mexico City then to Dallas, Texas. It was later determined that they were traveling on forged documents."

Arrio nodded. "And what else did you find out about them?"

David looked down at his glass. "Well, nothing."

Arrio exclaimed. "Damn! Any policeman his first week on the job can find out that much! Are you telling me that this Vicki is just a dumb little broad!"

David didn't like to be talked to like this. Not even by Arrio. As much as he wanted to shout at Arrio, or strike him, he had to keep

322

WOMAN IN THE MIRROR

his temper. "Yes, that's what I'm saying, just a screwed up little bitch!"

Arrio didn't like it that someone had been able to operate on his own home ground with impunity. "Well, this screwed up little bitch, as you put it, has really put one over on you." David by now had become very angry but didn't want to show it. He made a show of casually sipping his drink. Arrio continued to speak. "Perhaps you're right about one thing. I doubt that this girl Vicki put all this together. This took some organization with the resources, expertise and intelligence to pull it off. They knew everyone in your household, where they would be and what they were doing. Now, the government wouldn't be using private investigators. This wasn't the FBI, ATF or the CIA or any other agency in that alphabet soup in Washington. Now you had better find out who's behind this. I don't like someone that I don't know looking over my shoulder in my own backyard. That can be bad for business. Now, you just do what you must do, just find out who they are."

David planned to find Vicki and erase the stain on his honor. "Don't worry, Arrio, I'll take care of it. I'm going to find Vicki and kill her."

Arrio spoke with anger and authority in his voice. "I don't care about your personal problems. You find out who's behind this."

David said in a conciliatory tone. "But she made me lose face before my men. I must get her. It's a matter of honor."

Arrio exclaimed. "Your honor can wait! The business comes first."

David could say nothing more, Arrio was right. He must find out who was behind all of this.

323

CHAPTER FORTY-FOUR

Amanda and Cheryl took DNA tests to prove to the court beyond any doubt that Amanda was Cheryl's mother. Since Amanda had been the only parent of record, Cheryl's adoption by Sam should be no problem. Amanda had taken great care to explain to Cheryl what adoption meant, and how Sam would be her father. Cheryl liked Sam, but David was already her daddy. How could she have two daddies? Amanda explained to her that although David said that he was her daddy, he wasn't on her birth certificate, so he couldn't be her daddy. Cheryl then asked if Sam would be on her birth certificate. Amanda told her that Sam wouldn't be on her birth certificate, but that his name would be on other documents that would say that he was her daddy. Cheryl believed her, but needed time to sort it all out.

The next Saturday, Sam and Amanda took Cheryl to Six flags over Georgia. They took Cheryl on every ride that she wanted to go on, and they saw the puppet show. By that time Cheryl had reached the end of her endurance. They decided that the time had come to go. Sam picked up Cheryl, and carried her to the car. Sam and Amanda were deciding where to go for dinner. Cheryl wanted a happy meal, so they went to McDonald's for dinner.

That evening a tired, but happy little girl got ready for bed. Sam and Amanda knelt with Cheryl for her evening prayers. Sam and Amanda tucked her in. As Sam was saying good-night Cheryl said, "Sam, Mommy said that you're going to be my Daddy."

San adjusted the bed covers around Cheryl, then brushed her cheek with his fingertips. "Yes, Cheryl, I want very much to be your Daddy."

Cheryl, looking at Sam, smiled. "Mommy said that I should call you Daddy."

Sam still sat on the edge of the bed looking at her. "That's up to you Cheryl."

"Do you want me to call you Daddy?"

Sam smiled at her, and patted her on the shoulder. "Yes, I'd love that Cheryl"

Cheryl yawned, then said, "Okay, good-night, Daddy." Cheryl then closed her eyes.

Sam kissed Cheryl on the cheek, turned out the light, and left the room. Amanda had been standing in the doorway. She felt relieved that Cheryl had accepted Sam as her father. When they were out in the hall, Amanda hugged and kissed Sam. "Oh, I'm so relieved that Cheryl wants you to be her father."

Sam put his arms around Amanda's waist, and drew her close. "Well, I really worked hard for it. In fact there's only one other woman that I ever worked harder to get."

Amanda embraced and kissed him. "I love you Sam."

Sam, continuing to hold Amanda in a close embrace, said, "I love you too, but you're no longer the only woman in my life."

Amanda, with a devious smile, said, "Oh, do I know her?"

Sam laughed, letting Amanda have the last word. He felt proud that they were really a family now. He kissed Amanda again, then said, "Do you want to make out?"

Amanda snuggled up next to Sam, pressing her body against his. "What are you waiting for?"

At 10:00 PM on the same Saturday night they had a large crowd at the Lucky 7 Club. The alcohol flowed freely, and everyone was having a good time. Gloria had taken her turn on the runway to dance for the patrons. She already had several large bills stuck in her G-string. It looked to be a good night.

Eugene Deloatch, an enforcer for Jack Monroe walked in and sat

MICHAEL O. GREGORY

at the bar. The bar tender came up, and Eugene orders a beer. When the bar tender came back with the beer, Eugene told him not to leave, that he wanted to talk with him. The bar tender said, "Listen, Mac, I've lots of customers. I don't have time to talk."

The bartender started to leave. Eugene grabbed his wrist. "I suggest that you make the time."

The bartender had been angered by the rudeness of Eugene's action, and had been about to say something to him. One look into Eugene's eyes, and he could see that this would be no one to argue with, "Okay, Mac, what do you want to know?"

Eugene said, "We're looking for someone, a girl about twenty-five, good looking, about five-foot eight-inches, about one-hundred-thirty pounds, black hair, green eyes, calls herself Victoria Bujold."

The bartender nodded. "Yes, I remember, some old geezer came in here a couple of months ago. He had her photograph, and was looking for someone who knew her."

Eugene had heard this at other clubs, but here the bartender didn't finish by saying that no one knew her. Eugene asked, "Did anyone here know her?"

The bartender looked down, trying to avoid eye contact with Eugene, "No, everyone here said that they didn't know her."

Eugene could tell that even though he didn't lie outright, he hadn't told everything. Eugene knew that the best method to get information would be to be direct and forceful. He grabbed the bartender by the collar and pulled him closer. "Okay, buddy, do you want to answer my questions now, or do you want to answer them for my friends later?"

The bartender knew that nothing good could come from this Man's inquiry, and he didn't want to get Gloria in any trouble, but he realized that it would be in his beat interest to talk now. "Okay, as I said, he came in here asking if anyone knew her. No one said that they knew her. A couple of days later he came back. This time he had the girl with him, you know this Vicki."

Eugene realized that he had found what he had been looking for.

WOMAN IN THE MIRROR

"Yes, go on."

The bartender swallowed hard, knowing that he was about to betray Gloria, "Well, she wanted to see Gloria."

Eugene gave the bartender's collar another jerk. "Who's this Gloria?"

The bartender pointed at the woman dancing on the runway. "That's her right there."

Eugene took a look at Gloria, as she danced on the runway; then turned back to face the bartender. "All right, what's her full name?"

"It's Gloria Franklin." The bartender responded.

Eugene got right up into the bartenders face, and gave him an intense look. "Okay, you look like a real smart guy. If you want to collect your Social Security, keep your mouth shut. Understand?"

The bartender nodded nervously, he understood all too well.

Gloria finished work at 1:00 AM. It had been a very good and profitable night. She looked forward to treating herself to a day of shopping tomorrow. She could even get herself that designer handbag that she had her eye on. She dressed and left the club through the back door, and started walking to her car; she never made it. Two men grabbed her from behind. The last thing that she knew had been the odor of chloroform.

When Gloria regained consciousness, she lay on her back on a table, in what looked to be a storeroom. She was wrapped in what appeared to be a large table cloth. It was wrapped tight enough to keep her immobile, but not so tight as to leave bruises or other marks. She heard voices and looked around to see where the voices were coming from, as best as she could from where she lay. She had been wrapped so tightly that she could only move her head and toes. There were several men in the room. Most were in the shadows, so she couldn't see them well. There were three men standing close to her. She felt helpless and terrified. She just knew without anyone having to tell her, that these man could be killers. The man next to her head looked down and smiled. It was a cruel smile without warmth. "Hello, Gloria, good to see you with us at last."

327

MICHAEL O. GREGORY

Gloria would like to know who he was, but she dare not ask. After a few seconds she got the nerve to speak. "Why am I here?"

Still looking down at her, Jack Monroe said, "Well, we have a problem, and you can help us with it. We need to ask you some questions."

Gloria had no idea what these men could want from her. "Okay." She managed to say timidly.

Jack could see that she was sufficiently terrified to offer little resistance to interrogation, he began. "Someone came to see you a couple of months ago. It was Victoria Bujold."

Gloria wondered what Vicki had to do with this. "Yes, I remember her."

Jack said, "Okay, good so far. Now where did she come from?"

Gloria shook her head. "I don't know."

Jack got right in her face, and said in an icy-threatening voice that sent a chill along her spine. "That's not a good answer!"

Jack reached into a basin on another table next to him, and took out a small terry cloth hand towel. He rung out the excess water, then placed the towel over her face. Gloria didn't know for what reason the towel had been placed on her face, but she felt sure that it would be for something unpleasant. The towel felt cool to her skin. Cool and moist air filtered through the towel. Someone poured water on the towel. Gloria couldn't breathe. She tried to draw a breath, but air wouldn't come through the towel. It felt like she was drowning. She shook her head violently back and forth trying to shake off the towel, but someone kept pressing it to her face. Gloria panicked losing control of her body functions, and wet herself. Finally the man holding the towel removed it from her face. She tried to cough and breathe at the same time.

Jack said, "Okay, now be a good girl. Give me the answers that I want and we'll get along just fine. Now, same question, where did she come from?"

Gloria, in fear for her life cried so hard that she could barely speak between the sobs. "I don't know."

Jack put the towel back on her face and repeated the torture. When

328

WOMAN IN THE MIRROR

he removed the towel, and she got her breath back. Gloria continued to cry uncontrollably, shouting out between sobs. "I don't know! I don't know!"

Jack could see that he had so terrified her, that if she knew where Vicki was, she would've told him. His voice took on a soothing quality. "Okay, Gloria, relax I believe you. Now, what did you talk about?"

Jack's soothing voice did nothing to alleviate Gloria's terror. She still feared for her life, but thought that if she cooperated with these men, that she may yet get out of this alive. Knowing that her life depended on it, Gloria held nothing back, "She wanted to know how we knew each other. What she did when she was here in New Orleans."

Jack wondered if Gloria was trying to be evasive with him. "Look here, Gloria, you give me a straight story, or else!"

Gloria started to panic again, thinking that he would continue the torture. 'Please don't hurt me; I'm telling you the truth. She told me that she had amnesia, that she couldn't remember anything. She wanted to know where she had worked, where she had lived, and whom she had known. One other thing, she wanted to know if she had a baby while she lived here."

Jack wondered about this amnesia. He wondered how a woman could ever forget that she had a child. It had to be amnesia. It explained why she had been looking around New Orleans, instead of going straight to Lexington. "What did you tell her?"

Gloria had become a little calmer now. "I told her that she had no child while she was here in New Orleans."

Jack held the towel where Gloria could see it as a constant reminder to cooperate. "What else did you tell her?"

Gloria started to get excited again at the sight of the towel. "I told her that she had met this guy from Lexington, Kentucky, and had left New Orleans with him."

Looking into her eyes, Jack said, "Is that all that you told her?"

Gloria nodded. "Yes, that's all I told her."

Jack continued, "Now, did she say that she was going by any

329

MICHAEL O. GREGORY

other name?"

Gloria shook her head. "No, she didn't."

Jack wanted to test her to see if she had been telling him the truth. He put the towel back on her face again, and repeated the torture. Gloria had now become almost paralyzed with fear that these men were going to kill her. Jack removed the towel from her face. After she had quit gasping and coughing, he said, "Now, same question, did she give you any other name than Victoria Bujold?"

Gloria, crying hysterically, managed to say, "No, she didn't! Please believe me, I don't know any other name than Victoria Bujold!"

Jack's voice was soothing as he tried to calm Gloria. It took a couple of minutes before she had gotten herself sufficiently under control for him to ask any more questions. "Okay, I believe you. Now, was there anything different about her?"

Gloria nodded. "Yes, she now dresses, looks, and acts like a real lady. She said that she's married to a lawyer, and that she's pregnant."

Jack asked again, "Are you sure that she didn't say where she was from?"

Gloria shook her head. "No, she didn't say. I have no idea who, or where she is."

Jack regarded Gloria laying on the table bound up like a mummy, with just her head and feet showing; as he decided if he had all the useful information that he would get out of her, before he disposed of her. He made his decision and said, "Okay, I think that's all we need." He turned to the table where the basin of water sat, and picked up a syringe.

When Gloria saw the syringe she panicked, as she realized that they planned to kill her. As she spoke, it was with a quaking voice that she could barely control. "What's that for?"

With a sadistic smile, Jack said, "It's candy little girl. Hold her down!" Two men, one on each side of her, pressed her down against the table and held her immobile.

Gloria knew that they were about to kill her, and started to plea for her life. "No! Please don't! I won't talk!" Jack moved to her feet. Gloria's mind raced, trying to find a way out of her predicament. "No! Please don't do it! Please, I'll do anything! You can trust me, I won't talk!" Jack grabbed her foot, and held it immobile. Gloria tried to struggle, but she could only move her fingers, as she dug her nails into her thighs. Gloria's voice had now become a high-pitched squeal of stark terror, "Oh God, please, please, don't do it!" Gloria felt the sting of the needle as it found a vein on the top of her foot. She screamed. She was still crying when she lost consciousness forever.

Jack motioned to his men, "Okay take her out and dump her near a shooting gallery. Make it look like a junkie who has ODed."

That morning the police found Gloria's body next to the porch of an abandoned house used by junkies as a shooting gallery. Detective Sergeants Neal and Benning got the call. They arrived on the scene at 8:17 AM. The uniforms already had the scene taped off. Neal approached the senior uniform on the scene. "Anyone know who she is?"

The uniform officer shook his head saying, "No, I didn't see a purse. Some junkie must've taken it, if she had one."

Neal said, "Let's take a look at the body."

Neal and Benning, along with the senior uniform walked up to the body. The body lay on it's right side, in a fetal position. Her face had been partiality obscured by her hair. The body looked familiar to Neal. He took a pen from his pocket, squatted down, and pulled the hair back so that he could get a look at her face. He then stood up and put the pen back in his pocket. "I know this woman. She's Miss Gloria franklin. She was a dancer at the Lucky 7 Club. Now what in the hell is she doing here?"

Benning looked at, Neal. "What do you mean?"

Neal said, "Gloria wasn't a junkie. Her drug of choice was Smirnoff, not smack." Neal started to make a visual inspection of the body. There seemed to be something just under the helm of the skirt that he needed to get a better look at. He took the pen from his pocket, and squatted down again. The body was dressed in a miniskirt. With the pen, Neal raised the skirt a couple of inches. "Look, at this." Neal pointed to her

MICHAEL O. GREGORY

thigh, just below the helm of her skirt. On her thigh were four scratch marks that had ripped through her pantyhose, breaking the skin, he said, "Look, she deliberately dug her nails into her own flesh. Now, why would she want to do that?"

Benning shook his head. "I don't know, it's strange."

Neal took a closed look. "That's just where her hands would be if her arms were being held close to her sides. Look at her hair. It's been wet, but it didn't rain last night. Neal stood and put his pen away again, "When the Coroner gets here I want to know if she had scratch marks on her other thigh. This is no junkie OD. This is a homicide."

Chapter Forty-Five

The sun climbed higher into a clear morning sky. The ocean seemed to sparkle from the sunlight reflecting off it. A gentle breeze wafted across the patio. David Zamora sat at the table on the patio of his villa, having breakfast with Jack Monroe, Jack said, "I'm glad that I came down here. It's really beautiful here. Just look at that ocean."

With a wily grin, David gave Jack a playful slap on the upper arm. "I know why you really came down here. You want to chase the girls. You want to experience love Latin style."

Jack Monroe laughed. "Okay, well that too, but I did need to meet with you. Some of our merchandise is being intercepted before we get it. We need to work out new methods of shipment."

David did need to talk to jack about the problem of their merchandise being intercepted, but right now he had something else on his mind. "All right, we can work that out later. Right now I want to know what you found out about Vicki."

Jack put his fork down, and wiped his lips with his napkin. "As I told you, we found this private detective who had been looking for her, so we thought. It turned out that he had been working for Vicki. It's a long story, but to make it short, Vicki has amnesia, and was trying to retrace her life in New Orleans. The detective was a wash. He died of a heart attack before we could get anything out of him. Now with this broad Gloria, we got some information. We learned that Vicki knew of her daughter, but not directly. She didn't know when or where she had it. She didn't know the age or sex, obviously, but she did know that there was a child. Gloria didn't know where Vicki lives now, or whom she calls herself. Gloria did say that Vicki had changed, and that she's now married to a lawyer. She did tell us that she told Vicki about you, and that she went to Lexington with you. We checked Mr. Desormeaux's files, but we couldn't find out who he had been working for."

David continued to eat for a while, as he considered what Jack had said. He then put his fork down, took a sip of coffee, then dabbed his lips with his napkin. "You say that Gloria told Vicki that she went with me to Lexington?"

Jack nodded as he put his coffee cup back down on the saucer. "Yes, that's right."

David shook his head in puzzlement. "This is damn queer. I throw the whore out, and for almost a year and a half I hear nothing about her. Then all at once she shows up with amnesia, but she's looking for her kid; and she has the backing of an organization that we know nothing about. Well, if she went to Lexington, we may pick up her trail there. I don't know what to think about her. She moves around like a ghost. We can't get a handle on her anywhere. She has changed. The Vicki that I knew wasn't that smart. Did you find out anything about who's behind her?"

Jack shook his head. "No, nothing."

"What about Mr. Desormeaux and Miss Franklin? What did you do with them?"

"Mr. Desormeaux we fed to the gators. No one will ever find him. As for Miss Franklin, we made sure not to mark her up. We made it look like a drug overdose."

David nodded. "Okay, that's good. Now, if you'll excuse me. I have to make a call to Lexington. Then we can have more coffee in the living room; as we discuss our shipping problems,"

Ida had just returned from lunch, and had started to update her files and billing records, when there was a knock at the door. Ida called out, "Come in!" The door opened and, Patrick Fitzgerald walked in.

WOMAN IN THE MIRROR

Ida said, "Hi, Pat. What brings you here today?" The look on Patrick's face told her that this wasn't a social call, something had to be very wrong. "What's wrong, Pat?"

Without preamble Patrick came right to the point. "Ida, Hugh Desormeaux has disappeared. We believe that he's been killed, and that's not all. Miss Franklin is dead of a drug overdose. The New Orleans police are treating it as a homicide. Someone gave her a hotshot."

Patrick's news shocked her. Her relationship with Hugh Desormeaux had been professional, mostly on the phone or internet, but she still felt profound loss. To assimilate the information she wanted time to think. "Oh, Pat, please excuse my manners. Do you want a Coke?" Patrick nodded in the affirmative, and took a seat on the sofa, while Ida got a Coke from the refrigerator. Ida handed the Coke to Patrick, took a seat on the sofa next to him, and said, "Okay, what do we do now?"

Patrick took a swallow of Coke, and put the can on the coffee table. "We got your file from Hugh Desormeaux when we found out who we were up against; we don't however know what they found out from him before they killed him. You're going on a vacation right now. How do you like the mountains?"

Ida nodded. "The Mountains sounds okay."

Patrick smiled, put his arm around, Ida's shoulder, and gave her a friendly hug. "All right, we have a safe house in Tuskeegee, North Carolina. That's up in the Great Smokey Mountains. Now for your files, are they mostly paper, or are they on your computer?"

Ida smiled at Patrick's familiarity. Knowing him to be a widower, she harbored the notion that someday there could be something between them. She responded, "They're mostly on computer. However, I do have some paper files."

"Can you get everything in a van?"

Ida nodded. "Yes, it can be done."

Patrick, starting to stand, said, "Good, I have a van outside. We can get loaded up now. I want to be away as quickly as possible. Do you have your gun here?"

335

MICHAEL O. GREGORY

Ida, also starting to get to her feet with Patrick, said, "Yes, it's in the filing case."

With a nod, Patrick replied, "Good, get it and keep it on you at all times."

Ida got her gun out of the filling case, and put it in her purse. Patrick unplugged her computer, and started carrying it out to the van. Patrick and Ida together carried the file cases out to the van. Patrick said, "Now, is there anything that we have overlooked, like notes, or anything that can lead to Sam or Amanda?"

Ida thought. "Yes, there's my card file at home."

Patrick said, "All right, we're going there so that you can pack a bag anyway. We'll pick it up then."

They then left Ida's office, and drove to her home. There they packed a bag, and got the card file. Patrick and Ida then left Atlanta, driving north on Interstate 75, then Interstate 575, in route to the Great Smokey Mountains.

That evening they arrived at the safe house. The house was a three bedroom home of fieldstone and logs, with a large fire place. It was high up in the mountains, with limited access. The home belonged to a retired Army Major, and his wife. Ida would be their guest until she could safely return to Atlanta.

Patrick spent the night in Tuskeegee; then drove back to Atlanta the next morning.

Amanda had been fixing lunch for her and Cheryl, when the doorbell rang. She went to answer the door. She found Patrick Fitzgerald standing at the door. "Oh, Pat, how good of you to stop by."

Patrick said, "Hello, Amanda."

Amanda held the door open for him. "You're just in time for lunch. How does a cotto salami and cheese sandwich with potato chips sound?"

Patrick nodded. "That sounds really good."

Amanda took Patrick back to the kitchen, and offered him a seat at the kitchen table. She then started to make the sandwiches. "Oh, Pat, would you like lettuce and tomato?"

336

WOMAN IN THE MIRROR

Patrick nodded. "Yes, please. Where's Cheryl?"

Amanda took a quick glance out of the kitchen window at Cheryl, as she said, "She's in the backyard playing with Lady."

Patrick's tone of voice and manner changed. "This isn't just a social call Amanda. We have something serious to talk about."

A little frightened by Patrick's seriousness, Amanda stopped making the sandwiches, came over to the table, and took a seat across from Patrick. "What is it Pat?"

Patrick looked into Amanda's eyes to gage her response. "It's New Orleans. We had a problem there. Mr. Desormeaux is missing. We assume that he's dead."

The news of Hugh Desormeaux's possible death shocked Amanda. She found it hard to believe that anything had happened to Hugh Desormeaux. She asked, "How can you be sure that he's dead?"

Patrick responded, "Because that's not all, Gloria franklin has been murdered."

Amanda had a sudden profound feeling of remorse. She had a sick feeling in her stomach at hearing of Gloria's death. "Murdered! How?"

Still looking intently into Amanda's eyes, Patrick said, "It was meant to look like a drug overdose, but the police are treating it as a homicide."

Amanda looked down at the table, to avoid Patrick's continued gaze. "When did it happen?"

Patrick could see that Amanda had really been upset by the news. "Hugh Desormeaux has been missing for almost a week now. Gloria Franklin was murdered three days ago. Late Saturday night, or early Sunday morning."

Amanda just sat there for a minute looking down at the table, before looking back up at Patrick. "It's my fault. They're dead because they helped me."

Patrick reached across the table, took Amanda's hand in his, and looked into her eyes with understanding and compassion. "Amanda, listen to me. It's not your fault. Hugh Desormeaux was an investigator, he knew the hazards of his trade. As for Gloria Franklin, I do feel bad

337

MICHAEL O. GREGORY

about her, but neither you, nor she could foresee the danger at the time, so don't blame yourself. Gloria could have just kept her mouth shut. We all make our own decisions, for better or for worse. Just look at that beautiful little girl of yours, and tell me that we done wrong."

Amanda could see and accept the logic of what Patrick said, even if she didn't like it. "You're right, Pat. Regardless of the consequences, I had to do it. God forgive me."

Patrick released Amanda's hand and sat back in his chair. "Now, what I'm here for. It's time to make a decision. David Zamora knows that you were in New Orleans, and why you were there. You can also bet that he knows that you picked up the trail to Lexington. Now, one question, did you use your real name in New Orleans?"

Amanda thought for a moment. "Just to register at the motel. Mr. Desormeaux knew my real name. Everyone else called me Vicki. I just let it go at that."

Patrick nodded. "That's good. I've a feeling that they didn't get much from Hugh Desormeaux, or they would've gotten to Ida before I did. I just hope that they don't find your name on that motel registration card. Now, for Lexington."

Amanda was ready with an answer. "In Lexington Ida and I registered under our own names, and we used her business address. Ida gave the next door neighbor Mrs. Mitchell her card."

Patrick said, "We'll have to warn the Mitchell's, and get that card back, if she still has it."

Amanda responded, "You don't have to worry about that, I have the card. She wrote her address and phone number on the back, and gave it back to me."

Patrick relaxed a little, thinking that with luck they might just escape David Zamora's detection, "Okay, that's good. Now, is there any other place in Lexington that you used your real name?"

Amanda shook her head. "No, once we found out what David Zamora was, we were more careful."

Patrick nodded. "All right, there is the chance that they may not find you, but we must now assume the worst. That they'll pick up the trail, and that it will lead them to Atlanta. Now, you can do one of two things. We can move you and your family, and change your identity. Or you can stay here and see this thing through."

Amanda didn't have to think about it. She already knew what she had to do. "I'm not running. I'm not going to be looking over my shoulder, and be frightened of every sound in the night for the rest of my life. I'm staying right here and see an end to this."

Patrick had great respect for, Amanda. She had proven to be a person of courage and decisiveness, regardless of the peril, she had proven the equal of anyone that he had ever worked with before. "Good for you, Amanda. I knew that would be your answer. Now there are things that we have to do. I see that you have done everything that I have asked you to do so far. Now, we need to make this house a fortress, without it looking like one. That's my job. Do you have an empty bedroom?"

Amanda nodded. "We have the nursery."

Patrick replied, "It's not a nursery. That is, you're not using it as that yet."

Amanda shook her head. "No, we're not."

Patrick slapped his hand on the table. "Okay, then that will be your safe room. We need to have it empty. Then I'm going to bring in a prefab box. This is one of my bright ideas that I came up with. It's not big, just over five-foot square and four-foot tall. It's made of sections of one-quarter inch steel plate. It's brought into the house and bolted together in the safe room. It has no top or bottom, you don't need that, but it does have firing ports. I've used it before, and I can tell you that you are quite safe from gun fire in the box. It may be somewhat primitive, but it's effective. We'll set it up in the corner farthest from the door. That will be yours and, Sam's fallback position. If the house is attacked, my men will not enter that room; so anyone to come through the door is fair game. Keep the shotgun in the box, and your pistols with you." Patrick took a card from his pocket, and handed it to, Amanda, "If you see anything suspicious call this number.

339

MICHAEL O. GREGORY

You may not see me often, but from now on we're going to be with you twenty-four hours a day."

Amanda felt grateful to have someone like Patrick to look after her and Sam, "Thank you, Pat. Why do you do all of this for us?"

Patrick gave, Amanda a reassuring smile. "Because you need it, and I don't like to leave a job half done. As long as David Zamora is out there, the job isn't done. Now, how about lunch? I'm ready to visit with that lovely daughter of yours."

CHAPTER FORTY-SIX

At 11:00 AM two men wearing dark suits, and driving a dark-brown Ford Crown Victoria pulled up at the gate. The driver got out, pressed the intercom button, and identified themselves as Special Agents Stephen Carter and Roy O'Hern of the FBI. They were admitted to the house. The maid met them at the front door. They flashed identification at the maid. The man that identified himself as Agent Carter spoke, "Is this the Mitchell residence?"

The maid nodded ."Yes, Sir, it is."

Agent Carter said, "Is Mr. or Mrs. Mitchell in?"

The maid held open the door. "Yes, Sir, Mrs. Mitchell is in. Please have a seat in the hall. I'll see if she can see you." The maid led them into the hallway, showed the two agents to chairs, and then disappeared into the interior of the house. She came back in a couple of minutes. "Gentlemen, Mrs. Mitchell will see you now."

The maid took them back to the library. Mrs. Mitchell sat in a comfortable blue-leather upholstered chair waiting for them. She had dressed in a champagne-color silk dress, with a diamond and ruby broach. The two men shook hands and exchanged pleasantries with Mrs. Mitchell, then took seats in chairs facing her. With a pleasant smile, Mrs. Mitchell said, "Well, Gentlemen, would you like a cup of coffee?"

Shaking his head no, Agent Carter said, "No thank you Ma'am, we won't be long."

Mrs. Mitchell dismissed the maid, then turned her attention to the two agents. "All right, Gentlemen, now how can I help you?"

MICHAEL O. GREGORY

Agent Carter asked, "We're reinvestigating the people who use to live next door. Did you know them?"

Mrs. Mitchell replied, "No, not personally, but I did see them coming and going. I did know them by sight."

Agent Carter had his notebook out, and referred to it. "Now, the man who lived in the house, Mr. David Zamora, he left about nine or ten months ago?"

Mrs. Mitchell replied, "Yes, that's about right."

Agent Carter asked, "Do you have any idea where he moved to?"

Mrs. Mitchell replied, "No, Sir, I don't."

Agent Carter asked, "Now, as I understand, there were other men living there?"

Mrs. Mitchell replied, "Yes, that's right."

Agent Carter asked, "Have you seen any of these men lately?"

Mrs. Mitchell replied, "No, I haven't."

Agent Carter checked his notebook again, "There was also a young woman living there for a time, Miss Victoria Bujold. Did you know her?"

Mrs. Mitchell replied, "Only on sight."

Agent Carter asked, "Do you know at about what time she moved away?"

Mrs. Mitchell replied, "Oh, I'd say about one and a half years ago."

Agent Carter asked, "And do you by any chance know where she moved to?"

Mrs. Mitchell replied, "No, I have no idea."

Agent Carter asked, "One last question. Have you seen her since she moved out?"

Mrs. Mitchell replied, "No, I haven't."

Agent Carter said, "Thank you, Mrs. Mitchell. Can we question your maid?"

Mrs. Mitchell pressed the button. The maid came to the library. Agent Carter asked her the same questions that he had asked Mrs. Mitchell, with the same responses. After the two men were shown out, the maid returned to the library. The maid said, "They're gone

342

now, Ma'am."

Mrs. Mitchell responded, "Thank you, Betty."

"I don't like lying to the FBI." Betty said with a concerned look.

Mrs. Mitchell nodded. "I don't either, but they're not the FBI, they're gangsters." Patrick had warned her that something like this might happen.

After David Zamora's men, posing as FBI agents failed to turn up anything from the neighbors, they turned to looking for David's former domestic help. It took them three days to locate the maid and cook. The maid had no knowledge of Vicki. When they found the cook Roberta, she told them that Vicki had come to visit her at least three months or more ago. Vicki and the other woman had questioned her about David and Cheryl. Roberta told them that the woman that she knew as Vicki had used the name Vicki and no other. She didn't say where she lived now. The cook had a photograph of Vicki that she gave them.

With no other leads, they made copies of Amanda's photo, and started showing it in all the bars, clubs and other public places. They put the word out on the street that they were willing to pay for information.

One week later one of David's men walked into a Motel 6, and showed the photograph of Amanda to the desk clerk. The desk clerk took a cursory look at the photograph and shook his head. "No, I don't believe that I've ever seen her before."

David's man, still holding up Amanda's photograph, said, "Too bad. We're willing to pay good for information."

The clerk suddenly became very interested. "How much?"

David's man looked at him with a little half smile. "One hundred bucks."

The clerk put out his hand. "Let me see that picture again." The desk clerk took another look at the photograph, then tapped it with his finger. "Yes, I remember her now. She looked different from this photo, but it's the same girl. She was here close to four months ago. She was with an older woman." With the mention of the older woman, David's man knew that he had found what he had been looking for.

MICHAEL O. GREGORY

The clerk continued, "I remember them. They were here for two days. They made lots of phone calls, and were asking directions."

Taking Amanda's photograph from the clerk, and putting it back in his pocket, David's man said, "Do you have their registration card?"

He clerk checked the files. In a few minutes he came up with the card. "Yes, here it is, Ms. Ida Mae Wammock and Mrs. Amanda Tankersley of Atlanta, Georgia. The younger one, the one in the photo, is Mrs. Tankersley. Their address is on the card."

David's man took the card. He then took a one-hundred dollar bill from his pocket, and handed it to the clerk.

David Zamora had come to Arrio Jimenez's home for a working lunch. Lunch had now ended, and coffee had been served. Arrio lit up a cigar and exhaled a large cloud of smoke. He then turned to David. "That last shipment to new Orleans. Did you have any problems?"

David got his own cigar going before he answered, "No, everything went real smooth. We're ahead of the game again. It should take the pigs a long time to figure this one out and catch up again."

Arrio exhaled another large cloud of smoke. "Yes, we have a good thing going here. I produce it, and you ship it, and market it. We both get rich." Arrio took a hard look at David, "David, nothing can touch us. We have it made, but all this can be lost if you go out and do something stupid."

David knew what Arrio was talking about. He had been expecting this argument, and had been ready for it. "I'm not going to do something stupid."

Arrio had become concerned about David's behavior, when it came to Vicki and Cheryl. David had become so consumed with the thought of revenge, that he had divorced himself from reality. He felt that David would ignore unseen danger because he didn't want to deal with it. "I'm not so sure about that. You're becoming obsessed with this woman. You're letting your passions rule you."

David's rage had started to rise. He started to make wild gestures with the hand that held the cigar. "But don't you see that she has defied

WOMAN IN THE MIRROR

me! I can't let her get away with it!"

Arrio offered an alternative to what he knew David planned to do. "Why don't you just have the girl kidnaped, and bring her back."

David slammed his fist down on the table rattling the cups, and sloshing coffee into the saucers. "The girl! I don't give a damn about the girl! She was just the symbol of my complete domination over Vicki. Now, the only way for me to regain my honor before my men, is for me to kill Vicki, or as she now calls herself Amanda Tankersley. I know what name she's using now, and that she's living in Atlanta. As soon as my people locate her, I'm going up there to kill her myself. I want that whoring slut to know that it's me, and that I've defeated her. I made the mistake of not doing it the first time. That's one mistake that I'm going to correct personally."

Arrio exhaled another thick cloud of smoke. "If you are determined to do this, I can't stop you, but remember this. There's a phantom organization backing her up. We haven't been able to find out anything about it." Arrio waved the hand that he held his cigar with in front of David's face. "Now, listen to me good! If you go up there, you may be walking into a trap!"

David heard, Arrio's words, but disregarded them. He didn't care about anything except revenge. "We've been looking for this phantom organization and have found nothing. I don't think it exist. I just think that she found out where I was, and got some people to come down here and kidnap Cheryl."

Arrio felt that David had become so bent on revenge that he was in denial of the danger. He had become irrational. Arrio made one last plea. "Listen to me David. Just because you don't see it, don't believe that it's not there. Just let it go. It will end up killing you."

David shook his head in resignation, there being no way that he could back out now and maintain his honor. "I can't. I must do it."

There was nothing more that Arrio could say. He felt sad for what had happened to his friend David. It seemed like watching a train wreck about to happen, and not being able to do anything about it. He felt

MICHAEL O. GREGORY

that this would be the last time that he would see his friend David. "Okay, have it your way. Go with God."

After David left, Arrio called in one of his men. "Do you know the number of Jack Monroe in New Orleans?"

"I can get it Mr. Jimenez."

"Call him. Tell him that I have to talk with him. I think that we may need to start doing business with him soon." The man left to make the call.

When Sam got home from the office, Patrick Fitzgerald and Amanda were waiting for him. Amanda put Cheryl with Lady in front of the television. She then put on the DVD of Aladdin for Cheryl to watch. She then went into the kitchen with Sam and Patrick. As soon as they were seated at the table, Patrick started the meeting. "It's started. They know your name, and they know that you're in Atlanta. They were checking out Ida's office and home today. I'll give them one to two days before they find out where you live."

Sam looked at Amanda. "It's not too late for you to go into hiding."

She looked back at Sam, seeing the concern in his eyes. She knew that all he wanted would be for her to be safe. She put her hand on his. "I know that you worry about me, but this is something that I must do. Now, pat, please continue."

Patrick said, "All right, from now on you need to limit your movements. We want the only opportunity for him to get you is right here at home. Now, Sam."

Sam responded, "Yes."

Patrick continued, "You aren't the main target, but we'll still cover you. However, I don't think that they'd risk trying to hit you before they can get to Amanda. You'll have to do most of the shopping, and running of errands. I want Amanda to stay as close to home as possible. Amanda, when is your next appointment with the doctor?"

Amanda looked at the kitchen calendar that hung on the wall close by. "Eleven days from today."

Patrick nodded, "Okay, that's good. It should all be over with by

WOMAN IN THE MIRROR

then. I have a plan to get them. You don't need to know all the details yet, but the plan is to channel them into a killing zone, and kill them before they get to the house. So when things start going down, get to the safe room quickly. Now, I want to talk to you about Cheryl."

Amanda said, "Yes, what about Cheryl?"

Patrick continued, "It's time to get her out of harm's way. I assume that she'll be going to your mother's?"

Amanda didn't like to be separated from Cheryl, but she couldn't keep her here when there was danger. "Yes, I want her to go to my mother's until this thing's over with."

Patrick nodded, "Yes, that's the best place for her. We're lucky on this one. If she had been a boy, David would really want her back; but since she's a girl, he isn't too concerned about her, so we don't have to keep her as bait. You're the only one that he wants. He most likely wants to kill you personally."

Amanda asked, "Should I call my mother, and have her come and pick her up?"

Patrick shook his head. "No, Cheryl has to leave now. Call your mother, and tell her that we're coming. The dog will also come with us. It's best that she not be underfoot when things start to happen. After you call pack a bag for Cheryl, and an overnight for yourself. Sam, you'll have to cook your own supper tonight. We need to leave right away. It will be late when we get there, so tell your mother that we will be spending the night. We'll be driving back in the morning. Now, Amanda, once you leave Cheryl at your mother's, for their safety there can be no phone calls, no e-mail, nothing until this thing is over. Understand?"

Amanda nodded. "Yes, I understand."

Amanda got up to make the phone call to her mother. She then packed a bag for Cheryl and herself. Sam hugged and kissed, Amanda and Cheryl good-bye.

They all, along with Lady, got in Patrick's van, and drove off. Patrick drove through Atlanta, looping back on his track three times,

MICHAEL O. GREGORY

to make sure that he wasn't being followed. He then got onto Interstate 20 West and headed for Gadsden, Alabama.

CHAPTER FORTY-SEVEN

The focus of David Zamora's search shifted to Atlanta, Georgia. Every man from his organization, in the Atlanta area who could be spared, would be used for the search. David had been anxious to find Amanda as quickly as possible. They had two names, Ms. Ida Wammack and Mrs. Amanda Tankersley, but only one address. The address turned out to be the office of Ida Mae Wammack Investigations. First they had the office staked out to try to catch Ida coming to work. The second day they broke into the office. They found the office deserted, with all the files and records missing. They broke into Ida's home to see what they could find. They found no leads.

After finding nothing at Ida's office or home, they started trying to locate Amanda. They found no Amanda Tankersley listed in the telephone directory. They started to check out all the Tankersley's listed in the Atlanta telephone directory. On the second day they checked out the address of Samuel Tankersley. They found Out that he had moved, and had left no forwarding address. They checked with the neighbors at the last known address, and found that he had recently married, and that his wife's name is Amanda. None of the neighbors knew where they had moved to. However, they found out that Samuel Tankersley was an attorney in Atlanta. They checked with the telephone company to try to get Sam's and Amanda's new telephone number, but they had an unlisted number, and the telephone company wouldn't give it out. They checked the telephone book, and found the number and address of the law office of Tankersley and Zimmerman. They staked out the law office of Tankersley and Zimmerman, found out which one was Sam, and followed him to where he lived. Now that they knew where Amanda lived, they made their report to David Zamora.

David's men had been careful to not draw attention to themselves as they made their inquiries, so as not to alert their quarry, or anyone who might be protecting her. They were unaware that they had been under surveillance from the time that they had staked out Ida's office.

David Zamora sat in his favorite chair in the living room talking on the telephone. He finished speaking, hung up the telephone, and turned to the man sitting next to him. "I have that stinking little bitch now. We leave for Mexico City in the morning. We'll fly out from Cozumel."

David's man had been listening to David's end on the conversation on the telephone, and had an uneasy feeling. "I don't like it, Boss. I heard what you were saying on the phone, about that private investigator's office being abandoned and cleaned out. It's like they're one step ahead of us. Like they know where we're going before we get there."

David had become tired of everyone around him trying to dissuade him from going after that whore. He wasn't about to be dissuaded by any of his men. "Well, of course they were tipped off by the killing of that investigator and dancer in New Orleans. As for this so-called organization, most of that's speculation. Besides, they aren't the feds, or any other police. We can handle them if we have to." David had convinced himself that whatever obstacles were between him and the killing of Vicki could be overcome.

David's man had been caught between his loyalty to David, and a feeling of foreboding. "You know that I'm with you, Boss, but I wish that you'd just forget the whole thing."

All this talk had made David angry. He slammed his right fist into the palm of his left hand, then shook his finger angrily in the man's face. "Damn it! If you don't want to come with me, then don't! Just don't be here when I get back!"

The man became very apologetic. "Don't worry, Boss, I'm with you."

Henry Petrozello had devised a way to keep an eye on David

WOMAN IN THE MIRROR

Zamora. He had a routine that would allow him to retain his character and habits. The mornings were spent at the Tulum Mayan ruins. There he knew the members of an archaeological team working the site. He hung around and did whatever he could to help out. He would then have lunch in Tulum. After lunch he took his boat out to fish, or to dive. He wouldn't anchor in front of the villa, but would be close enough to observe any activity at the villa.

Henry also had a passing acquaintance with David Zamora's new cook, Isabell Zapata, a fifty-two year old widow who lived in Tulum. A petite woman five-feet one-inch tall, of one-hundred thirty pounds, with a compact, sturdy, but very well proportioned and voluptuous body. She was a woman who knew how to use her good looks and body to her best advantage. She dyed her hair black, so that no gray would show, and took great care of her appearance. She was an attractive woman who looked younger than her years. She had an interest in, Henry because he was about her age, attractive, unattached, had the virility to satisfy her and had money.

At noon on the day that David Zamora left for Mexico City; Henry had lunch at his regular place in Tulum. Isabell happened to stop by, and having a lot of time on her hands, sat with him, and they talked. He learned that David had gone on a trip, and that the villa was closed up. David had given Isabell two weeks of with pay. She told Henry that if he wanted a really good meal, to come by her place that evening, and she would cook for him. He accepted her invitation, knowing that a dinner wouldn't be the only thing from Isabell that he could look forward to that evening. Henry thought that if he ever got the urge to marry again, that Isabell would be a good choice. She certainly made it interesting in bed.

After lunch, Henry got into his car and drove north on highway 307. From what he could see of the villa from the road, it looked empty. He drove past, pulled off at a secluded spot, and walked back to the villa. He checked to make sure that the villa was unoccupied. He then picked the lock on one of the patio doors, and entered the villa.

351

MICHAEL O. GREGORY

A quick check of the villa revealed that there were no records or files. However, he did find a note pad setting on an end table in the living room, next to the telephone. Using a pencil, he brought out what had been written on it. It turned out to be an airline schedule for a direct flight from Mexico City to Montreal, Canada.

He went back to his car and drove home. He sent a FAX to Patrick about the information on the airline schedule. He then drove back to Tulum for dinner, and an evening with Isabell.

David Zamora, with his men, took a charter flight from Cozumel to Mexico City. From Mexico City they flew direct to Montreal, Canada. From Montreal they took a domestic flight to Toronto. In Toronto, David picked up forged Canadian identification for himself and his men. He also got a car.

He and his men crossed the border into the United States at Niagara Falls. David and his men took a flight from Buffalo, New York to Lexington, Kentucky. When they arrived in Lexington, David picked up two cars there, also more men, and weapons. They then set out for Atlanta.

When, Patrick received the FAX from Perrozeello, he started to put his plan into operation. The first thing he did had been to contact the FBI and the DEA. He let them know of David Zamora's intention of entering the United States through Canada.

He then assembled his team that he had picked ahead of time. The team had been organized in two parts, the blockers, and the kickers. The blockers were all retired Army. They were Sergeant First Class Snow, First Sergeant Avery and Sergeant First Class Miller. Avery and Miller were his snipers. They were both former members of the president's 100. The kickers were himself, Retired Marine Gunnery Sergeant Hanes and retired Navy Lieutenant Commander Kline, a former Navy seal commander. All of the team members would be armed with 12 gage shotguns, except for the snipers. They were to be armed with bolt-action rifles chambered for the 7.62 MM MATO round. The sniper rifles were fitted with starlight sniper scope, silencer and flash hider. The rounds

WOMAN IN THE MIRROR

were hand loaded to keep the muzzle velocity subsonic, so that there would be no sonic boom, or loud crack as the bullet passed through the air. All team members would carry side arms. There would be a third part of the team called the holders. That would be Amanda and Sam. They were just to stay in their safe room, and defend themselves in case anyone made it inside the house.

Patrick and his team were staying at a Residence Inn not far from Amanda's home. He had two buckets of KFC fried chicken, potato wedges, biscuits and plenty of chilled Cokes. The team had assembled in Patrick's suite for their briefing. Patrick had Amanda there for the briefing. He had her there for two reasons. One, to give her confidence in his team. Two, to let the team members see, and get to know her. Patrick introduced Amanda to the team members. He then started the meeting. "An announcement right off. We're going to be in a residential area. There are a lot of innocent civilians, so we'll have to limit our firepower. No assault weapons, and no rifles, except for the night sniper rifles. The offensive weapons will be twelve-gauge shotguns with full-capacity magazines. 00 buck up close is more than enough to get the job done. Up close it's devastating, but it won't carry far. We don't want to hit any civilians. For personal defense the sidearm of your choice. Everyone will have body armor. Wear dark clothing, and nothing that shines, or makes noise. Avery and miller will have their sniper scopes. The rest of us will have night-vision equipment. Everyone will also have a radio. Any questions?"

Amanda was curious. "I have one."

Patrick looked at Amanda. "Yes, what is it?"

Amanda said, "You said that Avery and miller were once president's one-hundred. What are the President's one-hundred?"

Patrick responded, "The President's one-hundred is the top one-hundred marksmen in the United states Armed Forces. They're Olympic-caliber shooters. Avery and miller can shoot the eye out of a squirrel at one-hundred yards, and do it consistently. They never miss."

Knowing that Patrick had the very best made Amanda feel a little more comfortable. However, she still had some concerns. "They really sound good, but you don't know how many men that David Zamora will have. Do you think that the six of you will be enough?"

Patrick could see that an explanation would be in order to allay Amanda's concerns, "Okay, look at it this way. David Zamora is a fool for attempting a thing like this anyway, but we must assume that he isn't a complete idiot. There are certain factors that will dictate the size of his force. It can't be too big, or they can't move fast enough. Too small and they can't get the job done. He'll use two to three cars or vans, at the most. More than that and he'll have problems evading the police. So he will have eight to ten men, twelve at the most.

"Now you aren't looking at just any six men in this room. Between the six of us we have over one-hundred fifty years of military service, mostly in combat arms with elite forces. We're all retired, but when we took off the uniform the training, knowledge and experience didn't stay with the uniform, it stayed with us. You can't find six men any better that what you have here."

Amanda could see the wisdom in what Patrick had told her, and felt reassured. "Well, thank you, Pat. That's all the questions I have."

Patrick looked around at everyone, 'Now, for the operation. Snow, you'll be with Avery and Miller as the blockers. You'll take up position on the other side of the creek from the, Tankersley's residence. I'll show you later today how to get to your positions without using the trail behind the house. We don't want David Zamora's men to find any evidence of our being back there. We hope to make him believe that the best way to approach the house is from the rear. So, Avery, miller, it will be your job to cut the size of his force right off before he gets near the house. If any turn back to engage you, Snow will be there to help out. I doubt that that will happen though. The only way out for them will be forward.

"Now, I'll have the kickers with me. That will be Kline and Hanes. We'll cover the front of the house. The feds have a car load of agents watching the front of the house. I can coordinate with them, and let them know that we're there to protect the Tankersley's. I know the local agents. We can work together. Any questions about the operation so far?" no one spoke up, so Patrick continued, "Now for the radio call signs. Snow, you will be linebacker six, Avery, linebacker five, Miller, linebacker four. I will be fullback six, Kline, fullback five, Hanes, fullback four. Amanda, you and Sam will be quarterback. You don't need any numbers. We'll know who's on the radio. I'll make frequent radio checks. If there's someone close by, and you can't talk, just key the mike two times. That about covers it. Amanda, do you know anything about radio procedures."

Amanda shook her head. "No, I don't."

Patrick gave her a reassuring smile. "Okay, now for a quick lesion on radio procedures. There isn't much about it, just a few words to remember, but first the transmit button. Press it down to talk. When you are through release it. As long as you have it down, no one else can use their radios. Now for the words to use. Over, means that you have finished transmitting, and you want the other person to transmit back to you. Roger, means that you understand the transmission. Wilko, means that you will comply. Out, means that the transmission is complete, and that no reply is expected. Now, if you say, over and out, I'll take your radio and hit you over the head with it." This got a little chuckle from Amanda. Patrick continued, "Now, if you want someone to repeat a transmission, you don't say repeat. The proper response is, say again. Only the canon cockers in the artillery use the word repeat. Now, do you understand that?"

Amanda nodded. "Yes, I do."

Patrick asked, "Okay, what does Roger mean?"

Amanda responded, "I understand."

Patrick asked, "And, Wilko?"

Amanda replied, "I will comply."

Patrick asked, "When do you say Over and Out."

Amanda, with a grin, said, "Never."

Patrick with a slight chuckle gave Amanda a pat on her shoulder.

MICHAEL O. GREGORY

"Okay, you got it." He then looked at each of his men in turn, 'Now, is everyone ready?" Everyone nodded. Patrick turned back to Amanda, "Are you ready?"

Amanda nodded. "Yes, I'm ready."

Patrick clapped his hands. "Okay, we'll start tonight. We'll be in position thirty minutes before sundown, and stand down after sunrise. So let's finish the chicken, then get some rest. Tonight will be a long night."

Chapter Forty-Eight

At 6:20 PM David Zamora and his party arrived at the Ramada Inn in Atlanta. They registered and David called a meeting with his Atlanta boss Clark Lydgate.

By 7:30 PM Clark Lydgate had started briefing David and his men on the Tankersley's home. David, Clark and a couple of David's men were sitting at a table in David's suite. The rest of David's men stood around the table looking on. Clark had laid out a drawing on the table. The drawing showed the Tankersley's house, with the adjacent houses, streets, woods and creek. Clark said, "This is it. The square with the X in it is their house." He ran his finger along the street in front of the house, as he continued to speak, "It's two blocks from the main road to the house. There's a cul-de-sac four houses down from their house, on the opposite side of the street. There are two ways out, back the way that you came from to the main thoroughfare, or down three streets, turn right, down two streets, turn left."

David had been studying the drawing, and pointed to the green shaded area. "You say that this is the wooded area?"

Clark nodded. "Yes, and this is the creek." Clark pointed to the blue line that ran through the woods across the back of the, Tankersley's house.

David pointed to a black line that paralleled the creek, between the creek and the house. "What's this?"

Clark said, "Oh, that's a track used by dirt bikers. At the point behind the Tankersley's house it runs about twenty-five yards from their back fence, and about ten yards from the creek."

MICHAEL O. GREGORY

David studied the track for a while, as a plan began to form in his mind. He then asked, "Where does it come from, and where does it go to?"

Clark replied, "It starts at the main road. I don't know how far it goes back into the woods."

David thought for a moment. "Is it very open? Can you move quickly down it?"

Clark nodded. "Yes, you can."

David took another look at the plan. "What about the woods behind the house?"

By now Clark knew what David had in mind. "Not much undergrowth. It's easy to get from the trail to their back fence; and there's enough moonlight for the next few days to find your way at night."

David wanted to know everything about this trail. "Have you been down this trail?"

Clark responded, "Yes, for the last two days."

Still looking at the drawing, David said, "Have you seen anyone else back there?"

Clark shrugged his shoulders. "Just a couple of neighborhood kids on dirt bikes."

David asked, "Have you been there at night?"

Clark shook his head. "No."

David thought for a moment. "Now, what about police surveillance?"

Clark said, "A car in the cul-de-sac day and night. Two, sometimes three suits, either Atlanta's finest, or feds. My money is that they're feds. A police, or Sheriff Cruiser makes a pass every thirty minutes."

David thought some more. "It's dark now. I'd like to see the trail in the dark."

Clark looked at his watch. "It's almost eight right now. We can look at the trail, and be back here by eleven-thirty."

David said, "Okay, Clark, you and I'll go and look the place over." David looked at the rest of his men, "The rest of you take it easy. We'll have another meeting as soon as I get back."

358

David went with Clark to check out the trail, and the Tankersley's house. His men went to find a bar and relax.

Snow had his team in position behind the creek. They had just made a 9:45 PM radio check. Miller spotted movement on the trail and called Snow on the radio. "Linebacker six, Linebacker four, over."

"Linebacker four this is, Linebacker six, over."

"Linebacker six, Linebacker four, I have movement on the trail. Two men unarmed, over."

"Linebacker four, Linebacker six, roger, break, Fullback six, Linebacker six, over."

Patrick answered the radio, "Linebacker six, Fullback six, over."

"Fullback six, Linebacker six, we have movement on the trail. Two men, no weapons, over."

"Linebacker six, Fullback six, do not interfere with them. Just monitor and report, out."

By now, Snow, Avery and Miller all had the two men under surveillance. They came walking up the trail from the main road. They left the trail behind Sam's and Amanda's house, and moved to the back fence. After a few minutes they returned to the trail. They then proceeded another two hundred yards up the trail, then double backed to the main road. Snow reported the activity of the two men to Patrick. Patrick acknowledged the report.

David Zamora could barely resist the urge to run up, burst into the house, and kill Vicki. His hands tingled at the thought of having them around her throat, chocking the life from her. It would be hard to wait until tomorrow night, when she was so close now. Reluctantly he left to go back to the motel.

David got back to the Ramada Inn at 11:15 PM. His men were waiting for him. He called the meeting right away. As soon as everyone had arrived in David's suite and gathered around the table, David begin. "All right, now here's the plan. We'll come up from the rear, by way of the trail. Clark!"

Clark responded, "Yes, David."

MICHAEL O. GREGORY

David continued, "I'll need two vans, each with driver and one man armed with an automatic weapon."

Clark nodded. "Okay, you'll have them."

David said, "I have five men with me. I will need four more men, armed with automatic weapons."

Clark replied, "Okay, you got them too."

David said, "And I'll need a car with three, or four men with automatic weapons."

Clark nodded. "Okay, is that all?"

David responded, "Yes, that's all. Now, let's get to the plan." David looked at the rest of the men, "We'll hit the place tomorrow night, or to be more exact, between two and three in the morning. That's the best time to catch her watchdogs off guard. The first part of my plan is the car with the three, or four men. They'll wait until the cop cruiser makes its drive by. Then they'll wait five minutes, then drive by the front of the house, and shoot it up. I want plenty of firing, lots of noise. I want her watch dogs to go after them. They need to lead them on a long chase, for about five minutes or more, then lose them. Can they do that?"

Clark nodded. "Yes, they can do that." He had seen right away that this would be a risky under taking, but didn't voice his opinion, knowing David's state of mind.

David continued, "Good. One thing I want them to understand, is that they are to shoot high. I don't want them to hit Vicki. I want that pleasure for myself. Once the drive by has her watchdogs looking the other way, I'll hit the house from the rear. We'll move about one minute after the drive by shoots up the house. By then her watchdogs should be in pursuit of the drive by vehicle. I want to take four minutes, five at the most. We need to be out of there fast. The two vans, with a man riding shotgun in each, will pull up in front of the house two minutes after the drive by. They are to be our get away, and to block Vicki's escape from the house. Now, if her watchdogs don't take the bait, we still have the firepower to take care of them anyway. Any questions?"

360

David paused to look around the table. When no one spoke up, he continued, "Clark, do you have some place for us to assemble before the job?"

Clark thought for a minute before he spoke. "Yes, there's an auto body shop just over two miles from the Tankersley's house. The owner has a sizeable cocaine habit. I'm sure that if I forgive a lot of his debt, that he will look the other way as we use his shop. We can assemble there before the job, and lay low there from the police afterwards."

David patted Clark's shoulder. "You're a good man Clark. I'll see that you get a good bonus for this after it's over with. Okay, we meet at the body shop at eleven tomorrow night. Now, everyone go out, have a couple of drinks then get some rest, and no booze tomorrow. I want everyone in good shape for the job. Understand?" David looked into the face of every man around the table to get a nod that they understood.

At 7:30 AM Patrick had his men stand down, and meet him at the motel. On the way Patrick stopped off at McDonald's for sausage biscuits, egg Mac Muffins and hash browns. When he got back to the motel suite, Avery already had the coffee on. They all helped themselves to breakfast, then the debriefing started. Patrick said, "Snow, what of the two men last night?"

Snow washed down a bite of egg Mac Muffin with a gulp of coffee, "I'd say that it was a recon of the area. It looked to me as if one man was showing the other the lay of the land."

Patrick looked at, Avery. "Avery, what do you think?"

Avery replied, "I concur with, Snow."

Patrick looked at Miller. "Miller, do you have anything to add?"

Miller shook his head. "No, I concur with Snow and Avery."

Patrick took a moment to think before he continued, "This night recon by those two men tells me two things. One, the man who was being shown around was most likely David Zamora. Two, the attack is going to come from the rear of the house, as we have been planning for. It will most likely come at night. It's my bet that it will come sometime after midnight. Any bets?" Everyone shook their heads, Patrick continued,

MICHAEL O. GREGORY

"Now they must know that the house is being watched day and night. I believe that they'll do something to draw off the surveillance before the attack begins. I'll coordinate with my contact at the FBI office to let him know about it. We need for them to respond to the diversion, then after two or three minutes double back. The bad guys won't be expecting that. We can catch them by surprise.

"Now, Kline, Hanes, we won't deploy from my van in the cul-de-sac until the diversion goes down. We'll then deploy to our forward positions." Kline and Hanes acknowledged, Patrick continued, "Good, now, Avery, Miller, when they get into position, hold your fire until you can see something going down. With the noise, and the dogs barking, you should be able to take out one or two each before they realize that someone is shooting at them. By the time they realize that they're losing people, they'll be committed to their own plan, and not be able to look back. Snow, that's when you cut lose with your shotgun. You should be able to get one or two more. The ones that you can't get, we'll stop at the house. By the time we're fully engaged, out FBI friends will be back. Any questions?"

Avery spoke up, "You know that some of them may be wearing body armor."

Patrick nodded. "Yes, that's right. Avery, miller, you need to go for head shots. That way even if they have body armor, it will do them no good." Avery and, Miller nodded. Patrick continued, "Now, remember that our adversary will give no quarter, so neither will we. This is a combat operation. We take no prisoners. Okay, everyone get plenty of rest. We have a big night tonight. I want every man alert." Everyone went to their room to sleep. Patrick had something to do before he could get some rest.

CHAPTER FORTY-NINE

1 0:20 AM a Roto Rooter truck pulled into Amanda's drive way. An elderly man in working clothes with the Roto Rooter logo got out of the truck. He took his toolbox from the truck, walked to the front door, and rang the doorbell. Amanda answered the door, and invited him in. "hello, Pat. Why the disguise?"

Patrick stepped inside, put his toolbox down, and closed the door. "Hello, Amanda, on the chance that someone may be watching, I'll arouse less interest if I come as a tradesman than as myself."

Amanda didn't have to look hard to see the fatigue lines on his face. "You look tired, Pat, come into the kitchen. I'll put on some water and make you a cup of coffee."

Patrick followed Amanda into the kitchen and sat at the table. After heating the water, Amanda made Patrick a cup of coffee and herself a cup of herbal tea, then sat at the table across from Patrick. Amanda said, "I know that this isn't just a social call. What's on your mind?"

Patrick sat his cup on the table, and looked Amanda in the eyes, "It's an excellent chance that the attack will come tonight." Amanda said nothing. She just looked at Patrick waiting for him to continue. Patrick continued, "We observed two men last night. They came up the trail from the main road. They left the trail behind your house, came up to your back fence, and stood there for about five minutes. It seemed to be a recon, one man showing the other the lay of things. We believe that the other man was David Zamora. We also believe that since he was making the recon at night, that he plans to strike at

MICHAEL O. GREGORY

night. We're almost certain that it will be tonight."

Amanda had been sitting unmoving with her hands around her cup listening to Patrick's every word. "Since you're so sure that they're coming tonight, is there something special that Sam and I should do?"

Patrick replied, "Just do as I have instructed you to do."

Amanda nodded. "Okay."

Patrick continued, "One other thing. I suggest that you and Sam sleep in your clothes tonight, that's if you can sleep at all. One of you must be awake at all times to listen to the radio. After the normal time for bed, even if you're still up, turn the lights out. Just leave on the baseboard night-lights, and stay away from the windows. We want to make them think that you're asleep."

Amanda nodded. "Okay, is that it?"

Patrick responded, "Yes, that's about it. We've done all that we can do. Now we must wait. Are you nervous?"

Amanda nodded. "Yes, and frightened too."

Patrick took Amanda's hands into his own. 'That's natural. We all feel that way when we go in harm's way. Now try to get some sleep today. I doubt that you'll be able to tonight. The police and feds have their eyes on the place. You'll be safe enough during the day."

Amanda replied, "Okay, I'll try."

They talked for a few minutes more, and then Patrick left. Amanda lay down on the sofa and tried to sleep, but she couldn't. She just felt too nervous to sleep.

When Sam got home that evening, Amanda met him at the door. After they had embraced and kissed, she started to tell him about Patrick's visit. "Patrick was here this morning. He said that there were men watching he house from the woods last night."

Sam placed his briefcase next to the door, and removed his coat. "When was that?" This didn't surprise him, but he still couldn't help feeling alarmed by the revelation.

Amanda continued, "It was about ten O-clock. He said that they were checking the place out. He's sure that one of them was David

364

WOMAN IN THE MIRROR

Zamora, and that we're going to be hit tonight."

Sam drew Amanda closer to show his support saying, "I guess that we're as ready as we can be. I'll be glad to get this thing over with."

Amanda put her arms around Sam and put her head on his shoulder and said, "So do I. I want us to have our life back."

At 7:45 PM, Snow, Avery and Miller took up their positions. Miller and Avery were about one-hundred yards back from the fence, on the right and left flanks. Snow had taken a position in the center, about twenty yards the other side of the creek from the Tankersley's house. They had taken care to choose their positions so as not to be seen, even with night vision devices. They made their radio checks with Patrick and waited.

Patrick waited with his half of the team in the van. They were parked in the cul-de-sac, not far from the FBI stakeout car. Everyone was ready to exit the van and take up positions as soon as the stakeout car moved. Patrick made a radio check with Amanda and Sam. Everything had been done to be ready. The trap had been set.

Amanda and Sam, feeling too nervous, didn't try to keep a normal routine; instead they spent their time in the bedroom. Amanda gained strength and comfort by his closeness. They were able to escape the seriousness of their predicament and relieve their tension and fear for a while in the act of love. Amanda finally did relax enough to get some sleep. Sam listened to the radio and maintained vigil while Amanda slept. Sam looked at her as she slept his only thought being her safety. If anyone tried to get to Amanda, they would have to come through him.

At 11:00 PM David Zamora assembled his men at the body shop. They all had automatic weapons, plus their side arms. The drive by team consisted of the driver and two shooters armed with AK-47 assault rifles. They had a stolen Ford Crown Victoria for the drive by vehicle. The team that would hit the house would consist of twelve men including David. Seven would go with him. Two drivers, and two gunmen would go with the vans.

The plan would be for the vans to let David's team out at 1:30 AM

365

MICHAEL O. GREGORY

at the head of the trail. The vans would then move to a position with the drive by vehicle, in a Kroger parking lot. There they could see the police cruiser as it went by after making its check of the Tankersley's house. Five minutes after the police cruiser passes their location, the drive by vehicle would go to shoot up the house to draw off the stakeout car. Two minutes after the drive by vehicle has left, the two vans would take off, drive to the Tankersley's house, and secure the front of the house. They were to block any escape from the house, and to pick up David's team. They were instructed to stay within the speed limit on their approach to the house, so there timing wouldn't be off.

Once dropped off David's team would move with stealth up the trail, to the rear of the Tankersley's property. They would wait at the back fence until the drive by vehicle drew away the stakeout car. Then they would rush the house, kill Vicki, take Cheryl if she were there, then make their getaway in the vans.

The whole operation would take five minutes, or less. David checked all the weapons, and questioned all the men to make sure that they knew what to do. He made sure that everyone knew that he wanted to personally take care of that bitch Vicki himself.

1:10 AM: David's and his men loaded into the vans and started for the debarkation point at the head of the trail.

1:23 AM: David's team is dropped off at the head of the trail.

1:38 AM: The vans took up position with the drive by vehicle in the Kroger parking lot, where they could see the police cruiser enter or exit the Tankersley's street.

1:52 AM: "linebacker six, Linebacker four, over."

"Linebacker four, Linebacker six, over."

"Linebacker six, Linebacker four. I have movement on the trail. I see three, no four men on the trail with automatic weapons, over."

"Linebacker four, linebacker six, over."

"Linebacker six, Linebacker four. I now have eight men, all armed with automatic weapons. I believe that's all of them, over."

"Linebacker four, Linebacker six, roger, out, break, Fullback six,

366

WOMAN IN THE MIRROR

Linebacker six, over."

Patrick answered the radio. "Linebacker six, Fullback six, over."

'Fullback six, linebacker six. I have movement on the trail. Eight men, all armed with automatic weapons, over."

"Linebacker six, Fullback six, roger. Keep me informed, out, break, Quarterback, Fullback six, over."

Sam had the radio in his hand when the call came in. "Fullback six, Quarterback, over."

"Quarterback, Fullback six. Have you been monitoring, over."

"Fullback six, Quarterback. Yes, over."

"Quarterback, Fullback six. This is it. Fall back to your safe room, over."

"Fullback six, Quarterback, wilco, over."

"Quarterback, Fullback six, out."

Sam woke Amanda up. They took their handguns, radio, cell phones and hurried to the safe room. When they got there Sam helped Amanda over the side of their little bulletproof box, then climbed in behind her. Once in the box they sat on the floor and waited.

Patrick got on the cell phone to alert the stakeout car as to what was going on.

2:03 AM: "Fullback six, Linebacker six. Enemy lined up along back fence, over."

"Linebacker six, Fullback six, roger, over."

"Fullback six, Linebacker six, out."

David and his men now waited behind the fence at the back of Sam and Amanda's house, waiting for things to start. They were not aware that at that moment they were being targeted in the crosshairs of night sniper scopes.

2:13 AM: A Fulton County Sheriff's Cruiser drove past Amanda's and Sam's house.

2:19 AM: The Sheriff's Cruiser passed the Kroger parking lot where the drive by vehicle and the vans waited.

2:24 AM: The drive by vehicle pulled out of the Kroger parking

MICHAEL O. GREGORY

lot, and headed for Amanda's and Sam's house.

2:26 AM: The vans pulled out of the Kroger parking lot and headed for Amanda's and Sam's house.

2:30 AM: The drive by vehicle pulled up in front of the house. The muzzles of two AK-47 assault rifles were thrust out of the windows of the vehicle and started firing. They fired one magazine each on automatic fire. After the firing, the drive by vehicle started to speed away. The stakeout car gave chase.

When the shooting started Sam and Amanda held each other close. They could hear the crack of the bullets as they passed through the walls. Dust from shattered wallboard filled the air. Pictures were knocked from the wall. One bullet smashed a lamp in the living room. Some of the bullets hit the kitchen cabinets, smashing dishes and throwing dishes, pots and pans out onto the floor.

Avery and Miller already had their first targets in the crosshairs of their scopes. When the first shots were fired from the drive-by vehicle every dog in the neighborhood started barking. You also had the noise of engines racing and tires squealing. Safeties were pushed off, sights aligned, breaths held, triggers squeezed and shots fired. No one heard he bullets as they passed through the air, or the click of the bolts as they recoiled and chambered a fresh round.

When David gave the word to move, four men didn't get up; they would never get up. As the rest of David's men started to climb over the fence, Snow broke cover, jumped the creek, and opened fire with his shotgun. One other man collapsed on the fence dead. Snow took cover behind a large oak tree.

David realized that he had fallen into a trap, but he couldn't turn back. The only way out was forward. David turned and fired a burst of fire, then continued to move forward. Snow fired again and another man went down, but got back up and kept moving forward, dragging his left leg. What felt like a sledgehammer punched David in the back, and knocked him to the ground, driving the air from his lungs. Thanks to the body armor that he was wearing, he would only have a bruise.

WOMAN IN THE MIRROR

He got back to his feet, and kept moving toward the house.

2:32 AM: The vans pulled up and stopped in front of the house. Patrick, Kline and Hanes were in position. The gunmen got out of the vans and positioned themselves on the side of the hood away from the house, unknowingly exposing themselves to the fire from Patrick's team. Patrick opened fire, killing the gunman next to the lead van. The gunman at the second van quickly moved to the other side to return fire. Patrick hit the ground, and rolled right to a position behind a pine tree. He got two quick shots off to keep the gunman's head down, and to keep his attention. Kline move left to come up on the gunman's right flank. Kline fired once. The pattern of buckshot hit the gunman in the right shoulder, neck and head. He fell to the street dead. The driver's panicked and took off. Now there would be no way out for David. Patrick, Kline and Hanes moved to the front of the house.

The vans didn't get far. Just before they reached the first turn, they ran into the returning stakeout car that blocked the road. The drivers died in a hail of gunfire.

Miller brought down the man with the dragging foot. David made it around the house to the carport with the one remaining man. There they encountered Hanes coming up the driveway with Patrick and Kline coming across the front yard. Hanes opened fire on, David's last man, hitting him in the chest. The man fell dead beside the carport. David had reached the carport and took cover behind the cars. He brought up his weapon to return fire. Patrick fired while running across the front yard. Two pellets caught, David in his left arm and elbow. It hit like a hammer blow, shattering his left arm. He felt intense pain, and he couldn't make his left arm move. He saw the door into the house. He fired a burst into the lock, shattering he lock, door and doorframe around the lock. He hit the door with the full weight of his body, and crashed into the house. He now knew that all escape had been cut off, and that he stood alone. All that he could hope for now would be revenge. He must kill, Vicki, that whoring bitch. She had been responsible for all of this. She would pay.

MICHAEL O. GREGORY

He could dimly see the interior of the house by the glow of the baseboard nightlights. He had found himself in the kitchen. He could see through the family room, down the hallway leading to the bedrooms. David shouted, "Vicki, You little whoring pig! I'm coming to get you! I'm going to blow your brains out!" David fired a burst through the family room, down the hallway. He then managed to change magazines on the kitchen counter with just one arm. He then proceeded through the family room, and down the hallway to the first bedroom.

Sam had his shotgun ready, and aimed at the center of the doorway. Amanda squatted next to him with her pistol at the ready.

David jumped into the doorway to the first bedroom, and fired a burst. There was no one in the bedroom. With his back to the wall, he eased up to the door to the second bedroom. He held his gun at the ready, sprung into the doorway, and fired a burst.

The first tightly packed pattern of buckshot struck, David in the lower abdomen and right hip, causing instant trauma to the lower abdomen. The right hip had also been fractured, and one pellet had smashed the second vertebra above the pelvis, severing the spinal column. David's legs immediately collapsed and he started to fall back. The second shot struck him full in the face. The third shot penetrated the abdomen, ripped through the intestines, liver, diaphragm and lungs, but he didn't feel it, David Zamora was dead.

After the gunfire the silence seemed profound. Patrick entered the house through the carport door. By the dim light of the baseboard nightlights he could see what a mess the house had become. He could also see a body lying in the hallway. He called out, "Sam, Amanda this is Patrick Fitzgerald. Are you all right?"

Sam and Amanda heard him. Sam called out, "Yes, Fitz, we're okay. We're down here in the bedroom."

Patrick called out, "Just stay there as I check out the house to make sure that it's clear." With his shotgun at the ready, Patrick checked out the living and dining rooms. He then came back to the kitchen and family room area, and started down the hallway. He checked out the

370

WOMAN IN THE MIRROR

first bedroom; then called out to Sam and Amanda that he would be passing in front of their doorway. He then checked the man's body in the hallway, to make sure that he was dead. He then checked out the master bedroom and bathrooms. He then returned to the doorway to Sam and Amanda's safe room. He called out, "Sam, Amanda, the house is clear. You can put away your weapons now. I'm coming in."

Patrick entered the room, felt for the light switch and flicked it on. The lights still worked, bathing the room in light. Sam climbed over the top of their refuge, then helped Amanda out. They were so relieved to finally have it over with, that they were a little giddy. Patrick said, "He was the only one to get into the house. You did a great job stopping him."

Sam smiled. "Thanks, I just did what you told me to do. Anyone coming through that door was fair game."

Patrick replied, "That's good. We got all of them. Now all we have to do is find out which one is David Zamora."

Amanda pointed to the body of David Zamora in the hallway. "I think that this one is David Zamora. When he came into the house, he was calling to me and cursing me."

Patrick nodded. "Perhaps so, but his face is a mess. The police will have to make an identification. One thing for sure though, it's ended. This thing with David Zamora had nothing to do with business. It was a personal vendetta of his. No one will mourn or want to avenge him. You don't have to look over your shoulder anymore. My job's done."

Amanda felt very spent now, and leaned against Sam for support. Sam had his arm around her to hold her up.

Police cars were starting to arrive outside the house. They could see the flashing red and blue lights from the police cars through the windows. One federal agent had been left with the getaway vans. The other two had come down to the house to take charge of the investigation.

Patrick got on the radio and told Snow, Avery and Miller to stand down, and to return to the motel. Kline had come into the house. Patrick told him to get Hanes and to get back to the van. He then spoke

371

MICHAEL O. GREGORY

to Sam. "I don't think that you and Amanda can stay here anymore; and I don't believe that the landlord is going to give you your deposit back. Why don't you take Amanda to a motel? You aren't going to get any rest here. I'll talk to the police about this."

Sam and Amanda put some things in a bag, and left to go to a motel. They were lucky that neither car had been damaged in the fight. They took Sam's car.

CHAPTER FIFTY

Sam and Amanda checked into a motel. Despite the early morning hour Amanda had to call her mother. Beth answered the phone. Amanda told her that everything had come to a successful conclusion. She then gave her mother a brief description of what had happened. She told her mother that she would call again later to talk to Cheryl.

That morning the news had reported it as a shoot-out between rival gangs. Sam and Amanda weren't mentioned.

The next day they started looking for a new home. Three days later they signed the lease and moved in.

Amanda wasted no time in going to pick up Cheryl. The next morning after they had their new home Amanda called her mother to let her know that she would be coming. She got away from Atlanta as soon as she could. She arrived at her mother's house in Gadsden at 11:00 AM.

As soon as Amanda pulled into her mother's driveway, she saw her mother and Cheryl come out the front door. As Amanda got out of her car Cheryl came running to her crying, "Mommy! Mommy!"

Amanda took Cheryl in her arms and held her close. They were so happy and relieved to see each other, that there were tears in both their eyes. Amanda said, "Oh, Cheryl, baby, Mommy's so happy to see you."

Cheryl said, "Mommy you were gone a long time."

With a hug Amanda replied, "Yes, Baby, but I won't be gone anymore." Beth stood beside them. Amanda stood up, still holding

MICHAEL O. GREGORY

Cheryl in her arms. "Hello, Mom."

Beth said, "I'm so glad that you're safe." Beth hugged Amanda. Amanda then put Cheryl down and they went into the house. Amanda had a seat in the family room with Cheryl. Beth went into the kitchen to get refreshments for everyone. She brought everyone a coke, then sat next to Amanda. Just then Amanda noticed a small-gold cross on a gold chain about Cheryl's neck. Taking the cross in her fingers, Amanda said, "What a beautiful cross Cheryl."

Smiling, Cheryl replied, "Do you like it Mommy? Aunt Audrey gave it to me."

Beth said, "When Audrey found out that Cheryl was staying with me, she came to visit Cheryl. She brought that gift for her. I'm proud at how much you have won Audrey over. She just loves Cheryl."

Cheryl then told Amanda that Grand Mommy had gotten her some water paints, and how she had painted with them, Beth said, "Cheryl, why don't you go back to your room, and get some of your pictures to show your mother? I'm sure that she would like to see them."

Cheryl said, "Yes, Grand Mommy." she then jumped up and ran back to her room to get the pictures to show to her mother.

As soon as Cheryl left the room, Beth asked, "Is it really all over?"

Amanda with relief was able to say, "Yes, Mom, it's finally all over. We have nothing more to fear."

"Are you sure?" Beth said with a questioning look.

Amanda nodded. "Yes, Mom, I'm sure. David Zamora is dead. It was his personal vendetta. His associates had nothing to do with it. It had nothing to do with business, and they are first of all businessmen."

With a smile, Beth replied, "Well, I'm glad that it's all over. Now we can go back to living like normal people again."

Amanda looked at her mother. "Believe me that's all I want to do, just have a normal life with my husband and children." Just then Cheryl returned with her pictures and showed them to her mother. Amanda said, "Oh, these are so pretty."

Cheryl nodded. "Yes, Mommy, I know. Grand Mommy told me."

WOMAN IN THE MIRROR

Amanda chuckled at Cheryl's proclamation, "Well, your Grand Mommy's right, you are."

Cheryl then said, "You know, Mommy, Grand Mommy let me sleep in your old room, and play with your Barbie dolls."

Amanda asked, "Do you like them?"

"Oh yes I do!" Cheryl exclaimed.

With a smile, Amanda responded, "Okay, then they're yours."

Cheryl jumped up into Amanda's lap and threw her arms around her neck, "Oh, Mommy, you're the best mommy in the whole world."

Amanda's love for Cheryl was boundless. To her Cheryl had to be the best daughter in the whole world.

When Ted got home, they all had lunch together. After lunch Ted went back to work. Amanda left for Atlanta with Cheryl and Lady.

In September Sam's adoption of Cheryl had been finalized. Cheryl was thrilled that Sam would now be her real daddy. She also liked having a new name the same as her mother and Sam's.

Sam really loved Cheryl and planned for as much time with her as he could. They went to Six Flags over Georgia and Stone Mountain. Cheryl also started kindergarten. She would be making new friends, and having a great time.

They went to Martinez to visit Sam's parents. Sam's parents took to Cheryl right away. Cheryl loved having so many grandparents who liked to play with her and give her things.

The first Saturday in November, Sam, Amanda and Cheryl went to Stone Mountain. They pulled into the parking lot and parked. Sam then said, "Now, how do you want to go by trail or by cable car?"

Amanda punched Sam on the arm. "Oh, you!" Cheryl giggle, Amanda continued, "I'm as large as Moby Dick and you want me to walk to the top!"

Sam now laughed. "Okay, we take the cable car."

They took the cable car to the top of the mountain, then went to their special place. Sam and Amanda explained about their special place to Cheryl. Cheryl thought that it was really neat.

375

MICHAEL O. GREGORY

The Monday after the trip to Stone Mountain, Beth came to stay with them. Thursday afternoon, Amanda went into labor. At 2:40 AM Friday morning she gave birth to Sam Jr., seven pounds three ounces. Sam was delighted; he could hardly wait to tell everyone about his son. Amanda had been relieved that everything went well, and that she had a perfect and healthy son.

In December Amanda went back to the clinic to see Dr. Weston. She had brought Sam Jr. with her. Amanda, as a new mother, took great pride in all the attention lavished on her and Sam Jr. by her friends and coworkers.

Amanda entered Dr. Weston's office with her purse and diaper bag on one shoulder, and, Sam Jr. in a carrier on the other arm. Grace took the diaper bag and purse, then helped Amanda get settled on the sofa, with Sam Jr. next to her. Grace took a look at Sam Jr. as Amanda straightened his blanket. Grace exclaimed, "Oh, what a beautiful baby! I'm sure that you are really proud of him."

Amanda nodded. "Yes, I love him more than I thought that I could ever love anyone. I had no idea that this kind of love existed."

Grace held out her hands. "May I hold him?"

Amanda nodded. "Yes, you may."

Grace picked up Sam Jr. from the carrier and cradled him in her arms. Sam Jr. loved all the attention that he had been getting. Grace held him for a couple of minutes, then put him back in his carrier. "I say, he's indeed a special child." Grace took a seat on the other side of the sofa from Amanda, them continued, "Do you remember our first meeting in this office?"

Amanda did remember. "Yes, I do. How could I ever forget? It was almost two years ago."

"At that time did you imagine that your life would turn out as it has?"

Amanda, remembering the metamorphosis that she had undergone since that meeting said, "Never in my wildest dreams."

Grace felt pride in Amanda's accomplishments. "I don't mind

saying that you have come a long way since then. We're proud of you."

Amanda blushed at Grace's complements. "Thank you."

Grace said, "To change the subject; the Chief of Nursing informs me that you won't be coming back to work with us."

Amanda had decided that she could no longer work full time with all the responsibilities that she had at home. "That's right. With Cheryl and Sam Jr. I already have a full time job."

Grace looked again at Amanda. "Okay, I know that you won't be coming back as a nurse's aide, but we do need you. We're about to bring a new candidate into project 'Trade In'."

Amanda responded, "I didn't know. What can I do?"

Grace had to convince Amanda that she would be needed. "Remember that Maryanne told you that we would need you as a consultant?"

Amanda recalled what she had talked about with Maryanne. 'Yes, I remember."

"Well, we've reconsidered, and we want you as a permanent member of the 'Trade In' staff. You'll be an assistant to Maryanne."

"That all sounds good, but…"

Grace interrupted Amanda. "Listen, we'll be paying you a regular salary for your services, and it will be a lot better that a nurse's aide. We can also be very flexible when it comes to your work schedule. We really need you."

Amanda thought for a minute before answering. "Okay, I'm with you. Who's the candidate?"

Grace felt relieved that Amanda had agreed to be with them as Maryanne's assistant. "I can't tell you yet, but the candidate is very wealthy. We can expect an endowment for the clinic in seven figures."

Amanda wondered if 'Trade In' would now be for only the very rich who could afford it. "Is that what it's for now, money?"

Grace was quick to reassure her. "Some will pay, so that others like you who need our services, but can't afford them, can be helped. We plan to start bringing in candidates as quickly as we can."

MICHAEL O. GREGORY

Relieved, Amanda replied, "That's great! It was a miracle for me. There are so many others who need a chance."

Grace asked, "Can you come in this coming Monday? I'd like to have you with me when I brief the candidate."

Amanda thought for a moment. "Yes, I can be here Monday anytime between nine AM, to two PM."

Grace gave Amanda a pat on the shoulder. "Good, then be here at nine thirty AM Monday."

Amanda started to get to her feet. "Okay, I'll be here. Now I must be going. I have to pick up Cheryl and get home to cook for Sam."

Amanda and Grace said their good-byes. Amanda got all her things in order, then left.

On her drive home, after picking up Cheryl, Amanda thought of her life these last two years; of how fortunate and lucky she had been. Of having a wonderful family with Beth and Ted. Of how she and Sam had found each other and how she had found Cheryl. Now she and Sam had Sam Jr. She knew that she had truly been blessed.

Printed in the USA
CPSIA information can be obtained
at www.ICGtesting.com
LVHW050954040624
782219LV00001B/6